MOVIN

MOVING ON

Peta Tayler

HEADLINE

The right of Peta Tayler to be identified as the Author of
the Work has been asserted by her in accordance with the
Copyright, Designs and Patents Act 1988.

First published in 1998
by HEADLINE BOOK PUBLISHING

10 9 8 7 6 5 4 3 2 1

British Library Cataloguing in Publication Data

Tayler, Peta
Moving on
1. House buying – Fiction 2. House selling –
Fiction
I. Title
823.9'14 [F]

ISBN 0-7472-2058-1

Typeset by
CBS, Felixstowe, Suffolk

Printed and bound in Great Britain by
Mackays of Chatham PLC, Chatham, Kent

HEADLINE BOOK PUBLISHING
A division of Hodder Headline PLC
338 Euston Road
London NW1 3BH

For Alan,

who after twenty-five years is still the best husband in
the world, as well as the best estate agent.

Chapter One

Beep beep. Beep beep.
'Hensham Homes, good morning?'
'Oh, hello, I wonder if you can help me?'

I wonder if I can, Paul Kingswood thought as he moved smoothly and automatically into his accustomed response to this opening gambit. Can any of us, really, ever help one another? Most of us can't even help ourselves. I certainly can't, so how can I possibly help you?

'Yes, Miss Chapman,' his mouth produced the words, 'yes, I understand. *Not* South Green or Elmwood. Three bedrooms, two reception rooms, downstairs cloakroom, garage, good sized garden, good condition, replacement windows . . .' Helicopter pad, his mind continued. Diamond door knobs. You have as much chance of getting them, poor deluded Miss Chapman, as you have of getting what you're asking for at the price you're offering. So I cannot help you, Miss Chapman. And nor can anybody else until you come to terms with reality.

Paul Kingswood talked to himself most of the time. Not just a monologue – he was capable of carrying on quite a detailed debate, involving two or more points of view, inside his head. He did it because he was lonely. He knew that this was so, but the knowledge carried no self-pity. Secretly, Paul Kingswood thought that he was a fairly amusing chap and quite good company. Good enough, at any rate, for a middle-aged, not very successful estate agent like himself.

More than twenty years of putting together the advertising copy every week had given him the habit of describing things, half ironically, in what he thought of as Agentspeak. Of himself he would have said 'Small semi-detached estate agent, in need of some modernisation; wiring and plumbing in good working order but roof in need of refurbishment (he was perceptibly balding); decor dated, but clean.'

Not much to look at, perhaps. At fifty-three he was resigned to being, if not short, at least not very tall. There wasn't much to be done about that, any more than he could cure the thinning of his once-thick hair. The gentle rounding of his figure was another thing, of course, but he had little time for exercise and living alone meant that his diet tended to be of the take-away variety. All he could do was to hope that people would see him as cuddly rather than fat, and go

1

along with the popular belief that plump people were jolly. Not that he felt particularly jolly most of the time, but he tried to be good company, even if it were only with himself. Better company, at any rate, than many of the people he met in his daily life.

It had to be admitted that he rarely met anyone, in the course of his work, with whom he could have a proper discussion, an exchange of ideas or a meeting of minds. He told himself that this was probably true for most people, but all the same it had to be said that the buying and selling of houses, involving larger sums of money than most people ever handled in their daily lives, tended to bring out the worst in people. There were days – particularly now, when he had rather too much time to think and to worry – when he wished he had never become an estate agent, that he had become a teacher or a bus driver or an anonymous person in local government.

It was probably too late to think of that now. In any case, he had never been one to go rushing headlong into new ventures. He thought of himself as someone to whom things happened: his philosophy was to accept what turned up and make the best of it rather than to remould the world in his own image. He had never set out to be an estate agent but it had happened, and on the whole he did not regret it. He would have denied that he was a fatalist, but buried somewhere deep within him was the feeling that his life was being directed, that there was a pattern which he could not discern but from which it was useless to attempt to break free.

In his early childhood, a rather lax Catholic upbringing (his mother had been a Catholic, a fact which she remembered rarely) had ensured that he would call the guiding principle God. Now, with his childhood faith eroded to the bones, he would be more likely to call it chance or fate. Nevertheless, he still looked for clues to the pattern, sought for the warp threads or the colour of the weft. He consulted neither clairvoyants nor tea-leaves – though one of the die-hard few who had resisted the lure of the tea-bag – but he took note of coincidences and found them significant.

There had been a time, long ago, when he had been embarrassed and even ashamed of admitting that he was an estate agent. Newly emerged from university with a degree in English, he brought with him in full measure the righteous scorn that the hippy generation felt for such people. He had worked in his uncle's agency during the long summer vacations but that was all right, because he didn't take it seriously and as a student he was entitled, nay duty bound, to screw as much money out of the system as it would bear. He built up a fund of anecdotes that were always good for a laugh at parties, and was able to buy himself a battered Mini which enhanced his desirability in the eye-liner and mascara-rimmed eyes of the long-haired short-skirted girls he was always eager to invite out.

It was the Mini, in the long run, that was his undoing. He always preferred to think that it was an excess of passion, but it had to be admitted that the exigencies of making love in so confined a space, with all the acrobatic contortions that entailed, probably contributed to the accidental leak of sperm that led, nine months later, to the birth of his elder daughter.

Fortunately for both of them, Jenny failed to realise that she was pregnant until they had finished their finals. Preoccupied with last minute revision she put down her late period and feeling of underlying malaise simply to exam nerves, and it was not until they were several days into the euphoric post-finals celebrations that it occurred to her that she had actually missed for the second time. A hurried trip to the university doctor – no discreet chemist-bought test kits in those days – revealed the alarming truth, and afterwards they sat in the Mini and tried to talk about it.

'I can't believe it,' said Jenny. 'I just can't take it in.'

'Nor can I.' He said it because he had to say something, but in fact he was so strongly moved that he was unable to find any words to express what he was feeling. In the past, imagining such a scenario after the inevitable panics and false alarms of student life, he had always assumed that he would be filled with fear or anger. Instead, what washed over him in a flooding wave was a feeling of astonished tenderness towards Jenny and, more particularly, towards the vaguely imagined little blob that was inside her that would, miraculously, grow into a baby. His baby.

He reached for her hand and took it with as much reverent care as if she had been the being he had called, in his childhood, Our Lady. Not ours, he thought, but mine. My Lady. His grip tightened.

'Don't worry, Jenny,' he said. 'I'll take care of you. We'll get married.'

Jenny, who had been half-inclined to have an abortion and had expected him to persuade the other half of her to fall into line, was vaguely affronted.

'I'm not sure that I want to go ahead with it,' she said wilfully. 'What about my future? My career?'

At any other time he would have answered, 'What career?' for Jenny had no plans at all for her future, assuming that once she had her degree excited employers would be contacting her immediately and pressing her to work for them. It was all very vague, and beyond the expectation of earning a great deal of money and having long exotic holidays, she gave no thought to the work itself. Paul, however, was too appalled to react to that.

'You don't mean . . . ? You don't want to get rid of it, do you? Not kill it, Jenny?'

She pulled her hand free.

'You're not coming over all Catholic on me, are you? I thought you

3

said you'd grown out of that sort of thing.'

'I have, I have, it's not that. You know I believe in a woman's right to choose, we've often said so. But that's when the woman hasn't any support or help, when it isn't possible for her to give the child a proper upbringing. Better no child than a neglected one, all that sort of thing. But our baby wouldn't be like that! I can work, make a good life for us all! Just think, Jenny. We'll be a real family. We can buy a little cottage, grow our own vegetables, have a cat. Or a puppy. They could grow up together, play in the garden, it'll be wonderful!'

Carried away by his vision, he failed to notice her lowering frown.

'Puppies grow up faster than babies. By the time the puppy has grown out of digging up the vegetables or piddling all over the carpet, the baby will be ready to take over.'

'No puppy, then,' he placated. 'You're right. It would make too much work, and you'd be busy with the baby. But I'll help. I'll change nappies, all that kind of thing. At least . . .' he caught himself up, realising that he was on the wrong tack. 'That is, if it's what you want. You're the one who'll have all the problems. It's your decision, and of course I'll support you, stand up for you, whatever you choose.'

Instantly, she softened. It had been the unexpectedness of it all, when she had assumed that she must accustom herself to the prospect of an abortion, that had thrown her off-balance – that, and the cocktail of hormones buzzing around her body. With a lightning change of mood, she turned a dazzling smile on him.

'It would be different, wouldn't it? Nobody else is getting married.'

'True. If you ask me, all that flower power and living in communes is getting boring. Old Hat. We'll set a new trend. Only one problem, though.'

'What's that?'

'Our parents.'

'Yes. They'll be so pleased. All that respectability.'

'Mm. Still, we can keep that quiet.'

Faced with the urgent necessity of providing a home for his little family, it had been only sensible to take up his uncle's offer of a job. It was at least familiar, work that he knew he could do and do well. Working in a small family firm was a benefit, too – he had no need to compromise his principles by fighting his way up a corporate ladder, and he was given a degree of independence in how he organised his time and his work. He found, rather to his surprise, that he was good at selling, and even rather enjoyed it. Certainly there was pleasure to be had from earning a comfortable and, as time went by, quite an opulent living. There was also a satisfaction in matching, from memory, the right buyer to the right house.

The birth, two years later, of a second daughter seemed to confirm Jenny in her role as mother and housewife. She showed no sign of resenting this: indeed, as time went by and she acquired a group of friends with children the same age she appeared more than content with her life. The small cottage, as they grew out of it, was sold to buy a larger cottage, and that in turn to buy an old farmhouse, with an acre of garden. By the time Paul's uncle succumbed to a heart attack, Paul was ready to take over, and for a few booming years there was money for expensive foreign holidays and to subsidise the purchase of some plots of prospective building land for which there was no planning consent but which might, one day, be granted it.

The collapse of the housing market, though he had foreseen it to a certain extent, still hit Paul badly. Having, by then, spent twenty years in the business, he had seen more than one cycle of boom and slump. Although it was obvious early on that this was going to be a bad time, it never occurred to him that it would last so long. A year, perhaps two, but surely after that the wheel would turn and things would improve. There was enough in the bank to tide them over, as long as they were sensible, and although it was a pity he had borrowed quite so heavily to buy the land it should be possible to keep up the repayments. The actual land, after all, was still valuable in itself, and if the worst came to the worst he could always sell it.

Two years later, he looked back and realised that he had been hopelessly optimistic. House prices were still going down, and as for building land, it was scarcely possible to give it away with a packet of breakfast cereal. The big building firms, who would once have snapped it up as an investment, were themselves lumbered with speculative land that was tying up their capital, and were looking for buyers rather than to acquire any more. Paul reduced the number of his staff, and took to waking in the night unable to get back to sleep.

After four years the number of employees was reduced to two and Paul was working a six-day week. They were long days, too: the less business there was, the more important it seemed to follow up even the most lukewarm sign of interest. By the time he did get home in the evenings he was tired with the leaden heaviness of depression and lack of sleep. More often than not he fell asleep as soon as he had finished eating his supper, a sleep from which he could scarcely rouse himself to crawl up to bed. Once there he would sleep until about two o'clock and then wake, to lie staring at the dark until six, when a too-short hour of unconsciousness would leave him to work like a zombie for the next day.

It was not very surprising, therefore, when Jenny told him, with the kind firmness of an old-fashioned nanny, that she was moving out. While the girls had been at school she had confined her activities to charity work and a busy social life. Once they had left home for university she dallied with several part-time jobs, mostly with friends, more as a way of filling her time than for the money they did not need. The last of these started out as a small shop selling furnishing fabrics and decorative objects, many of them imported from Italy and the Far East. It caught the peak of the housing boom and was a huge success. Jenny found that she had a natural aptitude for interior design. She did several courses on paint finishes and soft furnishing, and rapidly established herself locally as an up-market designer with an interesting and unusual slant.

The decline of the housing market, which hit Paul so badly, affected her not at all. Though the lower end of the market might be suffering, and though at the top end Lloyd's members were going down like ninepins and selling up, there were still plenty of people with money enough to spend on perfecting their dream houses. As her popularity grew she was able to pick and choose, and her work took her increasingly further afield. The times when she stayed overnight in London occurred more and more frequently. They saw little of one another, and although the money she earned paid their household bills and took some of the weight from Paul's shoulders, he could not bring himself to allow her to help the agency. It was a matter of pride, but also of common sense, because he saw no point in her putting her own money into something that increasingly resembled a Black Hole.

Nevertheless, though it might not have been a surprise, it was still a shock when Jenny told him what she intended to do.

'Moving out? But where to? And why?'

'Oh, Paul.' She was neither impatient nor resigned. Perhaps a faint hint of boredom clouded her fine grey eyes, but she swiftly veiled it with subtly made-up eyelids that showed only the finest of lines on their smooth half moons. Jenny had taken good care of face and figure: her flesh was firm, with no hint of flab or cellulite, her skin soft and smooth, her hair carefully highlighted to cover all but a sprinkling of grey hairs. 'You're surely not pretending this is coming as a surprise? You know we hardly see one another any more, and when we do we have nothing to say to one another, beyond talking about the girls.'

'Isn't that enough? Don't you like talking about them?'

'Of course I do. And surely we can still do that. I'm not going to Outer Mongolia, you know. Only to London. Less than an hour on the train, and fully equipped with telephones.'

'London.'

'Yes. You know I've had quite a few commissions there recently. There are more coming up. One thing leads to another, you know how it goes. And I need to be there, on the spot. I can't be stuck down here. I've got the chance of a flat, very central. It's large enough to use as an office and a work room, and when I've finished with it, it'll be worth every penny I put into it as a living advertisement.'

'And is there . . . someone else?'

Unexpectedly, that made her laugh. She hugged him briefly but pulled back when his arms went around her.

'You dear old-fashioned thing! No, there's nobody else, at least, not in the way you mean. No toy boy, no sugar daddy, no gipsy lover enticing me away. It's not like that. I'm going to be me. Not Paul's wife, or the girls' mother, or my mother's daughter. Just me.'

'I thought that was what you were. What you've always been. You're surely not saying, are you, that you've been living in my shadow?' He could not keep the bitterness out of his voice.

'Of course not.' The boredom was back. It was carefully hidden but he knew her too well. 'You've been a wonderful husband, a wonderful father. We've had a lot of good years together, had a good marriage.'

'But.'

'But. But it's over, don't you think? Oh, Paul,' she reached out and took his hand, holding it firmly in both of hers. 'I don't want to hurt you. I still love you so much, but as a friend, not a husband. We married so young . . . so very young. Haven't you ever wondered how things would have been if we hadn't?'

'Yes, from time to time.' He was always honest with her. As a matter of fact, he was always honest with everyone, something which he knew stemmed from a kind of revulsion from the 'lying estate agent' image people had of his work. And it was true that there had been times, during the long years of their marriage, when he had looked at other women with interest or even desire and wondered . . . He had never allowed his imagination to stray too far down that deceptively simple path. 'Your mother always said it wouldn't last,' he said wryly.

'Oh Paul!' She laughed, and her voice broke on a sob. This time she let him hug her, and they both wept a little. It was the funeral of something that had died, unnoticed, some while before.

Their daughters, when informed, seemed surprisingly unconcerned. Since they were, by then, twenty-eight and twenty-six and had left home years earlier, they could not be said to be much affected by the change. Even the prospective sale of the house, their old home, elicited little more than a request that they might be allowed to take a few items of furniture. It was all very civilised. Jenny took rather less than her half share of the house, and with his remainder Paul was able to clear some debts, and buy himself a pleasant little apartment in a new development on the edge of the town. After a few months he noticed with shame that he missed the garden more than he missed Jenny. He changed the flat for a tiny house with an equally tiny garden – all he realistically had time to care for – and his life settled into a new pattern.

Beep beep. Beep beep. Paul put his newspaper to one side.

7

'Hensham Homes, good morning? . . . No, I'm afraid I don't know what time the films start. No, this is not Hensham Cinema, this is an estate agency. Yes, really. No, I'm afraid you have the wrong number. The number you need is eighty four, eighty four, eighty four. Well, eight, four, eight, four, eight, four. Yes, I'm quite sure. Goodbye,'

'You're so patient with them, Mr K.' Paul wished that Rose would just occasionally omit her invariable remark. Partly because he felt it wasn't true – he might be patient on the outside but inside he was churning with irritation and resentment because the tiny surge of hope at the sound of the telephone had once again been dashed. Mainly, though, because he knew she was saying it to encourage him and he found that depressing.

With the office complement whittled down to himself and one other, it had seemed sensible to have two part-time people rather than one full-time. It spread the load when it came to holidays and illness, and also meant that clients felt the firm was larger than it actually was. Rose covered the mornings: middle-aged, dowdy, and sensible, her cosy manner went down well with the public and she was reliable, though plodding. Her slow, deliberate movement and speech made Paul want to scream from time to time, but it contrasted admirably with twenty-two-year-old Melanie, the afternoon girl.

Melanie did everything at lightning speed. Her fingers flew over the keyboard when she typed details on to the computer and, if the finished product was riddled with typing errors and spelling mistakes, 'Well, Mr K, at least it's *done*!' Melanie would cry cheerfully. Her energy made him feel middle-aged, but her rumbustious love-life and constantly changing hair and nail colour gave him much entertainment. She thought (and said) that Rose was past it, while Rose kept up a lofty superiority that failed to hide her paranoia where Melanie was concerned. They were both hard-working, fiercely loyal, and they both mothered him. Paul knew he was lucky to have them, and endured heavy home-made cakes that seemed to have set, like concrete, rather than cooked, and a hand-knitted pullover that made him itch (Rose) and magazine articles about the male menopause and offers to fill in a computer dating form (Melanie) with commendable stoicism.

'You'd think,' said Rose heavily, 'that with a number like ours, people would be able to get it right.'

Paul made the kind of agreeing noise that he hoped would not encourage her to pursue this well-worn theme.

'I mean, they're not even that similar, are they?' Rose, once launched, was not to be halted in her ponderous reiteration. 'Of course, it was easier before they put that eight in front of all the numbers. That was a real shame, when we'd had four double four double four for so long.'

'It cuts out the Tiny Tot calls, though.' Paul, giving in, reminded her once again. In the past he had wondered about parents' reactions to their suddenly increased telephone bills when their infant offspring, exploring, discovered that by repeatedly pressing the same button they could get an adult who would iterate, in tones ranging from the cajoling to the downright vicious, 'Where's Mummy, then? Go and find *Mummy*! Find *Mummy*! Go on, you little rat, fetch bloody *Mummy*!'

'I suppose so. Though I didn't mind those so much.' Rose's voice was wistful. She adored children, and her only son, Maximilian (Max the Knife, Melanie called him) was now nineteen, had shaved his head to a stubble and was working, spasmodically, as a barman. Rose, who had aspirations, had wanted him to go to university but he had so far resisted, although he had three reasonably good A levels. Rose was disappointed, but hoped it was a passing phase.

'The Tiny Tots were better than the . . . you know . . . the *nasty* ones.'

Paul nodded. He hoped his face was sufficiently serious. 'You haven't had any recently, have you?'

'Not *recently*. No. And I know Melanie thinks they're funny, but it's not very *nice*, Mr K, when he asks that sort of question . . .'

'No, of course not. You know, if it upsets you that much, I can contact the police.'

'Oh no!' Her response was uncharacteristically quick. 'No, I wouldn't want to do anything like that. Besides, it's not as if he *does* anything. You know.'

'I know.' Paul thought he had caught the note of sympathetic censure he was aiming for, but perhaps some of his underlying amusement got through because Rose turned suspicious eyes at him.

Rose's nasty phone calls were not, of course, funny. Not funny at all. In fact, when you considered the problem of a man who felt compelled to ring women up and ask them the colour of their underwear, before describing the particular feminine garments he was currently wearing, the thing took on an air of pathos. It was not, as Rose frequently said, as though he *did* anything. No heavy breathing, no masturbatory sounds, he did not even make any kind of lewd suggestion. He might have been a woman ringing up a female friend to discuss her day's wardrobe.

Melanie, on the rare occasions when she was targeted, was very sympathetic. She would listen intently, and describe her own underwear in return. Paul sometimes wondered whether the satin and lace creations she dwelt on were indeed what she had on beneath the crisp office suits she generally wore, but dared not ask in case she had a sudden access of feminism and decided this was sexual harassment at work.

9

'Poor thing,' she would say with brimming eyes when at last she put down the phone. 'Poor thing, you have to feel sorry for him. I mean, it's harmless, innit? Pathetic, really. It's a kind of social service listening to him, I reckon.' The trouble was that, however sympathetic she was, the caller undoubtedly preferred speaking to Rose, Presumably, Paul thought, because she was shocked, and showed it.

'You should be ashamed of yourself,' she would say crossly, after the first shocked gasp. 'Pestering people like this. You should go to your doctor, get yourself some help. It's downright disgusting. No, I'm not going to listen. And I'm certainly not going to tell you . . . No! I am not! I wouldn't dream . . . ! Well, really!' And she, who would not hang up on even the most abusive client, would clatter the telephone back into its receiver, her cheeks turning brick-coloured beneath the thick layer of powder that coated her rather downy skin.

Beep beep. Beep beep.
'Hensham Homes, good . . . afternoon?' A swift glance at the wall clock confirmed that the hour hand stood at one minute after midday.

'Estate agents?' The voice was elderly, educated, stern.

'I'm afraid so,' Paul admitted, knowing that his smile would be reflected in his voice.

'Well, someone has to do it, I suppose.'

'Like dustmen?'

'I was thinking of undertakers, really.' There was still no answering smile in her crisp tones.

'So was I,' he admitted, 'but . . .'

'But you thought that I, being elderly, might take fright at the word?'

'Something like that.'

A terrifying screech hit his ear drums. For a moment, head buzzing, he thought she had screamed at him in fury. Then the screech came again, slightly muffled, followed by a raucous demand. 'Give me a biscuit. Biscuit. Aaaak!' The tone was unmistakable to someone like Paul who had, since childhood, adored parrots.

'Sorry.' For the first time, his caller sounded unsure of herself. 'Bloody parrot. He knows something's up. I've covered him, he'll settle down.'

Please, thought Paul. Please let her want to put her house on the market. Please. Even if I can't sell it, at least I'll get to see the parrot.

'I have it in mind to move. My daughter thinks I should do it, that the place is getting too much for me. She fusses about me being on my own and I can't abide fuss. So I thought, why not? If I'm going to move on, I might as well do it while I'm still able to adapt to a new kind of life. And that means I must sell my house. My bungalow, I suppose I should call it, though I have never cared for the word.'

'I know what you mean.' Elation made Paul less careful than usual what he said. 'It's scarcely euphonious, is it? Though with pleasing Indian connotations, of course.'

There was a short pause, broken only by baffled complaints from the parrot.

'Are you sure you are an estate agent, young man?'

'Mostly. But I'm not very young, really.'

'Age is relative. To me, most people are young.' She said it without complaint, as one stating a fact. 'Do you mean, you are mostly sure, or you are mostly an estate agent?'

'Both, really. But what I am quite certain of is that I should very much like to value your –' just in time he stopped himself from using the word 'home' which, while a good word in itself, in this context had an unpleasantly agentish ring, '– your one-storey dwelling. If you would allow me to.'

'Very well. When would you do it?'

Paul looked at the virgin pages of his desk diary, open in front of him.

'I will come at whatever time is convenient to you. My time,' he said superbly, 'is yours to command.'

'Flummery. You mean you have no appointments. One may be living a little out of the world, but one still has some idea of the state of the economy. And even of what I believe they call The Housing Market.' She made it sound slightly obscene, which suited Paul's present mood. 'You may come at five. I have formed the habit of putting my feet up after lunch, and even the disgraceful way the BBC have moved Woman's Hour away from that time has not cured me of the habit. Not,' she added indignantly, 'that I listen to that dreadful afternoon thing. Cheapskates. All those ring-ins, or whatever they are.'

'Quite. So, what do you listen to? If you don't mind me asking? Radio Three?'

'Classic FM. It's not bad if you can ignore the advertisements, and at least they don't play things that sound like an orchestra being disembowelled with a cold teaspoon. Tomorrow, then, at five o'clock? We will have a cup of tea.'

'That will be delightful.' And the most delightful thing, he thought, as he noted down her name and address, was that he actually meant it.

He turned back to *The Times*. He had already finished the news section, and now he flicked through the business pages to find the 'Word-watching' at the end. He looked at it every day with as much attention as Melanie studied her stars in the tabloid she read. Although he would have dismissed the idea that an astrologer could predict his day, he nevertheless had a profoundly secret feeling that the words in the little feature sometimes had a particular significance.

'Circumforaneous', he read. 'Wandering from house to house'. Appropriate for an estate agent, at least. Was it, could it be, an omen?

Chapter Two

Roger leaned back in his chair, and crossed his long legs with an assumption of nonchalance. He noted with pleasure that the crease down the front of his charcoal-grey trousers was as sharp as if they had been made of good-quality paper, and his shoes had no smudges or scuffs to mar their perfect shine.

'I think I would like . . .' He heard the slight tremor in his voice and raised his hand to his mouth, giving a cough to cover the deep breath he drew in. 'I would like to make an offer on the flat in Shakespeare Court. Number forty-three,' he added, in case Paul had half a dozen flats for sale there. He noticed that his body had somehow rearranged itself without his noticing, so that he was leaning tensely forward, and hastily pushed his bony spine against the back of the chair.

There, he had done it. *Alea jacta est*, he thought, remembering one of the handful of Latin tags he had once learned to impress examiners. The die is cast. The biggest decision that he had ever made in the course of twenty-two years of life. It was out of his hands, for the moment, and in the (he trusted) capable ones of the agent.

It was ridiculous to feel so agitated. Anyone would think that what he was doing was unusual, or risky, or even illegal. And it was not as if the agent himself was at all intimidating. In fact, he had been glad to find something he liked that was being sold by this particular firm. For one thing it was small. The young woman who was there in the afternoons was rather alarming, it was true, with her brightly coloured hair and bold eyes, but he had soon learned to confine his visits to the morning when the older woman was there, the one they called Rose. A nice name, calling to mind the big cabbage roses his mother grew and cut to put in the vase in the front room. Actually, Rose herself reminded him a bit of Mum, with her dumpy figure in its shapeless knitted cardigan. He thought she would probably call it a woolly, like Mum did, and that she would have knitted it herself.

The agent himself was also far from alarming. He was older, for one thing, and Roger might have used the term fatherly if the word father had not been one connected, in the deeper recesses of his mind, with fear and dislike. Avuncular, perhaps, although his only uncle was his father's brother and was, like him, aggressive, stupid, and frightening. The man across the desk from him was far shorter than

Roger and, although cuddly was an adjective Roger would have hesitated to use, nevertheless he exuded a sort of benign cosiness that made Roger feel safe, as he rarely did with older men. He called Roger 'Mr Selby' too, and he himself was 'Mr Kingswood', unlike other agencies where sharply dressed young men bouncing with confidence introduced themselves as 'Darren' or 'Keith', and kept asking 'How *are* you?' with a spurious interest that Roger found impertinent.

Mr Kingswood was beaming at him.

'Splendid!' he said. 'How much did you want me to put forward, Mr Selby?'

Roger, imperceptibly leaning forward again, mentioned a sum which sounded enormous to him, small though it was in comparison with the heady prices attached to some of the houses depicted on the walls. It was three thousand pounds below the price being asked for the flat, and as soon as the words had left his mouth he wondered whether he had set it too low, and was making himself look embarrassingly stingy.

'That's my first offer, of course,' he added hastily. 'I might be prepared to come up a bit. Or something.'

'Of course. It's only sensible to make an offer, and nobody wants to pay more than they have to. Now, let's see, your mortgage is already sorted out, isn't it?'

Soothed, Roger leaned back again and agreed that yes, it was.

'And you've got a good deposit saved up,' mused Paul, scanning his computer screen. 'That puts you in a strong position. I'll give them a ring straight away, and see what they say.'

Roger flinched. Somehow he hadn't expected anything quite as sudden as this.

'They might not be at home,' murmured Paul, who had honed his mind-reading abilities to a fine pitch after so many years of dealing with clients in various stages of experience. He consulted the screen again, and dialled the number.

'Hello, Shelley? Paul Kingswood here, Hensham Homes. Yes, fine. And you? That's good. Yes, as a matter of fact I have. An offer for the flat, from the Mr Selby who you probably remember came to see it two or three times . . . yes.' His voice seemed to grow louder in response to her squawking tones. 'Yes, he's here with me now. Yes, that's right. No, I'm sure . . .' He paused and glanced at Roger. His client's remark, 'What, the long wet one like a bit of chewed string?' reverberated in his ear and his brain, but Roger looked quite blank. As Shelley's uninhibited shriek of laughter rang out Paul smiled, but Roger had retreated. Unable to bear to listen to this conversation he had allowed his mind to go back to contemplating the flat.

It had been one of the first he had visited. Though it had only one

14

bedroom, that one was a good size, and the building was separated from the road by landscaped gardens. Hensham, until twenty years before a sleepy little market town of a few thousand inhabitants, had benefited (or been ruined, depending on your point of view) from the arrival of a big electronics firm that had taken advantage of a cheap site and a convenient position to build a large factory. So successful had this proved that other smaller companies had arrived to pitch their tents nearby, to shelter or to bask in the reflected glow of prosperity. A sudden rash of new houses had hastily been built to accommodate the various workers and managements, and a local builder suddenly found himself so successful that he was able to drink himself to death in only three years, instead of the five his doctor had predicted.

The new homes ranged from an executive estate, where gardens were large enough to contain the swimming pools and tennis courts that success demanded, through the descending scale of semi-detached and terraced down to flats. Shakespeare Court was one of the more attractive blocks, of three stories only, the upper ones having generous balconies and the ground floor ones being allocated a small square of private garden, apart from the landscaped areas that were communally owned.

Roger's choice was on the ground floor, and it had been the little garden that had appealed to him. The large living room opened directly to it, as did the little kitchen next door, and although at present it was no more than a toy-strewn patch of rough grass and weeds, its main feature the fluttering washing on the rotating clothes line, in his mind's eye it was already burgeoning. He saw a little area of decking, such as had been displayed at Chelsea the previous year, with screening shrubs, pots for instant and renewable colour and even, if he could fit it in, what he named in his mind a small water feature.

Roger had thought long and hard about exactly what he wanted to buy. To begin with, when his mother had suggested he should look for a place of his own, he had been rather hurt.

'I thought you liked having me at home, Mum.' He had tried to make it sound jokey, but she knew him too well.

''Course I do, love. Nothing I like better than having you at home with me. But we can't go on like that for ever, can we?' Her shrewd eyes twinkled at him from her lined, yellowish face. He was so used to her bad colour that he seldom noticed it, but now he saw that her eyes had brownish smudges round them, and she had lost a bit more weight.

'You worse again, Mum?' She shook her head.

'Not worse, no. Just a bad day, that's all. We all get bad days.'

'Do I make too much work for you, is that it? I could do more, much more. You know I don't like you doing things for me all the time.'

15

She gave him a clout on the arm, hard enough to reassure him.

'Go on with you, you daft stick! Looking after you is the thing that helps to keep me going! Something to do, that's what I need. And don't think I'm going to stop doing it, just because you move out to a place of your own! You can bet your boots I'll be round there pestering you with crumbles and stews and my shepherd's pie, not to mention nicking your washing off the line so's I can iron it! No, I just reckon it's time, that's all. Time you spread your wings a bit. Stood on your own feet. You got to do it some time, why not start now? Meet more people. Find someone nice.'

'Oh, Mum!'

'Well, and what's wrong with that? Doesn't every mother want her kids to meet someone nice, settle down, all that? Why should you be different.'

'I'm twenty-two, Mum, not forty-two. I don't need to settle down.'

'P'raps not. So do the opposite, then. Sow a few wild oats. Fall in love, have an affair. Oh!' She laughed aloud. 'Listen to me! What would your Dad say to that, eh?'

Roger shivered.

'Don't, Mum,' he said uncomfortably. She stopped laughing, and taking his hand patted it between her own as if it were a piece of bread dough she was shaping.

'It's all right, love. I just want you to be happy, that's all. I can't hang around here for ever, when all's said and done. I'd like to know you had somebody . . . somebody nice . . . That's all.'

He smiled, because it was what he knew she wanted, though the effort made his face ache.

'Well, I suppose you're right, you generally are.'

'So you'll find out about a mortgage? And go and look at some places? Not too far away, mind,' she added with mock severity. 'I may be kicking you out of the nest, but I don't want you flying off, what do they call it, migrating?'

Any kind of change had always made him uncomfortable, but two or three days' thought had been enough to make him feel quite excited at the prospect of having a place of his own. For one thing, the money he could afford meant that it would necessarily be small, and this he found rather attractive. It was almost like the dimly remembered pleasure of playing in the Wendy House at his first school.

The flat at Shakespeare Court had appealed to him even before he visited it. He had always liked Shakespeare at school, and although he knew that desperate town planners, faced with naming a large number of new streets in one go, had simply taken the safe option and gone for English poets, he still felt that it was somehow significant to him. At first sight, though appalled by its untidiness, he had nevertheless liked the size and general layout. Visits to other, less

16

agreeable, flats had confirmed his first impression, though he had been careful to see this one more than once, at different times of day.

He realised that Mr Kingswood was speaking to him, and came back to himself with a start.

'Sorry. Miles away.'

The other man smiled.

'It was rather a long-drawn-out procedure. You know what Shelley's like – she loves to chat! By good luck they were both there, because her partner's on shift work and he doesn't start until this afternoon. They're very pleased that you're interested in the flat but asked me to tell you that they can't really afford to drop their price quite that far. I wonder whether we can reach some kind of compromise?'

Roger blinked at him.

'I expect you'd like to have some time to think about it,' said Paul resignedly. First time buyers and their ways held no mystery for him. 'It's a big decision. Though I have to say that it's a nice little flat, and in a particularly good area.'

'It needs a lot of work,' said Roger, seeing in his mind's eye the grubby carpets, the ceilings sepia-coloured from cigarette smoke and the scuffs and scratches on the wall.

'Cosmetics. Paint and paper job. The place is quite sound, underneath. Kitchen, bathroom, windows – nothing to do there. It does look a bit of a mess, I know . . .' And that's the understatement of the year, he thought, remembering the litter of abandoned beer cans, half chewed rusks, piles of washing, and heaps of magazines that covered every horizontal surface of the flat but the ceiling. 'I really don't think you'd be paying an unreasonable price. Eight years ago, they were going for twice that amount, and I think it's safe to say that prices can't go any lower. Well, they scarcely can, because they're more or less down to the same cost as building them new. Mortgages are cheap at the moment, and you're getting a good deal on yours.' Paul, watching carefully, could detect no sign of the 'you're an estate agent, I'm not going to believe a word you say' expression he knew so well. Encouraged, he continued. 'I think, unless it's going to eat too far into your savings, that the extra fifteen hundred is not unreasonable. Still, you must make up your own mind. Have a think about it, and give me a ring.'

Roger sat up straight.

'No,' he said. 'I don't need to think about it.'

I've blown it, thought Paul. Damn it all, after all these years you'd think I'd know better than to put pressure on a first-time buyer. They're all such delicate little blossoms, the smallest thing sends them screaming for cover. And *The Times* warned me, too. What was that word? Macrology – long and tiresome talk. And that's just what I gave him. My God, I'm getting too old for this game. In the old days I wouldn't have given a damn, just moved on to the next sale. But now – who knows when the next sale will be? And even if the fee on this will only be a drop in the ocean, it's still money coming in. Damn, damn and ultra-damn.

'I'll do it,' said Roger.

'I beg your pardon?' Paul was so busy cursing himself that he scarcely heard him.

'I'll pay the extra fifteen hundred. If that will do the trick.'

Paul smiled. For a moment he almost loved this thin young man who had folded his long limbs so neatly into the chair across the desk. Roger smiled back, elated.

'Great!' said Paul. 'That's great! I'm sure you won't regret it. Now . . .' He moved smoothly into the familiar routine of solicitors, mortgage broker, and possible moving dates. Macrology? he thought. Huh!

Shelley flung herself on top of Dave where he lay on the grubby sofa with a newspaper expertly folded into one hand, and a cigarette in the other.

'Whee! He's done it! Now, wasn't I right?'

'Steady, Shell.' He lifted newspaper and cigarette out of reach of her flying limbs. Shelley twitched the paper from his distracted grasp, and flung it over the back of the sofa. When he opened his mouth to complain she leaned forward and stuck her tongue into it, pushing her hands down to tickle his ribs.

'Aargh!' His voice was muffled by her tongue. He twisted his head to one side. 'Lay off, girl! Gimme back my paper!' Shelley, however, ignored him. She could feel how his body was responding to the pressure of hers as she rubbed her pelvis against his, enjoying the feel of the metal buttons on his jeans fly on her flesh. With the tip of her tongue still showing between her maroon-painted lips, she began to unbutton his denim shirt.

'Can't even have a quiet read of the paper,' he grumbled in mock disgust. 'Who's done what, anyway?' He reached out by instinct to the ashtray, and stubbed out his cigarette. 'And who to?' he added, with a grin, using his now freed hands to pull up her short skirt.

'That chap! The weedy one! He's going to buy the flat! Now we can find a proper house, be all moved in and settled before the baby comes! Mind my skirt!' She undid it and wriggled out of it, running her hand over her still flat stomach. 'Never think I was in the club, would you?'

Dave ignored this blatant demand for admiration. She felt his erection vanishing, and leaned forward to kiss him again.

'Don't worry, love,' she whispered throatily. 'You won't have to give it another thought. The flat's in my name, mine and Kev's, I'll

18

sort it all. And then we'll have a place of our own, a bit of privacy,' she wriggled again, 'so we can do what we like, won't have to worry about them upstairs making a fuss.'

'I'm not giving up my time off to drive you round all them places you want to look at,' he warned her. 'Not that I'll be able to take any time off, with all that money to find.'

'Skilled man like you, pay it off in no time,' she said admiringly. 'Proper jealous of me, all my friends are. Most of their fellers are on the dole. Not workers, like you.'

He was proud of his skill as a car mechanic, and the good money he brought home to her. She opened his flies, and smiled.

'That's my boy,' she said. In the bedroom her fourteen-month-old son woke and gave a fretful wail. He mumbled a query into her neck, but she straddled him and began the teasing approaches that always drove him wild.

'He'll be all right for a while,' she said. 'We got something to celebrate.'

Beep beep. Beep beep.

Paul, happily busy with filling in a sales schedule, left it for Rose to answer.

'Hensham Homes, good morning?' It was ten past twelve, Paul noted, but Rose had never mastered the intricacies of afternoon meaning just that. To her, it was morning until after lunch, which she ate in the office as did Paul and Melanie. Apart from five o'clock in the afternoon, when people began to leave work, it was the time when the office was most likely to be busy. Being there together also gave the two women a chance to catch up on what each had been doing, and to have a quick, pleasurable snipe at one another. Done, of course, beneath a superficially kind and friendly veneer, like splinters of glass embedded in a cake and hidden beneath a layer of sickly icing.

'No, I'm afraid this isn't the cinema. No, you want eight four, eight four, eight four. That's quite all right.' Rose was, if anything, even more polite to wrong number callers than Paul was. When she had first started working for him, he had pointed out that every encounter with the public, however mistaken, was a chance to gain the goodwill of a potential client. Rose had taken this much to heart.

'You know, Mr K,' she said now. 'I could easily ring the cinema, write down the film times from their recorded message. What do you think? As a kind of service to people?'

Paul spent a happy thirty seconds contemplating this. The local cinema, while showing all the general run of new releases, also had a club that showed more 'adult' films to late night devotees. He imagined Rose's face as she carefully enunciated 'and at eleven thirty, *Scenes In*

19

The Saucy Sauna – fun and games from Sweden for club members only.' Regretfully, he shook his head.

'It's a nice idea,' he said truthfully, 'but a bit impractical. It would tie up the phone for too long. And besides, the people who phone often want to book seats at the same time, so they'd still have to ring again. Clients,' he looked round the deserted office, 'assuming we had any, might think it a bit strange, too.'

Rose nodded regretfully, and returned to her computer keyboard. Each of them typed quietly for a moment, Paul almost as fast although he used only two fingers. Then Rose stopped, peered at the screen, and tutted.

'Really, Mr K! That girl! You'll definitely have to say something to her!'

'What's she done now?'

'It's just carelessness, there's no excuse for it. She should check what she's typed before she saves it, like I do. No pride in her work, that's the trouble.'

It was a familiar complaint. Only the sales schedule in front of him made it bearable.

'What's she put?'

'It not what she's put, it's what she's omitted.' It was typical of Rose, he thought, to use a word like 'omitted'. A sin of omission, he mused.

'And what has she omitted?'

'She's left out the a in insulated.'

He worked it out, and gave a snort of laughter.

'So it's insulted? What is it, an insulted loft? I suppose it's too much to expect that it's bored and insulted, instead of boarded and insulated?'

'No. It's the hot water cylinder. In the airing cupboard.'

Where they generally tended to be. He saw that she was annoyed by his amusement.

'Well, it's a good thing I've got you to check these things. You know how it is when you read through them – you see what you expect to see. I often do, at any rate.'

Rose opened her mouth to make a further complaint, but to Paul's relief the telephone rang, and he reached to answer it with more alacrity than he sometimes showed.

'Hensham Homes, good afternoon?'

'Would you be very kind,' said a woman's voice beseechingly, 'and come to value my house?' Paul, who at the beginning of her sentence had thought she was going to ask him to lend her money, glowed with pleasure.

'I should be delighted,' he said, meaning it. 'When would you like me to come?' The empty pages of his office diary gleamed at him, grinning like a set of false teeth inadvertently left in a skull.

'Well . . . It's a bit difficult. It's my husband, you see.'

Paul's elation subsided. That sort of remark often meant a divorce, and in his experience that led to problems. Very often one half of the couple would be pushing to sell, the other resisting. The agent, in the middle, often ended up as a combination of shoulder to cry on, whipping boy, amateur marriage guidance counsellor, or simply as a guided missile used indiscriminately by both sides. In any event, since the proceeds of the sale would have to be split between them to finance the purchase of two separate homes, the one thing they would inevitably agree on was that any price that gave even a faint hope of attracting a buyer would be wildly insufficient for their needs.

'The trouble is,' she confided, 'that he's rather stubborn, and rather deaf. Particularly when he doesn't want to hear something.'

'And he doesn't want to hear about selling your house?'

'No. That is, he knows that it has to be done, but he's trying not to think about it. In fact, it's not so much the house, it's the garden. The house is much too big for us now, of course, but you can close the doors and simply not use all the rooms. You can't do that with a garden, and he's killing himself trying to keep it as it's always been.'

Paul's spirits rose cautiously, reluctant to raise their heads above the parapet in case a hidden sniper might shoot them off.

Large house, large garden. Could this be a real sale, something that he could sell and actually make a decent fee from? It seemed too good to be true.

'Where are you, exactly?'

She told him. His spirits not only showed their heads, they actually jumped on to the parapet and started to dance on it. Outside the town, in the most exclusive (how he hated that word!) part of the outskirts, near enough to the town to be practical but far enough out to be considered 'country'. Something that would brighten up his weekly advertisement in the local paper, something that it would actually be a pleasure to sell.

'About how big is the house? How many bedrooms?' he asked, trying not to dribble into the telephone.

'Six. And two bathrooms. We built quite a bit of it ourselves. Had it built, I mean, when we first bought it forty years ago.' Good sized rooms, then, he thought, and solidly constructed. Thank you God, or Life, or Chance. 'And the garden,' she continued, 'is about an acre. Not including the paddock.'

'It has a paddock?' His heart was pounding. Ridiculous to be in such a state.

'Yes. And a couple of loose boxes.'

Paul would have thought he'd died and gone to heaven, if it weren't

21

almost certain that estate agents didn't go there.

'When would you like me to come round?' His voice came out pitched quite high, his vocal cords were strung up as tight as guitar strings.

'Could you manage this afternoon? My husband will be out then.'

'That sounds delightfully compromising.'

There was a short silence, during which time his blood congealed and sank into his feet, like poorly dissolved gelatin crystals. His traitorous tongue, clattering with joy, had betrayed him. 'Sorry,' he muttered. 'I don't know what got into me.'

'My dear man, you don't have to apologise. I knew your uncle. In fact, he sold us the house in the first place. That's why I wanted to come back to you. Sort of keep it in the family, you know?'

'Thank you.' He had never been so sincere. 'Um, what were you thinking of moving to? Perhaps I can find your next house, as well.'

She sighed.

'That's the depressing part. I don't really know. I can't imagine living anywhere but here, really. It would have to be something sensible, I suppose. Not too large, but with a reasonable garden – I don't think poor old George could survive without something to look after. He may have a dodgy heart, but he's not going to sit about waiting for it to pack up on him, and I don't blame him. So a small house, or perhaps a bungalow? Yes, maybe a bungalow would be the best thing. No stairs. Rest his heart and my knees, too. I don't suppose you could find us anything like that, could you?'

There is a heaven for estate agents, thought Paul, and I am in it.

'As a matter of fact,' he said with an affectation of nonchalance, 'I believe I could.'

Chapter Three

'That one might do. Mmm. Or that one . . . good position, house is a bit ordinary . . . Harry! Sit up straight, and for goodness sake stop messing that egg about and eat it!'

From behind the shelter of his newspaper, Alec glanced at his elder daughter. He wiggled his eyebrows at her, hoping to make her smile and to express his commiseration and encouragement. Harriet, who loathed eggs in general and poached eggs in particular, smiled wanly back. She straightened her spine but kept her head lowered over her plate, as if the egg would be easier to get rid of if she didn't have so far to lift it to her mouth. She looked at it in despair. Undercooked, the white round the yolk was clear and runny, dribbling in strings from the cooked part. She dabbled at it, knowing that if she had to put it in her mouth she would be sick.

'Mummy! Daddy's pulling faces at Harry!'

Georgina, Harriet's sister, was two years younger in age but about five years ahead of her in confidence.

'Don't be a sneak, George.' Christine's response was automatic, but her voice was mild, milder than her tone when she looked again at Harriet's plate.

'Come along, Harry. It's nearly time for school.'

Harriet looked up at her with swimming, myopic eyes. If her irises had been golden yellow instead of hazel, they would have looked exactly like miniature versions of the egg on her plate. Her glasses were missing, too – the frames must be damaged again. Christine suppressed the irritation that so often washed over her at the sight of her firstborn. As she frequently did she wondered how on earth she had managed to produce this skinny little waif, with her pale skin that never took the sun no matter where they went on holiday, her frail body, her wispy hair and the broad forehead that bulged over the hazel eyes that were her only attractive feature, in Christine's opinion. And even they must be hidden behind the wretched spectacles that were forever getting lost or broken.

'Do eat it, Harry,' she said, annoyed that the child flinched at her words even though they were spoken with brusque kindness. 'Eggs are good for you, you know the doctor said you need building up.'

'Like a house,' said Georgina helpfully. 'Harry's as thin as a

23

scaffolding pole, the wolf will huff, and puff, and blow her down. She needs some bricks and things, then she'll be built like a brick shit-house. What's a brick shit-house, Mummy? I mean, I know what a shit-house must be, but I thought they were made of wood, like the old outside loo at Gramps . . .'

'Really, George!' Christine's voice was indulgent. Georgina's sturdy body, the dark hair that bounced in lively curls round her pretty, vivid face, and her fearless approach to everything that life had to offer, made her precisely the daughter that Christine wanted. Alec rustled his paper.

'That's enough, Georgie. Harriet's egg is very runny, Chrissie. You know she hates them like that.'

'I've never known anyone as fussy as that child . . .'

'Well, you don't want her to be late for school. Let her dip her toast in the yolk and eat that, it's the yolk that's the nourishing bit, after all.'

His voice just stopped short of pleading. Harriet kept her head down. Her thin shoulders were hunched: he could see the knobs of her spine, the bones of her shoulder blades sticking out like hard little wings beneath her school pullover. He was overwhelmed by a feeling of protective tenderness, and cleared his throat gruffly. Beneath the edge of the tablecloth, Harriet's hand came out and touched his leg gently in gratitude. She began to cut her toast into neat pieces, and her mother watched with ill-concealed irritation.

'Don't cut them so *small*, Harry. It's going to take you for ever at that rate.'

Alec thought, as he so often did, that it was a pity that Christine was such a perfectionist. Other families, he knew, dispensed with a proper breakfast altogether. Many of his daughters' schoolfellows arrived at school in their parents' cars still chewing on a piece of toast, or even with a half finished bowl of cereal in their hands. Most of them, and their parents too, made do with a hurried snack in the kitchen. Christine, however, thought such habits slipshod, and insisted on a proper cooked breakfast every day, just as she had always eaten as a child, although she modified it in a token genuflection towards modern low-fat eating mores. Bacon and tomatoes were grilled, as were sausages and mushrooms, but even then Harriet picked off every speck of fat, and chewed the sausages suspiciously, nervous of pieces of gristle.

The table, too, was properly set each morning with a crisply ironed tablecloth and matching napkins. Butter was in a dish, toast in a rack, and jam decanted from its jars into cut-glass dishes. Alec knew that it required a lot of effort to see that this was done, but although he tried to be grateful to Christine he could not help seeing it as a kind of anachronism. He also felt that it was a subtle, perhaps unconscious, attack on him.

24

He, after all, had not been brought up to live like this. Although his grandfather had been a baronet, his father had been a younger son and everything, house, land and such money as was left, had gone to Alec's uncle along with the title. Alec's parents, cheerfully hard-working couple that they were, had been satisfied to eat breakfast around the convenient little breakfast bar in their formica-finished kitchen before hurrying away to work leaving Alec, whose school was nearby and whose journey was therefore shorter, to clear it away. He would linger over the last leathery slice of toast, dropping crumbs and blobs of marmalade on to his comic, then dash to pile the plates in the sink. He often thought that those pieces of toast, chewy and cold though they had been, had tasted far better than the crisp golden slices of healthy wholemeal that Christine served up.

It was true that his uncle had allowed them to have their wedding reception at the family house, but since that day they had scarcely set foot over the threshold. Christine had made an effort, sending Christmas cards and invitations to Sunday lunch, or dinner, or even for a weekend. They had never been accepted, and as the daughter of a wealthy industrialist she had very quickly decided, in her practical way, that he would be of no further service to Alec or to her, and she had abandoned her attempts.

Harriet had put her knife and fork together, leaving most of her egg on the plate. Alec stood up and began to pile the plates together. Clumsy with haste, he knocked Harriet's eggy fork off her plate. It left a smear of egg yolk on the crisp cotton of the tablecloth. Christine looked up from the property pages of the local paper that had been occupying eighty per cent of her attention throughout breakfast.

'*Do* leave that, Alexander. You know Mrs Mop will see to it in a moment. Look, what do you think of this one?' Christine frequently remembered to be tactful, and to behave as if it were his money and not hers that financed their home, if not their lifestyle. He put down the plates as Harriet darted from the room. Her black tights made her legs look even thinner, but he preferred them to the socks she had had to wear before, above which her legs had looked blotched and goose-bumped with cold for most of the year. Alec went round the table to look over Christine's shoulder. At forty he still kept much of the youthful good looks that she had found so attractive. Harriet's boniness was fleshed out by the muscles acquired during many years of tennis, running and rowing, and his hair was as curly as Georgina's, and still thick and dark as it had ever been.

'It's been very badly renovated,' he said mildly. 'Those plastic windows are completely wrong in a Victorian house. And isn't seven bedrooms rather a lot? Or are we going to take in lodgers?'

'Really, Alexander.' It was a routine expostulation, made so often that neither noticed it. 'The girls are growing up. They'll be going to boarding school in a year or two, and inviting all their friends back to stay.'

Her calm assumption annoyed him. He himself had been educated in the state system. His mother, a teacher herself, had felt strongly on the subject and his father had been relieved not to have to find the enormous sums necessary for a public school education. Alec thought that he had been well taught, and that looking back his schooldays had been as happy as anyone's he knew. He had very reluctantly gone along with Christine's choice of a small local preparatory school for his daughters, largely because the alternative primary school was very large and he knew that Harriet, at least, would have found it terrifying. The school was also nearer, another benefit, and the girls could have walked there if Christine had not thought it proper for them to arrive in her smart BMW.

That was all very well for now, but with Harriet now ten and Georgie almost eight, he was aware that he would soon have to make some kind of decision about their secondary school. While he could not feel that the huge Hensham Comprehensive would be anything other than an ordeal for Harriet, he was equally sure that she would be even more miserable at a boarding school. There was a small Catholic comprehensive school not far away, which was reputed to be good, but when he had suggested it to Christine she had dismissed it out of hand.

'Don't be ridiculous, Alexander. We aren't Catholics.'

'It isn't a requirement. They take plenty of Anglicans too.'

'You surely don't want her going over to Rome, do you?' Christine had all the horror of someone who only attended church at Christmas and Easter and Harvest Festival, for anything outside the straightforward Anglicanism she was vaguely familiar with. 'She'll be muttering rosaries and going on retreats and worshipping some kind of frightful doll covered with sparkly tinsel and artificial flowers. Besides, you're always going on about how clever she is, surely you want her to get the best possible education?'

'She's clever enough to do well wherever she goes, as long as she's happy and encouraged. And I don't think Catholic schools are quite like that now. Not in Hensham, anyway.'

'Well, it's still out of the question. And if you're worried about the fees, I'm sure The Trust would cough up.'

'I'm not worried about the fees.' Long years of marriage had taught him that Christine had no idea that she might be speaking tactlessly, she simply said what she thought. 'I would pay anything to give my daughters whatever is the best education for them. I'm just not convinced that a boarding school is the best thing for Harriet.'

'You don't seem very concerned about George.'

'Georgie will fall on her feet wherever she lands, she's that kind of person.'

'Well, I haven't got time to worry about it now. There's plenty of time, after all. They can stay at St Hilary's until they're twelve or thirteen. We can discuss it another time.'

Alec wondered whether what they had just had was a discussion, and whether in fact they had ever had such a thing. It was not that Christine dismissed his opinions, they just slid off her like an omelette from a teflon-coated pan. The main problem, of course, was the money. Not the lack of it – rather the reverse – but the unevenness of its distribution.

Alec earned what most people would consider a very good income from the small company of chartered surveyors of which he was a partner. It was enough for them to live in relative luxury, with two or three foreign holidays a year, meals out when ever they felt like it, a beautifully decorated home with part-time cleaner and gardener to keep it immaculate. The only problem (in Alec's eyes) was The Trust.

THE TRUST. He saw it like that, in capital letters. It had been set up by Christine's grandfather, a man who had made a tremendous amount of money out of the various business enterprises he had set up, and whose only big disappointment in life had been that he had no son. Distrusting women to function in any but a decorative fashion, he had tied his money up to ensure that his only child, a daughter, could not squander the capital. The beneficiaries were to be his grandchildren, and Alec had often mused that it was richly ironic that they, too, were females since Christine had only a sister and she, too, had no sons. More recently he had pondered on the fact that Christine had chosen to name her own children Harriet and Georgina, which were fine upper-middle class names that sounded well at school and the pony club, but always called them Harry and George. She herself had been called, as it were, after her grandfather, whose name had been Christopher.

Although successful, Alec knew that he could never compete with The Trust. Over the years it had financed the purchase of their first house, their second, and now their present one. With four large bedrooms, set in the middle of an attractive and extensive garden, it had already been a good family home even before Christine had added the conservatory and the little swimming pool that sat, neatly covered against leaves and other foreign bodies, below the terrace.

Of late, however, she had once again started to check the property pages of the local paper, and it was obvious that she was dissatisfied with where they were. Alec, who could have afforded to finance a mortgage on their present house though not, perhaps, on the kind of thing she had her eye on, knew that The Trust would cough up. Christine treated it as a sweetie jar to dip into, or rather as a useful

27

foliage plant, the kind you could always rely on for cutting to bring into the house, in the knowledge that it would soon regrow.

If, as seemed likely, Christine was set on moving to something more prestigious, she would borrow from The Trust without a second thought. Alec had sometimes wondered whether she realised that the pot was finite, and that the thousands of pounds of capital she would tie up in their home represented a substantial part of her eventual share. He supposed it didn't matter very much: his own income was more than adequate for their day-to-day needs, and allowed him to put money by also. If nothing else, they would be buying when the market was at a low ebb, and the differential between their present house and their future one would be small compared to what it would have been eight or ten years earlier.

'Can you take the girls this morning?' she asked now, reluctantly abandoning the newspaper and standing up. 'I want to get Mrs Mop started on turning out the kitchen cupboards. Oh, there you are, Mrs Mop. I thought we'd have a good go at the kitchen today, if that's all right with you?'

Alec winced. He could never feel happy about the way his wife called her cleaning lady 'Mrs Mop'. He himself always called her, meticulously, by her full name of Mrs Moppett, which always made him want to smile. Christine, when he had remonstrated with her, had been brisk with him. 'Nonsense, darling, you're being too sensitive. She knows it's a joke to call her Mrs Mop, and she certainly doesn't mind. It's not as if I treat her as a servant, or anything. I always have coffee with her, if I'm at home.' It was true that Mrs Moppett, fiftyish and cosy and smelling of clean washing, always seemed perfectly happy, but Alec still cringed. The children called her Mopsy, Harriet having named her after one of Peter Rabbit's sisters in honour of her Beatrix Potter-type name, and Alec sometimes wished that he could do the same.

'Yes, of course I'll take them. Good morning, Mrs Moppett.'

'Morning, Mr Blake. I'll just get the table cleared, then, and straighten up in here.'

'Right. Don't let Harriet forget her flute, Alexander, it's her lesson day.'

'Okay.' Alec marvelled once again, as he chivvied the children into the car, at how little Christine knew about her daughters. Harriet would never forget her flute. She loved it, and her lessons were the high point of her week. You might as well think of needing to remind Georgie to take her hard hat to riding on Saturday.

'We'll have a good clear out, Mrs Mop,' Christine was saying as he left. 'There are several things I never use that you might like, or they could go to the church bazaar. And next week, I thought we might go through the cupboard under the stairs.'

Alec sighed. All this clearing out, he knew, presaged the dire upheaval of packing to move house.

Beep beep. Beep beep.

'Hensham Homes, good afternoon?'

'Good afternoon. Is that Mr Kingswood?'

Paul rejected his jokey responses such as, 'I'm afraid so' and, 'It was when I last looked'. She didn't sound the type. Her voice was rather serious, educated and well-spoken. Genuine Georgian, he thought, not Neo. A classic facade of warm red brick fronting gracefully proportioned rooms. Altogether desirable, in residential terms.

'It is.' He spoke equally carefully, and since she had presumably telephoned with some specific purpose in mind which she would inevitably divulge, he refrained from asking whether there was anything he could do for her.

'My name is Beth Oldham. Mrs Oldham. I am Mrs Holt's daughter.'

He wondered whether this were some kind of test. If so, she wouldn't catch him out like that, as the unfortunate truth was that he had so few houses to sell that the name of any potential vendor was engraved on his memory in letters of fire.

'Five, Blackwood Lane. A bungalow, it should be easy to sell. I'm going to see it this evening. As a matter of fact,' he could scarcely keep the elation out of his voice, 'I already have someone who might be interested in it, if Mrs Oldham decides to sell through me.' I just hope that didn't sound like blackmail, he thought. Or pleading. Perish the thought.

'If she decides?'

'I got the impression that she was having several different agents to look at the place. Most people do.'

'That's not quite how I heard it.' Her voice – a pleasant voice, he thought – was not suspicious, thank goodness. Wary, perhaps?

'How did you hear it?'

'I rather gathered that you were encouraging her to sell her bungalow. Pushing her, in fact. That she had been reluctant, but that you had managed to persuade her.'

The words themselves sounded accusing, but her voice was carefully neutral. He thought back. Surely Mrs Holt had told him that her daughter was insisting she sell the bungalow, and move into sheltered accommodation?

'Um . . . do you have a sister?'

'A sister? No, I'm an only child. Why? Oh, I see. The old bat.' She was quick witted, and she was smiling now.

'Madam, be careful what you say. You are speaking of the woman that I love.'

'Because she has a bungalow to sell?'

'Partly. But mostly because she has a parrot.'

This time she laughed out loud.

'Did you believe her? When she said that I was making her sell up?'

'Not for long,' he answered. 'It seemed to me that Mrs Holt is someone who couldn't be made to do anything that she didn't want to.'

'How right you are.' The amusement was rueful this time. 'It's true that the place is getting to be too much for her. As a matter of fact, I'd been trying to persuade her to come and live with me.'

'And how does your husband feel about that?' Rather blatant fishing for information, but never mind.

'Pretty neutral, really. He's been dead for ten years.'

'I'm sorry.'

'It's all right. It was a long time ago. And besides, he was actually going off with someone else at the time.'

'Literally?'

'Yes, she was in the car with him. In fact, she was driving. She was only nineteen, and he let her drive his sports car. She took a bend too fast, and he was killed instantly. She was just bruised, poor girl, but very shocked, of course.'

'Of course. You're very forgiving.'

'Not really. Not at the time, anyway. I felt so guilty, because I'd been hating him so much that I got this irrational idea it was my fault, that I'd somehow ill-wished him. Then, of course, I realised that she was feeling even worse, because she really *had* killed him. And in the end, I was glad to be rid of him, though I wouldn't have wished him dead. And he was very well insured,' she ended demurely. 'Why am I telling you all this?'

'Because I'm going to save you from having your mother to live with you.'

'How do you know I don't want her?'

'I don't, but she does. At least, she says you think you do, but that you've had too many years of independence to go back to sharing your house with anyone, and so has she.'

'Goodness. It makes me sound like a dreadful misanthropist. But it's true I'm used to my independence.'

'No one else's washing up in the sink. Or socks – tights – on the bathroom radiator. Nobody finishing the last of the milk, or insisting on cooking you a three-course meal when you really fancy a nice boiled egg.'

'You've been there, then?'

'I'm practically the founder member.'

'Not one of those helpless men who can't manage their own laundry, and live out of a frying pan?'

'Not at all. I can cook, and wash, and clean.'

30

'*Where have you been all my life, Billie Boy, Billie Boy?*' Her singing voice was as pleasant as her speaking.

'Well, I can probably manage the Irish stew, but what on earth *is* a "singin' hinnie"?'

'Haven't the foggiest. One of those teacake things you're supposed to bake on a griddle, I think. Except that I don't believe I know anyone with a griddle. We've all got woks, now.'

''Appen we're in t'wrong part o' t'country, lass.'

'Aye, lad, 'appen we are.'

The telephone rang. With half an ear, Paul listened to Melanie answering it.

'Hensham Homes, good afternoon?' Her voice lifted, Australian fashion, at the end of each little phrase, making it sound like a question. She taped both the Australian soap operas each day, and watched them avidly when she went home after work. He had sometimes wondered how long it would be before she answered 'Hinsham Haimes, g'day?'.

'You're busy?'

'Nothing we can't handle,' he answered, listening to Melanie dealing with another cinema enquiry. Maybe Rose's idea wasn't such a bad one, at that.

'So, you think the bungalow will be easy to sell?'

'I know it will. When they built the new estates they were thinking of housing the people coming in to work on the industrial estate. But they forgot that people get older. There's a desperate shortage of good bungalows, in fact of bungalows of any kind.'

'Good. At least, I suppose it's good. It's just that I can't imagine her in an old folk's home.'

'Nor can I. But she doesn't have to make such an extreme change, does she? What about sheltered housing? There's a very good place in North Green, some flats but mostly small houses built like a model village, round little courts. There's a warden in case of problems, and all sorts of social clubs and visiting chiropodists and things, but they have their own front doors and so on.'

'That sounds more like it. What it is to have insider knowledge.'

'We have our uses. Believe it or not.'

'Oh dear. Are we bitter and twisted? Misunderstood?'

'Wouldn't you be, if you'd been an estate agent for thirty years?'

'I should think doing the same job for thirty years would be enough to make you a bit warped, no matter what it was.'

'Vicar? Nurse? Neurosurgeon?'

'*Can* you be a neurosurgeon for thirty years? You'd have to start rather young. Or live a long time. Still, I take your point. I suppose if it was something you really loved doing . . . but I wouldn't really know.'

31

'I imagine you're too young to have done anything for thirty years.'

'I'm forty-nine, so I suppose I am, really. But you don't sound old enough either.'

'Fifty-three. I started young. It's a long story, as you might say.'

'Great. I like long stories.'

The telephone rang again. Melanie answered it, but the sound continued and looking down at the telephone on his desk he saw that there were two lights flashing on the display.

'I'm sorry, I'll have to go, the other phone . . .'

'Of course, I've taken up too much of your time.'

'No . . .' But she was gone, with a decisive click. He cursed himself, for not asking for her telephone number. In case of any problems, he could have said. He also cursed the fact that she had called on a line that only took incoming calls, so he could not dial one four seven one and find out. For good measure he cursed people who telephoned him when he was busy.

'Hensham Homes, good afternoon?'

'Good afternoon, Mr Kingswood. This is Mr Selby speaking. Buying the flat in Shakespeare Court.' It was typical of Roger that unlike most clients he always assumed that nobody would remember who he was.

'Oh, Mr Selby, how are you?' Don't tell me, he pleaded internally, that you've changed your mind. Or that you can't get a mortgage after all. Not that. It happened all too depressingly often.

'I'm very well, Mr Kingswood, and thank you for asking. I just wondered how the sale is progressing? Have Mr and Mrs – have the owners of number forty three Shakespeare Court found anything yet?'

It was only a week since the offer had been accepted. First time buyers always thought things would happen at the drop of a hat. Either that, or they held things up for months because they couldn't be bothered to fill in any forms.

'I think we're progressing perfectly normally, Mr Selby. I've sent them quite a few details, and no doubt they've been in touch with other agents too. I'm sure they'll find something quite soon.'

'Oh, good. Only I wondered if I could go round there again this weekend.'

'For another look?' An alarming thought. Another look often meant second thoughts.

'Not exactly. I'd like to measure up the windows, that kind of thing.'

'I'm sure that would be fine. Would you like me to fix it for you? I could ask how they're getting on with their own house-hunting, at the same time.'

'That would be most helpful. Saturday afternoon would be best, really. Or Sunday morning.'

'Certainly, Mr Selby. I'll fix it up, and get back to you.' Mentally wiping a relieved brow Paul put down the telephone.

Chapter Four

Paul gave one last glance round the hall.

'Thermostat for the heating system in the hall,' he said into his hand-held recorder. 'Sorry, Rose. I missed it the first time round. Otherwise that's it.' He switched off the recorder, which was voice-activated, and slipped it into his jacket pocket. He looked hopefully at Mrs Holt. 'All done,' he said.

'You sound like a dentist. Are you going to offer me a nice rinse and spit?'

'I'm fresh out of mouthwash, I'm afraid.'

'Then we'll have to make do with sherry, unless you'd prefer another cup of tea. If you have time?'

Paul, who had carefully arranged to make the bungalow his last appointment of the day, gravely signified that he had time, and followed his hostess back into the living room. He would not, normally, have accepted such an invitation. A cup of tea or coffee, drunk on the move while he measured up a house, was the most he generally expected. It was usually better, he had learned, not to make himself too much at home in his clients' houses. It was, after all, primarily a business relationship, and although it was easier to be on friendly terms, too much friendliness could later lead to misunderstandings.

The sitting-room was large, extending right across the back of the bungalow. Its resemblance to a colonial dwelling was enhanced by the wooden veranda that ran along the outside, with wisteria and honeysuckle climbing up the posts and rioting on the roof. Even now, in September, there were still some flowers on the wisteria, and he thought that in early summer the whole veranda must be smothered in scented purple flowers. Against this background, the Benares brass trays on their carved wooden stands and the rugs on the wall looked as though the building had been designed specifically for them. The large metal cage, domed like a filigree Taj Mahal, and the parrot inside it, exotic in an average house, looked as normal as a budgie or a curled up cat. Unusual Two-Bedroom Home, thought Paul. Must Be Viewed To Be Appreciated.

The sherry was tooth-achingly dry, and there was a bowl of unsalted nuts to go with it. The parrot, which had kept its orange-rimmed eyes trained suspiciously on Paul, showed signs of excitement, bobbing its head and then climbing up to hang beneath the spire of the dome, stretching its wings out and shrieking. From the front it had appeared almost entirely green except for the flashes of blue, like eye shadow, over its eyes that were echoed on chin and flight feathers. From behind, however, its lower back and rump were red, and the tips of its short green tail were yellow. Paul checked it against his memory, and thought he had made no mistake.

'It's time for his bath,' said Mrs Holt. 'Do you mind if I . . . ?' She took up a plant sprayer.

Paul put down his sherry. 'Could I . . . ?'

'Of course. Let me just take out his food pots. There you are. From above, like rain. Go on, he loves it really, he's just pretending to be frightened.'

The parrot scuttled away down the walls of the cage, but when the fine mist from the sprayer began to drift down, he climbed crabwise up again and hung once more, wings spread wide as if to catch as much of the water as possible. He rotated slowly, silent except for an occasional mumble. Paul continued until his arm ached from being held up, his hand was tired from pulling the trigger of the sprayer, and the can itself was almost empty.

'That'll do. You're spoiling him. I don't normally keep it up for nearly as long.'

'I'm not surprised. How do you reach?' Paul was not very tall, but he was a head taller than Mrs Holt and the cage looked almost big enough for her to sit in.

'Stand on a stool. I know it's not recommended for someone of my age, but the alternative is to keep the cage on the floor and grovel about on my knees every time I have to put in food or water, or change the lining. Which, incidentally, I have to do every day. They say they only need spraying two or three times a week, but he does so love it. After all, where he comes from, it rains most days, I believe.' As she spoke she opened the door again, and took out the metal trays on the floor. Paul hastened to take them from her, as they were brimming with water, and tipped the wet sand, newspaper and birdseed husks out into the bucket she indicated.

'Thank you. Modern cages have a special opening, so you can slide the trays out without any risk of the birds escaping. I must confess this one is awkward, but it's so beautiful I couldn't bear to replace it.' With the ease of long practice she re-lined the trays, and put them neatly back. 'Besides, I don't worry about him escaping. I usually let him out at this time of day for an hour or two, and even when the french windows are open he never goes beyond the veranda. He's a bit of a wimp, really.'

Paul eyed the large, blackish beak. The parrot stepped out of the open cage, flew once round the room, and landed on the arm of the chair where Paul had been sitting. Hastily, though without any sudden movements, Paul resumed his seat.

'I'm honoured.'

'No, you have the nuts.'

The parrot eyed him.

'You,' it said. 'You.' Paul took a brazil nut from the bowl, as the largest item he could see and therefore offering the least risk to his fingers. The parrot, however, took it delicately, its head on one side. Standing on one greyish foot it took the nut in the other, and nibbled at it. 'Eureka,' it remarked, conversationally.

'Eureka?' It seemed one of the more unusual words to teach a parrot.

'His name is Archimedes.'

'Oh. Because he has principles?'

'Far from it. I'll show you why, later. Look out.'

The warning was too late. The arm of the chair, upholstered in glazed chintz, was protected by a kind of loose cover of clear plastic, as were most of the chair backs and arms in the room. The parrot, concentrating on the nut, was rather near the curve of the arm and his single foot had inadequate purchase on the slippery surface. Inexorably he began to slide down. Paul expected him to spread his wings and save himself, but Archimedes allowed himself to fall, still clutching his brazil nut, until he landed with a surprisingly heavy thud in the gap between Paul's leg and the arm. As if by the merest chance, which perhaps it was, the bowl was knocked from Paul's loose hold on his knee, so that the bird landed in a heap of nuts. 'Eureka,' he said again, reflectively, and after careful inspection took a walnut.

Paul wiped streaming eyes, and began to gather up the spilled nuts. The parrot eyed him balefully, and snatched at a passing peanut.

'Don't let him have too many. He's a greedy creature, he'd look like a rugby ball with feathers if I didn't watch his diet.'

'It seems unfair. It was a brilliant trick – was it a trick? It had that off-the-cuff spontaneity that you only get after a lot of practice.'

'Yes, he's done it several times. That's why I put you in that chair, and gave you the nuts. It always, er, goes down well. Get the nuts away from him, though, and we'll give him some fruit in a minute. He likes that even better. I spend a fortune on grapes.'

'Have you had him long?' Paul sipped his sherry, and absent-mindedly ate some of the gathered nuts.

'Twenty years. He was my husband's really. He drives me mad sometimes, and he makes a great deal of work, but I'm attached to him. You know what he is?'

Paul scratched the top of the parrot's head. 'A Festive Amazon?'

Her eyebrows shot up. 'I'm impressed.'

'You needn't be. I looked through the book last night, so it's fresh in my mind.'

'I'm still impressed.' She topped up his glass. 'And I assume you've forgiven me?'

'Forgiven you? For what?'

'I gather my daughter telephoned you.'

'Oh, that. Yes, of course I have. People like me forgive things ten times worse than that, every day of the week.'

'People like you? People who like parrots?'

'Estate agents.'

'There's more to you than just being an estate agent, surely?'

'I suppose so. Yes, of course there is. I just tend to forget it, that's all.'

'You should get out more. Meet people.' He raised an eyebrow at her. 'Yes, I know you're meeting the public all day long, but that's different, isn't it? I knew someone doing a job like yours, who had a name for members of the public who wander in off the street. He called them piles.'

'Why piles?'

'Because they're a pain, and they come in bunches.'

Once again, he laughed until the tears ran. It was not until he got home later on that he realised that he still didn't know why the parrot was called Archimedes. He thought, happily, that it might give him an excuse to go there again. He wondered, as he fell asleep, how often Beth Oldham visited her mother.

Roger knocked at the door. It wasn't a very loud knock, and he had already lifted his hand to try again when the door was opened.

'Mr Redman?' The woman's eyes travelled dubiously from him to Shelley, struggling up the path with a recalcitrant toddler hanging by one arm from her grasp. Roger backed away.

'Oh no. No. That's Mrs – er – Ms Redman. Her, um, her other half couldn't manage to get here, so I offered her a lift. I'm just . . .'

Her eyes lost interest in him, and focused on Shelley. There was a quality of desperation in them that he found disturbing. Shelley was dressed for the occasion in lime green leggings and a fluorescent-orange cropped top. The day was cool, summer's warmth chilling into autumn, but she showed no sign of feeling cold although the sight of her bare midriff made him feel quite shivery.

'Mrs Redman? I'm Louise Johnson. Do come in.'

'Call me Shelley,' she puffed as she lifted the little boy, who had gone alarmingly rigid and was screaming vociferously, into the air and looked him in the face, nose to nose.

'That's enough, Liam. This nice lady is going to show us her house, and on the way home we will stop at the ice cream van.' The screams stopped as if by magic, and though Roger winced at the thought of Liam eating an ice cream in his car, he was relieved. This was the fourth house they had visited in the last hour and a half, and he was almost as bored and exhausted as Liam was.

He still couldn't fathom how he had allowed himself to be put in this position. He had arrived at two o'clock, as arranged by Mr Kingswood, and had spent a relatively happy twenty minutes measuring the alcove (for his bookshelves), the windows, and (rather shyly) the size of the bed space between the fitted bedside cabinets.

'Get a double bed,' his mother had advised. 'No point in spending money on a single, and then finding you need a double later on. Oh, don't look at me like that! You know what beds are for, same as I do! And since you've got to sleep in one, you might as well have a decent size even if it is just for you, at the moment. Comfortable, you'll find it. Read a book, read the papers on Sunday morning – plenty of room.' He had blushed, but realised that she was right. Shelley and Dave's bed, he discovered, was a king-size, a fact which she told him with pride and he learned with embarrassment.

He had progressed to a minute inspection of the little garden. Shelley brought him a mug of tea – a good one, he was rather surprised to find, made just as he liked it.

'Nice little flat, innit?' she had asked, sipping from her own mug. He averted his eyes from the child, who was stuffing lumps of earth into his mouth, and agreed.

'And have you found anything yourself? Something to move into?' He felt more relaxed with her now, and the child, though disgusting, was still a kind of protection. 'I expect you'll be wanting something bigger.'

'Certainly will. Specially with another one on the way.'

'Another one?' She indicated the little boy with a nod of her head. 'Oh, you mean you're . . . expecting? Congratulations.' Covertly he inspected her, as if he thought she was going to swell under his eyes into an enormous, fecund shape.

'Yeah, thanks. My Dave's pleased. Our first, you see.'

'Your first? But what about – should he be eating that?'

'Oh, he'll be all right. He eats it all the time, funny little bugger. Makes his nappies dead gritty, but if it don't bother him . . . no, he's not Dave's, you see. Liam's dad was my ex. 'Course, Dave's fond of him, but it's not the same, is it? Like I'm quite fond of his two, nice little girls they are, when they come round. But this one,' she patted her stomach, 'that's our first together, see?' Her eyes were misty. 'Romantic, I call it.'

Roger wasn't sure that he would have called it that. An old-fashioned young man, he was inexperienced enough to think that 'romantic' involved flowers and candlelit dinners rather than babies, but he was touched that Shelley should think so.

'I hope you'll all be very happy together.'

'Yes, but we haven't found anywhere else, yet.' She turned brimming eyes on him. 'My Dave's so busy, comes home worn out every night, we've had no time to go looking. I'd go on my own, but he's got the car, and I can't get around much with Liam in his buggy. I had hoped to see two or three this afternoon, only Dave had to go out, so it doesn't look like I'll get there. Unless . . .'

Roger heard himself offering to drive her. Looking at the grubby child, he wondered whether he'd lost his head, but he told himself that it was important that Shelley should get on with finding a new house, so that his purchase should not be held up. A faint hope that it might not be possible to accommodate Liam in the car was dashed when Shelley produced a car seat that could be used with the rear seat belts – 'I just happened to bring it in from Dave's car . . . lucky, really.'

Now he trailed into the fourth house behind Shelley and Liam.

'It's Shirley, really,' Shelley was saying happily, 'but I changed it. More up to date, don't you think? Oh, hello. You must be Mr Johnson. Hi!'

He had the blond good-looks of a poster displaying the glories of the Aryan race. Shelley's first thought was that it had been peroxided, and she was impressed by how well it had been done – no roots showing, and the hair itself shiny and well textured. The colour suited him, however – the shortish hair stood up, golden yellow like a newly hatched chick, and contrasted with the darker brows and lashes that set off his bright blue eyes. So bright a blue were they that Shelley instantly, and shrewdly, diagnosed tinted contact lenses. Roger, less worldly-wise, was amazed by the limpid colour. Shelley, for once, would have been wrong. Both hair and eyes were entirely natural – in fact, disliking the attention they attracted, he had often been tempted to change them to something less noticeable.

The blond hair and blue eyes were set off by a skin tanned to a smooth brown that looked too perfect to be the product of simply being outside in the sun. He moved with the controlled power of an athlete, and that impression was confirmed by his well-muscled body. Shelley's widened eyes paid tribute to his beauty, but Roger noticed that in spite of his obvious good looks he lacked the 'look at me' manner of so many handsome young men or lovely young women. The blue eyes did not challenge, they were watchful but unrevealing, and he said little, seeming content to let his wife take the lead.

Shelley was shown round the house. Roger, feeling awkward, trailed round with them because he didn't know what else to do. Because he was not particularly interested in the house as such, he studied the people. It was easy because all their attention was concentrated on Shelley and her reactions.

He noticed that they never spoke to one another. Mrs Johnson – Louise, he remembered – did most of the talking, but occasionally Jason put in a few words of amplification about the wiring, or the heating system. She never asked for him to do this, even by a look, but simply left a space for him. On his side he never overtly corrected what she had said, his additions were carefully phrased and neutral. They never looked at one another, their eyes sliding over and away as if they were mutually invisible, but they were always aware of exactly where the other was, and took care never to close what seemed to be an exclusion zone of about four feet. On the one occasion when they miscalculated and arrived in a doorway at the same time, they bounced off one another before touching, as if they carried electrical charges that repelled as soon as they approached.

Shelley noticed nothing of this. Her attention was on the house and, to a lesser degree, on preventing Liam from doing any damage to it. Her conversation was punctuated by cries of 'Liam! Don't touch that!' She would probably not have noticed it anyway. Shelley found her own world, her own feelings and thoughts, satisfyingly fascinating. Her empathy was at so low an ebb that most people found her restful company. She never took offence at imagined slights, or asked impertinent questions, or gossiped. It never occurred to her that other peoples' lives could possibly be as interesting as her own, and in that respect she was an ideal neighbour.

When they finally left the house it was Shelley who was tired. Roger felt newly invigorated. The opposite of Shelley, he felt that his own doings were so dull that nobody could find them interesting. He never resented this – it was how he preferred to live – but he was inclined to fill the gap with the more fascinating details of other people's lives. He was never intrusive – his work-mates would have been astonished if they had learned with what fascination he followed their love lives and social relationships – but he was sensitive to the slightest nuance.

A young man whose strong principles had been inculcated at an early age by his mother, he would never have dreamed of speculating about a married couple, or even a couple who were in a settled relationship of any kind. This marriage, though, appeared to be already dead. Though they might still share the same house, Louise and Jason seemed to share nothing else. Roger had noticed, without appearing to, that two of the three bedrooms were being slept in. More poignantly still, in the bathroom, two toothbrushes and two tubes of toothpaste were neatly arrayed, in separate mugs, at the extreme ends of the bathroom shelf. The space between them, and between the two towels on the heated towel rail, was a gulf, an unbridgeable void.

Shelley collapsed into the front seat of the car, fanning herself with the sheaf of house details.

'I never thought it would be such hard work,' she said. 'It's all such

41

a muddle in my head, I can't remember any of them properly. How'm I supposed to choose?'

'You've only seen four, so far,' Roger pointed out. He had to shout above the clamour of Liam, who was howling 'Scream! Scream!' with the incessant beat of the jungle music his mother listened to.

'What d'you mean, *only* four? I've had it. They were all lovely, I'll pick one of them, no problem. Only which one? *Shut it, Liam!*' she shrieked above the clamour, without any real annoyance. In fact, a look of maternal pride spread across her face. 'He wants an ice cream, he's remembered I promised him one, bless him! All right, darling, you shall have your ice cream! The nice man will find the ice cream van for us!'

Roger looked at the inside of his car. Though he had bought it second-hand it was as immaculate as if it were fresh from the factory, and he vacuumed it scrupulously once a week and cleaned the seats with spray foam every month.

'I'll tell you what,' he said. 'We'll take him to the park, have a cup of tea for us and he can have his ice cream and a play on the swings, or something. Eat some sandpit. Then we can have another look at those details, try to sort them out. When I was looking, I made notes on the papers as I went round, that way you keep track of which place is which. Better to do it while they're fresh in our memory.'

Shelley looked at him with new respect and gratitude.

'That's really nice of you! I really appreciate that, Mr – oh, bugger it, I can't keep calling you "Mr Selby" if we're going to the park together! What's your proper name? Roger, isn't it?'

'Yes,' he agreed reluctantly, anticipating her giggles. To be fair, she made none of the comments that rose to her lips and managed to stifle her laughter to a fairly discreet snuffle. 'My friends call me Rog. To rhyme with dog.'

'Rog it is. And you know I'm Shelley. Off we go, then, Rog. I haven't been to the park for years – wouldn't mind a quick go on the swings myself, and all. And an ice cream! Treat's on me, of course,' she added scrupulously.

Roger put the car into gear and pulled smoothly away from the kerb. He was in no doubt as to which house was the best buy. Shelley's eyes had lingered on the second house they had visited, which was decorated to within an inch of its life with swags and frills and Victoriana. Behind the removable decor, however, the rooms had been smaller, and there had been an ominous crack zig-zagging its way up one wall. The last one, however, was beautifully maintained and had a good sized third bedroom, unlike the glorified cupboards so often found in modern houses. It was reasonably priced, too. He guessed that Jason and Louise – he had no difficulty in thinking of them by their first names – were desperate to sell as quickly as possible.

The final clincher was that it was the one being sold by Hensham Homes. An old-fashioned young man, he felt a strong instinct of loyalty for the agent who was selling him the flat. He thought that Shelley ought to feel the same – after all, Mr Kingswood had found them a good buyer, himself, at a time when flats were notoriously difficult to sell. He thought that it would not be unreasonable to persuade Shelley that this was the house for her. It was doing her a favour, really. Though modest, he was in no doubt that he could make her see it his way. In his own way, Roger had always been good with women, once he got to know them.

Saturday, Paul thought, was a funny day in the office. You never knew what to expect. It ought to be the busiest day of the week, the one day when most couples were both free to consider the most important purchase most of them would ever make. In practice, if was either frantically busy or completely dead, for no discernible reason. Frequently it was both, in patches. Days when you would expect it to be quiet, like Cup Final, were frequently quite busy. It went to prove nothing but the general perversity of the public. He remembered Mrs Holt, and smiled. Every time an empty office was suddenly filled with three groups of people all wanting instant attention, he thought of them as piles, and smiled at them all the more willingly.

Today had been very much par for the course. Perhaps a little busier – Melanie had commented, after lunch, that they had taken over an hour to eat their sandwiches. It was not a complaint, rather the reverse. Melanie and Rose were both strongly partisan, and rejoiced over sales almost as much as he did. On Saturdays they took it in turn to come in for the day, and Paul was grateful for their cheerful sacrifice of precious shopping and socialising time.

At her desk nearby, Melanie was talking into the telephone, running through a list of possible houses. He listened with half an ear. Her memory for what they were selling was amazing, her ability to pronounce the names of the streets less so. She had particular trouble with the group named after poets. Chaucer was always a worry, coming out in a variety of ways. Donne, of course, was known to nearly everyone as 'Donny', and he had given up any hope of changing that. On one memorable day, she had offered a house in Belloc Road as 'a very nice one in Bollock Place', which she had subsequently amended with shrieks of laughter. He had preferred not to tell Rose about that one. Rose never found that kind of thing amusing, any more than she smiled at the memory of the street that had been called, after a former mayor, Skinner Close. The name had been changed after strong representations to the Council from the owners of the second house on the left, who had violently objected to living at Four Skinner Close.

The telephone rang on another line – two calls at the same time! – and he picked it up.

'Hensham Homes, good afternoon?'

'Oh, hello, is that you, Paul?' He recognised Shelley's excited voice.

'Yes, it is. Hello, Shelley.'

'Listen, I've been to see four houses, and I've found one I like!'

'That's good.' It wouldn't do to get too hopeful. He had seen her working her way down the road known locally as 'Agents' Alley' and coming out clutching sheafs of details.

'Yes, that nice Rog – Mr Selby, you know – took me round this afternoon. Dave was busy. Well, out with the lads, really, but it's the same difference, innit? So Rog – that's what he likes to be called, because his name's Roger, did you know? Gave me a real laugh, that did. Talk about the wrong name! Anyway, that Rog, he came round to measure the windows and that, you know? And he said he'd take me, well, I asked him, but he could've said no, couldn't he? 'S'matter of fact, he was a real help. Noticed all sorts of things, like cracks and that. And replacement windows. And we went to the park and went through them all, and I made up my mind! I want to buy that one in Milton Place. Funny idea, naming a road after a disinfectant, but I s'pose they ran out of ideas. Anyway, stuff you can sterilise babies' bottles with is more use in the world than some old Prime Minister or something, eh? So, what do you think?'

Paul, reeling, realised that the house in Milton Place was actually one he himself was selling. Quite a good house, he remembered, and well priced. The owners were in a hurry to sell. Goodness, he thought. Two in the same chain. Things are looking up.

'I think you've made a good choice,' he said. 'So, how much do you want to offer?'

'Oh, I dunno. What d'you think?'

'What does, er, your other half think?'

'Dave? He doesn't think nothing, he's not come back yet.'

'Don't you think you ought to wait until he's seen the house before you make an offer? Suppose he doesn't like it?'

'Oh, he'll like it. Truth is, he don't want to move. I mean, he wants a bigger place, all that, but he don't want all the bother. Well, that's men, innit? Long as I pick something we can afford, and it's not something weird, he'll go along with what I like.'

Paul swiftly pressed buttons, summoning up her name on the computer screen. She could afford, he saw, to spend what the house was worth. At least . . .

'Have you actually spoken to someone about a mortgage? Filled in any forms, that kind of thing?'

'Oh, Dave does all that. Flat's mine – 'course, you know that – so he's a first time buyer, whatever they call it. The man said he

44

could get a good deal at the moment. Sounded like a load of gibble-gabble to me, but I never did have a head for figures. Just had a figure, eh!'

She was as uninhibited as a child, and he couldn't help liking her.

'The thing is, Shelley, you must remember that I'm working for the people selling the house.'

'But I put my name on your list? You're selling our flat, and I thought it'd be nice to buy through you as well. Mr – Rog – said it would be better that way, you could keep an eye on everything for us.'

'That's true. I would very much like to sell you your new house. But when it comes to selling, it's the owner of the property who pays the fee, and I'm working for them. Look, selling your flat, I'm working for you. It's my job to get you the best price I can, and to try to see that the buyer – Mr Selby – is actually in a position to buy. That's what you'll be paying me for, if the sale goes through. But when you come to buy something else, like Milton Court, then I'm working for the Johnsons. I owe it to them to get the best price I can.'

'So can't I buy it?' She was confused.

'Of course you can. All I'm saying is that I can't give you much advice on what you should offer. I can't say "Knock five thousand off the price and try them with that", because it wouldn't be fair to them. You see?'

'Not really.' She didn't sound very bothered. 'All right then, what about three?'

'Three thousand? Off the asking price?'

'Yeah, if you think that's OK.'

'I don't know if it is or not. I'll give it a try for you.'

'Great. Just think, when Dave comes home, I can tell him we've bought a house!'

'Hang on a minute! I said I'll give it a try! I'm not saying they'll agree. In fact, I honestly think the house is worth more than that. It's quite cheaply priced, for a miracle. But I'll put it forward for you, see what they say. Just don't be disappointed if it's no.'

'Right.'

'And meanwhile, when Dave gets home, do persuade him to go and have a look at it with you. Please?'

'Sure. Think they'll let me go round tonight? If I can drag him round there, that is.'

'I'll ask about that too. Don't worry, Shelley. I'm sure we can get this sorted out so everyone's happy.'

''Course we can.' She never really expected things to go any other way. And there's another word, he thought. Aprosexia – the inability to concentrate. If ever a word were appropriate to Shelley, that one was it. It even *sounds* right.

He gave himself a shake. To imagine that the 'Word-Watching' item in *The Times* was ruling his life was either paranoia or hubris. Or both. I won't look at it any more, he thought.

Chapter Five

'Do come in, Mr Kingswood.'
Paul stepped over the threshold, trying to look as though he valued six bedroom houses with a pony paddock three times a day and four on Sundays. Philippa Denton watched him warily.

'What a beautiful house,' he said, meaning it. It was a beautiful house. Kalopsia, he thought, forgetting the vow of the previous day. Last week's paper, not today's, but still. Kalopsia – the state in which things appear more beautiful than they actually are. It was true to say that given a house as expensive and saleable as this one, he would have found even brutalist concrete relatively attractive, but this was truly a delightful place.

'It was a cottage when we bought it. Two up, two down, Victorian. We extended it. No doubt you can tell the old from the newer, but most people can't.'

Now that she had told him, Paul could see that it was so. The original Victorian farm cottage was visible as the heart of the building to the discerning eye in the pattern of the roof lines and windows, and the arrangement of the rooms. The extensions had been so carefully done, however, that they blended seamlessly with the original. No expense had been spared. Old tiles had been used for the cladding and the newer roofs; old bricks and timber for the walls and joinery. Windows and doors matched up, all the proportions correct. Large though it was, it was rambling rather than imposing, an overgrown cottage instead of a small country house.

'We've been here for forty years,' said Mrs Denton. 'I'm not really sure I remember how we go about this. What do you want to do first?'

'If you'd like to show me round, and if it's not inconvenient I'll measure as we go.'

'Measure? Won't that take a long time? I suppose I could hold one end of the tape for you.'

Paul smiled. 'It's much easier than that. I have a sonic measurer.'

'What on earth is a sonic measurer? I believe I've heard of a sonic hedgehog . . .'

'That's more than I have.'

'Then you're obviously not a grandparent. Well, you're too young, of course.' She looked at him carefully, and he wondered whether she was going to have a look in his mouth to check his age by his teeth, like a horse. 'It's a computer game,' she explained.

'Ah. I'm old enough, but my daughters haven't obliged yet. Anyway, this is it, the measurer. It bounces a pulse off the opposite wall, like a bat, and you read the measurement off on this little screen in the handle. It's the boon of my existence, just as the old tape used to be the bane. So you see, it won't take very long.'

'Fascinating. It's not that I want to rush you. I've got plenty of time, it's just that my husband has gone to play golf, and I don't know what time he'll be back.'

'It's only ten thirty. Surely he won't finish a round this quickly – or did he start very early?'

'No, they were meeting at half past nine. It's just that he plays with an old buddy, and from time to time they fall out over something dire like which club is best to get out of a bunker, and then he comes stomping home early.'

'Oh dear.'

'Oh dear with bells on. But they play again the following week, and it's all forgotten. Still . . .'

'We'd better get on with it.'

'Thank you. Well this, as you can see, is the hall. You don't need me to tell you all this, do you? Presumably you've learned to recognise a kitchen, and a cloakroom, by yourself?'

'Just about. Perhaps you'd listen while I talk into my machine, and then if I miss something like an electricity meter, or a radiator, you can remind me about it. All right?'

'Splendid. I shall enjoy watching a professional in action.'

The house proved to be everything his first sight of it had led him to hope. It was true that the kitchen was old-fashioned, but the cream-coloured Aga was right back at the height of fashion, and it was immaculately cared for. He suspected that a surveyor would query the wiring, but he himself thought that the downstairs cloakroom and the bathrooms, equipped with sturdy white ware in no-nonsense shapes, still had a functional elegance which the more modern suites with their gold-plated taps often lacked. There were plenty of large cupboards, alcoves already shelved for books or display, and if the place was a bit over-furnished, well, what could you expect after forty years?

They had just finished the bedrooms when the front door opened and shut with a resounding slam.

'Oh *bother*! I should have known he would choose today to fall out with Colin!'

'Shall I shin down the drain pipe? Or hide in the cupboard?'

Her grin was surprisingly youthful.

'No, I think we'll just tough it out. As the grandchildren say.'

George Denton was tall, thin, and white haired. His first greeting to Paul was urbane, even charming, considering that he had just watched him come downstairs with his wife. His handshake was firm and vigorous, and the bushy white eyebrows that shaded his eyes seemed to direct his piercing look, like a beam of light bouncing off a mirror. His equally bushy white moustache shaded a mouth that looked as though it were used to giving orders, and giving them only once, at that.

'Kingswood, eh? That rings a bell.' His voice was loud, with the hard timbre of the deaf.

'You may remember my uncle, Simon Kingswood. I believe he sold you this house.'

'What's that? Speak up.'

Paul, who had thought he had spoken quite loudly, repeated his remark in what felt like a shout.

'Simon Kingswood? Remember him well. Not a bad chap, for an estate agent. Bloody awful at golf, but played a fair game of tennis. Simon's nephew, eh? And what do you do?'

Speaking as loudly and clearly as he could, Paul admitted that he, too, was an estate agent.

'Are you, indeed! And what are you doing here? Damned bloodsuckers, preying on the elderly, taking advantage of their weakness – I won't have you bullying my wife, you parasite. You hear?'

Since the speech was delivered in a resounding bellow, Paul thought that it was only the fact that the house was isolated in the centre of its large garden that prevented not just him, but half of Hensham, from hearing. Not very perturbed, he signified that he had heard.

'So you can clear off, uncle or no uncle!' The old man still said 'orf', like a caricature of a colonel.

'For goodness sake, George,' said his wife, 'you're making a complete fool of yourself. Just calm down, you know what the doctor said about your blood pressure.'

'To hell with my blood pressure! What's he *doing* here, Phil? Who let him in?'

'I let him in, you silly man. I told him to come and value the house, because I knew I'd have the devil's own job to make you see sense. And how right I was! But you're not to be rude to him. He's my guest. You know perfectly well you're just angry because you've had a disagreement with Colin, and it's spoiled your game. Now come and sit down, and I'll make us all some coffee.'

'I hate coffee. You know I never drink coffee.'

'Of course I know that. Coffee was just a manner of speaking, a generic term for a mid-morning drink. Mr Kingswood and I will have coffee, and you shall have a nice cup of tea. And we will discuss this, like reasonable beings.'

'Hmff. Hrrr. Very well. But I will not be brow-beaten.'

Paul tried to imagine himself brow-beating this splendid old man.

'I wouldn't dare to try, sir,' he said loudly. 'No one can make you do anything you don't want to do. In fact, I don't suppose anyone ever has done.'

A reluctant smile made the white moustache turn up at the edges.

'Not since I left the army,' he admitted. 'And even then . . .'

'Colonel?' hazarded Paul, and was rewarded with a brisk nod.

'By the end of the war. Don't use it. Never had any time for those chaps who hang on to their rank after they've come out of the army. Not if it was just a war-time commission. Different if they're regular army, of course. What about you? You're old enough to have done National Service, aren't you?'

'Yes, before university. I can't say I enjoyed it much, but I think I learned a lot. I'm quite glad I did it.'

'If only because it helps you deal with old buffers like me, eh?'

He led the way into the study that Paul knew they used as a small sitting room. 'Easier to heat,' Philippa Denton had remarked, 'and we keep the television in here. George thinks they're too ugly to have in the drawing room, but he loves to watch it.' George Denton sat in the sagging armchair that was obviously his usual place, feet in their highly polished brown shoes planted firmly apart, forearms resting along the chair arms with the hands grasping the front of them. They were strong hands, the skin roughened and stained by gardening.

'I love this place,' he said gruffly. 'Don't want to leave it. I know we'll have to, soon. House is too much for Phil. Garden's too much for me. Ought to go before it starts to get run-down, sell it while it still looks good. But . . . it's home, you see. Children brought up here. Grandchildren visit all the time. Tennis court. Old pony. That kind of thing. Bring their friends.'

Paul listened to what he was not saying. 'Do they come to see the pony and the tennis court, or you and your wife?'

The eyebrows wriggled like hairy caterpillars. 'What do you think?'

'I think,' said Paul, moderating his tone as he had noticed that George Denton, now that he was relaxed in his den and less angry, was finding it easier to hear him, 'that if they only come because you have a big house, and a tennis court, then they're not worth worrying about. But I can't believe that any youngster lucky enough to have a grandmother like Mrs Denton is capable of such behaviour. That's what I think.'

'Clever stuff.' The words were harsh, the voice mild.

'Yes, we're cunning, we estate agents. You don't want to believe a word we say.'

'Hrrmf.' His lower lip jutted out, blowing through his moustache as if it were a filter for his words. He levered himself out of the chair.

50

'Bloody thing. Springs gone, makes it too low. Come and see the garden.'

Paul glanced at the door. 'What about Mrs Denton?'

'Takes her hours to make the coffee. Aga's temperamental, took twenty minutes to boil the kettle at breakfast time today. Besides, she'll see us go. Eyes in the back of her bloody head, like a sergeant major.'

In the garden, he expanded. Even his sentences grew more complete, less telegraphic. The evidence of his loving hours was everywhere to be seen, in the striped lawn and neatly trimmed edges, in the careful slow shaping of trees and shrubs that had been pruned so that they looked as if they had somehow grown into the perfect form quite naturally. He pointed out the subtle positioning of foliage trees and plants, providing interest throughout the year and a background for the flowers. These were mainly of the old-fashioned variety: blowsy paeonies and hollyhocks, pinks and Canterbury bells, lavender and santolina and, everywhere, roses. Many were old types, grown for their scent, with a short flowering season but now bedecked with hips just beginning to flush with colour.

At the same time, Paul could see that the garden was on the verge of getting out of control. In the flower beds, clumps of perennials that should have been lifted and split were showing hollow centres. Brambles and nettles had sprung up in odd corners, and the hedges that had once boasted topiary shapes had sprouted so that they looked disreputable, like a neatly dressed man who has forgotten to shave for two or three days. The vegetable garden was weed-free but largely empty, and the edges of the tennis court were beginning to crumble where weeds had forced their inexorable heads through the surface.

The pony was old and fat. It stood dozing in the paddock, leaning contentedly against the post and rail fencing, but it seemed happy to amble over and eat the windfall that George Denton had picked up in the little orchard. It rested its head contentedly against his chest and blew while he ran his hand down its neck, under the rough mane.

'Loose boxes could do with a bit of attention,' George admitted. 'All right for this old thing, he's too lazy to do anything but eat, but anything more lively would push its way out through the walls. Still, the concrete base is sound, and I had those bricks put down in the yard outside. Good surface, that.' He sighed. 'I can't get proper help, you see. We had an old gardener – I say old, though he was younger than me – but he had to give up. Rheumatoid arthritis, poor chap. Shame, he'd been with us for years, and he was good with the ponies. A good handyman, too. There's plenty of people wanting the work, but they don't know how to do it, y'see. No experience, no knowledge. It takes years to teach someone how to care for a garden like this. Drives me mad, watching them do something I could have done myself in half the time, and better. So I get a bit irritable, and they don't like it.'

Paul nodded. He could well imagine the effect of 'a bit irritable'.

'The other problem is, where to go to.' Pushing the pony away George Denton turned round and leaned against the rail rather as the pony had done, looking back across the garden to the distant house. 'Difficult enough to imagine living anywhere but here, after all these years. We're not ready for some kind of ghastly twilight home yet – far from it, I hope. It's got to be something smaller, of course. Much smaller. But not poky. And with a bit of garden. I need something to potter in. It would drive Phil mad to have me indoors all the time, cluttering up the place, especially somewhere small.' He sighed again, and once more the air huffed through his moustache. 'We're used to our privacy. A little modern box, cheek by jowl with the place next door . . . not what we want.' He harrumphed. 'Champagne tastes and beer money, you'll be saying. Only it's not so much the money that's the problem – we ought to get a good price for this place, and of course we've long since paid off the mortgage. It's just finding something we could live in. See what I mean?'

'Of course I do. And you're right. There's no point in leaving here unless you can go into something that won't feel like a cage.'

The pony put its head against George's back, and nudged. Getting no response it sighed much as its master had done. Finding Paul's shoulder conveniently low, it rested its chin on it. Whiskery hairs tickled his neck, and the breath from its nostrils was warm and grass scented against his cheek. He reached up to rub its velvety nose.

'You think you've got something that might suit us.' It was not quite an accusation. Paul smiled.

'How did you know?'

'You sounded . . . not smug exactly, but "I know something that you don't".'

'Well, I have got a place in mind. And as a matter of fact, I do think it would be perfect for you. So much so that I'm almost terrified to show it to you, in case you don't like it. I'm also rather reluctant to appear to be putting you under any kind of pressure. It's just that the place I'm thinking of – it's in Blackwood Lane, by the way – is the sort of thing that will probably go quite quickly, even in today's market. So . . .'

'So we need to get on with it.'

'Well . . . yes. At least, you need to have a look at it, see if you like it. If so, I don't think there'd be any mad rush. The owner is as reluctant as you are to leave her home. If you could agree things between you, you could probably each take your own time, allow yourselves to become accustomed, discuss it with the grandchildren, all that kind of thing.'

52

'Sounds too good to be true.'

'I know. That's what terrifies me. I gave up believing in Father Christmas some while ago.'

'Oh, you don't want to do that.' Surprised, Paul looked at him. The pony, disturbed, flickered its ears, which tickled his hair. George's eyes twinkled below the frosted eyebrows. It occurred to Paul that if he had a beard to match the moustache, George would make quite a convincing Father Christmas himself, albeit a trifle tall and thin.

'Very well, then. Fix it up, and we'll go and look at this place of yours. If only to prove to your uncle's nephew that the age of miracles is not dead. On its knees, even in intensive care, but not dead yet.'

Back in the office, Paul looked at the careful list that Rose handed him of the people who had called while he was out. It was quite a long list, and he told himself that he should be pleased that there was more activity. Unfortunately, however, most of the calls meant trouble, in one form or another. Rose lacked the confidence to deal with any but the most simple of enquiries herself. People wanting to register as applicants, or wanting to arrange to view something, she could cope with. Anything else she regarded as beyond her remit.

'It's not that I don't *want* to, Mr K,' she would say earnestly. 'It's just that I might not do it *right*. You've got the *experience*. And you're a *man*. So I thought I'd better leave it for you.'

Resisting the temptation to pick out the less difficult ones, Paul pushed the buttons for the first number on the list.

'Mrs Attwell? Paul Kingswood here.'

'Oh, Mr Kingswood. I called you earlier, and you were *out*!' Her tone was outraged. Obviously he should have known that she might call, and stayed by the phone.

'Sorry about that, Mrs Attwell. So, what seems to be the problem? Not the survey?' As if I didn't know, he thought. If ever a house was doomed to have a dud survey, it's this one.

'It certainly is! That woman you sent round to buy the house, she's just been on the phone and she says they've found damp in the walls downstairs, and in the bathroom, and that the wiring isn't safe! And she says she wants five thousand off the price she was going to pay! It's disgraceful!'

Paul made soothing noises, and refrained from telling her that the surveyor wouldn't have found so much damp if her gutters had been cleared occasionally, and if she had opened the bathroom window from time to time to release the steam which had encouraged the growth of the sooty mould that rimmed the windows.

'You may remember,' he said mildly, 'that I did tell you at the outset that any buyer would need to have a survey done, and that the surveyor was likely to come up with things that needed attention. I believe I

53

did suggest that you have an electrician in to test the wiring, as there are no circuit breakers in the fuse box.'

'There's nothing wrong with our wiring! We've never had any problem with it!'

Paul suppressed the wish that she would electrocute herself with her outdated wiring, and continued to placate, to explain, and to cajole. After ten minutes he had got her to agree not to pull out of the sale altogether. Another five had her agreeing, reluctantly, that the house she was intending to buy in South London had also had problems with its survey, and that she was in turn reducing her offer.

'But that was quite different,' she said in self-righteous tones. 'It had a *crack*!'

When Paul finally put the telephone down, Rose brought him a cup of tea. Although he had had a cup of coffee with the Dentons, he was glad of it.

'Thanks. Thirsty work, talking to Mrs Attwell.'

'You're so patient.' She sounded depressed. 'It's a pity all employers aren't as patient as you.'

'Oh dear. Trouble?'

Her jowls wobbled as she nodded.

'Poor Maximilian has lost his job.'

'Oh dear,' he repeated. 'What went wrong?'

'They said he drank too much on the job. But if customers keep offering him a drink, what's he supposed to do?'

Paul refrained from making the obvious answer. He knew what Melanie would say when she heard the news. 'That Max,' she had said the previous week, 'he's always half cut. Beats me how he'd stay upright, if he didn't have the bar to lean on. And put it away – I've never seen anything like it! Max Capacity, that's what they call him. Like Max Headroom,' she explained, in case he had missed the joke. 'Only his headroom's unlimited, if you ask me. All empty space in there.'

'I suppose it is tempting for him,' said Paul.

'It's not so much *that*,' Rose said heavily. 'It's *politeness*, you see. He doesn't like to say no to them. Says it would be rude. He always had lovely manners, when he was a little boy,' she sighed, her eyes looking back over the years to a little boy with water-slicked hair who had never, in fact, existed.

'What's he going to do?' asked Paul, unwisely.

'Well, he's looking around. They offered him a labouring job, but they wanted him so early in the morning, and he's got accustomed to keeping late hours, in the pub. Besides, his hands wouldn't take it. Of course, he should really have something in an office.'

She looked at him with pale, spaniel eyes. Paul cursed himself, and thanked a benign providence (unusually) for the fact that in the present state of the market he certainly couldn't take on any new employees.

'I'll keep my ears open,' he promised her. 'Ask around,' he added mendaciously.

'I knew you would. You're such a kind man, Mr Kingswood.' Paul, feeling guilty, punched in the next number on her list.

Later that evening, he sat in his small living room looking out at his garden. He wondered what George Denton would make of it, and decided that given the undoubted limitations of size, it still was nothing to be ashamed of. The day had been fine, and he had left the french windows open. It meant sitting in semi-darkness because if he turned on the lights he knew he would be surrounded by moths and daddy-longlegs all eager to immolate themselves against the bulb or fall, concussed, into his microwaved lasagne. He didn't need much light to eat by, however, and the scented air coming in was more than compensation for the gloom. A magnolia grandiflora, trained up the rear wall, had three, white blooms just opening, and filled the room with their sharp lemon scent, more like lemon essence than the true citrus. In contrast, the tumbling petunias overflowing from the planted pots diffused a honey sweetness that would have been cloying on a woman, but was smooth as syrup on the evening air.

All in all, it had been a good day, Paul thought. The highlight of the day – the week? The month? The year? – had to be the Dentons' house. It was pleasant to think that Simon had been the one to sell it to them, like getting a late inheritance from the old fellow. A pleasant couple, too, and intelligent enough to see that their house needed money spending on it, and that the asking price should reflect this. Wonderful, he thought, not to be dealing with another Mrs Attwell. And if, as he hoped, they liked the bungalow, that would be two sales that ought to be relatively trouble free. They, on their own, would mean that for this month his sales fees would cover his outgoings on major items like rent, rates, and advertising. With the flat, and the little house in Milton Court, he might even succeed in nibbling a bit off the overdraft. Feeling expansive, he lifted the glass of red wine from the floor beside him, and toasted himself. Tonight, he thought, he would allow himself a second glass instead of his usual frugal one.

The lasagne finished, he sipped contentedly at his wine and watched the last of the light vanish from the garden. The mauve flowers of the petunias did their usual trick of glowing, as if internally lit, as did the white roses on the Iceberg. The sky changed from blue and green to deep indigo, and a glow reminded him that the moon was almost at the full. With the CD player turned up loud enough to drown out his neighbours' television without giving them grounds for complaint, reproducing the throat-aching tones of the Schubert violin quintet, he decided that maybe there was something in this Father Christmas stuff, after all.

When the telephone rang, he had a sudden intuition that it might be Beth Oldham before he realised that, of course, she didn't have this number. He had few telephone calls at home – his few close friends were from his school and university days, and were scattered round the country and abroad. The busy social life that Jenny had organised had diminished, since their divorce, to the occasional dinner or drinks invitation. He had never cared for the undoubtedly useful social and charitable clubs that many men in his position joined, and he admitted that he was lazy about meeting new people. Finding himself relatively uninteresting, he assumed that other people would do the same, and was largely content with his own company. Rather reluctantly he stood up and went to the hall. He had to switch on the light, and stood with his eyes screwed up in its sudden brightness.

'Hi, Dad! It's Judith!'

'Judith! How are you?'

'Fine, I'm fine. And you?'

'Yes, I'm fine. And how's John?'

'He's fine too. As a matter of fact, we're thinking of getting married.'

'Judith, darling, that's wonderful news. When?'

'Oh, round Easter, probably, when his divorce comes through. It won't be anything fancy, of course, under the circs, but I wanted you to know first. Well, after Mums. Although in fact I haven't actually spoken to her yet, she was out. I had to leave a message on the answerphone, ask her to ring me.'

'Well, you know how busy she is.' What am I doing, he wondered, making excuses for my ex-wife? And to our own daughter? 'Have you told Dizzy yet?' His elder daughter, Delia, had been christened long before the time when to be so named invited a flood of half-joking cookery questions. As a woman whose cooking skills went no further than opening carefully chosen packages from Marks and Spencer, she had recently resurrected her childhood nickname and started to use it again.

'Yes. she was very pleased, but we didn't talk for long. She wasn't feeling too good.'

'Really? Is she all right?'

'Yes, of course she is. It's quite normal to feel sick in the evening, instead of the morning, apparently. Oh, lord.'

'Ah. Do I forget I heard that?'

'Yes. I mean, no. Honestly, Daddy, she hasn't told anyone yet, only me and Mum, and that was only last week. She doesn't want people to fuss, after last time. You know.'

'Of course.' Delia, or Dizzy as she now preferred to be known, had had two early miscarriages during the course of the year, the second of which had left her very depressed. 'It's wonderful news, Judith. Do they think things are going to go all right this time?'

'The doctor says so, but of course she doesn't dare believe her yet. You're not hurt, are you? That she didn't tell you?'

'Of course I'm not.' He hoped it would soon be true. He had adored his daughters in their childhood, but since they had grown up and gone their separate ways, he found them rather alarming. Both intelligent, they had gone into high-powered jobs which they seemed to manage with ease, juggling with a full and complicated social life at the same time. They made him feel like a fuddy-duddy, or a dear old has-been. Which was probably what he was. Still, a grandchild . . . He remembered Philippa and George Denton. Should he, perhaps, if business improved, look for a bigger house? With parents and grandmother living in London, they might like to bring. the little one for weekends in the country. He saw himself pushing a swing, playing cricket, supporting a little figure on the back of a fat pony . . .

Hello, Father Christmas. Welcome back.

Chapter Six

Liz Hartwell looked at the test kit in her hand. She checked the instructions, then looked again. The liquid in the little container showed a clear blue. Not just a bit blue, either, not the kind of tinge you might have imagined because you wanted to see it, but a forthright blue that proclaimed itself like a summer sky, or a tropical sea. It was, though Liz didn't think of that, almost exactly the same blue as her own eyes when she lifted them to stare into the bathroom mirror. Even in the reflection the test kit was blue. She was definitely pregnant.

'You little beauty,' she murmured to it. 'You little beauty.' In moments of emotion her accent, which over the past year and a half had moderated, reasserted itself. She sounded exactly like her grandfather, who had spent his life running a sheep station in the outback for a rich businessman in Melbourne.

Afterwards, she was always glad to remember that her first reaction to the test result had been pure, uncomplicated joy. It was not what they had planned, of course. Mike understood her desire for a child, even shared it in a milder form, but they had both agreed that it was too soon. Better to wait, they had told one another wisely, until everything had settled down. Until things were a bit less stressed. Better for the baby. Better for them. Better, really, for everyone.

So they had decided and spoken, neither of them needing to put into words what they both felt. It was safer that way. Safer to refer generally to 'everything' and 'things', knowing all the time that what they meant was Ruth. Not Joseph, who had reacted with equanimity to his father's second marriage. Not his previous parents-in-law who, grieving for their daughter and anxious for her children, had given her a cautious welcome. Just Ruth, now thirteen, who had not yet come to terms with her mother's death three years earlier, who was fiercely possessive of her father and of her mother's memory, and who resented with every fibre of her being the woman who had come, as she saw it, to take her mother's place.

Liz looked once again at the test kit. She cradled it in her hands as though it held, not a specimen of urine and some chemicals, but the precious embryo itself, an *in vitro* creation yet to be implanted inside her. Whereas, in fact, the little creature had already alighted on its journey from her fallopian tubes, touched and clung, sent rooting tendrils into the lining of her womb, begun the miraculous process of cell division that would – should – might – end nine months later with the emergence into the world of a new person. Someone unique, someone who had in his or her genes elements of Liz and Mike, of the old world and the new, the symbol and result of their union.

'Ruth.' Liz groaned in a whisper, though she was alone in the house. 'What will Ruth say?' It sometimes seemed to her that everything she did or said or even thought was subject to this filter, this microscopic inspection. 'What will Ruth say?' was the first thing that came to mind when contemplating any action, from dusting the sitting room ('I don't want you to touch my mother's photograph') to replacing the lavatory roll ('We always have pink paper'). Liz had suppressed her desire to snap back – 'Do the bloody dusting yourself, then' and, 'Coloured paper isn't ecologically sound'. She told herself all the time that Ruth was at a difficult age, that she had watched her mother endure pain and sickness and had seen her die, that it was natural for her to have difficulty in adjusting to a step-mother and that, surely, everything would work out given time.

Nothing in life had prepared Liz for this. A childhood in the suburbs of Melbourne as one of a cheerful and friendly family, three years at university and then several years of varied employment, all of this had been uneventful and happy. Despite family problems – her older sister had inherited the farming gene from their grandparents and had invested everything in a small property where she raised horses and cattle, and battled endlessly with floods, droughts and the threat of fires, and her still older brother had been injured in a car crash and walked with difficulty – there had never been anything in her life that had led her to distrust her own ability to deal with it.

Faced with redundancy and the simultaneous fizzling out of a current relationship, Liz had decided to use the small redundancy payment to fulfil a long-deferred ambition to travel. Unlike many of her contemporaries she had not 'done' Europe during her student days, preferring instead to explore her own continent. This, she thought, was the ideal time. At twenty-nine, with no emotional ties but the deeply rooted certainty that she would soon meet Mr Right and settle down, she thought she would cut loose for a year.

After six months of roaming through France, Italy, Germany and Spain, she had come back to England for a rest, wanting to be somewhere where they spoke something at least approximating to her own language, and needing also to earn a bit of money. Europe had been more expensive than she had anticipated and she had not stinted herself. Being rather beyond the age to live out of a rucksack and a tent, and reasoning that she might not be back for decades, if ever, she had stayed at reasonably cheap hotels and visited as many places as possible. England, though still expensive, had at least a few distant relatives who would put her up for a little while, and maybe even find her some kind of job.

She had been lucky almost at once, getting a 'temporary' secretarial place that drifted unobtrusively into something that was, if not formally agreed as permanent, at least going to last as long as she would be likely to need it. Her boss, Michael Hartwell, had been pleasant and easy to work for, largely because he seemed so abstracted that he scarcely noticed what she did. Her early mistakes passed him by completely, though he thanked her with unfailing courtesy for anything extra that she did, like staying late to finish something, or fetching him sandwiches when she noticed that he had forgotten to go to lunch.

It was not long, of course, before office gossip informed her of his tragedy a year and a half earlier – the beautiful young wife with leukaemia; the endless treatments that caused so much discomfort but which never, it seemed, did anything to halt the progress of the disease; the rapid decline and the protracted death; all of this plus the worry of two young children left motherless. It was not surprising, she thought, that he seemed abstracted, and she correctly interpreted his distant manner as the combined after-effects of grief and shock. She found herself looking for things to cheer or encourage him, little articles in the paper that she would ring and leave for him to read, items in the local paper that advertised events that his children might enjoy, she even encouraged him to take them abroad on holiday, and booked them into a little hotel in France that she remembered from her own travels.

Almost imperceptibly, she found that they were friends. As she got to know him better, she discovered that buried beneath the quiet exterior was a sense of humour that inclined towards the surreal, and which she found irresistibly funny. At first he had found it difficult to laugh, as if to do so were somehow a betrayal of his dead wife, but gradually he relaxed with her, accepting that she was quick-witted enough to catch his more subtle jokes, and encouraging her to get as much pleasure from the bizarre in the everyday as he did. She noticed that however sharp his observation might be, it was never unkind. She began to realise that she had discovered a creature she had hitherto believed to be a myth – a man without prejudices and hang-ups who accepted the vagaries of human nature without regard to gender, age, class or nationality, and found his own vagaries more ridiculous than any other. When he turned to her, one day, and smiled a real smile because of a bit of business they had managed to clinch with a difficult customer, she realised quite suddenly that she loved him.

After that, terrified of rushing him and frightening him into retreat, she was patient and careful. All the hunting skills of her farming

61

grandfather were called into play, and she stalked him with the dedication of an aboriginal who knows that if he misses this one, he will starve perhaps for days, perhaps for ever. She never doubted that in time he would learn to love her. It was not possible, she thought, that she should feel such a powerful emotion without there being some kind of response. She waited for six months, fending off increasingly anxious enquiries from Melbourne (she had already been gone for longer than the original year she had planned for).

By that time he thought of her as a friend, they had been out for drinks and meals, she had visited his house and he hers. Only a man numbed by grief, she thought, could believe in such a platonic relationship between a man of thirty-eight and a woman of thirty-one, both single. His children accepted their friendship largely because, she thought, he himself was so transparently unaware of any alternative possibilities. The problem of how to break through the invisible barrier that stopped him seeing her as an available woman began to haunt her. She dreamed up stratagems that she knew she could not use, because to do so would be somehow to betray his trust in their friendship.

She began to sleep badly, and lost weight, and even began to lose some of her habitual optimism. Christmas came and went, a difficult time for him and the children, a lonely one for her thinking of her family celebrating in the heat of a Melbourne December – how had she ever complained about the heat? She mentioned that she might return to Australia, and was met by a look of resignation that caused her physical pain. Quite suddenly she wanted him to be the kind of brusque Aussie man that she had encountered at home, the kind of man who featured in the joke, 'What's the Australian man's version of foreplay? Brace yerself, Sheila'. She looked at Michael, and began to despair.

In the end, when fate took a hand, it was in so blatant a fashion that no one, she knew, would ever have believed it had not been contrived. They had worked late over a contract, and Michael had taken her to a pub for supper. It was Friday, and his children had gone to their grandparents for the weekend, so they lingered over the tough steaks and limp salad, both of them tired and one of them dispirited. She drank a bit too much, and he insisted on driving her back to the flat she had rented. Reaching it, he courteously saw her right to her door and even agreed to come in for a coffee.

They drank it, sitting primly on the sofa with a small gap between them that yawned, in her eyes, like the Grand Canyon. They talked easily, as friends do, and she longed to find him lunging at her. She thought of lunging at him, but dared not risk it. If he rejected her or, worse still, accepted her advances out of indifference or politeness, everything would be lost. So she sipped, and chatted, and when he rose to leave accepted the kiss on the cheek that was customary between them on such occasions. As she sometimes did, she turned her cheek as if accidentally so that her lips just grazed the corner of his, and as before he failed to turn his own towards her, so that their mouths could meet.

At the door of her flat she stood listening to his footsteps walking slowly downstairs. As the front door closed behind him she realised, with a lift of her spirits, that she had left her handbag in his car. Her keys had been in her pocket, and by some kind of Freudian amnesia she had left the bag where she had flung it on the back seat when getting in, as it was too big and too good to put on the floor at her feet. Leaving the flat door ajar she ran down the stairs to catch him. Wrestling the front door open – it was a close fit in the frame – she felt rather than heard the thud as the small movement of air from outside slammed her flat door shut. It had a good lock and the keys were on the inside.

Running down the path, fearing that he would have driven off, she knew that she was committed. She had known it when she pulled the front door closed behind her, knowing that she had no way of getting back in and that the other flats were either empty or lived in by people who, from deafness or bloody mindedness, would never answer a ringing bell in the middle of the night.

About to get into his car, Michael paused and turned as she ran towards him, calling his name.

'What's the matter?'

It was a clear, frosty night. A patch of ice by the gatepost where a dog had lifted its leg caught her unawares, so that she slipped and was only saved from crashing to the ground because Michael reached out and caught her. She clung to him.

'Oh, Michael!' She was half laughing, half sobbing. 'I'm sorry, I'm sorry, Michael!'

'What's the matter?' he repeated, his arms supporting her and showing no sign of letting go. She was shivering in her indoor clothes, not having bothered to take the time to get her coat, and he felt her shudder and held her more closely.

'I left my bag in your car, and now I've locked myself out!'

There was a pause. Liz rested her head against his shoulder. He smelled of the pub, and she breathed in the aroma of tobacco and warm beer as if it were pure oxygen.

'Well . . . you'd better come back with me,' he said. There was no more to it than that, and he neither kissed nor caressed her, but Liz knew that she had won. A month later, they were married in the same little church where his previous wife's funeral had been held. It had been bitterly cold, and Liz's family had all succumbed to local viruses the moment they reached England, so that their sniffs during the quiet ceremony were less of emotion than of the dismal effects of colds. The children had been subdued but polite, and Liz had been sure that as time went by they would accept her. Determined to do everything in her power to make them comfortable, she had reduced her working hours so that she could get home by three.

Joseph, rising ten, had been easy. His mother's death, a fifth of his lifetime ago, had already receded to a memory of sadness and he could scarcely recall the good times before she got ill. To have someone at home when he came back from school, to have home-made cake in the larder, his favourite suppers cooked for him, above all to have his father happy and making the silly jokes again that Joseph had almost forgotten he could make, all this seemed to him to be so obviously a good thing that he was unable to understand why Ruth was so upset. He didn't allow it to worry him. Experience, his own and his friends', had taught him that girls, especially older sisters, were strange creatures, given to moody behaviour and outbursts of inexplicable rage.

Liz treated him much as she would have treated a younger brother. As a little boy his mother and Michael had called Joseph 'Joey'; Liz, to whom the word joey meant only one thing, a young kangaroo, thought he had grown out of it. Joseph, who hadn't really thought about it, suddenly realised that it was a babyish name and demanded a change.

'Only not Joseph,' he said. 'Joseph just means I'm in trouble. Besides, it's too much "Mary and Joseph and the Baby in the manger".'

'Jo?' suggested Michael.

'Sissy,' said Joseph. 'There's a girl in my class called Jo. Two, in fact.'

'Joss,' offered Liz.

'Joss,' he repeated, tasting it in his mouth. 'Joss. Joss Hartwell. Yes, I like it. It sounds – grown up.'

'It sounds very grown up,' she agreed, unsmiling. 'What do you think, Ruth?'

'I think it's a stupid name. He's only a little boy, he's not grown up at all.'

Joseph – Joss – shrugged, not caring much. Michael frowned, but Liz warned him with a glance.

'Well, maybe you'll like it better when you get used to it,' she said peacefully.

'I'm not *going* to get used to it. Why should I?' Ruth slammed her way out of the room.

Patience, Liz thought. Just patience, and understanding. She ignored Ruth's outbursts, her rudeness, her attempts to come between Michael and Liz which sometimes succeeded because he loved his daughter so much, and he was so worried about her. Liz was careful not to try too hard. She made no attempt to ingratiate herself, to buy Ruth's affections with new clothes or CDs or treats. She was scrupulously fair in her dealings, siding if anything more often with Ruth than with Joss in disputes, once or twice backing Ruth against even Michael when she thought that he was being unreasonably over-protective. None of it worked, and if Ruth felt anything it seemed to be contempt for someone who would accept so much unpleasantness without hitting back.

Liz, whose security was based on the foundations of her parents' love for her and for each other, as well as on the good sense and sound values her upbringing had given her, felt at times a pity so profound for her step-daughter that she could have wept. The girl was so patently unhappy, so unable to let go of the past and move forward. Even her physical growth seemed to have been stunted by her misery. At ten, when her mother died, she had been tall for her age. Since then she had scarcely grown at all and was now the shortest in her class. While all her friends were wearing bras and moaning about the onset of menstruation and the eruption of spots, she had remained flat-chested as a boy until the last few months, when her breasts had at last begun to develop, delicate little pointed mounds that were so sensitive she took to walking with rounded shoulders to protect them. Refusing to allow Liz to buy her a bra she endured the chafing of her old vests, and wept when she caught sight of herself in the bathroom mirror.

Liz, remembering the competition among her own female classmates about who had a bra, and how big it was, understood and pitied her but was unable to help her accept her body's changes. Some tweezers left on the side of the bath, and several pubic hairs clinging to the tub, made Liz suspect that her step-daughter was fighting back against pubertal changes, but though her eyes watered at the thought she wisely said nothing.

Two weeks earlier, Liz had woken in the night to see a glow coming from the bottom of the bedroom door. Michael deeply asleep beside her, she had listened and been aware of someone on the landing. There was a creaking board just outside Ruth's door, so Liz was fairly sure that it was Ruth who went back and forth to the bathroom, finally locking the bathroom door and running taps in the basin. Quietly, Liz slipped out of bed and went out of her bedroom. All the doors were closed, the bathroom tap was still running. Greatly daring, Liz opened Ruth's bedroom door.

The bed had been stripped. Even the mattress cover had gone, and on the mattress was a tell-tale stain that Liz had no trouble in identifying. She fetched a wet cloth and the stain remover spray from downstairs, and set to work, then heaved the mattress up and over so that the damp mark was on the underside. By the time Ruth emerged from the bathroom, her arms full of damp sheets, the bed was made up afresh with clean linen from the airing cupboard, and a packet of sanitary pads – fortunately Liz had some as well as her usual tampons – was sitting discreetly on the bedside table. Liz herself was still in the bedroom, and Ruth paused in the doorway.

'How dare you!' she hissed. 'Get out of my bedroom.'

'I will, once I know you're all right.'

'Of course I'm all right. It's only a period, everyone gets them.' Ruth ignored the tearing pain in her insides, and the tears that kept flooding eyes that were already swollen and sore.

'It's still not much fun when they start in the middle of the night. Is it the first one?'

'Mind your own business.' Ruth wasn't going to admit that it was, nor that her first reaction on waking had been terror. She longed for her mother, for the feel of her arms warmly holding her, for the safety of childhood that had vanished for ever. Liz wanted to reach out and hug her, but knew only too well that the best she could hope for was a frozen endurance, the worst a physical rejection.

'Give me those, I'll put them in the wash.' Ruth dropped the sheets on the floor, and watched while Liz picked them up. 'Do you want anything? A hot drink? A pain killer?'

'No.' Ruth would have liked both, but wouldn't admit it. Liz left the room and heard the door close behind her. Oh well, she thought. At least she kept the pads.

Thinking about it now, she realised that at that time she must already have been two or three weeks pregnant, without suspecting it. It was ironic that the episode, which marked Ruth's entry into adult life, also marked the beginning of Liz's determination that they should move house. Her own pregnancy now made that determination even stronger. Their present three bedroom house was already full. With a new baby they would need a fourth bedroom. The thought of moving was exhilarating, like opening a window in a room that had been closed up for months and letting a gush of fresh air replace the stale miasma within.

In this house she would always be an intruder. At most she would be a kind of glorified housekeeper, forever surrounded by reminders of her predecessor. A first wife who had been divorced she could have coped with, even if it had meant visits from a bitter, resentful woman who tried to turn the children against her. A wife who had died, however, was a competitor she could never hope to overcome. Every corner of every room was full of her. Liz, cleaning the house, vacuumed her choice of carpets, polished her furniture, ironed her sheets. They ate off her plates and cooked in her saucepans. Mike, a far from insensitive man, agreed that the situation was intolerable and gave her *carte blanche* to change whatever she wanted, but Liz knew that to do so would be to invite open war with Ruth. When Liz bought some new plates, Ruth refused to eat. New towels (a wedding present) were not very mysteriously damaged with neat bleach, so that they burned into holes and their colour was patched and faded. When Mike suggested changing their bedroom, Ruth had looked at him with swimming eyes.

'How can you change it? The room where Mummy died?'

'It's not a shrine,' he pointed out gently. 'Mummy wouldn't want you to think of it like that. As a matter of fact, she said herself she was bored stiff with that old colour scheme. I would have changed it, only it was all too much of an upheaval while she was ill.'

'Don't change it, Daddy. *Please* don't change it,' she wept. Mike was firm, but Liz found herself unable to hold out against such desperation.

'We'll leave it for now,' she temporised. Mike's loving glance to Liz was negated by the look of malicious triumph that Ruth gave her. It was at about this time that Liz started thinking of Ruth, in the privacy of her own mind, as Ruthless. Ruth, cleaving to her mother-in-law or in tears amid the alien corn, was altogether too gentle a name for this spiteful little creature.

Liz put down the test kit, and spread protecting hands over her stomach. She could not believe that any child of Michael's could be fundamentally wicked. Mary, his late wife, had by all accounts been gentle and loving, and her own parents had accepted Liz with a kindness that she could not fault. But the thought of her baby, innocent and vulnerable, in this house, was untenable. The thought of letting Ruth babysit, or even change a nappy or, horrible thought, bath her little sibling, was equally difficult to contemplate. This has gone on long enough, Liz thought. I've tried patience, I've tried kindness, and it's got me nowhere. Somehow, before the baby is born, we've got to sort this out. And the first step is to find a new house, where we can all make a fresh start.

Beep beep. Beep beep.

'Hensham Homes, good afternoon?'

Not Mrs Attwell, thought Paul. Please not. Half an hour yesterday. Twenty minutes the day before. Just one day's peace, is that so much to ask for?

'Paul, how you doing?'

'Shelley!' Relief made his voice warmer than usual. 'I'm fine, how are you and Dave?'

'We're great. How's it going with our house? Have they found anything yet?'

'Not yet,' he said warily. 'Mrs Johnson has been looking, I know, but she hasn't seen anything she likes yet. I'm sure she will, though.

And you're not in too much of a rush, are you?'

'Well, I suppose, but I just want to be getting on with it, you know? Can't wait, really. And our little lad, the one who's buying the flat, young Rog – he's getting all keen, too. Says his mum wants him to move out. Funny, I thought it. She came to see the flat, seemed like a real old love, not the kind to kick her only one out of the nest, know what I mean? Only he says she's sick, wants to see him settled in a place of his own. Sad, that is. But lovely, innit? Wants the best for him, even if it means she's on her own. Got all choked up, I did.' Shelley, who rarely thought much about other peoples' feelings, had indeed been touched by this. 'Anyway, he says he'll take me round there again, give me a chance to measure up for a new suite. They've got a good offer on in town, did you know? Nice lad, really, for all he looks like a wimp.'

'Shelley,' said Paul sternly. 'Has Dave seen the house yet?'

'Well, not yet. But you know what he is, says he's too busy, wants to leave it all up to me.'

Paul clasped his forehead in anguish.

'It really would be a good idea for him to see it,' he suggested in as mild a tone as he could summon. Dismal memories of the collapse of previous sales because an absent partner had taken an irrational dislike to the other's choice danced like spectres through his mind. 'Please,' he implored.

''Course, sure, Paul. We'll do it this weekend. Or next, maybe. His team's playing away this weekend, he's sure to want to go.' Her tone was indulgent. Not for a moment would she have suggested that looking at their new home was more important than the football match of a third division team.

Paul felt demoralised when she rang off. He had seen too many apparently solid sales evaporate like morning mist for more trivial reasons than this. He opened the newspaper. 'Struthious', said 'Word-watching'. Ostrich-like behaviour. Well, that would have been appropriate on any day, since most of his clients displayed a similar inability to grasp life's realities when applied to themselves. And it would all, of course, be his fault.

'Never mind,' said Melanie. 'I'll make us a nice cup of tea.' Paul's mouth felt furred, and his bladder was bursting with the last two mugs of tea.

'No, thanks,' he said. 'I think I'll pass on that one.'

'You want to keep up your fluid intake,' she warned him seriously. 'Prostrate trouble, that's what you'll get, if you're not careful. Very common it is, in men of your age.'

Paul refrained from correcting her mistake, and also from informing her that his prostate was none of her business. He was relieved when someone came in, and he recognised one of the surveyors from a local firm. What was his name? Alec something. Their paths had crossed from time to time, as was inevitable. Alec – what the hell was his name? – was one of the few who refrained from putting the boot on sales by vicious down-valuations, he recalled, though his colleagues were less careful. The name came back to him in the nick of time – Blake. One the planners had missed, when naming the area known locally as Poets Corner. It would have been a better name, he thought, than Donne. Or even Chaucer.

'Alec,' he said with pleasure. 'Nice to see you. Is this a professional visit, or would you like a cup of tea? Melanie just offered me one, says I need it for my prostate.'

'Tea would be lovely,' said Alec Blake, smiling at Melanie. 'No, not a professional visit. Well, yes, but your profession rather than mine. My wife wants to move house.'

His tone was resigned, and Paul damped down his pleased response.

'Does she? What sort of thing would you be looking for?'

'Something imposing,' said Alec wryly. 'She's planning ahead for the girls' weddings, I think. Room for a marquee, that kind of thing.'

'But surely they're quite young?' Paul thought he had seen them, little girls still. The word wedding reminded him, guiltily, of Judith. Would she have liked a marquee on the lawn? He thought of his postage stamp garden, and grinned. Alec grinned back.

'Oh, you know Christine. I think she's bored with where we are now. It's a nice enough house, four bedrooms, pretty garden, but she wants something . . . well, more impressive.'

'And what do you want?'

'What she wants, of course.' They exchanged looks, the nearest Alec would go to outright disloyalty. 'I'd like something with a bit of character,' he said thoughtfully. 'If we must have all that upheaval, let's make it something really nice that we can stay in for a decade or two or three. You know what I mean. Something a bit older, perhaps. Not a land-based gin-palace.'

Paul lowered his eyes to hide his excitement.

'I might have something suitable,' he said cautiously. 'It's early days, though. An elderly couple, I don't want to rush them. Would she wait?'

'Probably not. Once she gets the bit between her teeth. If she could see it, of course, even on an informal basis . . .'

'I could try. And I suppose you'd be selling your present house?'

'Yes, we would. And of course I'd prefer to use the same agent for the sale and the purchase, if possible. So if you could come up with something . . .'

'Blackmail is an ugly word, Mr Blake.'

'It certainly is, Mr Kingswood.' They grinned at one another in something that could quite easily, Paul thought with surprised pleasure, become friendship.

Chapter Seven

L ouise Johnson was on the telephone.
'No, not yet,' she said. 'No, nothing. Yes, I know I need to find something, but I'm not going to buy something I don't like. Of course I don't want to lose the sale, but I'd be mad to go rushing into something. If nothing else, I should know about that . . . Don't be like what? Jilly, I intend to be like anything I want, in future . . . Yes, all right, well, sorry. But you're telling me something I already know, and I've got the couple who are buying this place coming back to measure up for furniture, and I know she'll go on about it too. At least, not the couple, just the woman and the young man who's buying their flat, he drives her around. Yes, I know, I thought it was a bit funny, but she's pushy and he's a bit limp . . . yes, I suppose the husband will come and have a look soon, but he doesn't care much either way, by the sound of things.'

There was a long, listening pause. The house was silent. Not even a ticking clock, or the purr of a boiler. No movement either, the air was still and odourless, as if the house had never been lived in, as if no one had ever fried onions, or worn perfume, or smoked a cigarette in it. Yet it was not empty. Jason was there, she knew that he was because his car was in the garage and there was a window open. He was listening, as she knew. In a way, she expected it. She even said unnecessary things over the telephone so that he would hear her. That was how they communicated, now. That, and the notes they left in the kitchen. Bald, factual notes for the most part, unsigned, unaddressed.

'Yes,' she said now, 'yes, of course I'm fine. Yes, I'm being careful. Don't fuss, Jilly! Everything's perfectly normal, I'm not ill. Yes, I expect he does know. No, I don't know what he thinks, and I don't care either. Well, that's how it is. Well, maybe. In time. But not yet. No, all right. There's a car, it'll be the buyers, I'd better go. Bye.'

She went to the door. Sure enough, Shelley was coming up the path, her high heels pock-pocking on the stone. Her blonded hair was swept up into a swirl like the whipped cream on top of a milk-shake, and her short jacket was shiny silver, like new stainless steel. She smiled at Louise, fluttering fingers with silver painted nails in a coy wave, and her eyes moved beyond Louise's shoulder. Louise,

71

though she had heard nothing, knew that Jason was there, a few feet behind her.

'Here we are again,' carolled Shelley, 'happy as can be!'

Roger loped behind her. Shelley had not been surprised by how willing he had been to bring her for another visit. She always expected men to do more or less exactly what she wanted, and although she did not take his help for granted she certainly did not look beyond her own mirror for a reason why he would accompany her.

'Hi, Louise! Hi, Jason!' Her friendliness was infectious, they both smiled back at her. 'Come without the ankle-biter today,' she pointed out. 'Left him up my sister's, give me a chance to concentrate, eh!'

She chattered like a starling as she whirled round the house. Louise and Jason accompanied her, mutually invisible, and Roger trailed behind writing down measurements in his small, neat script. He said little but smiled occasionally.

At the top of the stairs she caught her heel and tottered, arms flailing wildly. All three of the others started forward, but Louise recoiled at the proximity of Jason, and it was the two men who caught Shelley and steadied her.

'Thanks, boys!' She wiped her brow theatrically. 'Don't want to take a tumble down the stairs of me new home and lose the baby, do I? Bad joss, that'd be.'

'Bad joss?' Unusually, it was Jason who spoke. His voice was pleasant, low and soft. He kept his hand on her arm as she went down the stairs.

'That's what the Chinese say, it's like bad luck. Bad vibes, man.' She mimed a hippy, flickering fingers indicating straggly long hair. 'I used to do a bit of waitressing, worked in a Chinese restaurant for a while because they needed someone who could talk to the customers, help them with the menu. Nice, they were. Good food, too. Mind, the stuff they cooked for themselves was weird, you should have seen it, not like food at all. Duck's feet, all that.' She shuddered. 'Turns me up, just thinking of it.' She reached the hall, drew in a breath.

'You look a bit pale,' said Jason. 'Perhaps you ought to sit down for a moment, have a cup of tea or something.'

'I do feel a bit shaky,' Shelley admitted. 'P'raps I'd better. Not that I ever had any trouble carrying Liam, but you can't be too careful, can you?'

'Of course.' Jason steered her to the sofa. 'There you are. I'll put the kettle on.'

'Aren't you good!' Shelley marvelled. 'Just like a nurse!'

'As a matter of fact, that's what I am,' he said. 'I've got to go on shift in half an hour, I'm on nights this week.' He went to the door. Louise circled the room, sat down as far from the door as she could get. 'Will you have a cup?' he asked Roger. 'I'll make for all of us,

72

then. As a matter of fact,' he threw over his shoulder as he left the room, 'Louise is pregnant as well.'

Shelley, full of pleased amazement at this coincidence, did not notice that Louise's face hardened, momentarily, to granite.

'Are you really? Isn't that nice! When are you due?'

Reluctantly, Louise muttered a date.

'Only a week different! We might be in at the same time, that would be funny! Your first, is it?'

A peculiar expression crossed Louise's face.

'Yes,' she said, rather forcefully. 'Yes, my first.'

'Isn't that lovely! Over the moon, I was, when I fell for Liam. And this one too, for that matter. We're all like that in my family, we love babies. My Mum, she does fostering now, started doing it when we all grew up and left home. Hard work, that is, with some of those poor little mites. Damage limitation, that's what she calls it. Says you can't make them better, not really better, if things have gone wrong in the first years, but you can stop them getting worse, if you're lucky.' Jason came back in, carrying a tray. 'You must be ever so pleased, too.'

He smiled at her.

'I'm very pleased for Louise.'

'Only for Louise? What about you?'

'It's not his baby,' said Louise harshly. 'I don't want any tea.' She walked out of the room.

'Lor', I'm *sorry*. Me and my big mouth. My mum always said I only open it to change feet.'

'It's all right. You couldn't have known. We're splitting up, in fact.' Jason sounded quite unperturbed, which soothed Shelley at once.

'Oh, well, these things happen. 'Course, my Dave isn't Liam's dad either, so I know what it's like. Mind, he's been more of a dad to Liam than his real one, doesn't give a monkey's, he doesn't, except when the CSA come round after money. Screams blue murder then, he does. Still, that's men, innit? Present company excepted, of course.'

'Of course,' said Jason politely. His blue eyes met Roger's in a moment of shared amusement.

'Talk about embarrassing!' Shelley, in Roger's car, hugged herself and shuddered. 'I could have died!'

'I don't think they minded. I shouldn't let it worry you.' This from Roger, who frequently lay awake for hours sweating over gaffes that nobody but he had noticed.

'What do you mean, they didn't mind? After she slammed out of the room like that!'

'I don't think,' he said judiciously, 'that it was what you said that she minded. I think it was because it was him that told you.'

73

'Who, Jason? Her husband?'

'Yes. You know, they never speak to each other.'

'Don't they? I didn't notice. But then you know me, Mum says I'm always too busy transmitting to be able to receive. Funny things she says, my mum, sometimes. Not that she' s not right, though. I don't notice things about other people. Funny, that.' One of the more attractive things about Shelley was that in the middle of her self-absorption she was aware of her failings.

'I had more time to notice. I wasn't busy looking at the house.'

'I wouldn't have noticed anyway,' she said honestly. 'Still, if she's having someone else's baby, it's not very surprising, is it? I mean, he was nice about it, but he must be pretty well pissed off.'

'Mmm.' Roger was negotiating a roundabout, and put on a look of intense concentration to give him an excuse not to answer. It had seemed to him that far from being the angry, injured party, there had been something sad about Jason. In spite of his blond hair and his spectacular good looks, he seemed self-effacing, lacking in confidence, leaving all the talking to his wife. Towards her he had seemed, not resentful or jealous, but protective. At the same time, his expression was so controlled that he might have been a visiting stranger rather than a member of the family.

There was something else Roger had noticed, though he was perfectly sure that Shelley had not and he did not intend to tell her about it. In the kitchen, when Shelley was checking inside the cupboards to see how deep they were, there had been a piece of paper taped inside one of the doors. Louise had pushed it shut almost at once, but not before he had had time to see that it was neatly ruled into columns, like a school timetable. And a timetable was precisely what it was, with the days of the week on the vertical margin and the hours of the day, starting at seven in the morning and finishing at eleven at night, across the top. Spaces had been hatched in different colours, red and blue, orange and green. At the bottom, in the same coloured pens, were written two words. Bathroom, Jason, in blue, and kitchen, Jason, in red. Louise had the same words in orange and green.

Pondering, Roger considered this. He had an excellent visual memory – as a child he had often played Kim's game with his mother, and he had spent many hours of his boyhood practising to be a famous detective by noting down details of peoples' dress and mannerisms. Now, if he concentrated, he could almost reconstruct the timetable. It was a sharing out of the facilities of the house, he realised. Each of them had separate times to use the bathroom and the kitchen, coinciding with meal times, getting up and going to bed. He wondered what they did about the sitting room. There was a television in one of the bedrooms, he remembered. Perhaps Jason sat up there. Somehow he was sure that if anyone had the sitting room, it was Louise.

It seemed strange that Louise did not simply move out, and go to live with the father of her baby. Certainly she and Jason were not happy together, and sharing a small house under such circumstances must be so uncomfortable that it was difficult to imagine how it could be bearable. Poor things, thought Roger with easy sympathy. Poor things. He felt a quixotic urge to make sure that nothing went wrong with the sale that would release them from this purgatory. He turned to Shelley.

'That suite you were talking about should fit really well in the sitting room, don't you think?'

Shelley was startled. Even she could not have failed to notice that Roger was not very interested in her furniture.

'Yes,' she said cautiously. 'Yes, I suppose it will.'

'And Liam's going to enjoy that garden. You could get him a swing. Or a sand pit. Well, maybe not a sand pit,' he said, with visions of handfuls of gritty sand disappearing down Liam's throat. 'Tell you what,' he said expansively, 'if you've got time, why don't you come back and have a cup of tea? My mother would like to see you again.'

Shelley thought. Liam would be perfectly happy at his auntie's, and she had liked Roger's old mum. She was hoping, too, to persuade Roger to buy some of her old furniture. She really wanted everything to be new in her house. Perhaps she could get the conversation round to it, over tea.

'That'd be lovely,' she said with enthusiasm. 'Lead on, MacDuff.'

Changing gear with admirable smoothness, Roger headed for home.

Paul felt quite nervous when he took Alec and Christine Blake to see the six bedroomed house he had mentioned to Alec. He had liked Philippa Denton, and her husband George, so much at their first meeting and thought that their house was one of the nicest he had seen for a long time. He feared almost equally Christine's tactless pushiness, and George's bluntness, which might jeopardise what would otherwise prove to be an almost perfect sale.

'It's very good of you to let us come,' Christine Blake said graciously to Philippa Denton. Her graciousness, Paul was relieved to see, was slightly tempered. Secretly, Christine was rather over-awed by George and Philippa. The house might be shabby, but nothing could disguise the quality of the furniture which had the mis-matched elegance of inherited family pieces. Alec saw her eyes going round the hall, noting the Jacobean chest with the Hepplewhite chair next to it, the rugs on the polished floor that were balding in places but which still had the subtle colouring and intricate patterns of genuine Bokhara, and the two huge Chinese tulip pots from the openings of which sprouted, not flowers, but miscellaneous items including an old slipper, a yellowing copy of *The Times*, and a remarkably fine riding crop with an ivory handle bound with tarnished silver. It could not have been more different from Christine's immaculately tidy, carefully co-ordinated rooms, but it had an effortless harmony and charm that was as subtle as the smell of polish, pot-pourri and old mackintosh that somehow blended deliciously into the fragrance of an old and much-loved home.

Paul, following the family in through the front door, found that he almost wanted them to say that they didn't like it, that the house was completely unsuitable for their needs. Not very likely, he realised at once, seeing the acquisitive look on Christine's face. He didn't much care for Christine, and wasn't sure that he wanted to see her taking over this house and filling it with designer curtains and puffy Viennese blinds. Then he looked at Alec, and saw how he stood in the middle of the room, head back, breathing in the atmosphere as if he had been deprived of air for some years and had just found a place that was free of smog. He saw Philippa watching him. She closed one eye in a wink and he stifled a laugh.

He kept quiet as they went round the house.

'Of course I'll come along, if you want me to,' he had said to Philippa. 'You don't need me, though. The house will sell itself, you don't want some agent spouting Agentspeak all over it.'

'Is that what you do?' She had been amused.

'No. Well, not really. Not all the time. It depends on the people.'

'Well, I don't want you there for that. I want you there to keep them under control.'

'Are they likely to run amok? The children are reasonably well behaved, as far as I know, and Alec's a nice chap. Pretty mild, really. I don't think he's going to browbeat you into anything.'

'It's not him, it's her. I've come across her on committees. Terrifying woman, one of your true Juggernauts.'

Paul was astonished.

'You're surely not frightened of her? You? You could take on two of her, and eat them for breakfast.'

'Yes, but that's not the point, is it? If I eat her for breakfast, she's not likely to want to buy the house.'

'I thought you weren't sure you wanted to sell it. Or that George wasn't, in any case.' They had moved, almost at once, to first name terms, something which Paul seldom did with older clients but which had seemed natural.

'I don't *want* to, but I *need* to. I worry about George all the time, now. He's doing far too much in the garden, and it's never enough. And if we've got to do it, I'd rather get on with it. If these people are as suitable as you seem to think they are, then we might as well take the plunge. At least, that way, we won't have to endure endless people traipsing through, criticising the bathrooms and sneering at my kitchen. Not that Christine Blake won't sneer at it, of course, but I don't much like her so I don't care what she thinks.'

'If you don't much like her, could you bear to contemplate her living here?'

'Oh, that won't bother me. I've never felt possessive about this house. I mean, I love it, but once we leave I shan't haunt the place. She can do what she likes to it. Anyway, I don't believe she could spoil it, not really. And at least they're a family. I'd like to think of children growing up here.'

Paul looked at the children as he followed the little procession through the house. George had chosen to absent himself, saying quite rightly that he might frighten them off. The younger girl, he thought, was loving it. She bounced through the rooms, peering into cupboards and under furniture, standing on tiptoe to peer out of windows, asking questions in her clear, high voice. She exuded vitality and excitement from the mop of dark curls on her head to the thudding of her sandalled feet. Both the little girls wore sandals that looked remarkably like the ones Paul remembered his daughters wearing twenty years earlier. Surely most children wore trainers now, when out of school? The shoes were identical but Georgie, though younger, managed to make her footsteps heard in spite of rubber soles. It was not that she stamped or trod heavily, merely that her movements seemed firmer and more decisive. Harriet, on the other hand, crept from room to room on silent feet, only a faint mouse-like squeak betraying her when the soles turned on polished wood.

Paul found himself increasingly watching Harriet. He had several times had promising sales knocked down like ninepins because a small child in the family decided that the new house was unsuitable. He could not imagine Christine giving in to such foibles, or Alec either, but it was nevertheless clear that Harriet, if not Georgie, viewed the place with grave misgivings. He wondered why – he would have thought it a house calculated to appeal to children. Rambling and rather piecemeal, it offered plenty of secret corners and hiding places – it even had two staircases, something almost guaranteed to fascinate children who invariably were delighted by any possibility of a circuit. He saw her eyes lingering with pleasure on the numerous well-stuffed bookshelves, and once she reached out and stroked the cushions on a deep window-seat.

One of the bedrooms was slightly separated from the rest. The Dentons had wanted a cellar, and had constructed one beneath part of an extension. To save too much digging, and to allow for some daylight, the cellar was more of a basement, and as a result the two floors above were slightly raised. The bedroom on the top floor was approached by a short flight of four steps, and although not significantly higher it still gave the slight appearance of being a tower room. For one thing it was oddly shaped, having six walls instead of four with windows in three of them. All the windows had window-seats, and two alcoves were fitted with bookshelves above low cupboards.

'This looks like the room for you, Harriet,' said Alec.

'Yes, Daddy,' she answered politely, but her eyes slid away from him.

'It's not *fair*,' said Georgie. 'Why should Harry get the best room?'

'I don't know that it is the best room, really,' said Philippa peaceably. 'The one with the blue curtains is bigger, and you can see the stables and the paddock from it. This one looks over the orchard and the woodland.'

Mollified, Georgie signified her intention of returning for another look. Christine and Philippa went with her. Alec sat down on the window-seat.

'I rather like this room, myself,' he said to Harriet. 'It's just like a room in a story, don't you think? Good for reading and being quiet in. Nice and private.'

'Yes,' said Harriet unhelpfully. She twiddled with her hair, winding a stray lock round and round her finger in a way that drove Christine wild, and which Alec knew denoted anxiety. He cast a helpless look at Paul.

Paul turned to look out of the nearest window.

'Of course, some people don't much like heights,' he said. 'I'm not too keen on them myself. Makes me feel funny, being too high up.'

Harriet scowled at a table lamp as if she suspected it of having evil intentions.

'It's not the *height*,' she said crossly to the lamp. '*Heights* are all right.'

So, thought Paul. Not height, but . . . what? Distance, perhaps? He remembered, in his childhood, the comforting sounds coming from downstairs of his parents' voices and footsteps, and how worrying it was when a babysitter was there who made no noises, or different ones. This room was a long way from the living areas downstairs, and even from the other bedrooms.

'I suppose I might find this room a bit far away,' he said judiciously. 'It's a bit cut off from the rest of the house. It's nice to be peaceful, of course, when you want to read or be on your own, but if you wanted something, like a drink of water, or if you called out, you might feel that nobody would hear you.'

'Or if you had a bad dream,' said Harriet severely to the lamp.

'Yes, that kind of thing. Lots of people feel like that. Of course, you could have some kind of speaker system.'

'Like a baby alarm?' Harriet spoke scornfully, turning away from the lamp as if it had insulted her.

'Oh no!' Paul was shocked. 'No, I was thinking more like a kind of intercom. A sort of internal phone, like you have in rather grand hotels.' He spoke as though he assumed that she stayed in grand hotels all the time. Harriet said nothing, but she looked round the room as though seeing it for the first time. She nodded at Paul, an adult gesture signifying both acceptance and, he thought, gratitude. A glimpse of movement out of the window caught her eye.

'The others are in the garden. Come on.' She ran from the room. Alec and Paul followed more sedately.

'Thanks,' said Alec.

'Bright little thing,' said Paul. 'Imaginative, I suppose?'

'Very. Too imaginative, Christine says, though I can't see it, myself. She does get bad dreams from time to time, of course, and occasionally frightens herself into conniptions with ghosts in the roof or lions under the bed, but then when you see the pleasure she gets from reading . . . Christine thinks she reads too much, too. Always wanting her to come outside for a game of tennis, or a riding lesson. Of course,' he added fairly, 'she should be enjoying those things too.'

'Of course,' Paul agreed.

By the time they caught up with Philippa and Christine, they were already at the stables. As they stood on the brick courtyard, the pony came and hung its head over the stable door.

'Such a greedy little pig,' said Philippa affectionately, slapping its neck. 'I have to get him off the grass or he'd be as lame as anything. Ponies are the devil for laminitis.'

At the sight of the pony Paul saw Harriet, who had been running to join her sister, come to a sudden halt. She bent down to fiddle with her sandal, then edged slowly backwards until she was next to Paul, though she did not look at him. Remembering his own daughters at this age, Paul let his hand hang down as if by accident so that it was just beside her. After a tiny hesitation, during which he was careful not to appear to notice her, Paul felt her hand, warm and slightly sticky, creep into his. Almost imperceptibly she tugged him backwards. He went with her as if it were his idea.

'Come and see the water trough,' he said. 'There are fish in it.'

The large brick trough, tall enough so that Harriet had to stand on tiptoe to see into it, had several goldfish flitting through a healthy growth of water weed. 'Keeps the water cleaner,' Philippa had said. 'I put them in when we cleared out the fish pond one time, and never managed to catch them all again, so it seemed easier just to put in some weed and leave them to get on with it.'

'Doesn't the pony drink them?' asked Harriet dubiously.

'Presumably not. I think they sort of suck it in through their teeth. Like a tea strainer.'

Harriet giggled. 'Funny to find a goldfish in your tea strainer.' She dipped her finger in the water, drawing circles in it. 'I didn't know they had a pony here. I thought it was all empty. They're a bit old to have a pony, aren't they?'

'It's an old friend, I think. They keep it for their grandchildren.'

She digested this.

'Does that mean they'll take it away with them?'

'I'm not sure. I don't think they would have room for it.'

'They wouldn't have it put down, would they?'

'I'm sure they wouldn't. Not unless it was very sick, and in a lot of pain. How would you feel about it staying here?'

She stirred again, harder. The fish, which had come to investigate her finger for edible qualities, darted down into the weed.

'Georgie would like it.'

'But you wouldn't?'

'I don't really like horses much.' The confession came out in a rush, and she ducked her head so that her straggly hair fell about her face.

'That's all right. We all like different things. What is it you don't like about them?'

The struggle for words was visible in the tension in her thin body.

'They're so big. And they've got metal shoes on and if they tread on your feet, they could cut your toes off.' She wriggled. Obviously she had not yet reached the heart of the matter. 'And they twitch. When you touch them. Their skin goes all shivery.'

She sounded desperate, and he did not smile. He was reminded, vividly, of a thirteen-year-old Judith who had more or less been forced to have a French girl to stay on some kind of school exchange project. Judith had been appalled at the prospect.

'She has great long hairs under her arms,' she had wailed, 'and she eats her cereal out of a cup, with a *teaspoon*!' All her instinctive distrust of foreignness had been summed up in that cry, and it had taken all Paul's persuasive powers to make her agree that it was just possible, in spite of these grave defects, that the French girl might be all right. She had come to stay, and they were still friends now. Judith had visited her in Paris only three months earlier. He looked down at Harriet.

'You're probably being too gentle. If you stroke them gently it tickles, like a fly. You know how tickly it is if a fly lands on your bare skin?'

She nodded.

'Well, we can brush them away with our hands, but horses can't do that. They can flick their tails, but that's not long enough to reach the front of them. So they've learned to twitch their skins, to make the flies fly away.'

He saw her enter in her imagination into a horse's predicament.

'So it's not that they're cross?'

'Not at all. They can't help doing it. Have you ever had the doctor tap your knee with a little hammer, so that your leg jumps?'

'We do it at school, with rulers. You have to hit just the right place.'

'Well, that's called a reflex. It's a movement your body makes without you telling it to. And that's one of the horse's reflexes.'

She thought about it.

'I still don't really like horses all that much.'

'Well, you don't have to. Why don't you tell your parents that? Your father? They're not going to make you do something you really don't like.' And I hope that's true, he thought, remembering Christine. 'Of course,' he added, 'if you were to find you were really interested in something different, like dancing, say, or croquet, that might help.' He racked his brains for something as socially acceptable as horse riding. 'Sailing? They have a sailing club on the reservoir. You might like that. *Swallows and Amazons*. Long John Silver. Do you know,' he said, getting carried away in a connection of ideas, 'I know someone who has a parrot that talks. It's called Archimedes.'

Harriet thought about it.

'Archimedes was an owl,' she said decisively. 'Not a parrot. In *The Once and Future King*.'

'Seen the film?' He was clutching at straws.

'Read the book,' she said disapprovingly. 'So, why is the parrot called Archimedes?'

'I don't know.' In the face of her polite contempt he added meekly, 'But I really will find out. Perhaps you'd like to come and see it, some time?'

'Yes. Yes, I should like that. Thank you.'

'Not at all,' he murmured. She ran off to the others, who were going to look at the rest of the garden. Now what have I let myself in for, he wondered? Oh well, she'll probably forget all about it.

Chapter Eight

*B*eep beep. Beep beep.
  'Hensham Homes, good morning?'
  'Mr Kingswood.' He recognised her voice at once, from the rush of pleasure that went through him.
  'Mrs Oldham.' He hoped he didn't sound too eager.
  'Beth,' she corrected.
  'Paul, then. How are you? How is Mrs Holt?' Damn, I should have asked that first, when I know she's been ill. He had been unable to visit Mrs Holt or to show the bungalow to the Dentons because she had been in bed for the past week, prey to something she had referred to, tersely dismissive, as 'the horribles'. Paul, not knowing whether this meant arthritis, diarrhoea, the onset of cancer, or just a bad cold, had not liked to ask for elucidation. 'I'll let you know when I'm better,' she had said firmly, and rung off.
  'All right now, more or less. She gets these dizzy spells, and they make her feel terribly sick. They've done some tests, and it's not her blood pressure, but some kind of inner ear trouble which they say isn't serious. That's all very well, but at her age any kind of fall is potentially dangerous, so when she gets these attacks she just stays in bed until they go away.'
  'Nasty,' he sympathised.
  'Very nasty. However, the good news is that it always disappears as quickly as it comes on, and with no more reason. She's fine now. And so am I, since you asked.'
  'Good. Er, would you care to have lunch?'
  'Now?' Her voice was amused. It was ten o'clock.
  'Well, today. Or tomorrow. Or some time.'
  'That would be pleasant,' she said sedately. 'Only it will have to be some time. I'm actually in Penzance.'
  'Penzance? As in, Cornwall?'
  'The very same.'
  He had a sudden vision of the little town. He and Jenny had holidayed near Penzance when their daughters were small, young enough to enjoy the simpler delights of sea and sand in little rocky coves, and before the provision of some kind of night life became the pre-requisite of a good holiday.

'Lucky you,' he sighed.

'Yes. Well, it's pouring with rain, as a matter of fact, and I didn't bring warm enough clothes, but still . . . yes, it's lovely. You like Cornwall?'

'Love it. I always found it so exotic. Oh, perhaps not exotic, but different to Sussex, at any rate. I was always rather surprised to find that they spoke English, and used pounds, shillings and pence in the shops. It felt more like being abroad.'

'That dates you.' She was laughing at him.

'What does? Oh, pounds, shillings and pence. Goodness, it does, doesn't it? Funny how it sticks, though, what you were brought up with. All those sums we had to do at school, murder really. Or perhaps you don't remember?'

'I've already told you my age,' she reminded him. 'I remember perfectly well. Nice little sixpences for pocket money on Saturday. And lovely threepenny bits.'

'And half crowns,' he added. 'I had an uncle used to give me a half crown whenever he saw me. You felt really rich, with a half crown.'

'Aar, those were the days.' She was laughing at him.

'They certainly were. What can you get, now, for twelve and a half pee?'

'Not much. A small bag of shrimp sweets. A few seconds on the telephone.'

'Heavens, I'm sorry. Here I am gibbering on, and this call is costing you a fortune.'

'Not really. At least, it's tax deductible, so it's not quite so bad. A mobile phone is a necessary tool, like a laptop PC.'

'What do you do?'

'I'm a writer.'

Paul was faced with the problem common to those encountering writers and actors. Was the fact that he hadn't recognised her name a dreadful insult, or did it simply mean she worked under a different name? Should he say 'Of *course* you are!' in the tones of one who has been racking his brain to remember why the name was familiar, or would she catch him out? Probably the latter, he thought.

'Books?' he hazarded.

'Two. But mostly articles, short stories. Magazine fodder. Nothing very special, I'm afraid. I'm down here to interview a farmer who's sold up all his animals and gone into menhirs.'

'Men what?'

'Menhirs. Ancient standing stones, like you get in northern France and round here. And *Asterix*. Rather more like *Asterix*, really, because he's making them himself.'

'Out of granite? That must be rather a long job, even nowadays.'

'It would be, but no. Out of fibreglass. So you can carry them on your shoulder, like Obelix does. And they're selling really well, apparently.'

'Good for him. Er, who buys them, and what do they do with them?'

'Put them in their gardens, I suppose. Like a statue. Of course, you have to weight the base with concrete or something. I haven't actually met him yet, so I don't know the details. Still, you have to admire the enterprise, and the novelty value. Most farmers nowadays are racking their brains to find something they can do with their farms that doesn't actually involve crops or animals. Avoid the EC at all costs, and the animal rights lot too. You know what they're saying they're suffering from? Agriphobia.'

Fear of farming, he worked out.

'Good one,' he said. 'Your own?'

'As a matter of fact, yes,' she said modestly. 'It looks better written down. Clearer.'

'Have you always been a writer?'

'I always knew I wanted to. I did various jobs, secretarial, that kind of thing, but I always scribbled in my spare time. When I had my first book accepted I decided to give up the other jobs and go it alone. It's a bit of a struggle, sometimes, but I've good contacts in the magazine world and I can usually dredge up something to pay the bills. Most of the time.'

'Tell me about it. There should be a word for a phobia about opening brown envelopes. Though in fact the white ones are worse.'

'Yes, the professionals. Except, of course, for the ultimate terror.'

'OHMS? And don't forget the VAT office. You know what my daughters call me? The Hunchback of Hensham Homes.'

'?' She made an interrogative noise.

'The Bills! The Bills!'

She laughed. 'Can I use that? I'll give you a credit.'

'Of course you can. I'm honoured.'

'Oh dear, I better go.' He was pleased to hear that she sounded reluctant. 'Time for the fibreglass menhirs. And what I really called about was to say that my mother would be happy for you to go round again, and put the bungalow on the market properly.'

'I'd be delighted. Any excuse to see Archimedes again. And by the way, why *is* he called Archimedes?'

She laughed again.

'Oh, no, I'm not going to tell you and spoil her fun. Let her show you for herself. You'll enjoy it.'

'I'm sure I shall. Though not as much as our lunch.'

'Later,' she promised. 'When I get back.' He had to be content with that.

★ ★ ★

Liz Hartwell looked round the table at the people she thought of, resolutely, as 'my family'. It was easy enough to think of Joss like that, and of course Mike, but Ruth? Her heart pounded as she looked at the girl, knowing that Mike's announcement was certain to provoke an outburst of fury, or worse. Recently, since Liz had found her washing her sheets in the middle of the night, she had taken to a new tactic of silence. Her brother and her father she would answer, if spoken to directly, with as few words as possible. Liz's remarks and questions were ignored, and this had made Mike so angry that Liz found it better simply not to speak to Ruth, or to channel essential questions through Joss. The silence, which she would have expected to be easier to bear than the previous verbal attacks, was so heavy with unspoken menace that it made her ears ring.

Mike insisted that they should all eat supper together, regardless of television programmes, sporting activities or school commitments. It meant that they sometimes had to eat either very early or very late, to accommodate their various timetables, but it was the one thing that he would allow no arguments over. He had started it after Mary had died, when he had been forced to leave the children in the care of a housekeeper. Finding that he saw less and less of them, he had instituted family supper, saying that at least if they ate together he would have a chance to talk to Ruth and Joseph, and to listen to them, rather than simply sitting while they watched television. After he married Liz, Ruth had made a spirited attempt to break the pattern, but for once her father had been inflexible.

'Liz goes to a lot of trouble to cook us good meals,' he had said. 'The least we can do is to sit down and enjoy them together.' It was true that Liz, who enjoyed eating, was a good cook, and Joss at least had rejoiced at the exotic flavours she had introduced him to. Ruth had retaliated by announcing that she had become a vegetarian, but Liz had not spent a year sharing a flat with two vegetarians for nothing. Without fuss she had produced meat-free versions of the family meals, and though Ruth made a serious attempt to pick at them fussily, she was usually too hungry not to eat them. Her school canteen offered cheese salad or egg salad for vegetarians, day in, day out, and there were times when she regretted her stand. It was not in her nature, however, to go back on her decisions, though she indulged in the occasional burger when no one was looking.

'Family meeting after supper,' Mike announced.

'Oh, Dad! It's *The Bill* tonight!'

'You can tape it, and watch it later.' Mike spoke mildly, knowing that Joss's objection was a routine response, meant to be dismissed. 'Ruth?'

'Family meeting. That's so pathetic.'

'It was your idea,' he pointed out. 'You got it from *Neighbours*.'

'I don't watch *Neighbours* any more.' Her tone was lofty. 'Or *Home and Away*.' It was unnecessary to spell out why, and Mike was careful not to ask, knowing that she would make some damning remark about the Australian accents, or the Australian characters, in such a way that it was not quite an open attack on Liz.

'Well, whether or not, I've got something I want to tell you about. And something to discuss with you.'

Ruth pushed her bowl away, leaving her apple crumble half finished. Liz, despising herself, had nevertheless cooked Ruth's favourite meal. 'Let's get on with it, then,' Ruth muttered.

'When the table's cleared we will,' he answered. Since Liz had cooked the meal, it was the children's job to clear and stack the washing up in the dishwasher. When it was done and the table wiped, Ruth and Joss sat down again. Ruth, who had originally elected to sit opposite Liz so that she did not have to sit next to her, had realised that this meant she had to look at Liz every time she glanced up. She had moved back to her original place, keeping her chair as far to the other end of the table as she could, and turning her body slightly away and towards her brother. Mike reached out and took Liz's hand, and Ruth jerked her chair further away so that her arm was almost touching Joss's.

'Get off!' he said, shoving her away. She kicked him sharply. 'Ow! Dad . . . !'

'Stop it, you two. I've got something important to tell you.' Now it came to it, he was obviously finding it difficult to get the words out. He felt her tremble, and squeezed her hand. 'Some exciting news. Liz is having a baby.'

'Really?' Joss was surprised, but not particularly interested. 'When?'

'Not for quite a while. About May, probably.'

'Round my birthday.' He seemed to find this a cause for satisfaction. 'Cool.'

Mike looked at Ruth. Her face was the colour of lard, her eyes blank.

'Ruth?' he said gently.

Her lips worked. Without warning she shoved her chair back so hard that it fell over when she stood up. With her hand over her mouth she ran from the room, and they heard her retching and retching, then the splatter of vomit in the basin of the cloakroom.

'Yuck,' said Joss. 'Good thing she didn't finish her pudding.' Liz stood up, but Mike pushed her down into her chair again.

'I'll go,' he said. 'Stay here.'

Left on their own, Liz and Joss looked at one another.

'You don't mind too much, then, Joss?'

''Course not. Why should I? Simon, at school, his mum had another baby a few months ago. He reckons it's great. His dad's dead chuffed with himself, and his mum's so busy she hasn't got time to nag him, or notice what he gets up to. Not that he gets up to much,' he added hastily. 'You know. Just bed times and that. And when he takes the baby out in its pram, all these old ladies say what a good boy he is, and give him sweets. One of them gave him a pound coin even, only his dad made him put it in the charity box. Still . . .' He fell silent, his faraway gaze fixed on possibilities ahead. Out in the cloakroom a tap ran, and water splashed in the basin. Mike spoke, low and soothing.

'How could you?' Ruth's accusation was bitter. 'How could you? It's . . . it's *disgusting*!' Another murmur, still gentle. 'It's not normal! It's obscene! It's treachery! Don't you remember Mummy at *all*? How could you do that to her? You've got two children. You've got a son, and a daughter. Why do you want another one? It won't even be properly English! And it will have horrible red hair, like hers!'

Joss ignored the rising voice of his sister. He appeared sunk in profound thought. Then he frowned.

'Where will we put it?' he asked, looking vaguely around the room as though he expected some handy alcove or cupboard to materialise. 'I suppose it will go in your room.' He nodded at this reasonable supposition.

'That's the other thing, Joss.' Liz spoke quietly, her ears straining to the hall. 'Babies grow up quite quickly. He or she will need a room. Of course, we don't expect you to share, or Ruth. So it will mean we'd need a bigger house.'

'No!' Ruth stood in the doorway. 'Not that *as well*! You've taken everything else, you're not going to take our house!'

'What do you mean, taken everything else?' Joss was genuinely puzzled. 'What's Liz taken?'

'Only our *father*,' she hissed at him. 'Only our *lives*. Only our *mother's place*.'

Joss looked at her. Her eyes were red and bloodshot, her face greenish and sweating.

'You're potty,' he said. 'Cracked. Lost the plot. Out of your tree. One sandwich short of a picnic.' He looked ready to continue almost indefinitely.

'That's enough,' said Mike sternly. 'It seems to me that the only thing that Liz has taken is a great deal of abuse from you, Ruth. She's been patient, and so have I, but we can't go on like this. Liz is one of the family now, just as much as you and Joss and me. She's not trying to take your mother's place. Mummy's dead, we all miss her, and she's still part of this family, but life goes on. Mummy said that herself, don't you remember? She said, don't look back, don't go on being sad. Remember the good bits, the happy times, and then go on to new good bits and new happy times. It's not disloyal to bring Liz into our lives, or to have a new baby in the family. It's a positive thing, a new hope. And the sooner you learn to accept it, the better.'

'Never!' She was shrieking at him, lashing out with wild fists and feet. Mike took her by the wrists and held her away from him. 'I won't! I won't! And you can't make me!'

'No,' he said sadly. 'No, I can't. But nor can you make me not do it. And I tell you now, this house is going on the market, and we are going to find a bigger one. We'll take most of what's here with us, and nothing shall be got rid of without your agreement, but it's going to be different.'

'Can I have a bigger room, Dad? And bunk beds?' Joss, accustomed to Ruth's moods, took not the slightest notice of her frenzied attack on their father.

'Yes. Maybe. Not *now*, Joss.'

'Okay. Um, if that's all, I'll go and watch *The Bill*.' He gave Liz a pat as he passed her, as if she had been a pet dog. Liz smiled a wobbly smile at him. 'Cheer up, Sis,' he said, skirting widely round her. 'You know you're always saying your room is too small.'

'Oh you . . . you *boy*!' Ruth spat at him. 'You *baby*!'

'Not any more!' he riposted triumphantly. 'I'm not going to be the youngest any more!'

Ruth became incoherent, her words trailing off into sobs. She hung limply from Mike's hold, and he looked helplessly at Liz. Liz mimed a hug, and he gathered Ruth awkwardly into his arms. She tried to push him away, then collapsed sobbing against him. He sat down with her on his knee and she clung like a baby monkey, butting her head into his chest. Liz left them to it, and went out to the hall. The downstairs cloakroom smelled of sick, but when she looked at the clogged basin Liz's own stomach heaved, and she retreated to the kitchen where she put the kettle on and then finished clearing up the supper. As usual, the children had put the easy things in the dishwasher and left the crusted dishes as if they were invisible, though Liz had implored them times without number at least to leave them to soak.

Wearily she wiped down the worktops, then stood prodding half-heartedly at the burnt edges of the lasagne dish. Is this really worth it, she wondered? Is it ever going to get better? Or will we carry on like this until one of us cracks? Something tells me it's Ruth who's going to win this one. She's won already, really. After all, she's the one sitting on Mike's knee being petted, and here I am doing the washing up. Cinderella had it easy. She just had ugly sisters. I've got the step-daughter from Hell.

She shivered, although the house was warm. Back home, she thought, it's spring. Never mind the hot summers, the spiders, the bush fires . . . at least it's not bloody cold and damp for nine months of the year. At least you can plan a barbecue and not have to cook it under an umbrella and eat it indoors. And at least you don't have to share your home with some kind of malevolent gnome, intent on sabotaging your marriage and making your life a misery.

Another wave of nausea hit her. Curiously, though, instead of making her feel more hopeless than before, it cheered her up. Like receiving a garbled message from another planet, she thought. You're not quite sure what it's saying, but you know it's telling you that there's life out there. Or, in my case, in there. Here I am, it's saying. The creature from another world, coming to earth with who knows what powers? Weapons and abilities beyond our comprehension. A catalyst, a peacemaker, or maybe just the most powerful weapon of all, the nuclear deterrent that would enforce a peace, or win the whole war. Liz abandoned the half cleaned dish, and made herself a cup of instant hot chocolate to take up to bed.

Beep beep. Beep beep.
'Hensham Homes, good afternoon?'
'Timothy Goodard, Goodard & Smiley.' The voice was precise, introducing himself as if Paul might have forgotten the name of one of the leading local solicitors. Known locally as 'Good and Smelly', Paul always referred to them in his mind as 'Godot's', because he seemed to spend half his life waiting for them. Once, having been told three times that Mr Goodard would phone him back without, then, hearing a word, he had tried sending a fax. The first message had been ignored, and driven to desperation he had sent a second reading simply 'Hello? Hello? Is there anyone there?'. This had elicited a pompous answer which did not, in fact, address the basic problem at hand and he had since regretted his moment of levity. Mr Goodard and Mr Smiley were now, as far as he was concerned, permanently 'With a Client' or 'In Court', or simply 'Unavailable'. Which made the present call all the more unlikely, since Paul had not in fact tried to speak to them that day.

'What can I do for you?' Paul tried to keep the amazement out of his voice.

'Who,' asked Tim Goodard in portentous tones, 'is Claire?'

'Claire?' Paul thought frantically. 'Claire who?'

'Precisely.' The solicitor was triumphant. 'You can't expect us to help without a surname. Even if she is missing. Though why you should call us . . .'

'Hang on a minute!' Paul was thinking hard. 'Missing, did you say?' He heard the tremble in his own voice, and bit his lip. Tim Goodard's sense of humour was as small as his bills were large. 'I'm afraid there's been a misunderstanding. No one's missing. I asked Rose to call you this morning about Miss Sinclair.'

'Miss Sinclair? What about her?'

'Miss Sinclair. Missing Claire.' Paul spaced the words carefully.

'Well, really!' Affronted, the solicitor hung up, leaving Paul to enjoy his laugh until he realised that he still hadn't any answer to his question.

Melanie, who had missed this exchange, waited until he'd stopped laughing.

'There, that's better,' she said, as if he had been about three years old. 'Why don't we have a nice cup of tea? I've got some of those biscuits you like.' Paul would have been perfectly happy to do the tea-making himself, but neither Melanie nor Rose trusted him with something so important. His helplessness in the kitchen was one of the few things they agreed on. He sometimes wondered what they thought he did in the evenings and at weekends. There had been a time when they had shown an alarming inclination to cook him Sunday lunch each week, which he had escaped from by promising to call them if he was stuck.

Melanie stood up, then glanced at the door. 'Hello, dear, who are you?'

Paul also looked towards the door. It had opened such a small amount that he had not been aware of it moving, and a child had slipped through the narrow opening. Looking beyond her to see an accompanying adult, he did not at first recognise her in her school uniform.

'I'm Harriet Blake,' she said to him. She didn't seem to be surprised that he didn't remember her. It was as though she was used to being overlooked. Paul stood up.

'Harriet! Of course you are. Forgive me, I was miles away, and of course I didn't expect to see you. Um, shouldn't you be at school?' He glanced at the clock, which said half past three.

'School finishes at three,' she informed him. Unsure of her welcome, she stayed by the door.

'Of course it does. We were just about to have a cup of tea, and a biscuit. Perhaps you would like to join us?' He raised an eyebrow at Melanie. She, more practical, looked at Harriet severely.

'Does your mum know you're here? I always had to go straight home, when I was at school.'

'So do I. Mummy collects us. I told her I had extra orchestra practice, and that Daddy was picking me up later.'

'And is he?'

'He usually does. Half past five, at the school.'

'And I suppose the school think you've gone home?' Melanie was torn between disapproval and reluctant admiration. She, too, had been adept at playing school and home off against each other to gain her own ends, and she was surprised to see that this washed out little scrap had so much enterprise. Harriet nodded.

'I thought, perhaps, you could telephone Daddy?' She fixed beseeching eyes on Paul, but her whole body expressed the knowledge that he would probably refuse.

'What were you wanting to do instead?' he asked gently.

'I just thought,' she said forlornly, 'that we might go and see the parrot. Archimedes.' She looked down at the ground, not wanting to see the refusal in his eyes. One of her bony knees was scabbed where she had fallen over the week before. 'To find out why he's called that,' she said to her feet.

Paul thought.

'Well, why not?' he said at last. 'I really *should* find out why. And I ought to go and see Mrs Holt, now that she's better.'

'What about Mr Goodard?' Melanie was afraid she might have to deal with that herself.

'Mr Goodard,' he said grandly, 'can wait. We'll have that cup of tea, and I'll telephone Harriet's father and then if Mrs Holt doesn't mind we'll go and see her.'

'Are you sure? Who's Mr Goodard?'

'No one we need to worry about. At least,' he added, seeing Melanie's sardonic look, 'not until tomorrow. Sufficient unto the day is the Mr Goodard thereof. And the one thing you can say about Mr Goodard is that we're bound to have to call again tomorrow. And the next day, and the next . . . so just this once I shall copy Harriet, and steal a couple of hours for myself.'

'Good for you,' said Melanie. 'Time you broke out a bit. Come on, love. You can fetch the biscuits.'

Bemused but pleased, Harriet went with her. Paul picked up the telephone. AGENT IN KIDNAP SCANDAL, the headline blared in his head. A respected local estate agent runs away – no, absconds – with client's daughter. 'We only went to see the parrot,' claims Paul Kingswood, (53). He shook himself. He really should stop seeing things in terms of newspaper advertisements and headlines.

'What's *nefandous*?' asked Harriet. She was peering down at his newspaper, where he had idly ringed 'Word-watching'.

'It's what we're doing now, running away from school and the office,' said Paul. 'Unspeakably, unutterably wicked,' he added in hollow tones.

'Oh, good.'

'This is Harriet,' said Paul. 'Harriet, this is Mrs Holt.' He wondered for a second whether Harriet would be too shy to respond, but he had reckoned without Christine's strict training.

'How do you do, Mrs Holt,' said Harriet politely. They shook hands, and Harriet appeared to make one of her lightning judgments of character. She gave the same little approving nod she had once bestowed on Paul and a small smile.

'Do come in,' said Alice. 'I gather you're interested in parrots?'

'Well, I'm interested in the *idea* of them,' answered Harriet carefully. 'I've never actually met one before.'

'Then you must come and meet him at once.' Over Harriet's head, Alice's eyes met Paul's in a moment of shared pleasure in this pedantic child. 'Would you like anything to eat? I have some rather good chocolate biscuits I've been saving for a special occasion.'

Harriet's face turned pink. No one had ever suggested that a visit from her might be a special occasion.

'I did have some biscuits in Mr Kingswood's office, so I don't really need anything . . .' As ever, Harriet was to honest for her own good.

'Chocolate biscuits aren't about nourishment,' said Mrs Holt briskly. 'They're a form of celebration. I expect Mr Kingswood would like one too – I expect he's delighted to have an excuse to come and see Archimedes again. And we'll give a bit to Archimedes, so that'll be fair, don't you think?'

'Yes, perfectly fair,' said Harriet judiciously. 'After all, parrots don't really need chocolate biscuits either, do they? But I expect they like to celebrate.' As they walked into the sitting room, Harriet stopped dead at the sight of the cage. Her eyes shone behind her glasses. 'Oh, how beautiful!' she whispered. Alice Holt and Paul waited quietly until she drew in her breath in a deep sigh. Then Alice opened the cage door, and put in her hand so that Archimedes could sidle on to it. Paul wondered whether Harriet would be nervous of him – a child that feared ponies might easily find that large beak alarming – but Harriet approached without hesitation. Paul noticed that although obviously excited she stood quietly and without unnecessary movements. The bird cocked his head and eyed her. Paul was sure that he could see approval in those beady eyes.

'You can stroke him, if you want. Like this.'

Harriet copied Alice's caress. Her extreme stillness and carefulness was somehow more expressive of delight than any amount of talking might have been and Paul found himself more moved than he would have believed possible.

'Come and sit here, Harriet, and I'll put Archimedes on the arm of the chair,' said Mrs Holt, with a smile to Paul. He knew she was going to get Archimedes to demonstrate his falling off the chair trick, and he almost laughed in anticipation of Harriet's face. And then there was another thing, surely, that the parrot could do? Paul settled back in his chair, and prepared to enjoy himself.

Chapter Nine

*B*eep beep. Beep beep.

'Hensham Homes, good morning?'

'Oh, Mr Kingswood, this is Mr Selby.'

'Hello, Mr Selby. How are you?' Roger Selby, Paul thought, was rapidly taking over from other clients on the Frequent Phonecall stakes. Not that he was awkward – far from it – but he seemed to feel the need to discuss not only his own purchase, but Shelley and Dave's as well, monitoring the progress of their sale with as much care as his own. It was true that the Johnsons still had not found anything they liked, though Mrs Johnson had visited several houses. She was looking for something slightly more expensive than the two bedroomed house they were selling to Shelley and Dave, and Paul knew from Roger (though not from Louise herself) that she was not intending to share it with Jason, her husband. Paul had asked her, as a matter of course, how the new house was to be funded and had been told rather icily that she would be using money from a legacy.

'My broker tells me,' said Roger in his precise tones, 'that the mortgage lenders have taken up my references, and that I should be receiving a written offer very shortly.' He spoke with modest pride, as though he were to be awarded some kind of medal. Which, given the difficulties that lenders put in the way of potential borrowers, Paul thought, you could probably say that he was.

'Well done, old chap,' he said heartily. 'That's splendid.' It was curious, he thought, how Roger's pedantic speech patterns made Paul himself turn into a caricature of a bluff old uncle from somewhere near the beginning of the century. He just managed to stop himself adding, 'Jolly good show'. 'I'm afraid Mrs Johnson doesn't seem to have found anything that she likes yet,' he said, anticipating the next question. 'But I'm sure she soon will. She's certainly looked at several, they just haven't quite come up to her standards. Perhaps you should take her viewing – I always say it was really you that sold her house to Shelley and Dave! Well, to Shelley, anyway. Though I believe he's been to see the house now.'

'Yes,' said Roger. 'Yes, they told me. They called in to see us afterwards, me and Mum.' His tone was disapproving.

'Oh, good,' said Paul cautiously, hoping that the dour tone didn't mean that Dave had taken an irrational dislike to the house after all. 'And what did he say?'

'About the house? He said it was fine.' Roger, primming his lips together, was certainly not going to shock nice Mr Kingswood by telling him what Dave had said. With the same careless friendliness that Shelley always showed, he had invited Roger to go out for 'a quick one down the pub', leaving Shelley to talk to Mum. The two women got on surprisingly well, and when they left Mum had been getting out the photograph albums to show Shelley the pictures of Roger as a baby. Roger, who would ordinarily have turned down such an invitation because he disliked the taste of beer, was so eager to remove Dave from this embarrassing scenario that he had positively hustled him out of the door. Fortunately Dave was as anxious to get to the pub as Roger was to get him out of the house, so he saw nothing strange in this. The nearest pub, once The King's Head but recently renamed by the brewery The Hedgehog and Hollybush (which had at once led to the landlady being rechristened Holly by the regulars, so that they could make remarks about pricks and bushes) was only two streets away, but Roger suggested that they go in his car. This, as well as being a hospitable gesture, would enable him to have only one drink and make it last, the excuse that 'I'm driving' being an acceptable reason for sobriety even among the heavy-drinking fraternity.

Dave made himself instantly at home.

'Nice place,' he said approvingly, looking round at the new decor which included fake Victorian agricultural implements hanging from the ceiling, and a collection of equally fake leering Toby jugs which clustered along spurious beams. 'Good name,' he added with a grin. 'Reminds me of that joke about the difference between a Porsche and a hedgehog? Eh? Know that one, do you?' Roger shook his head, and Dave raised his voice. 'Thought everyone knew that one! Hey, you could adapt it for this pub – what's the difference between this pub and a hedgehog?' He looked round hopefully, collecting a few grins and nods. The landlady, her disposition already soured by being addressed all the time as 'Holly', wiped the bar down with a cloth that looked more of a genuine antique than most of the other things there.

'All the pricks are on the inside,' she said sourly, stealing his line. 'And you can say that again.' She looked pointedly at Dave.

'Touchy-toucheee!' Nevertheless, he led the way to a corner table. 'She always like that?'

Roger took a cautious sip of his pint.

'She's probably just having a bad day,' he said judiciously.

'Women, eh,' agreed Dave. 'Can't live without 'em, can't live with 'em. You got a bird, then? Someone moving into the flat with you, once you get shot of Mum?'

Roger winced. He hated to think of moving into the flat being called 'getting shot of Mum'.

'Not at the moment,' he said cautiously.

'Got something to look forward to, then, haven't you?' Dave spoke with simple envy. 'New flat, new freedom – you'll be having a ball, eh? Wouldn't mind being in your shoes! 'Course, I've got Shelley,' he mused. 'Lovely girl. And you've been really kind, driving her round and that.' Roger glanced at him warily over the rim of his glass. He hoped that Dave didn't mind Roger driving his, well, not his wife, but his lady friend, around. Dave, however, was sure enough of his own attractions not to fear competition from Roger.

'She tell you she's in the club?' he asked. Roger nodded. 'Bit of a turn up for the books, that – not that it's not to be expected, know what I mean?' He winked at Roger.

'Yes, she did just mention . . .'

'Pleased as punch, she is. Wants us to get married, do it properly, dress up like a meringue and put the little 'un in daft clothes. Women, eh?' He repeated indulgently. 'Still, I suppose I'll go along with it. Keep her sweet, all that kind of thing.'

'She's a lovely girl. My mum was ever so taken with her.' Roger spoke, for him, quite severely.

'Yeah, she's a smasher, my Shelley. She can cook, too, did you know that? Proper chips, things like that. None of your oven ones, all dried up. Real chip pan, she uses!'

Roger nodded his appreciation of this mark of culinary excellence.

'Little chap a bit of a handful? Young Liam?' The beer was beginning to taste better as his taste-buds accustomed themselves, and he found he was rather enjoying this man-to-man chat.

'No, no trouble at all,' said Dave airily. 'Not really. 'Course, I leave all that to his mum. I mean, that's her job, innit? Hey, that reminds me of another joke, new one. Listen, what's the word wife stand for? Eh?'

Roger was puzzled.

'Listen, you're going to like this one, it's good. Wife, see, W, I, F, E, know what it stands for? It's for Washing, Ironing, Fucking, Et cetera. Good, eh?'

Roger was embarrassed and affronted, but he pretended to laugh. Somehow, he had never managed to get used to the way people used such words in general conversation. He knew that he was old-fashioned, but he simply couldn't accustom himself to it. Fortunately Dave was so amused that his own laughter covered the lack of Roger's.

Roger, remembering this joke, felt his face grow hot and was glad that Mr Kingswood couldn't see him. He was comforted to think that Mr Kingswood would have been equally shocked. He was right, though Paul's reaction would have been to the lack of political correctness rather than the word itself. He regarded himself as rather a New Man, having been carefully educated by his wife and his daughters.

'Mr Selby all right, is he?' asked Rose as Roger rang off. 'Oh, Mr K, you really *must* speak to that girl!' She stared disapprovingly at the piece of paper in her hand, the newly typed details of the latest property.

'What's she done?'

'She's put *symphonic* WC in the bathroom. I ask you! And it's been mailed out, too!'

Paul smiled. Which symphony, he wondered? The *Appassionata*? The *Eroica*? The *Pastoral*, The *Surprise*? No, he thought. Just Number Two, in C. In WC, rather.

'Well, I don't think it's funny,' said Rose severely. 'What will The Vendor think?' She always managed to endow clients with capital letters, as if they were minor deities. Quite rightly, he supposed, as most of them seemed to think they were.

'They probably wouldn't notice,' he soothed. 'People see what they expect to see, after all. And most people don't read things carefully. Remember that time I put, "Ugandan Kitchen" in the advertisement, just for a laugh, and not one single person telephoned to ask me what it meant?'

Rose sniffed. She and Roger, though neither of them realised it, would have agreed on the subject of jokes.

Beep beep. Beep beep.

'Hensham Homes, good morning?' Paul was relieved to be let off the hook.

'I know you're keen to find a buyer for my mother's bungalow,' Beth Oldham's voice was warm in his ear, 'but don't you think ten years old is a bit young?'

He laughed.

'A bit, perhaps. But I think, if she'd had the money, she might have bought it! Though only if the parrot was thrown in, of course.'

'You don't behave like any estate agent I've ever known,' Beth remarked thoughtfully.

'Don't I? And how many have you known, exactly?'

'Well, none, really. I know, I know. Don't categorise. Estate agents are dishonest, engineers are boring, teachers are bossy . . . The trouble is, so often the stereotypes are there simply because they *are* true.'

'True. But how many people do you know who are strictly, one hundred per cent, honest and open in their business dealings?'

'Scarcer than hen's teeth,' she agreed. 'So it's all true, then? You are a liar?'

'So many of my clients assume that I am, I frequently find myself believing them. The trouble is, there are times when being a bit, well, *economical with the truth*, is the best way of doing things. Oh, lord, you're not going to put this into an article, are you? "Liars I have known", "Estate Agents Exposed", that kind of thing?'

'Of course I am. My tape recorder is running at this very moment.'

'Right, then. As a matter of fact, I lie to my clients very much less than they lie to me, on a ratio of about one to fifty. Generally, if I lie, it is unwittingly, because I am simply passing on some information I have been given, like, "yes, the house has been re-wired," or, "yes, these people are cash buyers," when in fact what they mean is that when or if they have sold their house, they will have the cash to buy a new one. I will hold back information from over-anxious vendors or buyers in order not to jeopardise a perfectly good sale, and I have spent the last seven years lying to my bank manager and assuring him that I really think I'll be able to repay my overdraft quite soon. Satisfied?'

'Not at all, not nearly sleazy enough. So, you now know about Archimedes?'

'Yes. Harriet loved it. Your mother put him through his paces.'

He saw in his mind's eye Harriet's thin face, unusually flushed with excitement, as she watched Mrs Holt take out the parrot's drinking bowl, and tip out some of the water.

'A lot of people recommend those special drinkers,' Mrs Holt said, 'but I'm afraid Archimedes doesn't like them. He's an old-fashioned sort of bird, he likes everything to stay the same as when he was young. You know that parrots can live to be very old?'

'Yes.' Harriet was solemn. To her, anyone older than twenty was quite elderly. She was entranced by the sight of the parrot cage, which would indeed have been quite big enough for her to stand up in. 'Is Archimedes very old?'

'He's nearly thirty. I think he would tell you that he is in the prime of his life.'

Harriet looked at Archimedes, who was preening one glossy wing and contriving to keep an eye, at the same time, on everything that was going on.

'Yes, I can see that he is,' she agreed solemnly.

'Now, watch.' Mrs Holt put the half-empty dish back in the cage. Archimedes glared balefully at it, and shifted crossly from foot to foot. He waited, like an impatient guest at a restaurant eager to be served, to see whether anything was to be forthcoming. When nobody did anything, he climbed wearily down the walls of his cage and stood by the dish, staring around in a pointed fashion. Finally, with an almost visible shrug and sigh, he walked with his rolling gait to another dish set nearby. It held something that Harriet had originally thought were nuts but which she now saw were small pebbles. Scrutinising them carefully, he selected one, picked it up delicately in his beak and placed

99

it in the water dish. He then proceeded to repeat this action, pausing from time to time with his head on one side to check his handiwork, and sometimes rearranging a pebble like a flower-arranger balancing colour and line. When he had finished, the level of the water was back up to the brim.

'Eureka,' he remarked smugly. Harriet's hands were clasped over her mouth, to suppress her laughter, but her eyes glowed. It occurred to Paul, rather too late, that she might not grasp the allusion, but he need not have worried.

'How *clever*!' she breathed. 'Archimedes and his bath!'

They had tea, and Harriet shared a small bunch of grapes with the parrot, then Mrs Holt sent her out to explore the garden while she talked to Paul. After a little while, Harriet came back and stood beside Mrs Holt's chair, waiting for a chance to speak.

'Yes, my dear? What is it?'

'Did you know that you have a door in your rockery?'

Mrs Holt did not smile.

'I *did* know, but I didn't know whether you would discover it. I know the cotoneaster has grown over it a lot, now that nobody goes there. It was built as an air-raid shelter, you see – you know about air-raid shelters?' Harriet nodded. 'It was very well built, so instead of pulling it down my husband used it to keep his wine in. My daughter used to have a den in there, when she was a child. She used to pretend it was a cave, or a dungeon, or a dragon's lair – you know the kind of thing.' Harriet nodded again. She knew exactly. 'Should you like to see inside it? There is a key hidden under the flat stone just to the left of the door, and you may take the torch from beside the back door.'

'Oh, *thank* you,' said Harriet, and danced from the room.

'Nice child,' remarked Mrs Holt. 'Reminds me of Beth, only Beth was always a plump little girl. She won't come to any harm,' she reassured him. 'It really is quite clean and dry in there, and perfectly safe.'

Harriet went home in a state of unusual satisfaction. She told Alec all about Archimedes in the car, but the air-raid shelter she hugged to herself as her own private secret. She resolved never to tell anyone about it. If their new house were to have something like that, she thought, she wouldn't mind moving nearly so much.

By chance she was at home when the Hartwell family came to look at her house. It was Saturday morning and Georgie had gone for a riding lesson, but Harriet had faked a tummy ache so convincingly that she had managed to stay at home.

Mike had insisted that both the children should come to look at the house.

'On paper, it's by far the nicest,' he said firmly. 'I want you both to see it, so we can make a decision together.'

100

'I don't need to see it to make my decision,' muttered Ruth. 'I'm not leaving this house, and that's that.'

Mike ignored her, and since he made it clear that he was prepared, if necessary, to put her into the car by force, Ruth reluctantly came along. She said nothing as they were shown round, sneering silently at every room. Christine entirely failed to notice the sneer, and was only impressed by how quiet and, in her eyes, well behaved she was. When Ruth turned down the offer of a drink and a biscuit, she suggested that both girls might like to go back upstairs.

'You could show Ruth your books,' she suggested vaguely, realising that Ruth was rather too old to be shown toys. Obediently the two girls trailed up to Harriet's room. Ruth sat on the bed and looked around. Harriet stood nervously by her bookshelves.

'You don't have to show me your stupid books,' said Ruth contemptuously. 'I expect they're all baby stuff, anyway. What's this?' She picked up a paperback from the bedside table. Her eyebrows rose. '*Animal Farm*? I suppose you thought it was all about cuddly lambies and dear little calves?'

'Not really,' said Harriet. 'I don't much like animal stories. But this isn't really about animals, is it? I mean, it's a kind of allegory, I thought.'

Ruth was reluctantly impressed. She had been studying *Animal Farm* at school.

'Who told you that?'

'Nobody. Well, it's in the preface.' Harriet sounded anxious, as though she had been caught cheating.

'Well, don't look so scared! There's nothing wrong with being brainy. I bet your parents love it.'

'Not really.' Harriet looked confused. 'I mean, Daddy understands about me liking reading, but Mummy always thinks I should be doing something. Riding, or playing tennis, or something. That's why she wants us to move, so that we can have ponies and things. Tennis parties.' She spoke as though her mother were proposing some complicated regime of torture rather than what Georgie regarded as a kind of attainable heaven.

'At least she wants nice things for you. Things she thinks are nice, I mean, even if you don't like them.'

'Doesn't yours? You're lucky having such a young mother. Doesn't she want nice things for you?'

'My *mother* wanted me to be happy, but that's got nothing to do with it. My mother can't help me any more. She's dead.'

Harriet's eyes filled with tears. She had never met anyone whose mother had died before, though of course it happened quite a lot in books.

'Oh, poor you! I am sorry!'

Ruth was pleased. In the months following her mother's death she

101

had received a lot of sympathy from everyone, but as time went by people expected her to have got over it. As if you could get over something like that.

'It's all right,' she said bravely. 'It was three years ago, now. Everyone's forgotten about her, except me. They just don't care any more. Especially now my father's married that – that woman. My step-mother.'

Harriet was appalled. Her life had been quiet and sheltered, and most of her knowledge of the world was derived from the books she had read. Solitary and imaginative, she had worked her way through all the standard children's fairy tales and classics, and in most of these step-parents, particularly step-mothers, had received a bad press. The name, to her, was almost synonymous with cruelty and wickedness. Some of her friends from school had step-fathers, she knew, and even step-mothers where their fathers had re-married, but since the marriages had broken up from divorce rather than death, none of them had to live with their step-parents on a full-time basis.

'How awful!' she breathed. 'What does she do to you?'

'She's trying to take my mother's place,' said Ruth bitterly. 'In fact, she has done. My father and my brother don't even remember her now, and they don't care any more. I'm the only one who remembers, and so she hates me. She pretends to be really kind, and really nice, but underneath she's not like that at all.' Ruth had told herself this so many times that it was easy to believe it, easier still to make Harriet believe it.

'How awful!' Harriet repeated.

'She'd like to get rid of me,' said Ruth, warming to her theme. 'She really would, only she can't. My father thinks she's so perfect and so wonderful, but he wouldn't let her do that. At least, not yet. So she's doing the next best thing, and getting rid of everything that reminds us of Mummy. That's why she wants to move. She wanted to change all the rooms, even Mummy's bedroom where she died, but I wouldn't let her, so now she's made them all think that we need a bigger house.'

'It's quite nice here,' said Harriet tentatively. 'You might find you liked it. It's a lovely house, really.' She looked round her room, where even the scuffs on the wallpaper and the scratches in the paintwork were familiar and, therefore, comfortable.

'Oh, I'm not saying it's not. But it's not home. Not *my* home, anyway. Not Mummy's home.'

'Like the house we're going to. It's very big, and if I were just going to visit it I expect I'd love it, but I don't want to go and live there. It's all going to be different. I'm going . . .' she paused, and swallowed before speaking the unbearable bit, 'I'm going to go to boarding school.'

They looked at one another, united in despair.

'It's not fair,' said Ruth fiercely. 'They shouldn't be allowed to do this to us.'

'There's nothing we can do. After all, it *looks* as though they're being kind to us. People would say that we're really lucky. They just don't *understand*.' Harriet's voice was resigned. Her previous ten years of life had not led her to expect that anyone, even Daddy, would pay much attention to what she might say.

'Then we've got to *make* them understand.'

'How?'

'I don't know. But we've got to do something to show them that they can't just do whatever they like to us. Something to make them see that we're not just going to lie down and let them trample all over us. Like going on a hunger strike, or something.'

'I don't think I could,' said Harriet honestly.

'Not even if we both did it together? We could encourage each other, keep each other company.'

'But we don't live together. We wouldn't be having our meals together, and that's when they'd go on at us.'

'No.' Ruth could see the sense of this. 'Still, we ought to be able to think of something. And if we both did it, surely they'd see that we really meant it.' She looked dubiously at Harriet, remembering how much younger she was. 'You can keep a secret, can't you? I mean, you won't go and say all this to someone?' She looked fierce, her thin face sharp and bony, even her hair looked prickly. Harriet shivered.

'No, I won't tell. I promise.' She found Ruth a bit frightening, but was flattered by having someone so much older bothering with her. Also, of course, she felt so sorry for her. It was easy for her to imagine how dreadful Ruth's life must be, and there was something rather exciting about knowing someone like her. It was like meeting a character out of one of her books. 'You can trust me,' she said firmly.

Philippa and George Denton would have been astonished if they had known how appalled Harriet was at the prospect of moving to their house. To them, as to their children and grandchildren, it was an ideal place for young people to grow up in, and even now the prospect of leaving it was something they both found hard to accept.

Philippa looked at George as they sat in the little room with the television. The slight breathlessness that they never spoke of was more pronounced today, she thought. As if he felt her glance – though he was watching the news on television – he put his hands down and clasped them casually round his knee, straightening his back in an effort to breath normally. Philippa's heart ached. After a few minutes he picked up the remote control – what a boon it was for the elderly, thought Philippa – and switched off the sound.

'Heard the headlines, that'll do me,' he said. 'Turn it back on again for the weather. Go on, then, ask away.'

'Ask what?' she prevaricated.

'You know. The house. Bungalow, rather. Place with the parrot. Don't you want to know what I thought of it?'

'Of course I do. Don't you want to know what *I* thought?'

'I don't need to ask,' he said with gruff fondness. 'Your idea to move in the first place. You liked the Holt woman, I saw that. Nod's as good as a wink.'

'None so blind as he that will not see,' she retorted sharply. 'Anyway, it was a lovely bungalow. Much better than I'd hoped. I loved the veranda, and I saw you poking around in the garden and eyeing up that rockery. You can't fool me.'

'I wouldn't try to. Anyway, I agree.'

'Is this going to be an "Anyway" conversation?' She blinked hard to clear the tears that had ambushed her at this unexpectedly reasonable answer. The family saying dated back to their children's early days, when sibling squabbles invariably started (and continued) with 'Well, *anyway* . . .'

'Not at all. I know you think I've been unreasonable –' he paused to allow her to deny it, but she folded her lips and merely look at him, '– and perhaps I have, but I just dreaded the idea of leaving all this and having to cram ourselves into some architect's idea of suitable packaging for the elderly. The only box I intend to be in is my final one. But I admit this isn't like that. The garden's not big, but it's interesting, and it's got potential. Enough to keep me amused, and not so much that I won't be able to manage it, with a bit of help. House is okay too.'

'Oh, you!' she said fondly. 'You don't care anything for the house, as long as the garden is all right.'

'True. But you mind about the house, and I mind about that.'

Philippa's face crumpled. 'Unfair,' she said huskily. 'You know I get all emotional when people are nice to me.'

'It's all right, I'm going to beat you later.'

'That's more like it.' She blew her nose and wiped her eyes. 'So, you think we should go for it?'

'I do. If we miss this one, we might wait years for anything as good to turn up. I did some asking around at the golf club – the price seems to be pretty fair. Not that I don't trust your chap,' he added to forestall her, 'but there's no harm in checking it out. With what we should get for this place, it should leave us with a tidy little nest-egg. Rainy days, and all that.' Philippa smiled, aware that such nest-eggs tended to dwindle in direct proportion to the sudden needs of impecunious children and grandchildren, but unable even now to worry about it very much.

'I'll tell him then, shall I? Paul Kingswood, tomorrow?'

104

'Yes, do that. Now, what about another drink? A toast to the future, that kind of thing.'

'Why not?' She smiled, holding out her glass. 'I'll drink to that.'

Chapter Ten

*B*eep beep. Beep beep.

'Good morning, Hensham Homes?'

There was a short silence. Not the cinema, Paul begged silently. Not a taxi order. It's only nine thirty, and I've had two cinema enquiries already. Why do people ring cinemas so early in the morning? Haven't they got anything better to do? Like moving house, for example? There was a click, and the line went dead. Well to hell with you, too, Paul thought sourly. It rang again, and he snatched it up.

'Hello?' he snarled.

'Dad?' His daughter's voice sounded startled. 'Is that you, Dad?'

'Oh, Dizzy, sorry. I thought it was another wrong number. How are you? How's the bump?'

'The *bump's* fine. Having a lovely time displacing all my insides and mucking about with my hormones. I tell you, Dad, this kid's going to be a research biologist or something. I *swear* it's using me as experimental material.'

'Poor old love. It'll pass.'

'I know it will. Anyway, I didn't ring just to have a moan at you. I really thought I'd better talk to you about Judith and John. The wedding, you know.'

It wasn't difficult to interpret her cautious tone.

'I'd really like to help. I can manage something, you know.'

'That's just it. They don't want you to feel you have to. All that father-of-the-bride paying for everything is distinctly *passé* now, you know.'

'I know, but then I'm pretty *passé* myself. I know I can't manage to do the lot, but I want to do what I can. Besides, things are picking up.'

'You always say that, you lying estate agent, you.'

'Ah, but the difference is that this time it's almost true. I've done a few sales this month, and I've got a couple of big ones that would pay for quite a lot of satin or tulle or whatever it is she wants to swathe herself in, if they come off. Which I think they will.'

'That's great, Dad. Nice houses?'

'Very. And nice people, too. And guess what – a parrot!'

'Dead or alive?'

'Definitely alive. The most tremendous character.'

'You'd better see if they'll sell it. I know how you've always wanted one. Perhaps Judith would like it as an extra bridesmaid.'

'It's male.'

'Page, then. Don't be awkward. Anyway, all I'm saying is, for goodness sake don't go overboard about the wedding.'

'I shan't. After all, I'll need to keep something back for the christening present, won't I? What do you think – a microscope? A chemistry set?'

'Something like that. Or just a nice presentation box of tranquillisers for me. See you, Dad.'

It was amazing how much better he felt after talking to Dizzy. It was true that although nobody could say that the market was lively, it was at least showing signs of coming out of its coma. Breathing on its own, he thought. Life support disconnected. If only I could find someone to buy the Hartwells' house! I know they'd offer for that place of Alec Blake's like a shot, and then the Blakes could buy the Dentons place with the pony paddock, and the Dentons could go for the bungalow. It's such a good chain, I *must* be able to tie it together. Why can't I find anyone to buy the Hartwells'? That bloody daughter of theirs, I should think. Every time I take anyone there she's scowling at them, playing her blasted music and generally making the place unpleasant. Extraordinary how she manages to make the whole house feel unhappy, as if she were haunting it. I must telephone round again, see if I can drum up some interest.

Beep beep. Beep beep.

'Hensham Homes, good morning? No, madam, I'm afraid I don't know the time of the late performance. But can I interest you in a delightful three bedroomed semi-detached house instead?'

It was a relief to Louise Johnson to have the house to herself. Jason's shifts had been daytime ones during the last few days, coinciding more or less with her own working hours. Stubborn in her misery, she had refused to go out in the evenings and he also had stayed at home. She told herself that he only did it to annoy her, to be in her way, refusing to admit what she really knew, which was that it was his way of looking after her. Jason, who was still the one person in all the world whose love she wanted, who had professed to love her but in whom she could not bring herself to believe. That he still cared for her, in the sense of feeling responsible, was a different matter. Caring for people was what he did, the way that he defined his place in the world and gave point to his existence. Even if he hated her, she thought, he would still look after her.

More than anything else, she wished that she could hate him. The idea, of course, was indifference, but she could not imagine a time when that might be possible. When he was in the house with her she was aware of him with every fibre of her body and spirit; the sound of his voice resonated in her ears though he seldom spoke; she was the Geiger counter to his radioactivity. It was exquisitely painful but dangerously pleasurable, she delighted in it as an addict delights in the drug that will, in the end, bring nothing but destruction.

She walked round the house. It was all very clean and inhumanly tidy. Sharing, as they did, the kitchen, the bathroom and the sitting room, each was careful to wipe down surfaces, to leave cushions smooth and furniture precisely arranged. It was as though both of them were intent on erasing their presence, and yet the effect was to highlight it. Only in her bedroom, the bedroom she had once shared with Jason, did Louise allow herself to be untidy. Behind its closed door books and newspapers littered the floor, clothes were strewn on chairs, even empty crisp bags and coffee mugs encrusted with dried on rings lay on bedside tables and windowsills. It was a kind of release to be able to do it, she almost revelled in the knowledge that the fluffy dust lay half an inch deep under her bed, that there was a heap of grubby clothes in the corner, and that the bed hadn't been made for several days.

In the past, she would never have let the room get into this state. They had bought the house four years ago, when they were first married. She still could not believe that she would ever know such happiness as she had felt during those early months, when they had shopped together for furniture, curtain materials, and all the little things that had been so lovingly chosen to achieve the perfect home. Together they had stripped paint and sanded wood, stained and waxed, repaired and renovated. Louise had taught herself about paint effects and stencils, Jason went to evening classes and learned to do cane and rush seating. They argued happily about colours and styles, sometimes disagreeing for the pleasure of it, always basically in accord.

Louise supposed she had always felt that she loved Jason more than he loved her. It wasn't something she dwelled on, it was merely implicit in their relationship. She always remembered her mother saying, rather sadly, something about how there was always one who kissed, and one who let himself be kissed. She had said it in French, which had made it sound more romantic and, somehow, more profound. Louise had known that her mother had been talking of Louise's father, who had allowed himself to be kissed for a short time and had then disappeared, leaving a baby Louise to be brought up by her mother. When Louise had been eight her mother had died, knocked down by a speeding car on a pedestrian crossing. Her grandparents were too old to take charge of her (and in any case they had never been fond of Louise, feeling as they did that she should never have been born) so Louise had been put into care.

Her first placement in a foster-home had been unhappy, as an only child she found the boisterous family of younger children impossible to cope with. After a few weeks, during which time she lost weight and began, to her shame, to wet the bed, she was moved, and moved again. With each change she lost confidence, and it was not until she was sent at last to a house where the children of the family had grown up and gone to college or out into the world that things improved. There, under the sensible care of older foster-parents who had already seen more than twenty children grow up, she had settled. It could not have been said that she thrived, but she grew and put on weight, and the bed-wetting ceased almost at once.

She stayed with the same family until she was sixteen. By then she had been with them for five years and, although the local authority had no further requirement to provide for her, the family told her she was welcome to stay on. She had sometimes wondered whether they might ask to adopt her, not realising at the time that they were too old for this to be possible, and because they did not she always had a deep-seated insecurity that she was only there as a temporary daughter. Because of this, and because they asked her kindly but not pressingly to stay, she had moved out and found herself a dark little room in a lodging house. With a job in the kitchens of a local hotel (which meant that she spent almost nothing on food since she was allowed to eat there) she felt that she had her life well under control.

At the same time, she always felt that there was something lacking, a kind of completeness the lack of which made her, in her own eyes, rather two dimensional. During her childhood and early adolescence she had always assumed that it was her mother she was missing. It was, of course, but as she grew up she realised that it was not merely her mother as a physical presence, but what she represented – the knowledge that there is someone in the world who loves you best.

Was it, she wondered, something lacking in her that kept her apart from the world? At school she had had friends, but never a best friend. Sheltered by her elderly foster-parents, her early encounters with the opposite sex were limited to school. Her interest in boys had been as a looker-on rather than as an active participator, and her early loves were images on television and in magazines rather than among her acquaintances. In the hotel kitchens she was shouted at by the chef and treated with teasing kindness by cooks and waiters. They took the place of her foster-parents, protecting and ignoring by turns, and since she usually had to work in the evenings her social life was practically non-existent. Sometimes, feeling like Cinderella, she would watch the guests in the dining room as though they were exotic creatures in a zoo, a separate species that was interesting but irrelevant to her own life.

Meeting Jason had been a revelation. Chopping vegetables for soup, her attention wandered and she cut her hand. It wasn't the first time – her fingers were almost always decorated with the blue plasters they had to use – but it was bad, the knife slicing deeply into the fleshy pad at the base of her thumb. It bled all over the vegetables (which annoyed the chef) and although it had not yet started hurting it was obviously beyond the first-aid box level of wound. One of the waiters, an elderly man whose increasing slowness of movement and tendency to muddle orders was making it obvious to everyone that he would soon be given his marching orders, was detailed to go to the hospital with her, and money was found for a taxi.

Outside the hotel, the ill-assorted pair looked at one another. Louise was clutching her wounded hand, holding a pad of cloth tightly over the flap of flesh that was beginning to throb.

'Are y'all right, girl? Sure, we should've phoned for a taxi while we were inside, should we not?' His blue eyes were watery with concern, the Irish accent stronger than usual. She thought his face was like a tortoise, thick gnarled skin above a wrinkled neck. His mouth, too – she remembered one of her foster-homes where she had given lettuce leaves to the tortoise and it had opened its lipless triangular mouth with just the same deliberation as he did when he ate. He looked at her hopefully.

'There's a bus goes to the hospital from the bottom of the road. I'll split the taxi money with you.'

'Aren't you the canny article, then? And you no more than a baby yourself.'

'Ach, bejasus, get away with you and your blarney!' She imitated his accent, and he grinned. His resemblance to a tortoise increased.

'Sure and somebody should have given you a rare skelping, altogether, you little devil! Let's be getting that bus, then.'

By the time they reached the casualty department she had to grip her lips together and breathe hard through her nose to stop herself whimpering from the pain. Her companion, feeling guilty about the pound coins that weighed his pocket so pleasantly, fussed over her unbearably until she begged him to go away.

'Go and have a cigarette outside. Go and have a beer – there's a pub down on the corner. I'll be fine.'

His face crinkled with guilty pleasure, and his eyes grew brighter so that she could see that the tales he told of his youth were more than the fantasies she had thought them. He patted her on the shoulder and she settled herself to wait.

When, in the end, she was shown into a curtained cubicle the wound had stopped bleeding and the pad of cloth was stuck to it. She gritted her teeth as a student nurse eased it gently off so that the doctor could look at it.

'Not very bad. Nice clean cut – knife?'

'Yes. I work in a hotel kitchen. I was . . .'

'Remind me not to eat there.' The doctor was abrupt, cutting across her nervous talk, but his smile was kind and there were deep bags beneath his tired, bloodshot eyes. 'We'll get that cleaned and stitched up. Tetanus up to date? Good. Jason will see to it . . .' He was gone, the curtain billowing from the speed of his passing. Louise looked round her vaguely.

'Lightning Lawrence, we call him,' remarked a voice from behind her right shoulder. 'He thinks he's on one of those TV dramas. He'd be whizzing round on roller skates if the administrator would allow it.'

Louise looked round and blinked at the most beautiful young man she had ever seen. Not attractive or handsome but beautiful, as an angel in a painting is beautiful. His eyes were very bright blue, and she spared a thought for her old Irish friend in his pub, whose eyes had never been as blue as these. They were set in a face that was faultless in its perfection and yet not cold or intimidating, as perfection sometimes is, and his hair was streaked the kind of rich gold that most girls dream of for themselves. In any other man she would have thought 'peroxide, what a vain git', but on him it looked as natural as rays of sunlight slanting through clouds and gilding a corn field.

'Hi!' he said. 'I'm Jason. Let's get started on that hand, shall we? I'll try not to hurt you.'

Looking at him, Louise thought that she wouldn't mind how much it hurt, so long as he was there with her, holding her hand with his that was warm even through the thin surgical glove. As he irrigated the cut and cleaned it gently he kept up a light flow of talk, and Louise struggled to answer.

'What's your name again? Louise? Nice name.'

'Do you think so? I hate it.'

'Why?' It was not just conversation, he really seemed to want to know.

'I got teased about it, when I was little.'

'At school? Kids can be right little beasts, can't they?'

'Yes. Not just at school. Everywhere.' It had been in her first foster-home where, miserable and confused, she had first started to wet her bed. One of the other children – she could not now remember whether it was another foster-child or one of the parents' actual children – had chanted 'Loo Wees, Loo Wees, you should be called Bed Wees, not Loo Wees'. The nasty little phrase had caught on, being of the simple lavatory humour appreciated by children that age, and had followed her to school. It was of short duration, a teacher heard it and spoke to the foster-mother. The perpetrator was punished and blamed Louise, hating her thereafter.

'Brothers and sisters?' Jason looked at the cleaned cut. 'Mm, pity, tape won't hold that together, not when you have to move your thumb all the time, it'll have to be stitches. I'd better get something to numb it.' He caught her confused look. 'Sorry, talking to myself. Silly, when I've got you to talk to.'

It appeared to be a mild flirtation, but he sounded as though he meant it, as though he really wanted to talk to her.

'Not brothers and sisters. I don't have any. I was in care, with a foster family. It was one of them.' She was astonished to hear herself saying it, she almost never talked about her childhood, and when she did it was of the early years, before her mother's death.

'In care? So was I.'

'Were you? Really?'

'Yes.' He looked amused. 'Did you think you were the only one?'

'It felt rather like it.'

'I know.' Looking at him, Louise saw that he did.

They were married two months later. Louise was entranced by him, dazzled by his beauty and fascinated by his quiet, almost secretive, nature. Outwardly friendly, he was very wary of revealing his inner feelings, which made it all the more rewarding on the rare occasions when he relaxed and let his emotions show.

She knew that she set too much store on how people looked. It was deeply ingrained in her, as it was in many children placed in care. Attractive children were more acceptable to foster-families, so the rumour went, and if you were really nice looking you might stand a chance of being adopted, even if you weren't a baby. Louise had seen herself that children newly arriving at school were more readily accepted by their peers if they were good looking, particularly the girls.

As a result she worried a great deal about her own looks, agonising over adolescent spots and scouring magazines for tips and hints on beauty aids. She taught herself dressmaking so that she could copy the high-street fashions she could not afford, and followed strict diet and exercise regimes. To her, being overweight or sloppily dressed meant a person without self-respect, almost immoral. She could never have been attracted to someone careless, and outward ugliness was, to her, the sign of inner badness. Jason was beautiful and therefore, in her eyes, perfect. She wondered endlessly why he had chosen her, of all people, but did not ask him because she was afraid that if he were to think about it, he might change his mind.

The hotel gave a reception for them, suggested by the kitchen staff who were delighted by their unintentional match-making. With an eye to the write-up they had already managed with the local paper, they would have liked a full scale wedding with the bride and groom emerging under an arch of crossed ladles, but Louise put her foot down and insisted on a civil ceremony. Even so it was much grander than she would ever have arranged for herself, and her foster-parents, now elderly, wept happily to see their last charge so suitably settled.

Looking back at the intense happiness of their first year together, it was difficult to see just where and when things had started to go wrong. Louise knew, of course, that no relationship could continue to be perfect for ever. She knew that the first rapture must inevitably dim a little, from time to time, that they would inevitably have moments of irritation or anger or even boredom. She knew that with her not inconsiderable intelligence, but with her heart . . . that was a different matter.

Had it, perhaps, been that holiday in Spain, when they had been married for just more than a year? Their first holiday abroad together, and for Louise her first taste of foreign travel. She had been bubbling with excitement for weeks, had read books about Spain, studied maps, even borrowed language cassettes from the library which she played whenever she was on her own, forcing herself to repeat and answer out loud, laughing at herself and yet dreaming that she would be able to impress Jason by her ability to ask directions, to order meals, or even to chat to friendly locals in bars or shops.

The reality had been so different from her imaginings. The pretty little fishing village that featured so prominently in the brochure still existed, but it was no more than a tourist attraction, a picturesque museum carefully preserved amid the ugly blocks of flats and the spreading hotels they were still building, so that their room looked out onto a dusty site that echoed to the sound of diggers and cement mixers that started up early in the morning, to catch the cooler part of the day. Louise, who had picked the place, was mortified. Jason told her that it didn't matter, that they could hire a car and go looking for the real Spain which he assured her existed only a few miles inland, but even this was soon out of the question.

On the evening of their arrival, desperate to get away from the concrete acres of their hotel, they had walked into the centre of the village. A dimly lit bar with rickety tables set up on the pavement seemed to promise local colour, but the dim lighting had concealed a very sketchy regard for hygiene, and during the night both of them were sick. Jason, who had travelled a fair bit and built up some resistance, was better by morning, but Louise spent the next few days between her bed and the bathroom, and for several days after that was liable to fits of nausea and giddiness that made it impossible for her to do more than flop in the shade of an umbrella on the crowded beach.

Louise had to admit that Jason did his best. He insisted on calling a doctor when Louise was still suffering from sickness and diarrhoea after thirty-six hours. The doctor – the only person they encountered throughout the holiday who didn't speak English – communicated in

114

sign language, and Louise wished that the tapes had taught her to say, 'I feel like death and I can't stop throwing up'. Jason would have stayed with her in the airless little bedroom, but Louise drove him out. He could do nothing for her. All she wanted to do was to lie as still as possible and groan from time to time and she hated him to see her like this. Reluctantly, he went to the beach, and by the time she was well enough to accompany him he already seemed to know several people.

It was only natural, she knew, that a young man on his own should be spoken to by single girls. It was all the more natural considering his looks. The blond streaks in his hair had bleached more dramatically in the sun, and he was the fortunate possessor of skin that tanned smoothly and evenly, without burning. He looked like an advertisement for something exotic and tropical, and Louise felt pale and limp and dull beside him. She saw how heads turned as he passed, heard the greetings called from all sides and mostly in female voices, and her heart seemed to chill and contract within her.

There had always been an element of 'why me?' in Louise's mind. Jason, whose initial response of 'why not?' had shown signs, not of irritability but of withdrawal, seemed unable to provide an answer and merely shrugged. Louise had stopped asking, but her insecurity did not vanish. Her experience of life had not encouraged her to believe in her own attractions, and she failed to see that Jason's own careful enhancements of his own good looks indicated a similar insecurity.

Louise made a big effort. Determined not to waste the holiday she forced herself to ignore how wobbly she still felt. She managed two days' worth of sun and sea before relapsing again, her still upset stomach rebelling and her skin, under-protected from her eagerness to lose what seemed to her its livid whiteness, red and sore.

Somehow they survived the fortnight, and during the last two days even managed to hire a car and visit some more unspoilt places, but it had to be admitted that the holiday had been a disaster. Jason joked about it, and Louise laughed, but inside she squirmed in agony. Afterwards she found herself hyper-sensitive, and had to struggle to control outbursts of jealous irritation which she knew would make his face close up as he withdrew from her.

Things settled down, but they were never quite the same again. The spontaneity had gone, for one thing, at least on Louise's side. She found herself always watching Jason for signs of being bored with her, of having met someone more amusing and exciting. Several times, Jason asked her what was wrong, but Louise only laughed it off and said he was imagining things, knowing as she did so that she was wasting an opportunity to talk things through, but unable to bring herself to do it. The effect was to make her feel edgy and also angry.

She wanted Jason somehow to sense what she was feeling and to reassure her, but couldn't bring herself to admit that anything was amiss.

Then, one day, she realised she was pregnant. Louise was never sure in her own mind whether this had been an accident or not: she told herself it was, but knew that somewhere along the line her subconscious had betrayed her into letting it happen. She waited until she was sure, then approached the subject in a roundabout fashion with Jason, bringing the conversation round to his childhood memories. They weren't happy ones. His mother had abandoned him at an early age but had refused to allow him to be adopted, so like Louise he had been moved several times from one foster home to another.

Jason's reaction, at the mention of babies, was to clam up immediately. Louise, who had been talking about a fictitious friend who had just found she was pregnant, felt as though he had slammed a door of ice in her face. Gritting her teeth, she jumped in with both feet.

'But you do want us to have babies some time, don't you? I mean, I know we never really discussed it, but I always thought . . . I know you like children, and you're so good with them, they always like you . . .'

'Some time, I suppose.' Jason sounded wary. 'Not just yet, though. For one thing, I don't see how we could afford it, not now we've bought this house. We need your income for a while, I'm afraid. Besides . . .'

'What?'

'Well, it's early days, isn't it? We haven't had a chance to get to know one another properly yet.'

Louise nodded speechlessly. Jason looked more closely at her.

'You're not . . . ? You didn't bring this up because you're . . .?' There was an expression in his eyes that she read as dismay, perhaps even horror. She shook her head.

'No. Oh, no,' she said firmly. 'Of course not.' She listened to her own words and wondered why she was doing this. Why could she not behave like an adult, tell Jason the truth? Something within her, however, would not let her take this way out. A kind of mad exaltation came over her, born of emotion and hormones and years of accepting what came along. For once, she was in charge.

The next day, she went to the doctor and said she wanted a termination. It was not as easy as she had expected, the doctor was reluctant.

'You're healthy, you have a home of your own and a splendid husband.' He had met Jason several times at the hospital. 'Are you perfectly sure you want to do this? Are there family reasons, perhaps?

116

Genetic problems? If so, there are tests, people who can advise and help you . . .'

'No, no, nothing like that. I just don't think we're ready. You know, neither of us had what you might call a normal childhood.' He nodded, since it was all recorded in her notes. 'Well, we don't want it to be like that for our baby. We want everything to be right, and if we went ahead now . . . I just don't think it would work out. It just frightens me too much!' Her last few words had the ring of sincerity in them, and the doctor backed down.

Louise had the termination without telling Jason anything about it, and told herself that she had done the right thing. Beneath the surface, however, Louise was miserable, confused and angry. Unable to show that she was mourning the baby, and unwilling to allow her anger a chance to express itself, she took refuge in silence, and any plans Jason might have had for the two of them to get to know one another better foundered on the rock of her inability to communicate.

Gradually, they drifted apart. Jason took on extra shifts at the hospital, and Louise half suspected that he might be more than friendly with one of the other nurses, but she was too unhappy to be able to do anything about it. To her minimal self-confidence she now added guilt and self-hatred, because she had killed her baby. She found herself blaming Jason, too, for what she saw as a rejection of their child. She took to goading him, trying to provoke him into a display of anger. The self-control, developed during his childhood as a protective device, kept him quiet and calm. Louise interpreted this, with her own irrational logic, as lack of feeling. Surely, she thought, if he really loved her he would react more strongly. She interpreted his lack of anger as indifference, and pushed him harder.

Their final row came, ironically, as the result of a celebration. Louise, who had attempted several times to contact her mother's parents and had been rebuffed each time, was astonished to learn from a solicitor's letter that they had died and left her a share in their estate amounting to almost fifty thousand pounds. Scarcely able to believe it she had telephoned the solicitor, and found that it was indeed true. Whether they regretted their treatment of her, or whether it was just that they had no other living relative to benefit, she could not discover, but the money was indisputably hers. She and Jason celebrated with a meal out and rather too much wine, which following on the bottle of champagne they had drunk earlier meant that for once Jason's control slipped. During the bitter row which erupted after their return home, when Louise had shouted at him that she hated him and that he didn't love her, he had snapped. Grabbing her by her shoulders he had pulled her roughly to him.

'I'll *show* you what I think of you,' he said, kissing her furiously. Louise struggled, though more for the pleasure of feeling his hold on her tighten than because she was frightened. Their love-making was violent and intense. Afterwards Jason, who remembered the evening only dimly, was shame-faced at the thought that he had lost control and raped her.

'Sorry about that,' he mumbled. 'It won't happen again. Are you all right? I mean, I didn't hurt you, did I?'

Louise had a powerful hangover, and her shoulders were bruised from his grip. She didn't know what she felt. She knew that for men, lust and love were far from being the same thing and there was also a nasty, niggling suspicion at the back of her mind. She took his awkwardness for some kind of disgust for her.

'I'm all right,' she said ungraciously.

He looked at her closely. 'And what about, well, consequences? We weren't very careful, were we?'

Louise chose to interpret this as unwillingness to have a child with her. Her mind went back to her earlier pregnancy, and her eyes filled with tears. She turned away so that he wouldn't see.

'I *said* I'm all right,' she replied brusquely. 'I can take care of it.'

Jason misunderstood. 'Yes, now that you've got the money . . .'

Louise rounded on him.

'The money! Yes, that's it, isn't it? You're not interested in me, just the money! Making sure you get your share, I suppose that's what last night was all about!'

Even as she said it, she knew it was unfair. One of her foster-families had had endless rows about money. Louise had absorbed their attitudes without being aware of it, and her rational mind was appalled by what she had said. It was too late to unsay it, however.

'If that's what you think,' said Jason quietly, 'then there's no more to be said, is there? I don't want your money, not a penny of it. And I'm not sure . . .'

'That you want me? That's the truth.'

'Truth?' His voice was bleak. 'What's truth? I don't know what I want, and I'm bloody sure I don't know what you want, any more.'

'I want you!' she wanted to wail, but pride and stubbornness held her back. He waited for a moment, then went out of the house.

Her next period did not come, but she made a great show of buying tampons and pretending to use them. There was no way she was going to use that weapon to bring him back to her. When, at last, she had to admit her condition, she pretended to him that she was several weeks less advanced than she really was, and let him think that the baby was someone else's. After that, of course, there could be no turning back.

Louise, in her untidy bedroom, looked around her in despair. She picked her clothes up off the floor, giving a little involuntary grunt as the movement made her head spin. She straightened up, dropping the handful of garments to press her hand over her mouth. The sickness itself was nothing, no worse now than a mild upset stomach: it was the fact that it was there which brought tears to her eyes. The future terrified her, with all the upheaval involved in buying a new home, even though she had the money for it. She dreaded the prospect of moving. She hated the idea of living on her own, and hated even more the prospect of sharing her home with someone else. She could see no pleasure in the thought of decorating and furbishing: all her skills had been learned in happier times and she had no wish to use them again. She kept postponing the moment, finding reasons not to go and look at possible houses. Deep within her the hope always lurked that somehow things would work out, but she knew that she must do something soon.

The telephone rang and she picked it up.

'Mrs Johnson? Paul Kingswood here. I thought I'd just ring you . . . there's a house I thought you might be interested in. It's a little over the price range you gave me, but I think it might be worth a look . . .'

Chapter Eleven

*B*eep beep. Beep beep.
'Harry! It's for you!'

Harriet, curled on a floor cushion in the corner of her room, put her book down reluctantly and looked nervously at the door.

'Harry! Oh, there you are.' Christine pushed the door open and held out the cordless phone from downstairs. 'I wish you'd answer when I call you,' she said crossly. 'I've had to come all the way upstairs and I was busy clearing out the hall cupboard.'

'Sorry, Mummy. I didn't hear you.' It wasn't true and Christine knew it but hadn't time to argue. Harriet stood up, and her mother held the phone out. Harriet edged away from her and put her hands behind her back.

'Who is it?' asked Harriet nervously.

'It doesn't *matter* who it is,' hissed Christine, covering the mouthpiece of the phone with her hand and thrusting it at her daughter. 'I've already said you're here, you can't not answer it.'

Harriet dithered from foot to foot in a way that made her mother want to scream, but Christine's growing irritation was enough to overcome Harriet's fear of the telephone. Reluctantly she held out her hand, taking the little plastic box with all the enthusiasm of a person being offered something wriggling and slimy. Christine gave a sharp tut of annoyance and bustled off downstairs.

'Hello?' said Harriet timidly. 'Hello?'

'Harriet? It's me.'

Harriet's heart sank still further. This was what she dreaded. Ever since, one day, she had answered the telephone and gone to her mother to say that there was a man on the phone who was asking about his mother's birthday and what should she say to him?

'For goodness' sake, Harriet! It's Daddy, didn't you recognise him?' Christine had been cross and Georgie had laughed, and Harriet had been mortified. Unable to say that the telephone made her nervous, that it distorted familiar voices she might have recognised if she hadn't been so anxious, she had from that day used the telephone as little as possible.

'Hello,' she now repeated, wondering who 'me' was. 'Um, how are you?'

'Oh, *fine*,' responded the telephone with heavy sarcasm. 'Absolutely *fine*. Some ghastly hag is coming to see my house, and you can just bet my step-mother will make her buy it, she'll probably just *give* it to her, and we won't even have *Christmas* at home, not that it would have been a proper Christmas anyway, because she's sure to want to change everything just because it's the way that Mummy used to do it.' The voice cracked a little over the last few words, but Harriet was so relieved to discover that 'me' was Ruth that she was less embarrassed than she would otherwise have been.

'Oh, poor you. That's awful.'

'Yes, it is. I don't know what to do.'

Harriet was flattered. People never asked her for advice and particularly not people of Ruth's age. She wished she could think of something very wise to say, something that would help Ruth and make her feel better, but the situation was outside her experience. In the books she read, children constantly came up with brilliant solutions to even adult problems, but she was clever enough to know that in real life there were fewer simple answers.

'Perhaps she won't like it,' she suggested hopefully.

'Why shouldn't she?' Ruth was instantly on the defensive. 'It's a lovely house. Of course she'll like it.'

'I didn't mean . . . I'm sorry.' Harriet, who had been luxuriating in being treated as an almost equal by someone of Ruth's advanced age, shrank like a salted snail.

'It's all right,' said Ruth gruffly. Her misery made her selfish and grumpy and the people at school who had once been so sympathetic had long since become fed up with her. She was, though she would never have admitted it, achingly lonely and she was dimly aware that even Harriet would be alienated if she wasn't careful. 'You've never seen the house, so you don't know,' she said forgivingly, and Harriet relaxed. She curled up on the floor cushion again, pushing her book aside in a way that would have pleased Christine, if she had been there to see it. Christine was convinced that Harriet read too much and that it was the books she read that made her, in Christine's view, over-imaginative and sensitive.

'Perhaps you could persuade her,' said Harriet with a flash of inspiration. 'Tell her there's something wrong with the house, or something. Not that there is, of course,' she added quickly.

'But I might not be there,' said Ruth gloomily. 'My step-mother is bound to arrange for her to come while I'm at school. She doesn't bother to go to work properly any more, now that she's got my dad to live off. She only goes to work in the mornings, I'm surprised anyone wants her at all, my dad only puts up with her because he was too sad about Mummy to notice how thick she is.' She paused for breath, and realised she had lost track of the subject. 'Anyway, she's bound to come when I'm not there, and she's bound to like the house. Besides, what could I tell her is wrong with it? She'd see it wasn't true.'

Harriet, in the course of Christine's obsession with finding a better house, had been trailed round too many unsuitable places to be thrown by that objection.

'The roof,' she said firmly. 'She won't be able to see whether it's true or not, and roofs are expensive. Or the drains. Grown-ups are always on about drains. I suppose you haven't got a willow tree in your garden?'

'No. Why?'

'Pity. We went to a house once with a willow tree, and my mother went on and on about how the drains wouldn't be any good because its roots would have damaged them. Daddy said, how would the tree know where the drains were unless they were leaking already, but she said that was silly, everyone knows that willow trees damage drains.'

'Pity. I suppose I could say that there *used* to be a willow . . . What else does your mother look out for?'

'Well . . . cracks in the wall, I suppose. Woodworm – you could do that, little holes with a drawing pin or something. Or . . . what about smells?'

'Smells? What sort of smells? You mean like farts or something?'

Harriet was slightly shocked that Ruth should think she would make such a suggestion, but subtly flattered too by its *risqué* nature.

'No, not farts. My mother always sniffs for something called dry rot, only I don't know what that smells like, but once we went to an old house and they'd been putting lavender on the fire, and making coffee in the kitchen, real coffee, not instant. It was lovely, the house smelled really nice, but my mother said they'd only done it to cover the smell of damp, and when the lavender wore off you could smell the damp smell.'

'Could you? What was it like?'

Harriet wrinkled her nose retrospectively. 'Horrid. Like an old dishcloth that's been left damp for ages.'

There was a thoughtful silence. 'I could do that,' said Ruth thoughtfully. 'There are some old cloths under the sink that she keeps for clearing up really bad spills, like oil, because she says she doesn't approve of kitchen paper. Typical, she's probably just saving the cost out of Daddy's money.'

'I don't think kitchen paper's very expensive, is it?' asked Harriet timidly.

'Perhaps not, but it all adds up,' said Ruth darkly. 'She's so stingy, you wouldn't believe what she does to save money. Do you know, she gets the butcher to give her bones and she boils them up, and makes soup! She even put in a poor little pig's trotter once, it was gross. I mean, when you think what it had been walking in, and things!'

'What was it like?'

'I don't know. I didn't eat it. Joseph did – that's my brother – but then he'd eat anything, even if it was full of bacteria.'

Harriet thought squeamishly of a pig's foot bobbing about in a pan of boiling water. 'It sounds disgusting,' she agreed. 'Mummy makes soup with vegetables sometimes, or we have it out of tins, mostly.'

'So did we, *before*. It's like I said, she'll do *anything* to save a bit of money. She's probably got it all hidden away in a Swiss bank account, and I expect she'll murder us all and get all the insurance money . . .'

This was a bit much for even Harriet to swallow.

'Ruth! Surely not!'

'Well, perhaps not quite that.' Ruth heard Harriet's shocked tones and back pedalled. 'Anyway, that wasn't what we were meant to be talking about. If I get those old cloths, and wet them with dirty water . . .'

'Put them in a plastic bag.' Harriet was relieved to be back on the original subject. 'Then they'll soon smell really awful. Then you can hide them round the place, like behind radiators or something. Then it wouldn't matter if you weren't there.'

'Brilliant!' Harriet glowed with pleasure at the praise. 'Pity we didn't meet sooner, we might have been able to stop her from making Daddy buy your house. Still, if she doesn't manage to sell this one, perhaps someone else will want yours and she'll be too late to get it.'

'Yes,' said Harriet forlornly. She was not particularly accustomed to have anyone consider her feelings, except perhaps her father, but even so it did seem that Ruth wasn't very concerned with anyone's problems but her own. Perhaps something of this penetrated the shell of Ruth's self-absorption.

'It was clever of you to think of the dishcloths. Can't you think of anything that would help you?'

'Not really,' said Harriet. It had never occurred to her that she could ever influence what happened to her. Disempowered by her age and her lack of self-confidence she felt, rather like Paul Kingswood but with perhaps more reason, that she was someone that things happened to. You enjoyed or, more often, endured what happened, but one way or another you had to accept the inevitable.

'Can't you tell your mother you smelled damp at the new house, or something, if she's so worried about that sort of thing?'

'She wouldn't take any notice. I mean, that house had lots of things that she'd normally hate, like an old-fashioned kitchen, and no double glazing, and she didn't seem to care at all. I suppose she thinks she'll do all that afterwards. It's a pity, really, it's much nicer as it is.'

'I thought you didn't like it?'

'Oh no, it's a lovely house, if you were just going to visit it. It's just that it's so big, and then it's got that pony . . . She's going to want us to be like that. Tennis and ponies and things. And boarding school . . .' Her voice trembled.

'It sounds great,' said Ruth enviously. 'I'd *love* to go to boarding school and get away from Her. Still, if it's not right for you . . .'

'No, it isn't,' said Harriet with unusual firmness.

'Then we'll just have to think of something.' Harriet's affection-starved heart warmed to that 'we', and she thought she would do anything to help her new friend.

'Yours is more important,' she said generously. 'Let's concentrate on that. I'll see if I can think of anything else.'

'I'm thinking of making an offer on that four bed detached in Oak Hill.'

Long years of experience kept Paul's face blandly interested, but inside he felt his heart drop. He had set his heart on selling that house to the Hartwells, who had seemed keen enough (apart from the ghastly daughter), but who still needed a buyer for their own house. Foolishly, he had allowed himself to believe that Louise Johnson would buy it, and thus give him the novel excitement of having a complete chain. Louise, however, had been hard to pin down, saying she would like to see the Hartwells' house but unwilling to make a firm appointment.

'Very nice house,' he said cautiously. 'In good condition.'

'Well, you would say that, wouldn't you?' Mr Jones, feet planted firmly apart, lifted on to his toes and rocked back on to his heels. The movement, in no way an attempt to mitigate his short stature, expressed supreme self-satisfaction. 'There's no point in you telling me things like that. I make up my own mind, that's the kind of man I am.'

'I wouldn't attempt to deceive you,' said Paul mildly. Mr Jones threw back his head in order to be able to look down his nose. It made his chin, already undershot, jut aggressively.

'You wouldn't be able to. No one's ever pulled a fast one on Paul Jones.' Paul was torn between a longing to prove him wrong, and a regret that they shared the same name. Paul Jones, too – the name brought back memories of dances in his extreme youth, of barging and manoeuvering to ensure that when the music stopped he would be opposite the pretty blonde and not the dumpy girl with sweaty hands. Mr Jones's parents had had no sense of humour at all, or too much.

'And how much were you thinking of offering for Oak Hill, Mr Jones?'

The jaw continued to jut, and the eyes narrowed suspiciously.

'It's no good you thinking you can pressure me into buying! I said I was thinking of making an offer, that's all. Seeing as how prices have come down to something halfway realistic. Mind you, it's over-priced,

125

that one is. Typical of you agents, always trying to push the prices up. You did it once, and where did it get you? Market blows up in your face, and all you hear is people whinging about negative equity. Fools, I call them.'

'Yes, I expect you do.' Paul glanced warningly at Melanie, who was shifting in her chair and whose face had assumed a glowing look of angry colour beneath her heavy makeup.

'I bought my house fifteen years ago. Sold it at the peak of the boom, and went to live abroad.'

'Tax exile?' Paul wasn't sure that his sarcasm was properly hidden but Mr Jones was well launched into the tale of his financial acumen.

'The company moved to Denmark, insisted I go with them.' Couldn't get another job, Paul mentally translated.

'And now you're back?'

'Took early retirement.'

'And how would you finance the purchase? If you made the offer, that is?'

'Cash,' said Mr Jones grandly. 'No messing about with mortgages, no chain.' He grinned, revealing large lower front teeth that almost covered the upper ones. 'Puts me in a strong position, of course.'

Paul couldn't deny it. Buyers in any shape or form were thin enough on the ground – buyers with no chain and no mortgage were almost rare enough to be considered a protected species. He should be pleased – and he was, if not for the orthodox reasons. It was quite obvious that Paul Jones's offer would be well below the asking price, possibly even ludicrously so. He was the kind of man who would regard it as sound business practice to make a first offer so low as to be positively insulting. Since he clearly regarded himself as God's gift to vendors, this tendency was bound to be even more exaggerated. With any luck, by the time Paul had negotiated him up to a halfway acceptable offer, the Hartwells would have a buyer for their house and could pip him to the post.

'So, what were you thinking of offering, Mr Jones?' He smiled gently. Melanie, who knew that particular smile, stopped fidgeting and allowed the colour to subside from face and neck.

Ruth opened the door, feeling suddenly nervous. It had all seemed so easy when the estate agent rang. She had assured him that her step-mother would be home by eleven o'clock, when the person wanted to come. She had wondered why he was so concerned that there should be an adult there and had a twinge of guilt that he might have guessed that she planned to sabotage the sale. It had not occurred to her that there could be any danger and it wasn't until the doorbell rang that she realised that she would be asking a complete stranger into the house. All the half-ignored warnings and unpleasant news

126

stories she had heard jostled uncomfortably in her head as she peered through the spy-hole. The woman looked harmless enough, but did that mean anything? As she looked the woman gave a half-shrug, and turned away. Ruth snatched the door open.

'Sorry,' she said breathlessly. 'Are you from the estate agents? I'm afraid I've forgotten your name.'

'Johnson. Louise Johnson. Aren't your parents in?'

'No, but it's all right, I can show you the house.' She stepped back encouragingly.

'I suppose, now I'm here . . .' Louise Johnson came into the hall and looked around her without much curiosity. 'Shouldn't you be at school?' she asked vaguely.

'I wasn't very well. Nothing catching,' Ruth added hastily, putting a hand on her stomach. 'Just, you know, cramps.' The other woman nodded, not very interested. 'Um, this is the hall,' Ruth said, and then felt silly. 'And the downstairs cloakroom,' she added with more authority, opening the door. The woman looked without going in, and turned away without a word. Ruth, forgetting that she didn't want her visitor to like the house, was annoyed. Her mother had redecorated the cloakroom before she got too ill to do anything, it was the last thing of that kind she had done. It still looked fresh and pretty and Ruth thought it deserved more than a perfunctory glance. Mrs Johnson, however, was already moving away. Ruth scurried round her to the sitting room.

The chill in the air made her shiver.

'Sorry it's a bit cold,' she said, glancing round to make sure she had remembered to shut all the windows again. 'The heating is on, but it doesn't work very well.' She was very proud of this touch – every window in the house had been wide open to the chilly October air until five minutes before the visitor was due to arrive. The radiators were working hard to compensate, and the warmth was releasing a very satisfactory stink from the smelly cloth that Ruth had tucked behind one of them.

'It's all right. I don't mind the cold,' said Louise Johnson, though her face looked pinched and white. Ruth led the way to the dining room, but stopped when she realised she was on her own. Louise Johnson stood stock still in the middle of the sitting room. She was bending slightly forward, her arms clasped round her front and her back rigid. Her white face was twisted, the lips clenched tightly and her eyes screwed up. Ruth hurried back.

'What's the matter? What is it?'

The older woman drew in a long breath, and relaxed. Her body straightened as the pain relaxed its grip.

'Nothing. It's all right.'

'Are you sure? You looked awful.'

Louise managed a pale smile. 'Thanks! No, it's all right, it's gone off now. Just a twinge, that's all.'

'Like I had? Period pains?'

'Rather the reverse,' said Louise wryly. Ruth, who had been feeling very adult and worldly-wise, had to work this one out.

'You mean – you're having a baby as well?'

'As well as what? Don't tell me you're . . . ?' Louise eyed Ruth's skinny little body in the school uniform she hadn't bothered to change out of. Ruth giggled.

'No, not *me*! My . . . my father's wife.'

'That's nice.' Louise's flat tone exactly suited Ruth's mood.

'Yeah. Lovely,' she said gloomily. Louise looked at her with more attention.

'Sulky little thing, aren't you? What's the matter – jealous of your dad's new wife?'

'No!' Ruth answered hotly, stung by the criticism. 'Of course I'm not jealous. And I don't sulk,' she added sulkily.

'But you don't like her. Why don't you clear off and live with your mum, then?'

'My mum's dead.' Ruth knew this was a clincher in any argument. Most people were so embarrassed by their *faux pas* that they didn't know what to say. Louise simply nodded.

'That's tough. My mum died when I was eight, so I know.'

'Did your dad get married again?'

'I don't know. He certainly didn't get married the first time, and he didn't hang around long enough for me to get to know him.'

'Who looked after you, then?'

'I was in care. Foster-homes.'

'Oh.' Ruth looked at her with shy respect. 'Was it awful?'

Louise shrugged. 'Some of it was, especially at the beginning. You get used to it, learn to be independent, look after yourself. It could have been worse. But it's not the same as having a real home, and proper family.'

Ruth scowled at the floor. 'You mean, I should be grateful for what I've got.'

'Nothing to do with me,' said Louise shortly. 'That's how it was for me, that's all.' In spite of her curt tone, she felt curiously sympathetic towards this plain, awkward girl. Her own unhappiness, the bitterness and hatred she felt towards herself, Jason, the baby, even the world, accorded with the similar feelings she sensed from the teenager. Her face softened. 'You have to move on, you know. Things change. People come and go. You can't fight it. Aah!' She drew in a sharp breath as the pain came back, worse than before. It gripped her like a wild beast, all claws and teeth. Little sparks danced against the darkness behind her eyelids, her ears buzzed.

'Sit down!' Ruth's voice was urgent in her ears, cutting through the buzz. 'You must sit down. I can't hold you if you fall.' Ruth steered her until she felt soft cushions against the back of her legs, and she let herself collapse backwards on to the sofa. From old instinct she put her head down to her knees, resting it there while the sick faintness ebbed and flowed. When she finally sat up Ruth was beside her with a glass of water, a damp face cloth and a dry towel. Gratefully she drank, the water sweet in her sour dry mouth, then wiped and dried her face.

'Thanks. That's just right.'

'Shall I call a doctor?'

'No.' The answer was immediate and instinctive. Louise saw that she had startled Ruth. 'No,' she repeated more quietly. 'It's all right. I'll just rest for a little while.'

'You should put your feet up,' said Ruth, bossy with fright. It was something her father was always saying to Liz. Louise nodded but did not move, so Ruth bent and lifted them for her, one leg at a time. It was only after the second leg was on the sofa that Ruth realised what the dark patch on the seam of Louise's grey trousers must be.

'You're bleeding,' she said. Her eyes flew to Louise's face. What she saw there sent her own hands flying protectively to hug her own stomach. 'You knew,' she whispered. 'You knew you were bleeding.'

'I wasn't sure.' Louise's voice was tired. 'I thought I might be . . . It's probably too late.'

Ruth thought she had never been so frightened. She hated Louise for making her feel this way, for allowing Ruth to see the hopeless despair she was feeling. At the same time she felt a kind of protective love, stronger even than she had felt for her dying mother, and for this, too, she hated the older woman.

'I'm going to ring for an ambulance.' She wanted to sound adult and in control of the situation, but her voice betrayed her by trembling into a childish whine. Louise caught hold of her wrist. Her grip was painful.

'Not yet,' she said. 'Please, not yet.' The pain was coming back. Louise knew she would not be able to hold Ruth, and she saw that Ruth knew this too and was preparing to break free.

'Please,' Louise said. 'Please listen to me. My husband . . . works at the hospital. I can't . . .' She paused, the breath hissing between her teeth as she struggled to master the pain. When it ebbed she was aware that Ruth was wiping her face again. 'I can't bear him to be there,' she continued when she could speak again. 'He'll be off duty in an hour. Just an hour, that's all. It won't make any difference, I promise . . .'

Ruth shook her head. She was out of her depth. She found herself longing for an adult – any adult – to appear and take charge. She remembered how Liz had appeared on the night of her first period, how she had re-made the bed and provided what was necessary, without fuss or questions, without being asked or thanked. If Liz had walked in at that moment, Ruth would have welcomed her with open arms.

'What shall I do?' She was asking Liz, not Louise.

'Just let me wait. That's all. It will be all right, I promise.'

'But your baby!'

'I think it's too late to save the baby.'

'Don't you *care*?' Ruth was angry again.

'Yes, I do. I didn't think I did, that's the trouble. I wasn't sure I wanted this baby. Now I know I did. Funny, isn't it?' Louise smiled mirthlessly. 'I've got what I thought I wanted, and now it's the worst thing in the world. Do you think it's my fault? Perhaps it knew I didn't know how to love it . . .'

'No, no, no!' The tears were running down Ruth's face, but she didn't feel them. 'It's not like that! It's not your fault!' She hugged Louise in her bony arms, held her against the tiny breasts that did not disguise the ribs beneath. 'Not your fault,' she whispered. She spoke to Louise, to the tiny undeveloped baby, to the ten-year-old Ruth who had feared, in the midnight dark of her soul, that her mother had died because she, Ruth, hadn't loved her enough.

They waited for the hour. The pains were less intense, came less often, and the bleeding got no worse. Louise, half out of her mind, whispered to Ruth. In short, half-formed sentences she told her, out of order and disconnected, about her childhood, about Jason, even about the other baby. Ruth, only half-understanding, knew that it didn't matter and asked no questions, merely nodded and murmured and made reassuring noises as if to a small child. At the end of the hour she rang for an ambulance and watched in outward calm while Louise was lifted into it on a stretcher. The ambulance men, preoccupied and hurried, established that she was not a relative, complimented her on being so sensible, and left with lights flashing. Ruth went back to the sitting room. There was a tiny spot of blood on the cushions of the sofa. Soberly, Ruth fetched a wet cloth and scrubbed at the mark until it was gone. Then, heavily, she picked the smelly cloth from behind the radiator, and carried it out to the dustbin.

Chapter Twelve

Philippa Denton looked down at the cloth in her hand. It was spotless. She realised that she had been over every surface in the kitchen twice, including the top of the old Aga. It was well known in the family that her response to any stressful situation was to clean something. The Aga, which combined the oily fluff that was produced by the burning process with the drips and spills normal to any cooker top, always seemed to need wiping, and was the thing she went for when really upset. 'Look out, Ma's cleaning the Aga!' was a familiar warning cry in the family, a signal to take cover from possible fireworks.

Now even the Aga was pristine. Philippa folded the cloth carefully in half, and put it over the rail to dry. She looked around. The kitchen was so clean and tidy that it looked unreal, a stage set of an old-fashioned kitchen where nobody had ever really prepared or cooked or eaten a meal, where no cat or dog had ever curled up in the warmth, no child had ever hung snow-crusted mittens to dry or left a trail of muddy footprints. Philippa's eyes filled with tears – tears of pity for an empty, soul-less room. The Aga purred gently, but the sound that had always soothed her now sounded like the slow, snoring breaths of someone unconscious or dying. She patted the smooth dome of the hot-plate cover, and wandered out into the hall.

Unable to settle, she strayed through the house. Now that she and George lived there alone it was seldom untidy, and never dirty. Untidy, of course, was a relative term. Neither of them had ever liked a house to be too perfect, regarding a scattering of books, newspapers, plant labels or any of the paraphernalia connected with their interests and hobbies as a natural part of a lived-in room. Now, Philippa twitched cushions straight, retrieved a pair of secateurs that had slipped down the side of the sofa, straightened a stack of gardening magazines to military precision, and adjusted the hang of a curtain. The bedrooms that had once been their children's were bare of all but a few balding soft toys rejected by the grandchildren, and some old-fashioned children's books of the heavily didactic variety.

In the doorway of her own bedroom Philippa came to a sudden halt. The room where she and George had slept for so many years was comfortably shabby, curtains and carpet gently faded, the furniture out of date, solid Victorian maple that had come from

George's family. The bed with the mattress that cradled her every night in the hollow her own body had worn had known their passion, their laughter and anger and tears. It was the place she went to for comfort whether the pain was physical or in her mind, but it could not comfort her now. From being her friendly lair it had become the place of nightmare, the place when she had first become aware that her body had betrayed her.

There was no pain, which would have alerted her sooner. Only the discomfort of clothes that had seemed suddenly tighter. She had assumed that she had simply put on some extra weight, not unusual at her age although she had never done so before, having the kind of metabolism that meant she had never had to worry about what she ate. She had cut down on butter, cheese and sweet things, and been pleased that she seemed to lose weight fairly quickly. Now, of course, she saw that easy weight loss as sinister. The absence of pain, which might have been encouraging, frightened her. Surely she had read somewhere that this was one of the signs of . . . of it. It – the thing that she couldn't bring herself to name.

How could she have missed it for so long? Her own body held no mysteries for her. Her childhood upbringing had been prudish and restricted, full of euphemisms and nods and unspoken words. Her mother had said, with some pride, that she had never allowed her husband to see her naked – she undressed in the bathroom, or if necessary under one of the voluminous nightdresses she always wore. Philippa remembered being made to change, as a small child on a deserted beach, under a damp, sandy towel, and wondering why all this discomfort was necessary. Mirrors in bedrooms and bathroom had been small, fixed high on the wall to show only decorous head and shoulders, and the single full-length one had been downstairs, in the hall. An only child, Philippa had satisfied her curiosity with surreptitious examinations of paintings and statues in art books in the library.

Marriage to George had been a revelation. From their first meeting she had felt a strong physical attraction to him, had found herself longing to touch him and, even more, to have him touch her. By the time she had walked, in virgin white, down the aisle on her father's arm she was as well acquainted with his body as with her own – better, in some ways. She knew the pleasant roughness of the hairs on his chest that contrasted with the soft skin of his belly and hips; the hard springy feel of muscles in legs and buttocks; the scratch of bristly morning cheeks and the tender skin in the hollow of his neck; the liquid slide of smooth ovoids within the wrinkled pouch of his scrotum and the hot satiny feel of his erection. Together they had explored and discovered, with rapture and awe and breathless laughter and he had banished for ever the childhood guilt and fear of her early masturbatory experiments.

Even now, although their love-making was infrequent and gentle, it was never perfunctory. The changes and indignities that age wrought on their bodies were matters for rueful laughter but were fundamentally unimportant. Never, until now, had she turned from his caresses or kept any physical secret from him. Her body had been so familiar to him that he had always known she was pregnant almost before she was aware of it herself and because of that she dared not let him touch her. He would feel it at once, that hard, rounded lump in the side of her abdomen – the more so since her loss of weight meant that there was little covering flesh to mask it. Pleading tiredness she had turned away from him in the bed they still shared, curling her body into the warmth of his, desperate for the comfort of his embrace in which, when it came, she could feel his surprise and hurt at her rejection.

How could she not have noticed sooner? Her mind kept coming back to that, scratching at it like a dog with a flea. For many years she had checked her breasts, finding the process dispiritingly easier as her once-full figure softened and deflated with time. She had always had regular smear tests, too, and it was no one's fault but her own that she had missed her appointment some months ago and never got round to making another one. The clinic had sent reminders, and she had been so sure that she would do it that she threw them straight in the bin. The truth was that she worried about George's health, not her own. She was aware of his vulnerability that she forgot that she, too, might be at risk.

Then again, if it hadn't been for the new shower . . . In the past she had loved her baths, loved to lie up to her neck in the steaming, scented water. Her family knew they could always please her with gifts of Floris bath essence, or extravagant scented soap. She would lie luxuriating, soaping herself and enjoying the slippery caress of her own touch. Like that, relaxed, she might have felt the lump more easily, but recently she had found her skin getting dry and itchy. The doctor banned anything scented in the way of bath essence or soap, and recommended a shower instead of a long soak. George had immediately had the shower enlarged and an electric pump installed, but even so the process was quicker and more functional. Her stomach muscles, still firm thanks to years of tennis and riding, would have been less relaxed than when she lay in the bath, and she had been aware of nothing.

So here she was, reduced to a state of abject panic by a lump. She, who had always prided herself on being level-headed in a crisis, was shaken to her foundations so that she thought she could feel her whole body faintly vibrating, an inner trembling that nothing seemed to calm. The fear was within her and without, it stalked her by day and by night, lurked in every dark corner of her soul. Fear not for herself, but for George.

She did not fear death. In fact, she had seldom thought about it, aware of its inevitability yet uninterested in what might or might not follow it. She feared pain, of course, as any reasonable being must do and part of her anxiety now was the prospect of prolonged and pointless suffering. From that point of view she would gladly have accepted some kind of euthanasia as an option, were it available, and were it not for George.

From time to time during their marriage they had said, half joking, 'I hope I go before you do'. In the past Philippa had thought she meant it. The thought of living on without George was unbearable, impossible. Now, faced with the fact that she might very well die first, she was filled with anguish for him.

To outsiders, even to those within the family, it always seemed that George was the one in charge. Not, perhaps, the stronger one – no one who knew Philippa could ever think of her as weak – but certainly the most powerful. Philippa was accustomed to deferring to him most of the time, not out of a desire to keep the peace but because she sensed his deep need to be the person who looked after things. More specifically, the person who looked after her. An old-fashioned man in this respect, he acknowledged her supremacy in the kitchen and the nursery, but expected to look after all the details of money, insurance, investments and major decision-making himself.

Only Philippa knew how much he depended on her. Even George himself, she often thought, was largely unaware of how often his decisions were influenced or formed by a quiet word from her. His strength was real, but it was built on the foundations she dug for him. In everyday terms, too, he was helpless. Cooking was a mystery to him, though he was an appreciative eater of everything that she produced. He polished his own shoes but had never used an iron; he treated supermarkets as warily as if they were uncharted, shark-infested seas and didn't know how to alter the timer on the boiler.

He could learn all of these skills, of course. The local education authority ran special cookery classes for men on their own: shirts could go to a laundry or be ironed by a visiting cleaner, and the service engineer could teach him how the boiler worked. The problem was that without her there to chivvy him Philippa feared that he simply wouldn't bother. Like many men, his friendships existed mainly outside the home, and had their focus in the pub or the golf club. His reading was restricted mainly to newspapers, a few magazines like The Spectator, and gardening catalogues. Without her there to fight with, to talk to, to laugh with, he would be lonely. Lonely, and lost. Philippa could not bear to think of it, but she had to. It occupied her whole mind, leaving no room for worry about herself or thoughts of what she should be doing.

She, who had always been the one to encourage her family to go to the doctor – 'No point in putting it off', 'Better safe than sorry', 'Might as well check it out in the early stages' – had been avoiding making an appointment for more than a week. In the past she had been scathing about people procrastinating in this way. Why couldn't they see that their best chance lay in getting treatment as quickly as possible?

Philippa was astonished to find herself behaving like this. Every day for a week she had got up in the morning intending to telephone the surgery the minute she got the chance. Showering, her fingers would explore the soft skin of her stomach, hoping each time that she had been mistaken, that there would be nothing there. Then, finding the lump, she would touch it delicately, as if too firm a pressure might awaken some sleeping demon within. Was it larger than before? Had it grown since last week? Once dressed, she would wait for George to leave the house. He knew her too well, sensing her agitation he hung around the house, reading the newspaper with extra attention and humming over the crossword. Once she had managed to chivvy him out to the garden or the golf course she told herself she must wait for half an hour, he was not above popping back to check on her. When, finally, she was free to telephone the task suddenly seemed beyond her, and she would busy herself with trivia.

As she came back down the stairs the telephone in the hall confronted her. The white plastic – it was a new set incorporating an answerphone, given to them the previous Christmas by one of their children – seemed to glint malevolently, it hooked her glance and held it. She veered towards the kitchen then remembered its antiseptic cleanliness and turned away again. Like a fisherman reeling in a difficult fish the telephone played her, drawing her inexorably towards it until she landed by the table. Her breath caught in her throat, she felt she was indeed gaping like a landed fish. Trying for some dignity, she picked up the telephone slowly, dialled with care.

'Mr Kingswood?' Her own voice sounded strange in her ears, it echoed round the hall. She was speaking too loudly. 'Hello, Mr Kingswood. It's Philippa Denton here. I was wondering, might I go back and have another look at the bungalow? Yes, as soon as possible. Yes, I'll be here all morning. Thank you.'

The small act of rebellion heartened her. Without giving herself time to think, she telephoned the surgery.

Paul's hand hovered over the telephone. Should he ring? It was several hours since he had made the appointment for Philippa Denton to go back to the bungalow – she must have left by now. He told himself that if there was anything wrong Mrs Holt would have called him but he was still uneasy. There had been something constrained

135

about Philippa's voice. She had always been friendly, even chatty, but this time she had cut short his polite enquiries as if she were frightened of speaking to him, of saying too much.

In his experience, this kind of behaviour meant only one thing – someone pulling out of a sale. The nicer the person, the more difficult they found it to say that they had changed their minds. An unexpected return to look at their purchase again often meant that they were having seconds thoughts, looking perhaps for something wrong that they could use as a let-out. Of course, the Dentons pulling out of buying the bungalow wasn't in itself a disaster – the bungalow was infinitely saleable, he could easily find someone else for it. What worried him was the thought that they might have changed their minds about selling.

Paul felt fairly sure that Christine Blake had only agreed to let him sell her house because she desperately wanted to buy the Dentons'. He was under no illusions there. Alec might like him, might treat him as a friend, but it was Christine's word that carried the day in that household. She had not troubled to hide the fact that she was unimpressed by his firm – which meant, of course, by him. Image and appearance were all to her. A tubby, balding, middle-aged man running a small business (albeit a long-standing family one) did not suit her ideas at all. A well publicised name, expensive shiny brochures, a large staff of young men and branches all over England sounded far more her kind of thing. It would be in vain for Paul to point out that branches in other counties would not know anything about her house, that prospective buyers visited the agents in the town they wanted to move to, not from, or that the bright young men were inexperienced, commission rather than client-oriented and that since they were all competing with each other they were not computer-based but kept all their customer information in little card indexes, jealously guarded.

If the Dentons decided not to sell, then it followed as a matter of course that Christine Blake would do the same, until something equally suitable turned up. It had to be admitted that 'something suitable', in Christine's terms, was more likely to be found in the glossy advertisements of his larger rivals, giving her a powerful argument in favour of selling her house, also, through them. Those two sales were the best he had had for a long time, and would have carried in their wake some useful publicity that might have picked up a few more, and the thought of losing them was profoundly depressing. Paul sighed, and withdrew his hand. Like Philippa, he was reluctant to have confirmation of his fears.

'Never mind, Mr K,' said Melanie kindly. 'It'll all come out in the wash. How about a nice cup of tea?'

Paul thought longingly of the merits of a strong gin, but accepted the alternative with as much gratitude as he could muster. As he drank it he watched the Christmas decorations going up in the street outside. Christmas decorations! Paul, like most estate agents, loathed Christmas with a hatred second only to that for the summer holidays in August. Both had the effect of dulling an already quiet market into catatonia.

The sight depressed him so much, he thought he might as well telephone Mrs Holt and know the worst, since nothing could make him feel any more dismal than he already did. She took a long time to answer the phone, and when it was too late it occurred to him that she might well be resting. If so, she was probably already disturbed so it was too late to hang up. Sure enough, when she answered she sounded breathless.

'Hello? Hello, who is it?' Archimedes, in the background, echoed the query in harsh, sarcastic tones as if he already knew the answer, and didn't think much of it.

'It's Paul Kingswood, Mrs Holt,' he said. 'I'm so sorry, I'm afraid I've disturbed you.'

'Not at all, Mr Kingswood. Is there some kind of problem?'

'I hope not. I just wondered how you got on with Mrs Denton?'

'Oh, I like her very much.' Mrs Holt sounded slightly confused by the question. 'Such a pleasant woman. She was here for quite a long time.' Her voice lifted in the slightest hint of a question. It reminded Paul of Melanie's unconscious imitation of Australian soap operas – he was pretty sure that Mrs Holt never watched *Neighbours*.

'And she seemed quite happy with the bungalow?'

There was a pause. I knew it, Paul thought. She sensed something wrong as well. Damn!

'She was perfectly happy with the bungalow,' said Mrs Holt carefully. The emphasis on the final word was so slight that Paul would have missed it if he hadn't been listening for the slightest nuance.

'But there is some kind of problem?'

'Well . . .' There was a thoughtful pause. 'There is something, but I don't know . . . it was a bit private.'

'Does it affect the sale? Oh, sorry, that sounds awful. Just like an estate agent.'

'Well, why not? To be honest, I don't know the answer to that. Probably not.'

'Good.'

There was perhaps more relief in his voice than he should have allowed himself to show. Mrs Holt thought for a moment.

'Would you like to call in, on your way home? Not if you're busy, of course.'

'I should love that. Is about half past six all right?'

'Splendid. Archimedes and I will look forward to it.'

* * *

Paul leaned back in his chair and sipped his wine, admiring its deep ruby colour and feeling his tension drain away. Archimedes clung to the rail of a nearby wooden chair, nibbling a large brazil nut. He had done his trick again, to Paul's applause, and had enjoyed the grapes that Paul had brought as an offering. He had also brought a bottle of wine for Mrs Holt, a robust Australian red that he had just discovered and which they were now drinking.

'I really don't think you need to worry about the sale,' said Mrs Holt. 'If anything, I'd say it's pretty secure.'

'Yes, I expect I over-reacted. It's just that sometimes, when people say they want another look at this stage, it's because they're having second thoughts. And she sounded a bit strange when she telephoned me. Distant, you know?'

'She's got a lot on her mind.'

Philippa Denton had sat where Paul now was, her hands playing restlessly with the rings on her fourth finger. Her questions had been disjointed – was the central heating boiler easy to understand? Did Mrs Holt have a cleaning lady, did she know of anyone locally? Had she lived alone in the bungalow for long? Was it easy to run?

Alice Holt had answered everything calmly and incuriously, seeing that the questions were only on the surface of the problem. She assumed that Philippa had reason to fear that her husband would not be living in the bungalow with her for very long. With profound sympathy she reassured as honestly as she could.

'Finding someone to clean is fairly easy – I have a very nice girl who does what we used to call 'the heavy' for me. The problem is more the garden. I've tried several people, they're all very willing but don't know the first thing, so beyond cutting the grass and basics like that I scarcely dare let them do anything unless I'm there to stop them digging up the plants for weeds, or pruning something that's just about to come into flower. Would that be a problem for you? The garden's not huge, but it's not tiny either.'

Philippa looked at her blankly.

'The garden? Oh, the *garden*'s not a problem, far from it. It's the house . . . the ironing . . . cleaning the kitchen . . . that kind of thing.' Her lips trembled, and she put up a hand to cover them. 'Oh dear. I'm sorry.'

'Let's have a drink.' Alice stood up as abruptly as her stiffening joints would allow.

Philippa looked worried. 'Oh no . . . it's all right . . . I should be going . . . rather early in the day . . . I'm driving . . .'

Alice disregarded her protests. 'It's not that early. One glass of sherry won't put you over the limit.' She was already pouring a healthy glassful.

Philippa sipped the sherry, not much liking the taste but finding its dryness bracing. It created a little nugget of warmth in her stomach, which gradually spread through her body. As always, drinking earlier in the day seemed to affect her more quickly. A soft fog pervaded her brain, and she felt her face glow as her skin flushed.

She knew, deep down, that she had come here because she needed to tell someone, and preferably someone who scarcely knew her and would not burden her with their own anxiety on her behalf. Somehow the fact of moving into this other woman's house carried with it a kind of impersonal intimacy, as though they were closely related but had only just met. When Alice Holt approached her with the bottle, she held out her glass to be re-filled without a murmur.

'I found a lump,' she said abruptly, then stared in horror at Mrs Holt.

'Oh dear. I'm so sorry. I thought it was your husband you were worried about.'

'It is. He's just not '. . . after all these years . . . I can't bear to think about it.'

'You haven't told him?'

'No. I haven't told anybody.'

'What does the doctor say?'

Philippa was silent.

'My dear,' Alice said compassionately. 'My dear, you don't need me to tell you . . .'

'I know.' Philippa wiped her eyes with her fingers. 'I know, it's so stupid, I kept putting it off and the more I left it, the more I couldn't do anything. You know?'

'I know. And now?'

'I've made an appointment. For the day after tomorrow. There weren't any spaces, and I want to see my own doctor, not one of the others who I don't know.'

'Of course. But surely if you were to tell them it was urgent . . . ?' Alice saw Philippa's face. 'No, well, I don't suppose two days will make any difference. And anyway, lumps don't have to mean anything bad.'

'I know. And I know I'm mad not to have had it checked straight away. If it's just a cyst or something I'll have had weeks of worry for nothing. It's just . . . I can't face it. I've never felt like this before. I didn't know I could. All I can think is, "No". Just that. If I were one of those science fiction creatures that can change its shape, that's what I'd change into, two huge letters. It's . . . taken me over.'

Silently, Alice poured more sherry. Philippa took a healthy mouthful and swallowed.

'I'll have to get a taxi home,' she said with the ghost of a laugh. 'Good thing George has gone to London for the day.'

'Stay and have lunch, if you like. I usually have a sleep afterwards, you can put your feet up and do the same. You'll be all right to drive later.'

'Are you sure?' Philippa sounded as uncertain as a child.

'Of course I'm sure. It's nothing much, just shepherd's pie, and some baked apples, but there's plenty.'

'I'd like that very much,' said Philippa, sounding surprised. She hadn't felt hungry for days, but suddenly shepherd's pie and a baked apple made her mouth water. It was so safe, so reassuring, like school lunches at her primary school. She hoped there would be custard, nice and yellow and made with powder. Would they, she wondered with a twinge of amusement, bicker politely over who would get the skin? Perhaps, if she let the older woman have it, she might agree to keep her company when she went to the doctor's. She suddenly felt that if Alice came with her she would bring her luck, as well as comfort.

Chapter Thirteen

'Mrs Redman? I'm Alec Blake.' The woman in the doorway looked blankly at him. Alec suppressed a sigh. 'I'm a surveyor. I had an appointment to look at the flat.'

Her face broke into a wide smile.

''Course you are! Forgot all about it, didn't I! Come in – Alec, did you say? And I'm Shelley. Cuppa coffee? Kettle's on. Watch you don't fall over the toys – just like his dad, Liam is, leaves things all over the place, bless him.' She kicked a battered toy car under the sofa, and stepped calmly over the small boy who was methodically tearing a magazine to pieces. 'Sugar in the coffee?'

'No sugar, thank you.' Alec was mildly amused. This was one survey where he would get to see the property in the raw. No one would have been drying out damp patches with a hair drier, moving large house-plants to cover tell-tale marks on the walls, or trying to disguise the smell of dry rot with coffee or scented candles. After one swift glance he ruled out the possibility that Mrs Redman – Shelley – might be pulling a double bluff on him. She wasn't the type to go in for such subtlety.

The flat, in fact, was in surprisingly good condition. Of course the outside was taken care of by the leasing company, and all the windows were new, low-maintenance sealed units. The black mould around the bathroom frame spoke of windows too infrequently opened to release condensation, and both walls and ceiling had the dingy brown patina of concentrated cigarette smoke, but with a good clean and some fresh paint or wallpaper it would be a pleasant home for the young man whose mortgage company had commissioned Alec's survey.

Christine, he thought, would have been disgusted by it. She would have had the place stripped out, the windows flung wide, and every flat surface scrubbed down to its undercoat, before the previous owners had unpacked their suitcases. And, to be fair, she would be perfectly happy to do it herself. Although she liked to leave the basic day to day cleaning to Mrs Moppett, she was not above rolling up her sleeves and setting to with sugar soap or a paint brush. She would have the walls rag-rolled or stencilled, the floor boards (nice, solid timber, he had noted) sanded, stained and sealed, the windows festooned with swags or blinds or swathes of fabric caught artistically over poles. It would be fresh and pretty, colours would be co-ordinated and the furniture carefully arranged so that the rooms appeared bigger than they were – it would look like an illustration in a magazine. But would it be a home?

Untidy and grimy though it was, the flat was very much a home. It exuded that air of fusty comfort that is found in the living rooms of elderly relatives, or the snugs of old pubs. The smell of chips and fried onions mingled with old tobacco smoke and the faint effluvium of nappies into something that should have been unpleasant, but was not. It was a place to kick off your shoes, undo the top button of your waistband and shirt, to slump in a chair with a pack of beers and watch an undemanding film on the television. Not something he wanted to do every day, perhaps, or even all that often, but still something that a tired, tense man could find himself feeling sentimental about.

He wandered back into the living room. The little boy, his face smeared with what Alec hoped was jam, had curled up on a crumpled cot blanket with his head pillowed on a greyish fluffy bear. His thumb was plugged into his mouth and his eyes almost closed. As Alec watched him he drew in a snuffling breath, snuggled his head round so that the little finger of the hand he was sucking could rub against the bear's fur, and closed his eyes with the finality of a stage curtain coming down at the end of a show. Alec made some notes on his clipboard – he generally used a hand-held tape-recorder, but preferred to make written notes in his squiggly, illegible handwriting when the owner was present. In the past he had more than once been attacked for mentioning defects that lowered the value of a house.

Shelley came back from the kitchen and saw him leaning over to write on the table.

'Sit down, why don't you? No point standing when you can sit, that's what I always say. And no point sitting when you could be lying down, eh?'

She spoke with a suggestive lilt and a wink that was so obviously habitual that it was not at all provocative. She dumped two mugs of coffee on the table, reached across to snare an opened bag of sugar with a spoon stuck in it, and retrieved a packet of biscuits that she had tucked under her arm.

'There you go!' She spooned sugar into one of the mugs, stirred vigorously, gave the spoon a cursory shake and stuck it back in the packet again. At least she didn't lick it as well, Alec thought without disgust. It reminded him of his student days, when washing up was something you only did when every plate and bowl in the house was coated with ancient food, and when changing the sheets was regarded as so dangerously adult that it was practically middle-aged.

The coffee, however, was hot and strong, the biscuits ginger nuts. Alec sat in an armchair, balancing his coffee with difficulty when the cushions and springs sagged beneath him. He sank so far down that he wondered how he would ever get out again, but it was surprisingly comfortable. At Shelley's encouraging nod he had taken four biscuits. Following her lead he dunked the first one, enjoying the contrast between soggy and crunchy as he bit into it, and ended by fishing uninhibitedly with his teaspoon for the bits that had fallen off.

He couldn't remember the last time he had dunked a ginger nut. Christine would have been appalled – even more appalled than by the state of the flat. Eating biscuits in the middle of the morning was bad enough.

'If you eat a proper breakfast it should keep you going until lunchtime, there shouldn't be any need for snacks. Biscuits and sweet stuff just rot your teeth and make you fat,' she would say firmly to the girls when they asked for something to take to school for their mid-morning break.

'Everyone else has something,' Georgie would argue, 'why can't we?'

'It's no good telling me about everyone else,' Christine would respond without heat. 'We don't need to copy all the things that other people do, do we? If you must take something, you can take an apple, or a banana.'

'You can't eat a *banana* in break,' said Georgie crossly. 'You'd be called a monkey.'

'How very rude.' Christine wasn't really listening. 'You shouldn't take any notice of that kind of thing. Sticks and stones may break my bones . . .'

Georgie had continued to argue, but Harriet had turned away despondently. No one knew better than she that words *could* harm you. In fact, she thought she would prefer a stick or a stone any day, even if it did break her bones. At least with broken bones nobody could expect her to go to her riding lessons, or play hockey. That kind of pain, the merely physical, was bearable. Words, that stuck in the mind and festered like a splinter in the flesh, were far worse.

Alec, whose memories of his own childhood were still vivid, knew that it wasn't hunger that motivated his daughters. In the complex, shifting structure of playground society, the snack you brought to school was one of the things that defined your position in the hierarchy. It gave you status, it was something to trade, to withhold, to give as a favour to one below you, as a bribe to one above, or to share with a friend as a symbol of closeness. Knowing this, he kept a small store of snack bars hidden under a duster in the side pocket of his car, and gave them out on the mornings when he took his daughters to school. Nothing was said – he would never openly encourage the girls to

143

disobey their mother – but he knew this was something they didn't mention to Christine. He despised himself for going behind her back instead of standing up to her but knew that she could bring the heavy artillery of dentists and nutritionists to bear against his puny footsoldiers of childhood memories and it seemed to him all that he could do.

'Flat all right, then?' Shelley finished her biscuit and sucked her fingers clean. 'No woodworm or nothing?'

'Nothing. The flat seems fine. Perfectly sound.' Normally Alec preferred not to get involved in such discussions with owners, it only led to problems, but this case was so straightforward he couldn't see any harm in it.

'Needs decorating,' said Shelley judiciously.

'Well, most places do, I find.' Such diplomacy was second nature to Alec. 'And of course, most buyers want to change things like colour schemes, in any case.'

'I reckon young Roger – that's the fella that's buying this place, you know – he'll have this place looking like something in a book. You know, them shiny ones they have down the dentist's. *Homes and Gardens*, and that.' Shelley invariably referred to magazines as books, a real book being something so pointless in her eyes as to be almost invisible. Apart from an occasional foray into a romantic novel, she regarded reading for any purpose other than getting information – the television guide, a recipe, or how to use the contents of a home hair colouring kit – as a waste of time. In that one thing, had she known it, she and Christine would have seen eye to eye. 'Make it lovely, Roger will,' Shelley continued. 'Not my cuppa tea, though, really,' she added, looking fondly at the clutter.

'No,' Alec agreed, rather forcefully for him.

'Really?' Shelley looked at him, examining again the well-cut tweed suit, the shirt with double cuffs and silk tie, the well polished expensive shoes. 'I'd have thought you'd have lived in a house like that.'

'I suppose I do. My wife's very good at all that kind of thing. Co-ordinated colour schemes. Special paint finishes. Themed pictures and ornaments. Everything just so.' He couldn't keep the depression out of his voice.

'Bet it's really nice.' Shelley's voice was completely free of sarcasm or envy. 'She must be really clever.'

'She is. Very clever.' Alec felt, and looked, more miserable than ever. Shelley, never particularly sensitive to the moods of others, was concerned.

'Make you another cup of coffee, shall I?' Alec shook his head. 'Biscuit, then? Go on, nothing like a nice ginger nut, as the actress said to the red-haired bishop.' She came close to him, offering the packet of biscuits. 'Go on, take one.'

'No, really, thank you.'

Shelley took one herself and perched on the arm of his chair. The flat was warm and her legs were bare below an abbreviated lycra skirt. He could hear the smoothness of their skin against the nylon upholstery. Christine's legs were often prickly to his touch, and he couldn't help wondering about the difference. Above the tiny, clinging skirt Shelley wore a baggy chenille pullover in vivid sugar pink. She smelled pleasantly of some kind of spicy scent. He had a sudden longing to bury his face in her pullover as the little boy had snuggled into the toy on the floor, and flinched away from her in reaction.

'Is it difficult, what you do?' Uninhibited as a child, she spoke through a mouthful of biscuit and he was soothed.

'Not particularly. It's quite a long training, though – a lot of exams to pass. You have to be very thorough, very careful.'

'Sounds tricky to me. Your wife must be very proud of you.'

'Mm.'

'Course she is.' Her tone was encouraging, as to a child.

'Maybe at the beginning she was. I don't think she thinks about it much now.'

'Really? Dead chuffed, I'd be, to have a fella with a job like yours, and looking like you do.' He was actually aware of the nearness of her body, but felt no sense that she was making a pass at him. It was by no means unusual for him to be offered such favours. It was an occupational hazard, as it must be for any man whose job entails visiting a house at a time of day when a woman is more likely to be there on her own.

Generally such invitations were easy to resist, the more so since the element of bribery was usually implicit, if not explicitly set out. There had been several women who thought they could buy a good survey with the use of their bodies, an exchange which he was too professional to contemplate and which was, in any event, scarcely flattering. One or two women were simply bored, lonely or looking for a way of getting revenge on an erring husband – they, too, were not difficult to refuse.

Only twice had he been tempted, and given in to temptation. Looking back he realised that both occasions had coincided with times when Christine had been arranging another advance from the Trust – once for their present house, and the other time for extra money to build a conservatory. In retrospect he saw that his marital lapses had been rather pathetic attempts to shore up his male pride. Neither episode had been particularly pleasurable, a combination of guilt and shame numbed all but the most basic of feelings so that the couplings had been hasty, an animal gratification that left him empty and depressed. On both occasions he had sworn he would never succumb again. He had resisted the urge, not particularly strong in any case, to confess to Christine and had vowed that in future he would say no.

145

This time was different. For one thing, there was no question of Shelley wanting him to gloss over structural problems with the flat – he had already told her that the survey was all right. Nor did he feel there was anything sexually provocative about her nearness – she sat near him as a child might have done, or even a friendly pet. Her flattery, though blatant, had an innocence about it that was appealing. More than that, what she had was something he suddenly longed for, not the physical excitement of sex but the cosy warmth that Shelley seemed to offer. He remembered a friend from college days who had maintained that the best relationships were 'all cuddles and farts'. At the time he had thought it shallow and silly, but now it expressed something basic that he realised was missing in his marriage.

Unfortunately, it was difficult to see how he could say this to Shelley. 'I don't want sex but I'd love a cuddle' sounded a bit feeble and perhaps a bit insulting too. He turned his face to speak to her, but as he did so his arm caught the fabric slip cover of the other arm of the chair, where he had perched his unfinished coffee mug. The mug slid towards his lap and he watched it in the kind of frozen helplessness of such times, knowing that he should try to catch it but knowing also that he would probably knock it flying. Shelley was not so slow. With her characteristic lack of inhibition she leaned across him and caught the mug in the nick of time.

Alec, not daring to move, found that she was lying almost across his lap, and that his face was against her side. More embarrassing still, he felt his body responding to the touch of hers, and knew that she must be aware of it. He felt such blood as was not otherwise relocated rushing to his face. Opening his mouth to speak, he found it full of chenille-covered breast.

'Hmum. Fuff,' he said. The fluffy sweater was as soft as he had imagined it. He turned his face to take a breath, and for a moment allowed himself to relax against her, luxuriating in the feel of it against his skin. Without any sign of embarrassment Shelley giggled.

'Well, I saved the mug, anyway, but now I'm stuck! Give us a hand, Alec!' Blushing still more he took the mug from her, and helped her off his lap. He knew he should leave at once, but the evidence of his arousal made him cringe at the thought of standing up.

'Sorry about that,' he said, ashamed. Shelley took the mug, which he had forgotten he was still holding.

'That's all right! You couldn't help it.'

The ambiguity of her reply, which could have related to his clumsiness with the mug or to his excited state, was so exquisitely tactful that he was able to look at her. She smiled at him with the calm, radiant smile of a goddess, then bent and kissed him swiftly on the cheek.

'You're a lovely man,' she said gently, 'and your wife's very lucky.

146

Know what? I could be really jealous of her, no kidding.'

His embarrassment subsided with his penis. He stood up.

'I'd better be going. You're a pretty special lady yourself, Shelley. You tell that man of yours to take good care of you, or he'll have me to answer to!'

She grinned at him.

'No hard feelings, eh? As you might say!'

He gave her a gentle slap on the bottom, and she giggled.

'You're a shocker, Shelley!' He put all the liking he felt for her into his voice. 'I don't know why I like you . . .'

'But I do!' she chimed in tunefully.

Unexpectedly, he experienced a surge of elation. Shelley's gentle dismissal, rather than belittling him, suddenly made him feel quite different about himself. There was a kind of self-confidence that he had not known since the heady days of young manhood, an inner strength so that he thought he could, at that moment, have done almost anything. Run a marathon, swum the channel, written a best-seller – the world seemed within his grasp again. He stood up, stretched his whole body as if testing the new-found elasticity of his muscles, and gave Shelley a brief hug.

'Thanks, Shelley. You're a great girl.'

'That's me,' she agreed cheerfully. 'And you're a great guy, too.'

'Yes, I believe I am!' he answered, laughing aloud at himself.

Beep beep. Beep beep.

'Ruth! Telephone!'

Ruth scowled at the door. She hated having calls when Liz was at home. The downstairs telephone was in the hall, where anyone in any of the downstairs rooms could listen, and upstairs was in the main bedroom. Ruth refused to go in there since Liz had moved in and polluted the memories of Ruth's mother's last days with her presence. She had begged her father to buy a cordless phone, but he had said all that must wait until they moved into the new house.

'Ruth!'

'All *right*! I'm *coming*!'

Ruth thought it would probably be Harriet. Nobody from school ever telephoned her nowadays, and her grandparents always telephoned after six o'clock, when it was cheaper. If it was Harriet there wouldn't be much point in talking, with Liz in the kitchen with her ears stretched (Ruth was convinced) to catch every word.

'Hello.' The word was a growl.

'Hello, Ruth. This is Louise Johnson.'

'Who?'

'Louise Johnson. I came to the house two days ago. I wanted to thank you for taking care of me.'

147

'Oh, that. It's all right.' Ruth was embarrassed, but pleased to be thanked. Since the ambulance had carried Louise away she had replayed the events several times in her head, fascinated and appalled in turn. 'Um, how are you?'

'I'm all right. They're keeping me in hospital a couple more days, though. I lost the baby.'

'Oh. Sorry.' Ruth wriggled, her body expressing her mental discomfort. What were you supposed to say? She remembered how awful it had been when people talked to her after her mother died, saying things that were supposed to be comforting but which invariably made her feel angry or more miserable.

'Shall I . . . would you like me to come and visit you?' Ruth was astonished to hear herself saying the words. No sooner had they left her lips than she wished them unsaid. She hated hospitals. The smell of disinfectant was, to her, the smell of death, and the flashing, beeping machinery promised miracles but were no more than an empty mockery. She'll probably say no, she comforted herself. She won't want me visiting her, she doesn't know me.

Louise, however, was lonely. Longing for Jason to visit her she had nevertheless forbidden his presence. She had never had many women friends, and after her marriage had been so tied up with Jason that she had allowed the friendships to lapse. Besides, she felt strangely drawn to this plain girl. Perhaps it was her obvious unhappiness that gave Louise a fellow-feeling, but she felt protective towards her, as if she had been a younger version of herself. Ridiculous, of course, when Ruth had a father, a brother, a real home of her own, and yet she had the lost air of a displaced person.

'Yes,' said Louise. 'Yes, if you can, I'd like to see you.'

'I'll come after school tomorrow. About four o'clock.' Ruth's tone made it clear that she wasn't seeing this as something to look forward to, but Louise ignored it.

'Nightingale Ward, then.'

Ruth arrived at the hospital with a feeling of heaviness in her stomach which had been growing all afternoon. The hospital was familiar – most of her mother's treatments had been carried out in London, but she had still spent time here. Ruth had visited her often enough to know every inch of the approach road and entrance. Even the faces at the reception desk looked the same. Ruth put her head down and hurried past, not wanting to have to speak to them. Once in the corridors she had to look for signs, Nightingale Ward being unfamiliar territory.

Her school shoes squeaked on the polished floor tiles, her school bag bumped painfully into her leg as she walked, being overloaded with large books for her geography homework. Feeling she should bring something with her but not knowing what, she had stopped at a greengrocer's on the way. Grapes, of course, that was what you were supposed to take, but the only ones available looked shrivelled and unappetising. In the end she had picked the most interesting thing there, a large pomegranate. She had loved them as a child, and her mother had always bought them for her as a treat. In the shop it had seemed exotic and clever, but now the thought of it embarrassed her.

Walking into the ward, she had a moment of terror that she wouldn't recognise Louise. With relief she heard someone call her name, and recognised her erstwhile visitor.

Louise, sitting up in bed in a pale blue nightdress, looked much younger than when Ruth had seen her before. Her face was pale, but she had brushed her hair and put on some lipstick.

'Ruth! I wondered whether you'd be able to manage it. No detention today, then?'

Ruth frowned, then saw it was a joke. 'Not today,' she said carefully. 'Today, I got away with it.'

Louise gave a little smile. The curtains to either side of her bed were drawn shut, giving an illusion of privacy. Louise had made it clear that she didn't welcome neighbourly chat. There was a chair, but she patted the bed. 'Sit down.'

Ruth perched awkwardly, worried about jarring the bed. The cotton blanket was slippery and the bed was too high for her feet to touch the floor, so she was forced to wriggle herself backwards. Then she remembered the pomegranate and got off the bed again to rummage in her school bag.

'I got you something . . .' The fruit was still in the crumpled brown paper bag from the shop. Ruth saw a ribbon-decked basket of fruit on the bedside locker, and was ashamed, but it was too late to withdraw. Louise opened the bag.

'A pomegranate! And what a beautiful one! It's almost too perfect to eat.'

Her pleasure was genuine. Ruth looked again at the fruit, saw how the golden skin flushed with vivid russet, how the place where the flower had been rose from the sphere into a perfect little crown.

'I read somewhere that pomegranates were the original Apples of the Hesperides,' she growled, 'and maybe the fruit in the Garden of Eden, too.'

'Well, it's certainly more tempting than a dreary old Golden Delicious,' said Louise. 'They never taught me things like that at school. All I ever knew about pomegranates was that the infant Samuel had them embroidered on his robe. Golden pomegranates, I always thought that sounded wonderful. His mother sewed them for him when he was sent away to live with old Eli. I liked that.'

149

Her face was wistful. Ruth didn't know whether she should be flattered or uncomfortable, and felt both.

'We don't do much about the Bible at school,' she muttered. 'Just comparative religions, that kind of thing.'

Louise looked down at the pomegranate that she still held. 'Do you know, I've never actually eaten one of these. What are they like?'

'Lovely! At least, I always used to like them. Mummy used to get them for me. They're a bit messy, though. Do you want me to show you?'

'Good idea. I've got a plate and a sharp knife in the locker – they came with the fruit.'

Ruth cut through the hard skin, and split the pomegranate into quarters to reveal the jewelled inside like a thickly encrusted geode. Having something to do made her more relaxed, and she picked the little fleshy seeds apart and removed every bit of bitter yellow pith. Louise, mildly amused, picked one up and ate it.

'Nice,' she said. 'Sweet, and the seed's like a little nut. You have some too.'

They shared the fruit, laughing guiltily as little pink blobs fell on the floor and rolled in all directions. Ruth looked at her fingers.

'They'll think I've been smoking,' she said in some satisfaction, displaying a yellowish stain.

'I hope I didn't frighten you too much, the other day,' said Louise, feeling that the time was now right.

'No, not really.'

'I'm afraid I probably told you rather more than I should have done. I was in a state, and to be honest I can't remember things all that well.'

'It's all right. I didn't mind.'

'And the miscarriage didn't bother you too much? I mean, it doesn't happen all that often. Most people don't have any trouble when they're pregnant, or not much. You don't need to worry about your step-mother, for instance.'

'Worry, about her?' Ruth's voice was scornful. 'I was just sorry . . .' She stopped.

'Sorry it wasn't her, instead of me?' Ruth looked defensive, but Louise's words were entirely free of condemnation.

'If she wasn't having the baby, we wouldn't have to sell the house,' Ruth muttered.

'It would probably happen anyway. They really want to move, you know. Make a new start, like me.'

'You don't need a new house, now.'

'Well, as a matter of fact, I do. Even without the baby, I have to move on. So do you.'

'But I don't *want* to!'

150

Louise looked at her, and saw herself. Quite suddenly, she saw that while Ruth's problems were different from her own, they stemmed from the same insecurity, the need to cling on to something outside herself, to be carried by someone else's certainty. She felt uncertain about her own ability to come to terms with this, but she found that she wanted to help Ruth even more. Hoping that she wouldn't do more harm than good, she carried on.

'What about when you get older, when you're grown up? Are you still going to be staying in that house trying to be a little girl? Are you going to spend the rest of your life there, trying to hang on to the past? It can't be done, believe me.'

'What do you know about it?'

Louise ignored Ruth's aggressive tone.

'Not much, perhaps. But I do know that you have to let go of the past.'

'I don't know what you mean.'

'I know you don't want to listen to me. And I know I don't have any right to say these things to you. But I'm saying them anyway, because someone has to.'

'But I don't have to listen! Anyway, what about you? Isn't it time you started taking some of your own advice? All this "I know he doesn't love me" and "I know he doesn't want our baby" stuff, it's enough to make you puke! How do you know, if you don't talk to him? So don't give me all that stuff about hanging on to the past, when it's exactly what you're doing yourself! Just because your grotty old grandparents didn't want you doesn't mean everyone has to feel like that.'

Ruth slid off the bed, knocking the pomegranate plate to the ground. Little bits of pomegranate went everywhere and Ruth squashed them under her feet as she grabbed her school bag. 'Mind your own business!' she shouted. Her feet slipped on the shiny flooring, and her school bag dealt her a vicious blow on the shin, but somehow she fought her way out of the curtained area and ran out of the ward.

Louise looked at the messy floor round her bed, and up at the curtains that still swayed in the movement of Ruth's passing. She wasn't sure whether her desire to help had backfired on her or not. Certainly what Ruth had said, though painful to hear, had needed saying to her as much as her words to Ruth. She had little doubt that each had found what she heard equally painful. So . . . what? Did she, perhaps, have to consider Ruth's criticisms as carefully as she would wish Ruth to consider hers? It felt like a bargain, though Ruth had not meant it that way. More, perhaps, a thing of checks and balances. Perhaps one only had the right to give advice if one had the humility to accept it from others.

Louise sighed. It was all a great deal more complicated than she had ever expected.

151

Chapter Fourteen

'Mr Kingswood. I thought I'd just pop in and see you.' Roger folded himself neatly into the chair opposite Paul's desk. He called in as often as he could, and was thoroughly at home in the office now.

'Good morning, Mr Selby. You've had the report back on your survey?'

Roger proffered a brown envelope.

'Yes. I've brought it to show you. I think it's all right . . .' He jittered, obviously in need of reassurance. Paul thought, not for the first time, that what many first time buyers needed was a kind of nanny to reassure, cajole or (at times) bully them through the obstacle course that was buying a property. He took the envelope and glanced through the papers.

'Well, that all seems very satisfactory. Not that I expected anything else – I've sold several of those flats and never had any problems. Who did the survey? Oh, Alec Blake. That's funny.'

'Is it, Mr Kingswood?'

'Well, he wouldn't be aware of it, but there's a chance that he might be involved in your chain.'

'Oh, I see.' Roger looked anxious. 'It doesn't matter, does it? I mean, you don't think the building society might mind, do you?' He spoke with respect, as one fearing the unpredictable wrath of an easily roused deity.

'I wouldn't have thought so, For one thing, he was completely unaware of the connection, and for another it's still a bit of a polo.' Roger looked confused. 'A hole in the middle,' Paul amplified. 'I was hoping that the people up the chain from you – in the house that Shelley's buying – would buy the house of the people who are wanting to buy Alec Blake's house, if you follow me.'

'It's complicated, isn't it? Like one of those puzzles, you know, who is my father's daughter's brother's child?'

'Yes, or one of those awful problems they used to give us at school – if it takes ten men eight days to fill a bath with a teaspoon, how many chimpanzees will do it with a ladle. And sometimes it seems just as impossible as that.'

Roger looked at him with respectful sympathy.

'Is that usual, to have all the houses being sold by you?'

'No, far from it. I can't remember it happening for years, at least not a chain as long as this one – if it even happens this time. I'm not too sure about the house in the middle, the one the people are selling who want to buy the surveyor's place. I've had quite a few viewings there, but none of them seem to jell. I really had high hopes of Mrs Johnson. You've met her, haven't you, when you took Shelley round there? I really thought the house would suit her. She went to see it the other day, but I haven't heard a thing.'

'Well, you wouldn't have done. Didn't you know? She's been in hospital!'

'Who, Mrs Johnson?'

Roger hitched his chair closer, and leaned forward confidentially. Paul found himself leaning forward in emulation and pushed himself back against his chair.

'Yes, that's right. Shelley went round there a couple of days ago to measure up again, and he told her. Mr Johnson. Said she'd had a miscarriage. Seemed quite upset, Shelley said, though of course it wasn't his baby.'

Paul felt that he shouldn't really be gossiping about his clients, but he supposed that what Shelley knew was pretty soon common knowledge.

'Really? I didn't know.'

'Didn't know it wasn't his?'

'No, I didn't know about the miscarriage. She did tell me about the baby. How on earth does Shelley find these things out?'

'People tell her things.' Roger sounded wistful. He would have liked to have been the kind of person people told things to, but he suspected that he never would be.

'Yes, I suppose they do. Well, it's not surprising I haven't heard from her, then.' An unpleasant thought struck him. 'They are still planning to move, though? Losing the baby hasn't made her change her mind, decide to stay put?'

Roger shook his head.

'Oh, no. That was the first thing Shelley asked – she's quick, isn't she? Doesn't miss a trick. But he – Mr Johnson, that is – said they'd still be selling. Of course, they're splitting up . . . um, you did know that?'

Paul admitted that yes, he had known that.

''Course Shelley's getting worried that they haven't found anything yet. It wouldn't matter, only I've got a special offer on my mortgage that's only going to last to the end of next month.' He spoke as though it were two pence off a packet of biscuits, but Paul understood the urgency. It seemed extraordinary, in this time when there were so many houses on the market and so few people wanting to buy them, that Louise Johnson couldn't find a house to suit her, but it wasn't the first time he had known a chain to founder for this reason. He sighed.

'I'd better check it out, I suppose. Difficult situation, though. Is Mrs Johnson at home, do you know?'

'I think so. They kept her in hospital for a few days – Shelley says that means she was quite poorly. I'm sure you can do it, though, Mr Kingswood. You've got such a tactful way with you.'

Paul noticed that Melanie was giggling quietly behind her computer monitor. He subdued a tendency to smile, and thanked Roger with a straight face.

'You want to watch out, Mr K,' said Melanie after Roger had finally left. 'I reckon he fancies you.'

'I can't help it,' said Paul with a smirk. 'Some people just find me irresistible. Usually the wrong people, unfortunately.'

'Heard from Mrs Holt recently? Or her daughter?'

'Melanie!' Paul's shock was unfeigned. 'Whatever are you talking about?'

'Can't fool me. Parrots, indeed!' exclaimed Melanie cryptically.

'But I like parrots! I always have done!'

'Of course you do,' she soothed. 'Anyway, shouldn't you be checking up on young Roger's bit of goss?'

'Get back to work, you eavesdropping hussy.'

'Mr Kingswood?'

'Mrs Oldham?' Paul glanced across the office, though he knew perfectly well that since it was the morning it was Rose at the other desk, not Melanie. Rose would never dream of admitting to listening to his conversations, or of teasing him about them afterwards.

'Beth, since you asked me out to lunch.' Her voice was warm with laughter.

'Paul, then, in spite of the fact you've never taken me up on it.'

'Circumstances, not excuses. I have to go where the work is.'

'And where is it now?'

'Mold.' Her voice fell dramatically into a deep, trembling contralto.

'I beg your pardon?'

'Clwyd. Welsh Wales. Scene of devastating flooding some years back, and home of an excellent small theatre.'

'And which are you writing about, floods or thespians?'

'Thespians, though the floods will get an honourable mention. It's a great place, the people give you such a warm welcome.'

'Good.' Surely he wasn't feeling jealous, at his age, about a woman he'd never even met? But how warm a welcome, exactly?

'Yes. Anyway, I thought I'd better tell you that my mother has another bee in her bonnet and has decided to make over the ownership of the bungalow to me.'

'Oh?' Does that mean she's not going to sell, he wondered gloomily? I should have known this chain was doomed. It all seemed too good to be true. Or does it mean that she will be coming to live here? In his mind, the 'she' was unambiguous.

'Yes, oh. It doesn't make any difference, does it? It's not some kind of tax fiddle – well, I don't think you can do that sort of thing now, can you? It's not even so she can claim to be destitute and get the local authority to house her. It's just to simplify things.'

'In what respect?'

'Her dizzy spells have been getting worse, and though they keep telling her it's nothing serious, she's convinced she could drop dead at any moment. She doesn't want everyone to be inconvenienced by having to wait months while her estate goes into probate.'

'That's very thoughtful of her.' Paul didn't know whether to be relieved or worried. He had become fond of Mrs Holt.

'Yes, isn't it.' Beth's voice was reserved. 'It's not like her at all, though.'

'Really? I'd have said she was a very considerate person.'

'Oh, yes, I didn't mean that! It's just that there's no real reason for her to *be* so considerate. These dizzy spells have never worried her much in the past – she'd have ignored them completely if I hadn't physically taken her to the doctor to have them checked out. She's always had good health, and never been one to fuss over it. I don't know why she's suddenly decided she's on the way out.'

'You're quite sure . . . would she keep it from you, if there were really something wrong?'

'I wondered about that too. But I'm sure she wouldn't. It's just not her style, if you know what I mean. And besides, I know her so well. I can't believe she could be that ill without me noticing something.'

'A premonition? That doesn't seem like her style either.'

Beth's laughter rang in his ear. He liked her laugh. It was hearty, uninhibited without being loud.

'Goodness, no! She makes a point of walking under ladders, and would no more consult her stars for guidance than she would ring the speaking clock to get directions to Liverpool. In her book, magpies are just black and white birds, black cats are dark coloured felines, and spilled salt is a gritty nuisance underfoot to be swept up as quickly as possible. No, I'm sure it's nothing like that. And the funny thing is that she doesn't seem worried in the least. If anything, I'd have said she was rather pleased with herself.'

'Maybe it's just a whim, and she won't do it.'

'She's already done it! At least, she's instructed her solicitor, and it's all in hand. Without even consulting me, though I suppose I can hardly object.'

'You'll be landed with dealing with the sale. Technically, if we get an offer, I shall have to refer it to you, and then there's all the paperwork and so on.'

'She's never minded paperwork, any more than I do. Oh well, it's keeping her amused, at any rate.'

'Yes.' Now that he didn't need to worry any more, Paul was rather pleased with the prospect of having an excuse to telephone Beth. And an estate agent has a legal obligation to convey any offer he receives, he thought happily. I wonder if I can persuade people to make silly offers? 'I'd better have a note of your mobile number.'

Louise parked the car, not in the drive but a little way down the road despite the showery rain that came and went so unpredictably. Even now she wasn't sure that she wanted to go back there. It was not so much the memories of her miscarriage that deterred her – though it was true that the house was inextricably linked in her mind with the pain and fear she had experienced there – as the thought that Ruth might be there. Louise had specified a morning appointment, trusting that Ruth would be at school, and it was true that Mr Kingswood had told her it would be Mrs Hartwell who would be there, but she could not rid her mind of the feeling that Ruth would hear about it, and manage to appear.

And yet, strangely, it was largely because of Ruth that she had come back. She still felt a disturbing mixture of anger and pity for the girl. Part of her wanted to see and even buy the house only because Ruth was so against it. Why, thought Louise, should she allow a girl of that age to manipulate her? Louise wanted to punish her, but at the same time she wanted to help her. She thought of Ruth as a kind of hermit crab, clinging to a shall it had long since outgrown.

The wind, that was whirling the lumpy clouds across the sky, was fitful at ground level. Blustering in fits and starts, it caught the stationary car and pummelled it. As if herself shaken loose from her hiding place, Louise impelled herself out of the car and down the street. She was reaching for the bell almost before she got to the door, knowing that if she gave herself the slightest delay she would turn round and go again.

'Mrs Johnson?' The woman who opened the door was not obviously pregnant. Perhaps, if you were looking at it, you would see the slight thickening of the waist, the glow of skin that had never entirely lost its Australian tan. Looking at her made Louise feel like a washed out monochrome picture, limp and faded and empty. But even before she had lost the baby, she thought, she had lacked that gloss of fulfilment and joy that made the other woman seem almost luminous.

A sudden gust of wind spattered them both with rain as vicious as thrown gravel, and impelled Louise in through the door. Liz struggled to close it against the onslaught. Louise put out a hand to help, but as she did so the wind dropped as quickly as it had come and the door shut with a bang.

'Good grief!' Liz leaned against the door for a moment. Several wet leaves, torn from the beech hedge by the violent weather, had been carried in and Louise automatically bent to pick them up. Liz did the same, and the two women almost collided. Louise stepped back and stood up, putting out a hand to steady herself against a door frame. Straightening up too quickly still made her feel dizzy.

'Steady!' said Liz. 'Are you all right?'

Louise nodded.

'Sorry,' she said. 'I keep forgetting I'm not supposed to do things like that.'

'I was sorry to hear about the baby.' Liz had all the directness of her Australian upbringing. 'It's brave of you to come back here.'

'I wanted to see the house. And lay the ghost.' Louise stopped, aghast. She never said things like that even to people she was close to.

'Yes, I can imagine.' Liz was neither surprised nor embarrassed. 'I think I'd feel the same. Come on, then. Let's do it.'

She led the way into the sitting room. Louise went straight to the sofa and stood by it, her body stiff. Then she bent slowly, almost hearing her spine creak, and put her hands on the cushions, stroking them gently. Her legs felt weak: she let them buckle beneath her, supporting herself on her hands until she knelt by the sofa, leaning over it protectively as if over a cradle.

A dark mark appeared on the fabric of the cushion; her first thought was that it was blood, and it wasn't until a second drop splashed down that she realised she was weeping, the tears running unheeded down her face and dripping off nose and chin. She put up a hand and smeared them off. Her nose was running, she needed a handkerchief. Tears were one thing, but to have her nose dripping on to the cushions was unthinkable. She rummaged in her pocket, but Liz thrust a handful of tissues into her hand. Louise tried to speak to thank her, but what came out was a moaning wail.

She buried her face in the tissues, and her body sagged down until she was half lying on the sofa. The effort to hold back was making her feel dizzy – the only way she could stop the sobs was to stop breathing. She felt Liz's hand on her back, and shrank from the kind of clumsy embrace that, in her experience, was what women offered one another at such times, but Liz merely left her hand where it was, in the middle of her shoulders below her neck. The touch was firmly reassuring, a little patch of warmth that seemed to dissolve the tightness within her. Louise let go, sobbing luxuriously, noisily, for once allowing her body free rein to express what she felt. It reminded her, incongruously, of her first sexual experience with Jason, when led by him she had abandoned her inhibitions to cry out at the moment of climax.

The result was the same. When she finally stopped crying she felt exhausted, drained of all emotion but peaceful. Her body ached, her knees were locked and stiff, but in spite of that she seemed to be floating, cushioned against physical discomforts. She drew in a breath that seemed to go right through her body, to the end of every extremity, and sat up.

Liz handed her a damp face cloth, and a dry towel. Louise wiped her face, as gently and carefully as if it had been a child's. The cloth was cool against hot, puffy skin, and she held it for a moment over her eyes, breathing slowly through a nose that was beginning to unblock. She patted her face dry with the towel.

'Thanks,' she said gruffly, hauling herself creakily up off the floor. Sitting on the sofa, she dabbed at her eyes with the damp cloth once more. Liz, who had gone through to the kitchen, came back with a tray which she put on a small table between them. Louise looked down at the face cloth and the towel.

'That's what she brought me. Ruth.'

'Did she? Good.'

'She said it's what her father does for you, when you feel ill.'

Liz smiled wryly. 'I wouldn't have thought she'd have noticed.'

'Well, she did. She was very sensible, really. It was all a bit frightening for her, and I wouldn't let her call an ambulance straight away. I was . . . a bit strange, I'm afraid.'

'I don't know that that would worry Ruth all that much. She's pretty strange herself.' As a rule Liz never allowed herself to criticise her step-daughter to anyone, but she felt oddly close to this woman.

'Yes, she's a funny kid. Reminds me of me at her age, in a way. My mother died when I was quite young, too.'

'Did she? And did you have a wicked step-mother as well?'

'No. I never knew my father. I went into care. Foster-homes, that kind of thing.'

Liz shivered.

'That doesn't sound like much fun.'

'Not much. Oh, it wasn't that bad, don't get me wrong. I wasn't badly treated, they were good to me, really. It just wasn't . . . home.'

Liz looked down at the mug of tea in her hands.

'I don't know that this is home for Ruth any more, now that I'm in it.'

'She doesn't want to leave it, though. Um, is there anything wrong with the heating?'

Liz blinked.

'No, nothing at all. Why, are you cold?'

'No, but when I arrived last time the house was icy, and she said the heating didn't work properly. Looking back, I think she'd had the

159

windows wide open. The air smelled more like outside than cold inside, if you know what I mean.'

'I certainly do. Wretched girl, no wonder she told the agent it would be all right for you to come! I thought at the time it was strange, when he told me afterwards. Up till now she's done her best to discourage people from coming round at all. *Bloody* girl!'

'Yes. It warmed up after a while, of course, but by then I wasn't in a state to notice. And . . . there was a smell.'

'A smell? What kind of smell?'

Louise wrinkled her nose.

'Nasty. Old sink drains. Slimy dish cloth.'

Liz flushed with annoyance. 'I could kill that girl! I wondered where that old cloth had gone! What d'you suppose she did with it?'

'Put it behind the radiator, I should think. The smell got stronger as the room warmed up.' Her lips twitched. 'It's quite clever, really. It could have worked, too, under different circumstances.'

'Well, I don't think it's funny!'

'Nor do I, really. But it shows you she's serious.'

'Well, so am I serious. Seriously pregnant, for one thing. It's not just that, though. We could probably manage if we had to, at least for a year. But I can't stand it! It's a nice enough house, but it's not mine! I'll always be an interloper, and outsider. I want a home of my own!'

'So does Ruth.'

'And it's mutually exclusive.' Liz spoke bitterly. 'I know she's had a bad time, and I'm sorry for her, but . . .'

'Not that bad. I told her that.'

Liz looked at her with awe.

'Did you? How brave!'

'Not really. And anyway, it's true. Losing her mum is bad, of course, but she's not the only one. At least she's still got her dad, and her brother . . . and you.'

'But I'm the one that's causing all the problems!'

'No you're not. She is.'

'Yes, but—'

'But nothing,' Louise interrupted. 'You mustn't let her bully you. It doesn't do her any good, and it will only make her despise you.'

'She already does.'

'There you are, then. Stand up to her. And make sure her father does, too.'

'She gets so angry.'

'She doesn't *get* angry. She *is* angry. Angry with everyone and everything. Angry with life. Angry with her mother.'

'But Ruth adored – adores – her mother!'

'Exactly. And her mother went and died on her, left her behind. Of course she's angry! It took me years to stop being angry with my

160

Mum for being so careless, for letting herself be run over. Oh, I didn't admit it, of course. And I hated myself for feeling like that, and that made me even more angry. She can't admit it either, so she takes it out on all of you. On you most of all, because she knows you won't fight back.'

'I don't want her to hate me . . .'

'Well, she doesn't really have any reason to, does she? I'd say it isn't you she hates, not really. You're just convenient.'

Liz sighed.

'You make it sound so simple. But what do I actually do about it, when all's said and done?'

'Stick to your guns. Let her know that you know what she's been up to. That the sale will go ahead anyway, whatever she does to prevent it. Tell her what's going on. Talk to her, even if she doesn't seem to be listening. She's frightened of the future. Tell her about the new house, tell her what furniture and stuff you'll be taking from this one, that she can have her mother's things, that you're not just going to chuck it all out and start again – I assume you're not?'

'No, of course not!' Liz was shocked. 'I wouldn't dream of it! I just don't see why every cracked cup, every wobbly old saucepan, has to be treated like a holy relic.'

'There you are, then. She's not a stupid girl. Rather the reverse, I'd say. She won't want to see it, but one of these days she's going to have to admit that you're right.'

'You think?'

'Well . . .' Louise grinned. 'Maybe not. But what have you got to lose? At least this way you keep your self-respect.'

Liz nodded. 'I suppose I have let her get away with a lot. It's just . . . I really wanted her to like me.'

She sounded forlorn. Louise nodded.

'I know,' she said. 'But think about the teachers at school. Which were the ones you liked and respected? The ones who let you get away with anything, or the ones who let you know where the lines were drawn, and then stuck to them?'

Liz nodded.

'Yes. I see what you mean.'

They drank their tea, each silently engrossed in her own thoughts.

'Listen to me, laying down the law,' said Louise. 'My own life's in such a muddle I feel like one of those flies that's been caught by a spider, all tied up with sticky web. I don't know what makes me think I can tell you how to deal with yours.'

'I don't know. Seems to me it's the people with problems themselves who can understand about other people's. Anyway, I'm grateful. It's good to have someone to talk to. I just wish I could help you with your problems too.'

161

'So do I.' Louise shook her head. 'Trouble is, my problems are in my own head, not other people's. And even saying that,' she admitted, 'is a step forward. So you see you have helped me, after all. Now, don't you think I ought to look round this house?'

Chapter Fifteen

'. . . So I'm not going to tell him,' finished Philippa defiantly.

There was a thoughtful pause at the other end of the telephone.

'Ah.' The voice was carefully non-committal.

'Or the children.'

'Mm.'

'You think I'm wrong.' Philippa knew she was sounding defensive. Well, she was defensive. She had already battled this one out with her doctor, and a battle it had been, too. That was the trouble with having had the same doctor for years – they started to think they could run your life for you, tell you what to do . . . She remembered with a twinge of shame how cross she had been with him and how patiently he had responded to what he obviously considered her unreasonable recalcitrance. The only time he had come close to losing his temper was when she had warned him not to go behind her back and tell George himself that she was going into hospital.

'You're surely not suggesting that I would violate patient confidentiality . . . ?' He was almost spluttering, and Philippa saw with shame that he was more hurt than angry.

'Sorry, Malcolm, sorry,' she said quickly. 'I'm just getting paranoid about it. I know you wouldn't do anything like that.'

'Unfortunately, I couldn't,' he said darkly. 'I can only beg you to consider how George will feel when he finds out.'

'You do think I'm wrong, don't you?' she said now into the silent telephone.

'I've no idea. Not if that's how you want it to be. I'd say it's your decision.'

'George will be very hurt.' The lack of opposition, oddly, was making Philippa question her own actions. 'And so will the children.'

'They'll get over it.'

'Yes. I suppose so. It's just . . . I can't stand them *fussing*.'

'No. I know what you mean.'

'No point in worrying them yet . . .'

'Quite.'

Philippa knew that she had no need to justify herself, but she couldn't leave it alone. Like someone with a jumpy tooth, she had to keep prodding it with her tongue to test whether it was still hurting.

'It's – what's that word they use now? Denial, that's it. I'm still in denial. If I talk to them about it, what I will see in their eyes, hear in their voices and in what they don't say, will make it real. And I can only cope with it by pretending it's not really happening.'

'Fair enough. So, who have you told? Apart from the doctor, that is?'

'Nobody. Well, you.'

Alice Holt was silent again. This was the first time she had spoken to Philippa since the day when they had sat together in the bungalow, drinking sherry, and Philippa had told her she thought she might be ill. A woman with a strongly developed instinct for privacy, she could well understand why Philippa would prefer to keep her condition to herself, at least until she had definite knowledge of what precisely that condition was. At the same time, to be the only person who knew . . . it was a responsibility, a burden, even. One which was not particularly welcome.

'When do you go into hospital? Next week?'

'Yes. Only for a few days, they said. Probably. They'll take out the . . . the lump, and do some tests. Perfectly straightforward.'

'Mm. And where are you going to say you're going? I mean, you can hardly just vanish, can you?'

'Well, I thought of saying I was going abroad – Paris, say, or Venice – with a friend. But George is mad on travel, he'd think it odd of me to go without him. If nothing else he'd want to drive me to the airport, and then there's all the fuss about insurance, and travellers cheques and things. So then I thought somewhere like a health farm.'

'And he'd accept that?'

'No, of course not. That is, he'll roar with laughter and tell me I'm potty, at my age. I've never really bothered much with that kind of thing, I'm afraid.'

'So why would he believe you're starting now?'

'Well . . . I was going to blame it on the friend I'm going with. I mean, that I'll say I'm going with. That she doesn't want to go on her own, that kind of thing.'

'He's not likely to say he wants to come too? Out of curiosity, or something?'

'Not very. Anyway, I can say it's a special week, concessionary prices, for women only.'

'You've got it all worked out. And – the friend? I thought you said you hadn't told anybody, except . . . oh.'

'I know it's an awful nerve,' said Philippa miserably. She suddenly felt reduced to the status of a naughty child. Then she realised that Alice Holt was laughing.

'My dear – me! At a health farm! A funny farm would be more likely! You wouldn't like to say you've booked in to have a short course of psychotherapy, or something? I mean, look at me!'

'It isn't just about how you look, you know. It's about how you feel. Massage, aromatherapy, that kind of thing. Pampering yourself.'

'What my grandmother would have called wicked self-indulgence. She would have been appalled. In her book, if you enjoyed it then it must be sinful. She used to try to terrify me into good behaviour when I was a child, but I'm afraid she made heaven sound so utterly dull that I rather preferred the idea of a bit of hell-fire and damnation. As a result I'm afraid I always went for the entertaining option over the sensible one. Perhaps I should go and try out a health farm, after all.'

Philippa was amused. 'Why not? Use the sauna to get into training for the hell fires. Perhaps I should come with you.' Her amusement faded as reality returned. 'Then again, I may not be able to. Anyway, I don't mean to involve you. It's just that you're the only person that George hardly knows, or who doesn't have a husband he plays golf with. Not that he'd check up on me, of course, but you know how these accidental meetings seem to happen at the most inopportune moments.'

'Of course. Shall I go away?'

Philippa was shocked. 'Of course not! I wouldn't dream of putting you to any trouble!'

'Oh, it wouldn't be any trouble. I've been thinking of going to visit my daughter, anyway. I might give her a ring and see if she's going to be at home.'

'Now I feel guilty.'

'Don't. She's been asking me for ages, and I've been lazy about doing anything about it. Not that I don't want to go, you understand – just inertia.'

Philippa's mind came back like a yo-yo on a string to her own preoccupations.

'If you were in my position, would you tell her? Your daughter?'

Alice thought about it.

'Yes, I probably would.' She thought again. 'There are just the two of us, you see. I was over forty when she was born, and right from the start we were, well, friends. That sounds dreadful, I know. I've never been keen on those mothers who say, "Oh, my daughter's my best friend, we do everything together." I have visions of mothers going round in unsuitable clothes and muscling in at the discotheque. It wasn't like that. It's just that we thought the same way, found the same things funny, things like that. We're very close, and yet . . . in a funny way, we're very separate. We don't depend on one another much, but we both know the other would be there in a flash, if needed. You know how it is with some old friends – you don't see them for years, but when you do you pick up just where you left off, and it's as if no time has passed? It's a bit like that.'

'It sounds wonderful. Is she married?'

'Not any more. And no children, which is a pity. I should have liked some grandchildren.'

Philippa thought gratefully of her own family, her children married and with children of their own, preoccupied with their own lives, sharing, perhaps, their problems and anxieties with her with as much difficulty as she was now feeling about sharing hers with them.

'The only thing is,' Alice was saying, 'that if I go to stay with Beth, I won't be able to come and visit you.'

'I wouldn't expect you to do that! Visiting people in hospital is ghastly, one never knows what to talk about.'

'I rarely have that problem. Won't you mind, not having anyone come and see you?'

'Not really. I don't expect to be in very long, in any case. They kick you out almost before you've come round from the anaesthetic these days.'

'Well, good luck, then. Let me know how you get on.'

'Yes. And . . . thanks.'

'It's a disaster,' said Ruth. 'A total bloody disaster.'

She ranged around Harriet's bedroom, unable to settle, kicking at the floor cushions as she passed. Harriet was thankful that there weren't any books on the floor, Mrs Moppett having 'done' the room that day and piled them neatly on the bedside table and the desk. She thought that otherwise the books might have been flying round the room like footballs.

'Well, you knew it was likely,' she said soothingly.

'And her of all people!' Ruth continued, ignoring Harriet. 'That cow I looked after! I should have left her to it, let her bleed to death or something. Cross-eyed bitch!'

Harriet rather liked that last phrase, and repeated it silently to herself.

'If it wasn't her it would have been someone,' she pointed out reasonably.

'Not if I had anything to do with it,' responded Ruth darkly. 'It never occurred to me she'd come back. How could she bear to, after last time? And I went to so much trouble, opening all the windows so the house was cold, and putting the dish cloth behind the radiator . . . then she had to come back while I was at school, and talk to Her. My step-mother.' She punched one hand into the palm of the other. 'That's it, of course. She talked her into it. Probably bribed her, said she could have the house really cheap. Uh!' She punched again. Harriet's hands ached in sympathy.

'That means you'll be coming to live here,' she said sadly. 'Can I come and see it, sometimes? Perhaps you could have this room.' She brightened at the thought. 'I'd like that. Maybe she – the person who's buying your house – will let you go and visit too . . .' She broke off as Ruth came to a halt, shuddering.

'It's *our* house. Our *home*. You don't really expect me to want to see it all different, with someone else's things in it, do you?'

Ruth hung her head.

'No. Sorry.' Ruth, caught up as she was in her own feelings, nevertheless felt a pang of pity at the sight of the younger girl. Her straight, brownish hair hung forward, parting at the back to reveal the nape of her neck, naked and defenceless in its skinny whiteness. It pulled at some basic instinct deep within that Ruth wasn't even aware that she possessed; something akin to an animal's response to the submissive rolling over of a young creature to display its vulnerable belly. She stopped pacing, and flung herself on the bed next to Harriet.

'Sorry,' she said gruffly. 'Didn't mean to take it out on you. You're the only person who really understands.'

A tide of pink flowed up Harriet's pale face, and her head raised as if a puppeteer had pulled a string and lifted her drooping body.

'I know it's not so bad for me,' she said. 'I wish I could help you. There must be something we can do. Can't you talk to your father?'

Ruth shook her head.

'He's as bad as she is, now. Worse, really. I mean, she's only my step-mother, nobody expects her to be nice to me. But he's my father. You'd think *he*'d care about how I feel.'

Harriet thought of her own father, who surely cared but seemed powerless to protect or help her. Perhaps, she thought, all fathers were like that.

'There's nothing we can do, then,' she said forlornly.

'There must be something. We've got to make them take some notice of us.'

'How? We're children. Well, I am, anyway. We can't make them do anything.'

Ruth thought. 'We need something that will show them straight away that we're serious. Like the suffragettes, chaining themselves to the railings.' Harriet looked anxious. Ruth could see that the younger girl, though willing to help, would not be able to withstand her parents' disapproval. Not unless she were out of their sight . . .

'I know! We can run away?'

'Where to?' asked Harriet, unusually practical.

'I don't know . . . anywhere!' Ruth dismissed such paltry details with a wave. 'The point is, they'd see we were serious. They'd be worried about us, and they wouldn't be able to make us change our minds, because we wouldn't be here! It's perfect!'

'I don't want them to be worried . . .'

Ruth struggled for patience.

'They've got to be a bit worried, otherwise they won't take any notice. But we can telephone them or something, so they know we're all right.'

Her enthusiasm was beginning to be infectious.

'It would be exciting,' Harriet admitted. 'We could tell them we wouldn't come back unless they promised not to punish us. We could say they should put a notice in the newspaper to let us know they're going to do what we say . . .' The romance of it was carrying her away. It was like one of the adventure stories she used to read when she was younger. She saw herself and Ruth camping in a hidden bit of countryside, sitting by a camp fire while bacon sizzled in a pan, filling kettles from a sparkling stream . . . no, a spring that bubbled, pure and sweet, from the hillside . . . A flurry of wind rattled the window, and she came back to earth. Her vision of camping out vanished in the grey light of a chilly wet November day. 'Where could we live?' she repeated. 'We've got to go somewhere, and they'll be looking for us.'

Ruth frowned.

'Haven't you got any friends we could go to?'

'No one that would keep it a secret. Have you?'

'Not really.' Ruth did not want to admit how few friends she actually had. Besides, it was quite true that nobody's parents would be at all likely to be prepared to hide the two of them. 'What we need,' she said, thinking aloud, 'is something like an empty house, where we can live without anyone knowing about us.'

Harriet shivered.

'It sounds a bit creepy,' she said, her vivid imagination going into overdrive and coming up with large echoing rooms hung with cobwebs, miles of creaking corridors and damp, rat-infested cellars.

'Well, we can't exactly camp in this weather, can we? And I'm certainly not suggesting we go and live in Cardboard City. I do have *some* sense of responsibility. What about the place your parents want to buy? That has stables and things, doesn't it? Outbuildings?'

'Yes, but nothing very warm. And there's a pony, so the people are always going out there. They'd be sure to find us. Oh!'

'What's the matter?'

'I've just thought of something. Quiet, let me think.'

This was so unlike the usually meek Harriet that Ruth was silenced.

'Yes, I think it might work! There's this place I know, an old lady lives there, with a parrot, and there's a thing in the garden . . . it's an old air-raid shelter.'

'It might do, I suppose. But what about the old woman?'

'Well, she said she doesn't go out into the garden much at this time of year. And she never goes into the shelter. It's inside a sort of rockery, and the door faces the other way, away from the house, and it hasn't any windows so we could have lights in there at night, and nobody would see.'

'Yes!' Ruth was impressed. 'That sounds good. Well done, Harriet!' Harriet glowed.

'And she told me – the old lady, that is – that it's never damp in there, and it doesn't get very cold either, that's why her husband used to keep his wine in there. And then her daughter used it as a, you know, a kind of play house when she was little. I've been in there, it's quite clean and it's empty.'

'Doesn't she keep it locked? You wouldn't keep wine in a place without a lock.'

Harriet looked almost smug.

'Yes, but the key is hidden there, by the door, and *I know where it is*!'

'Brilliant! Let's go and have a look!'

'What now?'

'Yes, why not? It's only two o'clock, it won't be dark for ages yet. We can say we want to go for a walk. Is it a long way?'

'Quite long. The only problem is, I'm not sure of the address. When I went before I was in the car, and I didn't go from here. And if we do find it, supposing she sees us in the garden?'

'Old people nearly always have a rest after lunch. Do you think we can get into the garden without going through the house?'

'I think so. If we can find it. There's a kind of path along the back.'

'Phone book. You remember her name, don't you? And then a map. Come on, Harriet, I'm sure we can do it.'

Ruth was quite put out to find how many Holts were in the telephone book, and still more put out that none of them seemed to be the right one.

'Oh, come on, Harriet. Look, that one's a Hensham number, are you sure it isn't that?'

'No, I know that road, someone in my form lives there. She's not here.' Ruth looked so depressed that Harriet was driven to new heights of inventiveness.

'I could ring up Mr Kingswood,' she suggested tentatively.

'Who? You don't mean the estate agent, that Mr Kingswood?'

'Yes, he's nice. He's the one who took me to the bungalow, to see the parrot.' Her fingers were already flicking through the pages of her mother's telephone book.

'What will you say to him?'

Harriet hushed her, she had already called the number.

'Mr Kingswood? It's Harriet Blake, Mr Kingswood. Yes, that's right. The parrot. Yes. Well, that's why I was . . . I wanted to write and thank

Mrs Holt, and I don't know her address . . . yes, I've got a pencil . . .' She wrote busily. 'Thank you very much, Mr Kingswood. And thank you for taking me, that day. Yes, it was lovely. Thank you. Goodbye.' Gleefully she waved the piece of paper at Ruth.

'Goodness, Harriet. That was brilliant!'

Harriet glowed. She rarely received such unstinted praise.

'There's only one thing,' she said, with mock irritation.

'What?'

'I'll have to write the letter.'

This, for some reason, struck both of them as wildly funny. They giggled helplessly, leaning against one another and gasping for breath.

'Now then, you two.' Christine came out of the kitchen. 'I don't want you frowsting indoors all afternoon. Why don't you go out for a while? Get some fresh air?'

She was vaguely surprised to find that this elicited, instead of groans, more gales of laughter. Funny little things, she thought, more indulgently than usual where her elder daughter was concerned. Harriet looks quite normal, for once. That strange Ruth girl must be a good influence.

'Good afternoon, Mr Jones.' Paul knew that his voice didn't sound very welcoming, but he thought that even managing to be polite was pretty amazing.

'What about my offer, then?'

'What offer, Mr Jones?'

Paul Jones shook his head.

'No wonder you lot are always complaining about the state of the market! Here I am, cash buyer, and you can't even remember that I made an offer on that place in Oak Hill. More than a week ago, and not so much as a phone call since. I suppose you forgot to tell them about it, didn't you? I could have the law on you for that.'

Paul leaned back in his chair. Generally he stood up for customers, but staying seated was his unspoken gesture of dislike.

'I remember very well, Mr Jones. You told me that you were thinking of making an offer. I took you to mean that the offer was not, in fact, yet on the table. I did, however, mention it to the owners.'

'You did, did you?' There was disbelief in the small eyes.

'I did. And as I believe I made clear to you at the time, they told me that they were not interested in any offer as low as that. Since you had told me that under no circumstances were you prepared to pay any more, I saw no purpose in wasting your time with a telephone call. You had been most insistent, as I remember, that you should not be pressured in any way.'

Mr Jones glared at him with a kind of baffled malignancy. His undershot jaw was thrust further forward, his lower lip pulling slightly down to reveal the yellowing, crooked teeth that met tip to tip with the upper ones.

'Don't you go putting words into my mouth! I know what I said! So you didn't bother to tell them about my offer?'

'Not at all, Mr Jones. As I said before, I told the owners that you were thinking of making the offer, and they informed me that if you did so, it would not be acceptable.'

'But I'm a cash buyer!'

'Even so, I'm afraid. They have now accepted another offer, in fact.'

'Oh yes? How much?'

'I am afraid I am not at liberty to disclose that, Mr Jones. Suffice it to say that it was substantially higher than yours.'

'Influenced by you, I suppose! You agents, you're always trying to push the price up!'

'If I were selling your house, Mr Jones, wouldn't you want me to get the best price I could for it?'

Paul Jones glowered.

'I wouldn't want you to get any kind of price. Catch me using an agent to sell my house! Did it myself last time, sold my house in Beech Road in three days.'

'Well done. What did you get for it?'

Paul Jones bridled, but told him. Paul, whose memory for such things was phenomenal, cast back and worked out that the house should have been worth at least ten thousand more.

'That sounds very moderate,' he said in an admiring tone. As had happened before, Mr Jones listened to the tone rather than the meaning of the words. He looked as pleased as it was possible for him to do.

On the whole, thought Paul as his irritating customer left, there had been some satisfaction in the exchange. When the telephone rang again he picked it up jauntily.

'Hensham Homes, good afternoon?'

'Daddy! It's me! I mean, it's us!'

'Dizzy darling! Is everything all right?' Not another miscarriage, or she wouldn't be sounding so elated. Or saying things like that, surely?

'Yes, everything's fine. More than that. At least, I think so. Brace yourself, Grandpa. It's twins!'

'Twins! You mean . . . *two* babies?'

'Yes.' She was on too much of a high to pick up on this remarkably silly question. Melanie was staring at him, her face breaking into a wide smile. 'They didn't realise before – one of them was hiding the other one, or something. But this time there they were on the scan, I've seen them, Daddy, it's just . . . just miraculous!' Her voice was husky with emotion, and he felt his own throat tighten in sympathy.

'It's like, well, it's like a kind of bonus, to make up for the miscarriages. Like getting them both back again, in a way.'

'And feeling okay? Not too uncomfortable?'

'No, not yet, though of course I'm bound to get very big. But they say everything's going right, no sign of any blood-pressure problems or anything. Of course they'll probably be born a bit early, that's normal with twins, but the doctor said they were the liveliest he'd seen for a long time!'

'Oh, Dizzy, I'm so happy for you. And is Jeremy pleased?'

Dizzy sounded rather shamefaced.

'As a matter of fact, he doesn't know yet. He was supposed to be coming to the clinic with me, but he was summoned by the Big Cheese to discuss some frightfully crucial new client, and I told him not to make waves by saying he couldn't. But I had to tell someone, so I rang you!'

Paul felt extraordinarily flattered. Somehow, being the first person in the family to hear about the twins made them even more special to him. For the first time he really felt like a grandfather. I must do something, he thought. Make them something. I used to be good at woodwork . . . After Dizzy rang off he sat in a happy trance, making little sketches on a piece of paper. When the telephone rang again, he jumped and came back to earth with a bump.

'Mr Kingswood.'

'Mrs Holt! Is everything all right?' Now that the complete chain was set up he had a superstitious terror that something would happen to destroy it.

'How clever of you to know who I am. Yes, everything's fine. I just thought I should tell you that I'm going away for a few days, to stay with my daughter. I'll drop a key off with you, in case you need to get in while I'm not there, for a survey or something.'

'That's great. Thanks for letting me know. You'd be amazed how many people think that once they've found a buyer, it's all over. Um . . . who's looking after Archimedes? Does he go to a – what? A parrotry?'

'I'm afraid they don't really exist, for parrots. He'd hate it, anyway. If I'm going to be away for long, I usually get someone to come and live in. As it's only a few days, my cleaning lady will go in every morning and see to him. I'm afraid he gets a bit lonely and crotchety but he'll appreciate me all the more when I get back.'

'Of course. Only I wondered . . . since I'll have the key, perhaps I could drop in on my way home, spend half an hour with him, give him his bath . . . I'd be happy to do it.'

'Well, I know he'd love it, but are you sure? I know how busy you are.'

'Not that busy. And my evenings are my own.'

'Then I accept with the greatest pleasure on his behalf. If you will help yourself to a sherry, or what ever you fancy, as a reward for your good deed . . . ?'

'I don't need a reward, I'd love to spend time with Archimedes. If I bring him some fruit, is that all right?'

'Lovely, but don't spoil him. Archimedes is very keen to develop champagne tastes at my expense. Should I give you Beth's number, in case you need me?'

Paul felt himself blush, and was glad he was on the telephone.

'As a matter of fact, I've already got it. I, er, I gather you're making the house over to her?'

'Yes. It seemed like a good idea. In all sorts of ways.'

With this slightly cryptic remark, she rang off.

Chapter Sixteen

'Louise.'

Jason stood in the doorway of the sitting room. He never voluntarily entered any room where she was, halting in the entrance as if at some invisible force-field. She knew very well that he did it out of consideration for her but it still made her edgy. Her deep-seated lack of confidence made her feel that he couldn't bear to be in the same room as her, and she hated herself, and therefore him, for minding. She spoke without looking up at him.

'Come in, for goodness sake, if you've got something to say.' When he did approach she allowed herself to flinch away from him and felt a fierce little flame of pleasure at the pain he was not quick enough to mask. 'What is it?'

'As they say on the soap operas,' he said lightly. 'I think we need to talk.'

'I don't see that there's anything to talk about.' As the words left her mouth, Louise saw in her mind's eye Ruth's furious face. You're a fine one to talk, said her look.

'I'm sorry about the baby. Both the babies.'

The colour drained from Louise's face so rapidly that he put out his hands to support her. This time, when she flinched from his touch, the movement was involuntary and for some reason he did not find it so hurtful.

'Here, sit down.' He guided her into a chair. Louise put her head down to her knees and waited until the grey buzzing had abated. She licked dry lips.

'How did you know?'

'Someone at the hospital mentioned it. One of the midwives – it was on your notes and she just assumed I would know. Of course that sort of thing shouldn't happen, but busy people make mistakes. Oh, Louise, what happened? Can't you tell me about it?'

'What's to tell?' Her voice was dreary. 'I was pregnant, and you didn't want the baby, so I got rid of it.'

There was silence. If Louise had expected denials, she did not get them.

'You were right,' he said at last. Louise, astonished, looked at him for the first time, her mouth falling open in amazement.

175

'You were right,' he repeated. 'I'm not saying you did the right thing – how could I, my own baby? But you were right that I didn't want it. All those excuses I made, about money and not being ready – they were just a cover up. The truth is, I'd have been so jealous I don't think I could have borne it.'

'Jealous?' Louise's throat had closed so tight the word was scarcely audible. 'Jealous? Who'd you be jealous of? It would have been your baby!'

'Yes, I know. Of course I don't mean I'd have thought it was someone else's. I'd have been jealous of the baby, that's all.'

'But . . . why?'

Louise felt that she had somehow strayed into some kind of surreal other world, where familiar words had unfamiliar meanings.

'Because you'd have loved the baby more than me.'

The quiet words rang through her head like a tocsin. Louise shook her head, unable to speak.

'I'd never had anyone else, before, who really loved *me*,' he said quietly. 'The real me, not just because I was good looking or whatever. Someone who understood where I came from, who spoke the same language. Someone who knew what it was like to be rejected. Someone who hadn't had a family, who hadn't even had one of those "single mums" they're always going on about. Single mums! I'd have given my soul for a single mum of my own, even if we did have to live off social security in a B & B. Being married to you, belonging together, it was like . . . I don't know . . . like a dream come true.'

'But you didn't love me!'

Again, she did not get the answer she expected.

'Perhaps not. But only because I didn't really know you. That part of what I said was true enough. But I loved the *idea* of you, if you like. I just didn't know how to tell you. And I was afraid, if I did, that you wouldn't want me any more. And I was right, wasn't I?'

'No, no, it wasn't like that! I thought you just didn't care about me, that you were just being kind to me because you were stuck with me. You didn't seem to mind what I said, nothing touched you, you never got angry or anything.'

'I couldn't.' He struggled, the effort to reveal his feelings apparent in his face. 'Being angry, showing my anger . . . it terrifies me. The more I feel, the less I show.'

'But you didn't even seem to mind when I said I was having someone else's baby.'

'Oh, Louise.' Amazingly, he was smiling, though his eyes were pink rimmed. 'I am a nurse, after all.'

'You mean . . . you knew it was yours?'

'Well, I was pretty sure. All that messing about with tampons . . . but you didn't wear those old knickers you usually keep for then, and

176

you just didn't seem like you generally are when you have the curse. Besides, I didn't see how you could have managed it without me noticing you were seeing someone else. Even if it was happening at work – and don't forget, I know everyone at the hotel pretty well – it just didn't feel right, if you know what I mean. I may not always understand what you're thinking, but I do know you pretty well. You just never behaved like someone with a lover.'

Louise gave a wan smile.

'I suppose not. So, why didn't you say anything? Why go along with the separation, and everything?'

This time it was his turn to shake his head.

'I didn't know what to say to you. You seemed so angry all the time, and then I thought I'd raped you that night, and that was why . . . I was frightened of pushing you. At least while you were still living here in the same house, there was some hope of sorting things out. I kept thinking that one day something would happen that would give me a chance to talk to you. And it has, I suppose. Only I wish it wasn't that, not our baby . . .'

Somehow, without knowing quite how it had happened, Louise found that he was holding her hand.

'You didn't rape me, you must know that. I wanted it as much as you did. That was one of the things I was angry about, really. I thought my body had betrayed me, but I suppose my instincts were wiser than my brain. But then, the next day, you were so strange that I thought you were disgusted by me, that you thought your body had betrayed *you*. So I thought I had to choose, that I couldn't have you and the baby. I chose the baby, this time, but I kept thinking I'd been wrong . . . there were times when I hated the baby for making me choose, and then when I lost it . . . it felt like it was my fault. I've been so stupid. And so horrible to you.'

'No more stupid than me. There now, is that another thing we have in common? Our poor children are going to find us very irritating.'

He felt her shudder.

'I feel in such a muddle. I never thought this would happen. What are we going to do? What about the house? Those people want to buy it. Are we going to tell them they can't?'

He stroked her back with his hand, a gesture she always found soothing and which now made her almost melt.

'Only if you really feel desperate to stay here. But I think perhaps it's time we moved on – in all senses of the word. Let's buy that other house, if you like it.'

'Only if you like it too.'

'Only if I like it too.'

'Are we really going to do it, then?'

177

Ruth stifled her irritation. 'Not if you *really* don't want to,' she said deviously. 'I don't want you to be frightened, or anything.'

'I'm not frightened exactly,' Harriet countered quickly. 'It's not that. It's just . . . well, I don't know, it's not something I ever thought *I* would do. Running away, I mean.'

'This isn't running away.' Ruth put every ounce of reasonable persuasiveness she could muster into her voice. 'Running away is going to London, living on the streets and begging and things. This isn't like that, we've got somewhere to go, somewhere that's not too far away, and it's perfectly safe. You know it is. This is a protest.'

'I know, but . . .'

'Running away is for people who don't know what to do. People who protest are people with a cause, something to fight for. You know, like the road protesters. Just think – they lived in trees, all out in the cold and the wet. We've got a nice little house to go to.'

'Yes . . .'

'And think of all the trouble we've gone to, getting it ready. I even went and bought the camping gas for the light and the stove, and you got all that food . . .'

'Mm . . .' This was a powerful argument. The trouble was that the imaginative Harriet had found it all too easy to get carried away by the sheer fun of planning it all. It was like bringing an adventure story to life, like having a day-dream. Oh, the pleasure of making those lists and gradually assembling the things – ground-sheets and cushions and sleeping bags, candles and matches and camping gas appliances (taken from the depths of the understair cupboard by Ruth, whose parents had once been intrepid campers). The water bottles, the packets of soup and dehydrated meals, the cunning little saucepans that fitted inside one another. The joy of suddenly remembering something, like a tin-opener and of Ruth's praise when she did so.

They had smuggled their collection into the shelter, on Saturday afternoon when Mrs Holt was 'putting her feet up'. They had picnicked there, once even using the camping stove to cook a meal, and it had been like a cross between the *Famous Five* and playing in a Wendy House. It had been so much fun that Harriet had completely forgotten, or had managed to edge out of her mind, the serious purpose behind it all.

Now, however, the preparations were finished. It was Saturday afternoon, and the two girls were in Harriet's bedroom. Georgie had gone to visit a school-friend with a pony, a friendship encouraged by Christine who was too thankful to have Harriet safely occupied with someone to wonder why a girl of Ruth's age should want to spend so much time with someone at least three years younger. Christine was happily occupied in the sitting room with a batch of new interior design books that she had had sent from a specialist shop in London. She was physically present, but her mind was busily roaming round the new house trying out colour schemes.

'Not today,' said Harriet. 'We can't go today. It's Daddy's birthday, we're having a special supper.'

'No, no, not today,' Ruth soothed. 'Tomorrow. Monday morning. We go off to school as usual, only it won't be as usual. You get taken in the car, right?'

'Yes . . .'

'Well, don't worry about that. I go on the bus, so it's easy. I'll come along to your school, wait near the gates. When your mum's gone, we go. Easy. Then we've got the whole day to get ourselves sorted out. We can lay a false trail – go to the station, or something, so they think we've gone by train. Then we can get down to the hideout and be well out of sight by the time they start looking.'

'But I can't just walk out of the school again! Someone will see me! Besides, we wouldn't have the whole day. Don't they have registration at your school? Everyone will have seen me arriving – if I'm not there when they do the register, there'll be a dreadful fuss.'

Ruth was taken aback. She wasn't used to Harriet standing up to her so firmly. She had to admit that the younger girl was right, too. She hadn't seen the school, but she knew from what Harriet had said that its small classes and protective atmosphere were a world away from her own bustling comprehensive.

'Well, couldn't you wait a bit and then say you feel sick or something?'

'Then they'd ring my mother, and keep me there until she came to fetch me.'

'Fussy, aren't they.' Ruth didn't bother to hide her scorn.

'It wasn't so bad before, but there was a girl in the year below me who was taken away by her father last term. He was German, or something, and they were divorced, he took her back to Germany and her mother blamed the school for letting her go. There was a huge row, it was all in the papers, and after that all the teachers were told not to let us out of their sight. They cancelled a school trip to London, even, and then all the other parents started complaining.'

'Goodness.' Ruth was impressed. 'Did they get her back?'

'Yes, in the end. Her mother went over to Germany and fetched her.'

'Is she still at the school?'

'Yes. Her mother didn't want her to, but she was really upset when she got back home and the doctor said it was important for her to go back to the same place. She still cries a lot.'

'Is she frightened it'll happen again?'

'No. She wants to go back to her father in Germany.'

'Oh. Well, anyway, how can we do it? It's no good waiting until the end of the afternoon. There must be times when people go out of school in the day time. How do they do it?'

Harriet thought.

'A girl in my class went to the dentist, the other week. Her mother was late, so they sent a taxi for her.'

'A taxi. I wonder . . . it wouldn't be too expensive, if it wasn't too far. How much money have we got left?'

'Not much.' Harriet scrabbled for her purse, and they examined their resources. 'I could break my piggy bank.' She looked at the china pig on her windowsill. It had her name painted on it, in a little wreath of flowers. It had been a present from her godmother, and it had no opening other than the narrow slot in its back. Ruth picked up the pig, and shook it. It gave a satisfyingly heavy clinking sound.

'What about a knife? Sometimes you can get the coins to slide out that way.'

Harriet shook her head.

'I tried that, last Christmas. You can only get the little ones, fives and ones. All the others are too fat.'

'We'd better leave it, then.' Ruth found that she couldn't bring herself to push Harriet too hard. The trouble was, the younger girl was too malleable. Ruth knew very well that she could make her break the piggy bank, but there was something about Harriet's very defencelessness that made Ruth feel protective, almost motherly, towards her. 'I'll think of something.'

Had she known it, she could not have picked a better way of persuasion. Harriet, braced for a forceful attack, crumbled in the face of this moderation. Without giving herself time to think she took the pig from Ruth's hand, and cracked it smartly against the edge of the bedside table, with the same brisk movement her mother used when breaking an egg. The pig obliged by flying into several pieces mixed up with a heap of coins.

The destruction of the pig marked the turning point for Harriet. He could not, she felt obscurely, die in vain. She put aside all her doubts and fears, and addressed her considerable intelligence to making sure that their escape went smoothly.

Beep beep. Beep beep.

'Hensham Homes, good morning? Mr Kingswood? Yes, he is. I'll put you through.' Rose's finger stabbed the button. 'It's the woman from Shakespeare Court.' Her face was heavy with disapproval. Paul picked up his own phone.

'Paul!'

'Hello, Shelley. Everything all right?'

'Well, I dunno, Paul. We got problems with our mortgage.'

It was bound to happen, thought Paul. I knew it was all going too smoothly.

'What sort of problems, Shelley?'

'They won't give us one, will they.'

'Won't give you one? Why not?'

'I dunno. We got this letter.'

Past experience made Paul wary. People who had been refused mortgages were usually a bit cagey about saying why, usually because they had some kind of unresolved problem with their credit record. Like having county Court Judgments, or being undischarged bankrupts. Although nowadays the lending companies were so neurotic it sometimes appeared that they would turn someone down for eating the wrong kind of breakfast cereal.

'Let's see, who was arranging your mortgage for you?'

'Friend of Dave's, from down the pub.'

'Yes, of course.' Oh dear, thought Paul. Save me from the friend who offers to do it for you on the cheap. 'And what does he say?'

'Dunno. I rang you first. Ask your advice, like, as it's to do with the house.'

'To do with the house? In what way?'

'Because of the tree in the garden.'

'Ah!' Light dawned. Paul realised with much relief that it was not Shelley and Dave who had been refused a mortgage, but simply that the survey had thrown up a query on the house. 'Tell me, Shelley, did they send you a copy of the survey report?'

'Yes. Dreadful, it is. Might be problems with this, and could be problems with that.'

'Might be and could be aren't the same as "are".'

'Yeah, I know. I was dead worried at first, then I looked at it again and I reckon they was just covering their arses.' She giggled. 'Oops, sorry. Language, Timothy.'

'No problem. You're quite right, too.' Shelley, he reflected, was not short on native wit. Plenty of people more experienced than she had been thrown into complete panic by a report like this. 'So what was this bit about the tree?'

'Said they wanted a specialist report, in case of something or other.'

'Subsidence?'

'If you say so. Yeah. So what do we do?'

'Give them what they want. A report from a tree specialist. It shouldn't be too expensive – I've got a tame one I can contact for you. I might even be able to persuade the Johnsons to chip in with part of the cost. Leave it with me. Everything all right otherwise?'

'Yeah, fine – now that young Louise has found a house. That going okay, is it? Dead cagey, she is, can't get a word out of her about it.'

'Oh yes,' said Paul blithely. 'Yes, that sale's going fine. It's in the bag.' He caught himself clutching at the wooden edge of the desk as he said it. I shouldn't have said that, he thought. Asking for trouble. But the chain was all right, wasn't it? 'Yes,' he said, reassuring himself as much as Shelley. 'Yes. Safe as houses. As you might say.'

Afterwards, looking back, he resolved never to use that phrase again.

Ring ring. Ring ring. Ring ring. Ring ring.

'Hello?' Philippa spoke warily. George, she knew, was safely in London for a regimental reunion lunch. He had left in good time that morning, and Philippa had seen him go with very mixed feelings. Rather to her surprise he had refrained from teasing her about the health farm, merely telling her to have a good time, and not to overdo that dieting nonsense.

'Ridiculous, at our time of life. You look very nice as you are. Matter of fact, you've always looked nice. To me, anyway.'

'Oh, George!' Philippa had blinked back a rush of tears. 'Such praise! Still, there's always room for improvement, isn't there?'

'Hrrmph. Well, I'll see you soon, anyway.'

Philippa resisted an urge to cling to him and blurt out where she was really going. She watched him walk down the path to the garage, then listened to the sound of his car receding as he drove away. She shivered, and felt very alone. For the first time ever the house seemed too large, too empty for her. She found herself thinking with gratitude of the little bungalow, and took herself briskly upstairs to fetch her overnight bag.

When the bedside telephone rang, she jumped. It couldn't be George, of course. He was on the train. One of the children, ringing for a chat? Not likely, at this time of day – the evening was their time, when work was finished, children were in bed, and calls were cheaper. Not, she begged silently, *not* the hospital to say that her operation was cancelled, her bed no longer available. She was aware that by turning down the earlier appointment she had put herself in a weak position.

'Philippa?' A woman's voice, familiar. 'It's Alice Holt.'

After saying goodbye to George, the pretended trip to the health farm was still real in her mind and she found herself feeling faintly apologetic for not being ready to leave.

'I'm just ringing to wish you luck,' said Alice warmly.

'Oh, thank you!' Philippa was touched.

'Well, since I'm the only person who knows, it's the least I can do. How do you feel?'

'All right. Not as nervous as I thought I would be. It all seems a bit unreal.'

'Got something to read? It's all hanging around, in my experience. Once you've filled in the forms, that is, and answered all those dreadful questions about your personal habits.'

182

'Yes, I know. I've got a nice cosy Maeve Binchy book – not too demanding, and wonderfully relaxing.'

'Good. Well, I'll be leaving in a little while, for my daughter's. I gave you the number, didn't I? Do give me a ring, let me know how you get on.'

'I will. And . . . thank you.' Philippa was unable to find the words but Alice was cheerfully brisk.

'No need to thank me, I'm looking forward to going. It will be nice to get away for a few days, have a change of scene. Not that I don't love this place, but . . . I'm beginning to feel it's time to leave, if you know what I mean.'

'I know. I'm beginning to feel the same.'

'That's good. I like to think of you living here.'

'So do I.' I like to think of me living, full stop, thought Philippa.

'Well, that nice Mr Kingswood is going to pop in while I'm away, to visit the parrot, so the bungalow will be well looked after. Not that we have much trouble round here. Not many break-ins and of course you don't need to worry about things like squatters, not like in the cities. So it'll all be here for you, when you're ready.'

'Yes. That's rather a comforting thought. Thank you.'

Beep beep. Beep beep.

'Hello? Oh, hello Louise. How are you?'

'I'm all right.' Liz thought that Louise sounded surprised to hear herself saying this. Her voice was different – lighter, more alive.

'You sound better. Is that vitamins, Prozac or lurve? It can't be the weather.' Liz glanced at the window, against which the wind and rain beat relentlessly. Louise gave a giggle.

'As a matter of fact, I think it's lurve.'

'Goodness, how exciting! Do you mean you've met someone else?'

'No, it's Jason. We had a talk, and sorted a few things out. As a matter of fact, it's partly thanks to your Ruth. She told me I should stop faffing around and talk to him and, thanks to her, I did.'

'Goodness,' said Liz carefully. 'I'd never actually seen Ruth as a counsellor.'

'Well, I had the nerve to tell her what I thought she should be doing, and nobody could have been making more of a mess of things than I was, so why shouldn't she have a turn? I was in just as much of a muddle inside as she is and with far less reason, really. Looking at where she was going wrong helped me to see that in some way I was doing just the same – I had an idea fixed in my head, and I twisted everything Jason did and said to fit in with it. I can't believe I was so stupid.'

Liz sighed. 'The light on the road to Damascus, in fact. I wish Ruth could have a revelation too.' She caught herself up. 'Anyway,

I'm delighted for you. So, do you want to come and have another look, show it to Jason?'

'Yes, that's what I was ringing about. I must have been in a bit of a fog when I came before, I find I've forgotten how the rooms are.'

'I hope he won't hate it.'

Louise sounded surprised. 'No, I'm sure he won't. I really feel this is the right house for me. For us. I just want him to see it too and to have a clearer picture of it in my mind and, perhaps, do a bit of measuring up.'

'That's all right, then. Not that I want to put pressure on you, or anything, of course. I just dread the thought of going through that round of people wanting to come and view, and trying to fix it so that I'll be here but Ruth won't, and all that.'

'Oh yes, Ruth. I've been thinking of her so much, and feeling rather bad about her. How has she been?'

'Well,' Liz spoke cautiously, 'she's been a bit easier, as a matter of fact. Surprising really but I think perhaps she's beginning to come to terms with the whole thing, to accept that we're going to move. I couldn't really say she's been nicer, exactly, but she's been a lot less nasty. Mostly she ignores me, which isn't too bad, and I think she must be getting more involved in her school work, she's always up in her room writing.'

'That must make it easier for you.'

'Yes, much. And she's made a friend, too, so she's out much more. Strange, really, it's the little girl who lives in the house we're buying, and she must be at least three years younger than Ruth. Funny little thing, very bright, I believe, and rather shy but perfectly nice. Ruth's taken to going there quite a lot, which must be a good sign, don't you think? At least she's getting to know the new house, getting to feel at home in it, which must be a step forward.'

'That's extraordinary. You'd think it would be the last place she'd want to be. Still, it's good if she's got a friend, even if there is an age difference.'

'Yes. I really think we've turned the corner now. I think Ruth is finally accepting the move. Who knows, in time she may even come to accept me!'

184

Chapter Seventeen

Alec Blake was sitting in Paul's office when his mobile telephone rang. He had called in to discuss the valuing of an Edwardian house similar to one that Paul had sold six months earlier and stayed for a cup of tea. They had spent a pleasant half hour inveighing against the iniquities of the Government's handling of interest rates, from which they had moved to fish (the Government's iniquities in handling the fish quota), to Hong Kong (the Government's iniquities in the hand-over to China) and from there, for no apparent reason, to music. When the phone rang they were deep in the relative merits of Haydn and Mozart, and it took them a few moments to come back to earth.

'Sorry,' said Alec, fishing in his coat pockets. 'Bloody awful things, I hate them.'

'Necessary evil,' agreed Paul, turning courteously away while Alec answered his call. For all that, it was impossible not to hear Christine's voice, high and tense, as she spoke.

'Alec? Have you got Harriet with you?'

Alec's first thought was astonishment that she should have shortened his name – she hadn't called him anything but Alexander for years. Then he noticed that against her usual habit she had failed to shorten Harriet's name as she usually did. The wrongness of it worried him more than the question itself.

'No, of course not. Was I supposed to pick her up?' He was fairly sure he wouldn't have forgotten – he loved collecting the girls from school, having them to himself in the car and hearing their stories of the school.

'No. Oh God, Alec, she's gone.' Her voice rose in panic. Alec felt a sick lurch in his stomach, but damped his own voice down, flattening it deliberately to the slow, deep tone he found useful when defusing arguments with awkward clients.

'Steady on. Tell me just what happened. You went to collect her from school?'

'Yes, as usual. And I waited outside for ages, because I thought she was just being slow – you know how dreamy she can be. In the end I sent Georgie back in to tell her to hurry up, but she couldn't find her. I couldn't go in – I was on a double yellow line, and you know how difficult they are about parking round there – so I sent Georgie back to ask her teacher. Harry's teacher. And she came out and said she wasn't there, she hadn't been there since the middle of the morning when she went off to the dentist. She was horrible, all sniffy and cross, saying that I should really have sent a proper note in with Harriet instead of a last minute phone call, it was awful, I didn't know what to say because I knew she wasn't going to the dentist and I hadn't telephoned and she just looked at me as if she thought I was lying to her, it was so awful, and then she said I'd better come and check with the office, so I went in but the secretary had gone home, wretched woman, and all there was was a note to say that someone had telephoned about Harriet going to the dentist and a taxi coming for her, and the teacher said Harriet seemed to know all about it, and perhaps it was you that fixed it up, and she looked at me so strangely so I said yes, that must be it, and now I'm at home and she's not here . . . Oh Alec, you don't think she's been kidnapped, do you?'

'No, no, surely not. We're not in that league, surely. Um . . . have you called the police?'

'The police!' Her voice rose to a shriek. 'So you do think she's been kidnapped, then? Oh, God . . .'

'No, no, no,' he soothed. 'Not kidnapped, no. But she *is* missing, we must inform the police.'

'But the police . . . It's so . . .' Christine struggled for words, unable to express her feelings; because they were in such turmoil. If anyone had ever asked her, she would have assured them that she was equally devoted to both her children, and she would have done her best to believe it but deep down, she would have known that Georgie was her favourite. Now, faced with Harriet's disappearance, a little worm of guilt and self-doubt was stirring within her. It was not a feeling that she was accustomed to. Christine, like Georgie, lived her life very much on a practical level. She had no time and saw no necessity to look below the surface. Self-analysis, in her book, was another name for self-indulgence.

If it had been Georgie who had disappeared Christine would have been frightened and distraught, and certainly angry, but she would not have panicked as she was now doing. Georgie was like herself, practical, level-headed, a survivor. She was perfectly capable of playing a naughty trick like this just for sheer devilment, only to reappear a few hours later, giggling cheerfully and wondering what all the fuss was about. Harriet, on the other hand, was a worrier. Her over-active imagination made her see potential dangers in every situation and the nervousness that sometimes drove Christine wild now made the kind of escapade that Georgie would revel in completely out of character.

Beneath it all was the guilt that Christine could not cope with. It was all the more unbearable because she really didn't know why she should feel guilty. Somewhere along the line, her subconscious mind told her, she had failed her daughter and the feeling was unbearable because unfamiliar. Her usual ordered mind was thrown into turmoil and this inability to think and plan frightened her more than anything else.

'The police . . .' she repeated helplessly. 'It seems so . . . final.' Part of her was still hoping that Harriet was just reading in a corner somewhere, that Christine had somehow just missed her in her search round the house. Calling the police meant admitting to herself that Harriet was truly lost.

Alec drew in a deep breath before answering. He told himself that Christine was in a state of shock, that she scarcely knew what she was saying.

'I'm coming straight home,' he said. 'I'll be with you in a few minutes.'

'We should be out looking . . .'

'Looking where? There's no point in running about the town in a panic. The first thing is to check all the possible places, ring all her friends, find out as much as we can. Why don't you sort out as many phone numbers as you can, start ringing round?'

'Yes. Yes, I should have thought of that.' Christine sounded better now that she had something to do. 'And you'll come straight back?'

'Right away. Try not to worry. I'm sure it's all a mistake, she'll turn up right as rain and wonder what all the fuss was about.'

'Wretched child! I'll *kill* her. Oh, Alec . . . you don't think . . . she hasn't been . . . all those awful stories in the news . . .'

'Don't think about that. Concentrate on finding her.'

Alec came off the telephone. Paul and Melanie were both staring at him, appalled and concerned. Alec grabbed for his coat, searching for his car keys with a shaking hand.

'Sorry. There seems to be a bit of a crisis . . .'

'My dear chap . . . if there's anything we can do . . .'

'Oh, Mr Blake, it's not Harriet, is it? Not your dear little girl?' Melanie's eyes were round and shiny with tears. Alec blinked at her.

'How do you know Harriet? Oh, she came here, didn't she?' The thought encouraged him – this wasn't the first time Harriet had tricked her way out of school and gone on her own private affairs. 'The parrot! You don't think . . . ?'

'Mrs Holt's away,' said Paul tersely, scribbling on the back of one of his cards. 'Look, I'll be here until six, and then I'll go straight home – this is my number. If there's anything I can do . . . Helping with searches, I mean, or telephoning, or something . . .' His voice turned husky, in his mind's eye seeing those clips of television news, lines of concerned neighbours and friends combing the countryside for a missing child that so often, dear God, so hideously often was found

187

mutilated and dead. Or, perhaps even worse, was never found at all.

'Thanks.' Alec took the card and pocketed it. Paul longed to offer comfort and support. He put his hand for a moment on the other man's shoulder, gripping it in the inarticulate way that came naturally to him, wishing they were women so that they could hug one another.

Afterwards, Alec wondered how he had reached his house without crashing. He had no memory of the journey, and thought it likely that he had scarcely slowed down for junctions, never mind stopping and looking. He parked – or rather abandoned – the car in the drive and ran into the house.

'Alec!' Christine was in the hall, just replacing the telephone. 'Oh, Alec!' For the first time in many years she clung to him for support. 'I've rung everyone I can think of, she isn't with any of her friends and none of them know where she is!'

He held her tightly, pushing down his own terror and trying to think.

'The school said there was a telephone call, and a taxi, and that Harriet seemed to know all about it?' he thought aloud. 'That doesn't sound like a kidnap, anyway. Harriet wouldn't go along with anything that wasn't safe.'

'But she's such a dreamer!'

'A dreamer, yes, but she's very sensible. She's also quite nervous of things – she'd be frightened to do anything like going off with a strange adult. And you've always taught them not to go with anyone who says they've come from us, unless they give the code words you agreed with her and Georgie. Where is Georgie, by the way?'

'Upstairs. I told her to have a look in Harriet's room, just in case there was anything there to give us a clue. Not that there's much hope – Mrs Mop does the bedrooms on Mondays, she'll have tidied and cleaned everything.' She gave a sad little smile that moved Alec more than her tears. 'I never thought I'd see the day when I'd regret having such an efficient cleaner,' she said sadly.

Georgie came down the stairs. Her eyes were red and swollen, her cheeks sallow. She too ran to Alec. He picked her up and held her, clasping the solid weight of her firm little body as if she, too, might disappear.

'Oh, Daddy!' She clung to him, her arms hard and her fingers clutching at his hair, his clothes, his neck. He could feel her trembling.

'It's all right, Georgie. It will be all right, don't worry, I'm here, we'll find her. . .' The soothing words flowed on meaninglessly, but Georgie relaxed a little in his arms. She was too young, he thought, to face something like this.

'Would you like to do something to help, Georgie?' She nodded. 'Well, poor Mummy's very upset. I think a nice cup of tea might help her, make her feel better, don't you? Do you think you can put the kettle on, get things organised?' She nodded again, and he kissed the top of her head. 'Good girl. You go and do that, and I'll take care of Mummy and everything. All right?' He put her down, and she ran to the kitchen looking, he was glad to see, less anxious now that she could help. While she was out of the room Alec telephoned the police.

'They'll come straight round,' he said quietly to Christine. She sat down suddenly on the stairs, putting her head down to her knees. 'We have to tell them,' he said gently, going to sit beside her and putting his arm around her. 'We need their help, everyone's help.'

'I know.' She shuddered. 'It's just . . . I feel so helpless.'

'I know. It's a nightmare. Shall we ring Mrs Moppett, while we're waiting, ask her if she saw anything when she did Harriet's room?' Christine nodded hopelessly, but did not stir. Alec telephoned, then came back to Christine.

'She's coming straight round. She sounded very upset.' Christine looked at him in dismay. 'I couldn't stop her. She wants to help.'

It was only a few minutes before Mrs Moppett arrived. She looked strangely unlike herself in a pair of leggings and a baggy pullover – she always came to work in a sensible skirt and blouse, with an overall to protect them. She carried a plastic carrier which she held tightly, twisting the handles between nervous fingers.

'Mrs Blake, dear, I'm so sorry, poor little Harriet, whatever can have happened to her?'

Alec shook his head slightly, and nodded towards the kitchen. It occurred to him that it might be a good thing having Mrs Moppett here – her familiar presence might well be able to comfort Georgie while he and Christine were busy with the police.

'Georgie's just making a cup of tea for us all,' he said.

'That's nice.' Mrs Moppett was quick to take his hint. 'I'll go and see if she needs a hand, only I brought this.' She indicated the bag she carried, without giving it to them. Her manner was anxious. 'Oh, Mrs Blake, I'm sorry if I did wrong, only when I did Harriet's room this morning I found her piggy bank broken in her bin I thought she must have had an accident and I picked out the pieces because they weren't too bad, and I thought I'd have a go at gluing it together for her.'

Christine stared at the cleaning lady as if she were speaking in Mandarin.

'That was very good of you, Mrs Moppett,' said Alec. 'I know Harriet will be grateful.' He was hiding his impatience with difficulty, listening out for the police car to arrive.

'Yes, but that wasn't it. Thing is, there was an envelope on her table, and I thought . . . I thought . . .' She scrabbled in her pocket for a handkerchief and snuffled into it. 'I thought she was worried about breaking the pig, you see, afraid that Mrs Blake would be . . .

189

well, and when I saw the envelope with Mummy on it I thought it was to say sorry, sort of, and I thought if I stuck the pig carefully it wouldn't notice where it was broken, and nobody need know, so I . . . so I put the envelope in her drawer, you see, and I was going to tell her she needn't be frightened about it, we could keep it a secret from . . . well, I never thought . . . I only wanted to help her, poor little thing . . .'

Christine was already on her feet and running up the stairs to Harriet's room. Alec took the plastic carrier from Mrs Moppett's shaking hands. He took out the ball of newspaper and gently unwrapped it. The pieces of pig were all there, its face with the slightly quizzical expression looking up at him. He turned the pieces with careful fingers. Harriet's name, painted in gold within the little wreath of flowers, had been carefully glued together so that only a faint hairline crack could be seen running through the middle of it. Mrs Moppett gave a sob, and put her handkerchief up to her face again.

'I only . . . I only wanted . . .' she said, hiccupping. 'She was always polite to me,' she burst out. 'I was . . . I was sorry for her . . .'

Christine came rushing down the stairs, clutching a piece of paper. 'She's all right! She's all right! She's gone with Ruth!'

Alec took the note from her, and read it, frowning.

'Dear Mummy and Daddy,' in Harriet's sprawling handwriting. Her thoughts always ran so far ahead of her hand that her writing was all over the place. 'Please don't worry about me, I'm fine and I'm not by myself, I'm with Ruth who is much older so we're perfectly safe. I'm sorry but I don't want to move to a big house with horses and tennis courts and have to go to boarding school, and this is a protest to show that I really mean it. Please don't be cross with me, if it's all right you can put a notice in the paper and we'll come back, lots of love, Harriet. PS, *please* don't be cross.'

'Who's Ruth?' asked Alec, confused.

'She's that older girl, you know, the one whose parents want to buy this house. She's been round several times, and they've been going for walks together.' Christine was frowning. 'But I called them! They said they hadn't seen Harriet, and they never said anything about Ruth not being there! Do you think they're . . . do you think there's something funny about them?'

'I wouldn't have thought they were child abductors, or anything like that,' he soothed. 'Let's give them another ring.'

Liz was alone in the house when the telephone rang. Afterwards she was convinced that she had felt a shiver of premonition at the sound, at the time her first thought was that it would be Joss, ringing to say that his football training session had finished early. She sighed, getting up from the sofa where she had been enjoying half an hour with her feet up and a cup of tea, and remembered guiltily that she hadn't even started thinking about preparing supper yet.

Expecting to hear Joss, she could not at first take in who Christine was or what she was asking.

'I'm afraid you have the wrong number,' she said. 'There's no one called Harriet here.'

The woman at the other end launched into a garbled explanation, interrupting herself with frantic questions.

'Ruth?' Liz picked out the one name in the jumble of words. 'You want Ruth? I'm afraid she's not back from school yet.' She glanced at her watch – it was later than she had thought. She tried to remember whether Ruth had said she had something happening after school; very often now she seemed to need to go to the library to look something up. Liz had never checked up on this, feeling that she had to display some trust in Ruth.

There was the sound of voices in the background, and then the muffled crackling sounds that indicated that the other telephone was being transferred. A man spoke.

'Mrs Hartwell? Alec Blake here.'

'Blake? You mean, the house in Oak Hill? The one we're buying?'

'That's right. Our daughter Harriet . . .'

'Has made friends with Ruth,' finished Liz. 'Sorry, I didn't catch on straight away. Is there some kind of problem?'

'I'm afraid there is.' His voice was heavy. Liz felt as though it entered through her ear and sank, like a stone, to the middle of her body where it sat cold and hard and implacable. 'Do you know where Ruth is?'

'She's not back from school. I thought she'd gone to the library.'

'Is that what she told you?'

'No. She didn't tell me anything. I just assumed it.' Liz was embarrassed. She thought she sounded as though Ruth was allowed to do whatever she liked, that nobody bothered to make sure she was all right. 'She's a very sensible girl,' she heard herself making the excuse. 'I've never had to worry about her. Well, not in that way, at least.'

He sighed. 'Well, I'm afraid we're going to have to start worrying now. She and Harriet have run away.'

'Run away? Why? Where to?' Liz immediately realised what an idiotic question that was, but her brain felt numb. 'I'm sorry, that was such a stupid thing to say. I'm just . . . I don't know what to say.'

'I know. I suppose your husband isn't home?'

'No. I'll call him at once. We must go and look for them . . .'

'Hang on. No point in rushing out in a panic. Harriet left us a letter, but unfortunately we've only just found it. I suppose Ruth didn't leave anything?'

Liz looked wildly round the hall. She knew there was nothing there,

or in the other downstairs rooms, but . . . Ruth's bedroom? She seldom
went in there, even to clean. Ruth had made it clear that she would
clean the room herself, rather than have her private place polluted by
the presence of her step-mother.

'I'll check her room,' she said. 'Don't go away . . .'

Running up the stairs was like running up the Empire State Building
– the stairs seemed to go on for ever. Ruth's room was tidy, the carpet
hoovered and the photographs and ornaments carefully arranged on
her dressing table. A space in the middle marked the place where a
framed photograph of the late Mary Hartwell had stood. In its place
was an envelope. Nothing was written on it, but it was sealed shut.
Liz ripped it open and ran her eyes over the short, scrawled note.

Running back down the stairs she tripped, and only saved herself
from falling by grabbing at the bannisters. By the time she reached
the telephone again she was shaking and breathless.

'A note in her bedroom,' she said, her voice hoarse and shaking.
'Didn't see it before.'

'Sit down,' he said soothingly. 'Catch your breath. You're having a
baby, aren't you? You must be careful.'

'I'm all right. She says . . . oh, blast the little cow . . . sorry, she's
just such a nightmare, she hates me . . . she says she's not going to
come back until we say we won't sell the house and move. She says
they're quite safe and we're not to worry. Or rather, her father's not
to worry, she doesn't mention me. I suppose she thinks I wouldn't
care, or else she just likes to think of getting me in a panic . . . sorry,
I'm so sorry. It's not Harriet's fault, I'm sure of it, she's so much
younger and Ruth can be very domineering, oh *damn* her, how could
she do this? Where the *hell* can they be?'

'Harriet said much the same thing. At least they're together, and it
sounds as though they've found somewhere to hide out. At least they're
not roaming the streets of London or Brighton.' He hoped it was
true. Surely Harriet had more sense than to do that? She was a nervous
little thing, he couldn't imagine her agreeing to do anything so
frightening.

Remembering her peaky little face, her skinny body and those
anxious eyes, he felt his heart melt with tenderness. That she could
have been worried enough to be driven – or even led – to do anything
like this filled him with anguish and guilt. Couldn't she have talked to
him, if she was that worried and unhappy? Honesty compelled him
to confront the fact that he would probably not have understood the
depth of Harriet's dismay at her mother's plans for their future. He
certainly would have been unlikely to have confronted Christine over
the matter.

'I must call my husband,' said Liz.

'Yes, of course. We should keep these lines as free as possible,

192

anyway, in case they try to ring. Do you have a mobile phone?'

'No, but Mike does.'

'Good. Give me that number, and I'll give you the number for mine.'

Liz rang Mike. Unable to find a gentle way of breaking to him that his daughter had run away, she told him the bald facts.

'Are you all right?' In the midst of her worry she felt a little glow of warmth that he could spare some thought for her.

'Yes, I'm all right. Sort of.'

'I know. I'm on my way, I'll be with you as quickly as possible.'

The next few hours passed in a kind of blur. Liz telephoned the mother of Joss's best friend, who willingly said she would collect him from football training and keep him overnight.

'If there's anything we can do . . . would you like me to come over, be with you?'

'That's so kind.' Liz blinked away hovering tears. 'I think I'd better say no, though. It's better for Joss to keep everything as normal as possible, don't you think?'

'Poor old Joey.' Her son and Joss had been friends for years. 'He's been through a fair bit in his short life, hasn't he? Don't worry, I'll keep him as long as you want. Um, if you need people to help look . . .'

Liz shuddered.

'Thank you . . .' She sat down on the stairs, unable to leave the vicinity of the phone, waiting for Mike. When he came in he hugged her briefly, keeping one arm tightly around her while he read Ruth's note.

'Have you called the police?'

'No. They've done that. The other girl's parents. I expect they'll be here any minute.'

They sat down on the stairs together. Liz leaned against his sturdy warmth.

'I'm sorry,' she said awkwardly. He gave her a little shake.

'Not your fault. If anything, it's mine. I should have seen this coming. I kept hoping things would settle down, that she'd come to her senses. I should have done something about it, perhaps got her some professional help. I always had the feeling that things were worse than you were letting on, but I didn't ask – I suppose I was trying not to know. It wasn't fair on you' He scrubbed his face with his hand, as if clearing something sticky and clogging from it.

'You're not to blame,' she reassured him. 'You did your best, you always supported me.'

'Of course I did! You're my wife! Not just a kind of glorified nanny for the kids! I want you for me, not for them, and if that makes me a selfish bastard, then that's what I am.' He sighed, and Liz echoed his sigh though there was a little patch of warmth in her mind that she thought would never leave her, whatever might happen.

The police were brisk, courteous, and gave the unspoken impression that this was likely to be a storm in a teacup, and that the girls' parents were largely to blame for their children's behaviour. They took away a photograph of Ruth, and promised wearily to institute an inquiry at any of the places where the girls might have been seen.

'Railway station, bus station, shopping mall, cinema, recreation ground . . .' they intoned, a familiar list to them. They left looking efficient but bored. Mike used his mobile to telephone Alec Blake, and they arranged that the two men should go out to look for the girls, while Liz and Christine stayed at home in case of telephone calls.

Liz spent the first hour checking Ruth's room, and on the advice of the police she also checked for what might be missing from the rest of the house. She was very encouraged to find that both the sleeping bags had gone from their place at the back of the linen cupboard. The understair cupboard, too, looked as though someone had been rummaging in it. Liz, who had checked in there recently so that she would have some idea of what she was going to have to clear out when they moved, soon realised that the camping lamp and stove had also gone. She risked a quick call to Christine.

'Yes? Harriet, is that you?'

'I'm sorry, Mrs Blake. It's Liz Hartwell. Ruth's . . . Ruth's step-mother.'

'Oh, yes.' Christine's voice was icy. 'Have you heard from her? Did she say what she's done with Harriet?'

'No, I haven't. Mrs Blake, I'm sorry that this has happened. I think Ruth is to blame, and of course we're responsible for Ruth. She still hasn't got over her mother's death, and I'm afraid she's very bitter against me, and the new baby.'

'I should have known.' Christine had scarcely listened to her. 'I should have known there was something odd about it, her coming round all the time when she's so much older than Harriet. It's just . . . they seemed happy together, and I . . . I don't understand Harriet at all, really. I was just glad she was keeping herself occupied, making a friend, even if it was someone so . . . unlikely.'

'I know. I felt the same. That's not why I phoned, though. I've been looking round the house, trying to see if they've taken anything, and they have. Both our old sleeping bags have gone, and the camping stuff – gas lamp, and gas cooker. I think a few tins have gone from the larder, too, though we don't use a great deal of tinned stuff.'

'No . . .' Christine sounded bewildered. Clearly she couldn't see the point of what Liz was saying.

'Don't you see? At least it means they planned this. They must have been preparing for several days, to get all this stuff out, and they must have had somewhere to hide it. Somewhere safe, where they could leave the things. So at least they're not out on the streets, or living rough in London – they wouldn't take camping gear there, surely? I think it's a good sign, it means they're probably safe.'

'Probably.' Christine's voice was sarcastic, but she sounded interested. 'If you call it safe, a thirteen year old and a ten year old camping out, in November. Still, I see what you mean. But where could it be?'

'I don't know. Ruth doesn't tell me anything.'

Christine thought about that.

'Nor does Harriet, I suppose,' she admitted. 'I never thought about it before. Georgie's always chattering on about what she's up to, but Harriet . . . I always thought it was just because she never did anything except sit around with her head in a book.' She fell silent for a moment. 'If we get her back, I'll never tell her off for reading again.' She sounded tearful.

'When,' said Liz firmly.

'What?'

'When you get her back. Not if.'

'Yes.'

'We'd better get off the phone,' said Liz, reluctantly. She had never felt so lonely before.

'Yes. Yes, we must. Will you tell the others, or shall I? About the sleeping bags and things, I mean.'

'I will, if you like. I really think it's a good sign.' Liz put all the encouragement she could muster into her voice.

'Yes. Well . . . goodbye.'

'Goodbye.'

Liz stood for a few moments, watching the telephone and willing it to ring. It remained obstinately silent. In the end she went, drearily, into the kitchen and made a cup of tea which grew cold and formed a skin on top as it sat, undrunk, on the table beside her.

Chapter Eighteen

Paul sat in his office. Melanie had gone home – it was long after closing time. All the other offices in Agents Alley were closed, the bouncy young men had roared off in their Ford Escort Cabriolets to do whatever bouncy young men did to fill up their evenings – Paul had an image of strangely coloured cocktails in crowded bars – and the streets were silent in that limbo time between people going home from work and going out for the evening. Alec called once, briefly, on his mobile.

'You're still there? Good of you. It looks as though it's more of a childish prank than something more serious. She's gone off with that Ruth girl, the one whose parents are buying our house, you remember? They've been quite friendly, getting together at weekends and things. She left a note, Harriet did, I mean, said it was a protest, that she didn't want to move house and do all the things her mother's planned for her.'

'She was worried about the pony. Surely she wouldn't run away just about that?'

'No, that's just part of it. I think boarding school is probably the big worry. I blame myself – I knew it wasn't right for her. I should have put my foot down, let her know she wouldn't have to go away if she hated the idea that much. Anyway, I'm going out looking, and so is Mike Hartwell. Christine and his wife will stay at home, by the telephones.'

'Can I help? Do you want me to go and look?'

'Good of you, but no. The police are out, they more or less told us we were wasting our time, we should leave it to the professionals.'

'Well, ring me if you need anything. I'll be here or at home, you've got the number.'

'Thanks.'

Paul sat on, unable to bear the prospect of going home. His heart smote him when he thought about Harriet. She was so different from his memories of his own daughters, who had been self-sufficient and outgoing from an early age, more like the younger Georgie. Despite this, there had been something infinitely touching, to his way of thinking, about her earnest, slightly anxious expression. Her obvious intelligence, her over-active imagination, and her delight in Archimedes the parrot, were all very endearing to him although he could see how irritating she must sometimes have been to her practical, straightforward mother.

He found it hard to believe that Harriet could be quite so desperate as her actions seemed to imply. The other girl, of course, was an unknown quantity. Paul had scarcely spoken to her, except the one time when he had made the appointment for Louise Johnson to visit the house during which, as he had later heard, Louise had suffered her miscarriage. His image of the girl as a bad influence had been powerfully strengthened by this event, though of course he knew that she couldn't be blamed for Mrs Johnson's troubles. As thin as Harriet, the skinniness which in the younger girl was touching, seemed to him in the older one to indicate something sharp and prickly. He felt that she was powerfully manipulative and was perfectly sure that she was the instigator of this escapade. He only hoped that she was responsible enough to take proper care of Harriet.

The telephone rang a few times, mostly with enquiries for the cinema but one or two for business. He was constantly amazed, on the occasions when he stayed late at the office to work on the VAT or the end of year accounts, that customers showed no surprise at all at getting an answer to a late evening call. Perhaps they thought that he lived above the office, or just assumed that he didn't go home at all, just propped himself up against the filing cabinet like a furled umbrella, waiting to be used again. Or, more probably, they didn't think about it at all. After all, who cared about the social life of a tubby, middle-aged estate agent?

As an antidote to self-pity he phoned both of his daughters. Predictably, neither was at home, but he left messages on their answerphones. They were perhaps slightly more effusive than usual, he was obliged to use answerphones all the time when contacting clients, but had never quite got over the feeling that they were a business tool, lacking in privacy or a personal touch. This time, feeling grateful that each was safe and (presumably) happy, he allowed a certain amount of sentiment to creep into his words.

As he put the telephone down again the door rattled. He looked up, resigned. If he was going to hang around the office, he supposed he might as well have something to do, though it was difficult to imagine that anyone seriously looking to buy or sell a house would be setting about it at this time of the evening. The tall figure outside, however, resolved itself into Roger Selby. Paul beckoned him in. I should have known, he thought. Most people would simply have marched in, whatever the time, since the light was on and the door unlocked. Only Roger Selby would wait, politely, to be invited in.

'Is anything the matter, Mr Kingswood?' He wiped his feet carefully on the mat. 'I was on my way to my evening class, and I saw you were still here. I'm not disturbing you, I hope?'

'Not at all,' said Paul, explaining the circumstances. Roger looked shocked.

'How very dreadful,' he said, shaking his head. 'Two young girls, and on a night like this, too. What can they be thinking of? Their parents must be frantic.'

'Pretty much, I imagine. As a matter of fact, the father of one of them – Harriet, the younger girl – is the surveyor who checked your flat for you.'

'Goodness!' Roger was rather excited at being involved, even if so tenuously, in something so dramatic. He remembered something else. 'Isn't he involved in my chain, too? I thought I remembered you telling me that.'

'Yes – and the other girl, too. She's the daughter of the people that are three up the chain from you. They're selling their house to Mrs Johnson, that Shelley is buying from. I'm afraid you could almost say it's all my fault: the girls met when the parents were looking round your surveyor's house.'

A faint look of alarm crossed Roger's face, which Paul interpreted correctly. Roger Selby, he thought, was too nice a young man to voice any selfish anxiety over the fate of his own purchase when the lives of two children were in jeopardy.

'I'm sure everything will be sorted out,' Paul said soothingly. 'It won't make any difference to the chain.'

Roger smiled ruefully.

'I shouldn't be thinking about that at a time like this,' he said.

'It's only natural. You don't know the girls, after all.'

'No, but . . . I'd like to help, if I can.'

'What about your evening class? What are you studying?'

'Cookery. It was my Mum's idea, said every man should learn to cook.'

'She's quite right. I should be doing the same. Is it a good class?'

Roger's face lit up with enthusiasm. 'Oh yes, very good! We're doing pastry tonight! Not that that matters,' he added, 'if I can help at all.'

'It's very good of you. I believe the police are out searching, and the two fathers, of course. I don't really know why I'm still sitting here, I don't suppose there's anything I can do. No, Mr Selby, you get along to your class. I'm sure everything will soon be all right.'

Roger left. Paul knew that he should do the same. Sitting around the office was pointless, he might just as well go home. Being hungry and tired and uncomfortable wasn't going to help Harriet, and it certainly wasn't going to do him any good. Somehow, though, the thought of eating turned his stomach, even the glass of wine he usually relished in the evening felt like a kind of betrayal. There was Archimedes, of course. He had fully intended to spend at least half an hour with the bird every evening while Mrs Holt was away. But thinking of Archimedes brought Harriet back too clearly. He didn't think he could bear to be in that room remembering her too poignantly, in school uniform bought for growth which had not yet happened. There where she had laughed and been happy. He sat on.

'This is fun,' said Ruth firmly.

'Yes,' Harriet agreed, without much conviction. She looked round the little room in the air-raid shelter. It was true that the earlier part of the day had been great fun. Going off to school had been awful. It had been her father's day to take them, he had been in a particularly jolly mood and had made them both giggle with his jokes. Harriet had noticed that he had seemed more cheerful recently. She assumed that he, like her mother, must be excited about moving to the new house and the thought made her feel guilty. It was even worse when they arrived at school and he pulled, not just his usual single snack bar out of their hiding place, but a whole packet each.

'There you are,' he said. 'Treat your friends, or have a good pig out. Party on!' He had driven off before they could thank him, and Harriet, who had wanted to give him a proper kiss goodbye – in case he never forgave her – was left on the pavement looking after him an feeling a bit tearful.

'Come on dopey,' said Georgie, tugging at her arm. 'Why are you always in such a dream?' She sounded exactly like their mother, and Harriet pushed her away with unaccustomed roughness.

'I'm not dreaming, I'm thinking,' she said crossly. 'You wouldn't know about that, of course.'

'Well, I don't know what you've got to think about that's so important,' returned Georgie with spirit. 'Anyway, thinking is all you can manage. You never *do* anything.'

'That's what you think,' said Harriet meaningfully, then caught herself up. Georgie might not be brilliantly clever, but she was very quick. It wouldn't do to give her the idea that Harriet was planning anything. 'We'd better get into school, the bell will be going.'

Harriet sat through the first part of the school morning with increasing agitation. Every time anyone opened the classroom door her heart lurched, and it seemed that people did nothing but call in – two sets of parents, being given the guided tour, no less than three notes from other members of staff, and a delivery of new maths books. By the time the message arrived that she was to go to the dentist, she had begun to think that Ruth had changed her mind about the whole thing, or unaccountably forgotten about it, and had started to relax. As a result she was able to act more normally than she would have done earlier, and went off under a barrage of envious or sympathetic glances, depending on whether the other girls disliked school more than dentists, or vice versa.

Fetching her coat from the cloakroom, she found the packet of snack bars that she had left in her locker. the sight of it filled her with guilt, she couldn't bring herself to take her father's gift with her, so she slipped it into Georgie's shoe bag. The taxi took her to the dentist's proper address – this had been Harriet's own suggestion – and Harriet paid him herself, saying that her mother had given her the money. Once the car had driven off, Ruth emerged from behind the hedge and they skipped off, giggling with pleasure at their success. Harriet had never felt so elated, in retrospect, the escape from school had been like an adventure game. They made their way to the bungalow, using a circuitous route that brought them to the hidden footpath without, as far as they knew, anyone seeing them. Worming their way through the gap in the hedge, they hid for a while watching the house – reconnoitring, as Harriet put it. It was quiet and still. Even the music they had often heard coming from it was silent. In the end they ran to the door of the shelter, keeping the bulk of the rockery between them and the bungalow, and let themselves in.

Unpacking and sorting out everything they had brought was fun, and so was the picnic lunch, but after that the afternoon dragged a bit. They dared not have the door wide open, in case anyone should take it into their heads to walk round the garden, so they kept it pushed three quarters shut, leaving as wide a chink as they dared to admit some light. It was rather gloomy, but they decided that they must save the torch batteries and the camping gas as far as possible. Harriet had brought a couple of books, but there wasn't enough light to read and in any case it seemed rather unsociable. In the end they played cards, wrapped in their sleeping bags for warmth, competing for matches instead of money. Their hands got very cold, so they made themselves tea, and very soon the inevitable happened and they both found they needed the lavatory.

This was a problem they hadn't really thought about. Of course, in books it simply didn't arise. People in adventure stories never seemed to need to pee, leave alone anything more serious.

'It doesn't matter, we can just go behind a bush,' said Ruth.

'That's all right if it's just once,' objected Harriet, 'but it won't be, will it? Anyway, I want to go properly. You know.' Harriet's stomach was very sensitive to her moods – any kind of upset was inclined to bring on an attack of diarrhoea, something which she had forgotten until now, when her insides were sending her increasingly urgent messages. Ruth frowned.

'We'll have to dig a hole, then. That's what proper campers do.' She looked around.

'There's a trowel by the back door,' said Harriet, eager to be helpful.

201

'I could creep and get it. It's beginning to get dark, already, I'm sure nobody would see me.'

'Well . . .' Ruth wasn't sure.

'It's probably safer now than when it's properly dark. It's so cloudy, there won't be any moonlight, and we'd never be able to find the trowel without using the torch. Mummy always says this is the worst time of day when you're driving, it's much more difficult to see things in the half-light. If Mrs Holt has the lights on inside, she won't be able to see anything out here.'

'All right, then. But don't make any noise.'

Outside, it was darker than Harriet had realised. The short winter day was already almost over, little pinpoints of light showed where the next door bungalows had turned on their lights. Built in a more spacious age, each bungalow was in the middle of its plot and therefore widely separated from its neighbour, a fact which had encouraged Ruth and Harriet to choose their hiding place.

There were no lights in Mrs Holt's bungalow. Harriet crept through the garden and peered through the thickly twining trunks of the wisteria that grew up the pillars supporting the veranda roof. The rooms were dark. A sudden movement made her jump, then freeze, until she realised that it was the parrot, spreading his wings while he hung upside down from the roof of his cage. The sight was somehow reassuring, reminding her of a happier past, and she would have stayed to watch the dimly seen bird had not a sudden gurgling from her stomach reminded her of an increasingly pressing need. She darted to the back door and took the trowel, then carried it back in triumph to the shelter.

'There's no paper,' said Ruth gruffly. She knew she should have thought of that.

'It's all right. I'll use newspaper,' said Harriet, who couldn't wait around talking about it. 'That's what they used in the olden days, anyway.'

'Make sure you dig a proper hole, then.'

Harriet found a place in the middle of an overgrown patch of rhododendrons, where the soil was soft enough to be easy to dig. It wasn't very comfortable, being cold and draughty, but she was too relieved to be free of discomfort to mind very much. The torn up bits of newspaper were harsh, to one used to the good quality quilted paper that Christine bought, but the experience had a certain ruggedness that made Harriet feel that she was a survivor, marooned on a desert island or in a trackless jungle, living on her wits.

Her mother's training, allied to the fact that her hands were dirty from the trowel and from pushing her way through the rhododendrons, made her creep back to the bungalow where she stealthily washed her hands at the outside tap. Without soap she feared it wasn't very thorough but the cold water was better than nothing. She shook them, then wiped off the worst of the water on her track suited legs – they had decided on track suits, as the most comfortable clothes for sitting around in. Shivering a bit, she made her way back to the shelter.

By now it was dark. The faint reflected glow of the street lights was just about enough to enable her to find her way but inside it was pitch black and she hesitated in the doorway, nervous of blundering in and knocking something over.

'Ruth? Where are you?' There was a little quiver of anxiety in her voice.

'Over here. Shut the door, then you can put the torch on.'

Harriet bit her lip. She had left the torch where she had put it down by the tap. 'I've left it behind,' she admitted. 'I'll go back for it.'

'No, it's all right. I've got the matches. Shut the door, and I'll light a candle.'

In the darkness, the flame seemed brilliant. They had put candles in some of the old wine bottles that they had found stored in the corner, and with three of them lit the place took on a bohemian air. It was rather romantic, and when they put the candles up on the shelves, to be out of harm's way, it was surprising how much light they gave. The flames gave an illusion of warmth, too, which was very welcome to Harriet as she wrapped her sleeping bag round her again.

'I think Mrs Holt has gone out,' she said. 'There aren't any lights on, and I'd have seen something, even if she'd been in one of the front rooms. There'd have been some light showing under the doors, or something.'

'Great. We must still be careful, though. They'll know we've gone, by now.'

'Yes . . .' Harriet sounded wobbly again; Ruth was quick to change the subject.

'What shall we have for supper tonight? You can choose.'

Harriet thought about it. They had prided themselves on being very sensible about food. They had agreed that they mustn't only have the sweet things like biscuits and cakes and sweets. Things like bacon and sausages (which Ruth ate when away from home) they had, reluctantly, abandoned because the smell of them cooking might carry too far and alert someone of their presence. They decided on baked beans and scrambled egg, with toasted marshmallows for pudding.

Harriet's eyes shone, little candle flames reflected in them as she smiled. 'Yummy! I love toasted marshmallows, and if we have an apple afterwards it won't be so bad for our teeth.'

'Only you must be careful not to burn yourself,' said Ruth conscientiously. 'Hot sugar is much hotter than boiling water, you know.'

203

They decided to start cooking at once. Talking about supper had made them feel hungry, and with only one little camping stove it would take quite a while to prepare. With the door closed, the heat produced by the camping gas soon warmed the little room to a comfortable temperature, and by the time they had eaten they both felt warm enough to take off their track suit tops and sit in tee shirts. They turned the gas down low, not to use up the cylinder too fast, and used their forks to spear the marshmallows. The delicious smell of burning sugar overlaid the savoury aroma from the baked beans, and they giggled as with lips pulled back from the heat they nibbled crunchy, browned bits of crusted mallow, the gooey inside stretching out in strings that stuck to lips and chin.

'I don't think I can manage another one,' said Harriet regretfully. She sucked the last bit of sticky burned sugar from the prongs of the fork, and licked round her mouth. 'I'm really thirsty, aren't you?'

'Yes,' agreed Ruth. 'I'll get us some water.' She stood up and went to fill their two mugs from the plastic bottle at the side of the room. She gave one to Harriet, drank her own quickly and then went to refill it. She stood where she was, head tilted back to drink. As she drained the mug she was aware of a curious, flickering light on the opposite wall. Harriet was staring at her, her eyes round and appalled, her mouth dropping open to cry out.

'Your hair! Your hair!' Ruth looked at her blankly, and Harriet leaped to her feet and blundered across to her. She knocked over the gas cooker, luckily no longer burning. Ruth opened her mouth to warn her but before she could do anything Harriet was beside her, beating at her head with her hands. Ruth, fortunately, was so surprised that she made no attempt to fend her off. Harriet was whimpering in panic, her hands hit and flailed about Ruth's head. 'Your hair! Your hair!' she repeated. 'Your hair's on fire! The candle!'

Ruth, understanding her at last, turned her head towards where the candle stood on the shelf behind her. The tall candle, which had once been well above their height, had burned down while they cooked and ate so that it was just the right height to catch the loose ends of her hair. As she turned her head the hair moved towards it again, and Harriet swung her arm to knock the candle out of the way. Her bare arm caught the bottle with some force so that it smashed against the wall behind, driving a piece of glass deep into the soft flesh.

Harriet looked down at her own arm, more surprised than horrified. 'It doesn't hurt,' she said dully. 'It can't be bad.' Without stopping to think she pulled the piece of glass out with her other hand. At once the blood, which was already trickling down and dripping off her fingers, gushed out in force. Harriet looked at the jet, black in the light of the two remaining candles. Her knees began to buckle. Ruth caught hold of her arm, squeezing her fingers as hard as she could over the cut. It felt slippery, as though it would slither through her fingers like jelly, but she hung on with all her force. Harriet was on the ground, half-sitting and half-lying against the wall, with broken glass all around her. Ruth hoped she wasn't being cut anywhere else, but she couldn't spare a hand to do anything about it.

'Harriet!' she said urgently. 'Harriet, try not to faint, please Harriet, open your eyes. Harriet!'

Harriet mumbled, her eyelids flickered. Ruth, who had hoped that Harriet could hold the wound for long enough to enable her to get help, realised that she was on her own. Crouching beside Harriet she squeezed the arm as hard as she could with her right hand, and reached out behind her, searching for something – anything – that she could use to wrap the wound. She touched something hot, jerking her fingers away and realising that it was the metal top of the camping stove. It seemed impossible that it should still be hot enough to burn her, it seemed like hours since she had turned it off. Leaning as far as she could, she swept her hand further out, and felt cloth. Grabbing it, she realised it was her tracksuit top – not ideal, but better than nothing and at least it was big.

Wishing she could see better she used her left hand and her teeth to tie a knot in one sleeve, then she pressed the hard lump down on the wound and swiftly bound the rest of the garment as tightly round Harriet's arm as she could. In the dim light she couldn't see whether it was enough to control the bleeding, but she knew she couldn't afford to take time to find the torch. Gripping the cloth-wrapped arm and hoping that she was keeping the knotted place tight over the cut she pulled Harriet upright.

'Come on, Harriet. Come *on*,' she muttered vehemently. 'Help me, please help me. Just stand up for a second. *Please*, Harriet.' Harriet moaned, but though she swayed she stayed upright for long enough for Ruth to get in front of her, crouching down to get both Harriet's arms over her shoulders so that Harriet's head rested against the back of her neck. Still hanging on to the bandaged arm with her right hand, Ruth straightened her legs so that Harriet was almost off the floor. Then Ruth walked to the door. She had to let go of Harriet's left arm so that she could free her own left hand to open the door. It grated noisily over the ground, and Ruth crouched again to step out.

'Help!' she called. 'Help!' Her own voice sounded thin and breathless. She could see the whiteness of her own breath in the frosty air, her bare arms puckered into goose-flesh but she felt nothing. Her voice seemed as powerless as the dissipating steam of her breathing; the lights of the neighbouring bungalows looked no more than a distant glow. The owners, cosily tucked up in front of their televisions behind carefully closed curtains, could not possibly hear her. She set off towards the bungalow, Harriet's feet trailing on the path behind her.

Every step was an effort, she could hardly see anything, it was like walking through water or thick, dark treacle.

As she neared the bungalow her eyes began to adjust to the dark. No good knocking, and it had taken her too long to get this far, she couldn't risk trying to get to a neighbouring house. She saw the trowel by the back door, where Harriet had left it. Her back felt as though it was breaking. Ruth let Harriet slip to the ground, keeping the arm she held up in the air and still hanging on tightly to it. Then she bent for the trowel and used it without a second thought to smash the glass in the back door. She put her hand in without a thought that she might cut herself in turn, and found with relief that the key was still in the lock inside. It turned sweetly, there were no bolts. The door opened and Ruth half stepped, half fell inside. She didn't even try to pick Harriet up again, knowing that she wouldn't manage it, but simply kicked the mat with its litter of broken glass aside with her foot, and pulled Harriet over the threshold and into the warmth of the kitchen.

Switching on the light blinded her for a moment, she stood blinking and amazed at the normality of it all, the tidy kitchen with every surface wiped, every door and drawer shut, the dry dish cloth and tea towel neatly draped over a rail. Ruth wondered whether she should use them as bandages, but when she looked down at the track suit top, which still appeared dry and unstained by fresh blood, she thought it safer to leave it in place. Instead she dragged Harriet over the floor and into the hall, where she picked up the telephone.

Nine nine nine. This was the second time she had done this, but this time she was almost beyond speech. When the calm voice asked what service she wanted she muttered 'Ambulance' so quietly she had to repeat it. The questions they asked seemed to be in gibberish, she couldn't answer them, couldn't remember where she was, not the name of the street or anything sensible. The voices were suspicious, wary of childish pranks. In the end, shaking her head in an attempt to clear her mind, she pressed the handset button to disconnect, then dialled the only number she could remember.

It was answered before the first ring had finished sounding.

'Hello? Ruth?'

Ruth gave a little sob.

'Oh, Liz,' she said. 'Liz, please help me.'

Chapter Nineteen

'Ruth! Oh, thank God, where are you?'
'I don't know!' It was the tearful wail of a lost child. The sound of a familiar adult voice, a voice which she thought she hated but which now sounded reassuringly like home, put Ruth straight back into the dependence of childhood. While she had been alone and responsible she had been strong but her strength was used up. All she wanted was to hand over to someone older.

'Are you in a call box?'

'No, a house. I broke in . . . I had to . . .' Ruth was sounding increasingly hysterical. Liz flattened her voice, sounding as matter-of-fact as she could.

'That's all right, that doesn't matter now. It's an empty house, is it?'

'Yes, she's gone out. Or away. Liz, Harriet's bleeding, I think I've stopped it but I don't know, it was very bad and I'm frightened to look in case it starts up again, she's fainted but she might be unconscious, you don't think she'll die, do you?'

'No, no, not if you stopped the bleeding. Have you called an ambulance?'

'I tried, but I don't think they believed me and I couldn't tell them where we are.'

'You must know roughly. Think, Ruth. Where did you go, after school?'

'Here. We've been here all the time.'

'In the house?' Surely they wouldn't just have broken into an unfamiliar house?

'No, in the garden, there's an air-raid shelter . . . Harriet knew about it . . .'

'She knows the people who live there? Would her parents know them?'

'I don't think so . . . there's a parrot . . . the agent knows.'

'The agent?' For one moment Liz wondered wildly if Ruth had gone off her head, was imagining herself in some kind of spy story.

'The estate agent. The one who's selling our house. I can't remember his name . . .'

'Don't worry, I'll find it. I'll get an ambulance there as quickly as I

207

can. Just hold on, darling, it'll be all right. I'll have to hang up now. All right?'

'Yes. Be quick, Liz. Please come . . . I'm frightened . . .'

'Oh, Ruth . . . I'll be as quick as I can.'

Liz rummaged through the telephone table drawer.

'Where's that bloody detail, I know I put it in here, damn, damn, damn, can't find it . . .' She tipped the drawer out on to the floor, and pounced on the copy of the sales particulars of the house. As she dialled the number she glanced at her watch and nearly put the phone down again. Of course nobody would be there at this time of the evening, she should be phoning Mike, telling the police. As her hand hovered over the disconnect button the telephone was answered.

'Hensham Homes, good – good evening?'

'Oh!' Liz was startled. 'You're not a machine?'

There was a smile in his voice. 'Far from it. Human and fallible, I'm afraid. Er, have you got the right number? This is an estate agency.'

'Yes. Oh, yes. It's Liz Hartwell, you're selling our house—'

He broke in before she could say any more.

'Of course! Is there any news of the girls?'

She was too flustered to question how he knew.

'Yes, Ruth's just rung. She says they're at a place Harriet knows, a place with a parrot. Does that mean anything to you?'

He groaned. 'Yes. Is Harriet there too? Are they all right?'

'Harriet's hurt. Bleeding. Ruth said she thought she'd stopped it, but she sounded terrified. I must ring for an ambulance. Can you tell me the address?'

'Of course.' He did so. 'Look, I've got the key. Mrs Holt – that's the owner – is away. How did they get in?'

'Broke in, I'm afraid. I'll ring Mike, and then I'll go down there.'

'Yes, I'll come along too. If they've broken in I'll have to do something about fixing it up. All right?'

'Yes. Thank you.' Liz was impatient to be gone. 'I must ring for an ambulance.'

'Why not let me do that? Then you can go straight round there.'

'Would you? That would be wonderful.'

'You know how to get there?' He gave her swift, clear directions. Thank God for estate agents, she thought wryly. At least they know where places are.

When she telephoned Mike, and found that he and Alec Blake were right over on the other side of town, she was thankful that Paul Kingswood had offered to come along. Not, of course, that she was old-fashioned enough to feel the need of a man's support at moments of crisis, but still . . . it would be good to have someone else around.

When she screeched to a halt outside the bungalow, an ambulance with its lights flashing blue was already there. She ran to the door of the building, rattling at the handle, but it was firmly locked. A dimly seen face looked at her through the thick glass panes of the door.

'You a parent?'

'Yes,' she called back. This was no time for the minutiae of family relationships.

'Round the back, then. Door's open.'

Liz stumbled down the path at the side. Luckily there were outside lights switched on, as the street lighting didn't reach the garden. The kitchen door with its broken pane was wide open, and in the hall two uniformed men crouched over Harriet. One of them was holding up a plastic drip bag, the other was talking to her in a loud, encouraging voice. Liz felt she had stepped into an episode of *Casualty* – it was all so unreal. When one of the men turned his head she was surprised to see that he wasn't the familiar actor of the television series. She looked round for Ruth, and saw her huddled in the corner of the room. Liz edged past the men, and as she reached her Ruth looked away from the tableau in the middle of the room and saw Liz. Her face crumpled like a child's.

Tentatively, Liz put her arms round the girl, not pulling her close or applying any pressure but scarcely touching the stiff, skinny form. She hadn't forgotten the coldness of Ruth's rejection when, in the early days, Liz had attempted to hug or kiss her. Ruth had gone rigid and without actually pushing Liz away had removed herself from Liz's reach giving the impression of someone brushing off a distasteful touch.

This time, to her amazement, Ruth's stiff body immediately melted against her. She tightened her arms, as much to hold Ruth up as to comfort her. Ruth clung to her, pushing her head into the side of Liz's neck like a small child. Liz held her firmly, rubbing her back with the instinctive caress of a mother winding a baby. She rested her cheek against the top of Ruth's head.

'Ruth, Ruth, little Ruthie, it'll be all right, don't worry, I'm here, it'll come right, you'll see, she'll be fine . . .'

One of the men looked round.

'You the mother, love?'

'Yes,' said Liz without thinking. 'Not Harriet's mother,' she added quickly. 'Her parents are on their way, they'll be here in a few minutes. Is she all right?'

'She'll be fine. She's had a nasty shock, and lost a fair bit of blood, but she'll do. We'll get her to hospital so they can clean the cut and stitch it, give her a bit of a check over. They'll maybe want to keep her in overnight, just to be on the safe side, but she'll be fine. She'll be right, eh?' he imitated a broad Australian accent.

'Ruth?' It was Harriet's voice, very wavery. 'Ruth, are you there?'

209

Ruth turned her head towards where Harriet lay. Liz slackened her hold, but Ruth still clung to her so Liz kept her arm round the girl's shoulders and went with her. When they reached Harriet, now wrapped in blankets and looking very small and white, Ruth crouched down. Liz stood beside her, keeping a hand on her shoulder in token support.

'I'm sorry, Harriet. It was all my fault.'

A small puzzled frown creased Harriet's forehead. Her face was grubby, she looked very young indeed.

'Not your fault,' she whispered. 'You saved my life. They said so.' She made a tiny movement of her head towards the men.

'That's right, love,' said the man who had spoken before. 'Bled to death, your little friend could have, if you hadn't managed to stop the bleeding so quick. You did a grand job, I reckon, all by yourself, getting her in here and calling us up.'

'But I couldn't even remember the address. I thought they didn't believe me.'

'People making hoax calls don't forget the address, and they don't sound as worried as you did, love. They get a feeling for that kind of thing – sort of instinct, like. Traced the call, got the address, no problem. Had us here in a trice. No, you did a good job, love. Quick thinking, that knot was. Done a first aid course, have you?'

'Yes, at school.' Ruth was hardly listening to him. His praise, which in different circumstances would have pleased her so much, passed by her unnoticed. 'If we hadn't been here, you wouldn't have been hurt. You'd never have done it, without me leading you on. I'll tell your parents, say I made you do it, then they won't be so cross with you . . .'

Harriet shook her head, a tiny movement. One of the men put out his hand to prevent her from moving, but Ruth was before him. With a gentleness Liz had never before seen her display, Ruth put her hand to Harriet's cheek.

'Lie still,' she said. 'Don't forget, you saved me first. I might have burned to death.' She put up her hand to feel the back of her head, her burned hair forgotten until now. She was amazed to find that it felt no different to usual. 'It's all right! I thought I'd be half bald! You put it out so quickly, it was brave of you, braver than I've been. You're a heroine, Harriet.'

A faint tinge of pink coloured Harriet's cheeks.

'Do you really think so?'

'Yes, I do. And I'll tell you what else. You don't need to run away and make protests like that to make people take notice of you. You're brave. You can tell them, make them see that you really mean it.'

'I don't know . . . and what about you? You're just as brave as me. Braver. Will they listen to you?'

'I don't know.' Ruth hung her head. Liz opened her mouth to speak, then wisely closed it again.

'Perhaps,' said Harriet hesitantly, 'perhaps they will, if you listen to them too, do you think?'

There was a bustle of arrival. The front door, double locked, was undone and opened. Paul Kingswood stood aside for Christine, Alec and Mike who rushed through then stopped in the doorway, transfixed by the uniforms and the medical formality. Christine gave a little whimper, and clutched at Alec's arm.

'It's all right,' he said, encouraging himself as much as her. 'She's all right.'

'Daddy?' The relief in Harriet's voice was like a knife in his heart. 'Is that Daddy?'

'Yes, darling.' He tiptoed forward, as though a heavy footstep might damage her. Christine followed him. Ruth, who had stood up as they came in, stepped back into the shelter of Liz's arms, and they moved out of the way as Alec came to kneel by his daughter. Across the room Liz met Mike's eyes, and a moment of complete understanding passed between them, so that for the first time since she had got there her eyes filled with tears.

'I'm sorry, Daddy, I'm sorry,' Harriet was saying. 'I didn't want you to be worried, I didn't mean to upset you.'

She was becoming distressed, and he was quick to soothe her.

'I know, darling, it's all right. Nobody's cross with you, just as long as you're all right.' He glanced up at the ambulance men, who responded with the same information they had given Liz. Ruth pulled away from Liz, who immediately dropped her arms to release her. Ruth, however, gripped Liz's hand before stepping forward.

'I'm sorry, Mr Blake. It was my fault we ran away, it was my idea. I thought I could look after Harriet, keep her safe, but I couldn't. I'm sorry.'

Christine rounded on her. Liz took a step forward ready to defend Ruth but Alec was before her. He still kept hold of Harriet's hand, but he looked up at his wife with an expression she had never seen on his face before.

'Christine.'

It was all he said, but his firm intention was clear. His wife looked at him in amazement. He locked eyes with her, and it was her glance that dropped. Liz relaxed.

'Mummy . . . ?'

Alec Blake continued to look at his wife. She crouched down beside him.

'Here I am, darling.' It was the gentlest voice that Harriet could ever remember hearing from her mother. 'Don't worry. We'll come to the hospital with you, stay with you while you're there.'

'Only room for one in the ambulance, madam,' cut in the uniformed man, who was now preparing to take Harriet out on a stretcher. Harriet's eyes moved from one parent to the other. She said nothing. Christine saw how her daughter's eyes lingered on Alec. Her lips trembled, but she pressed them together for a moment before she spoke.

'Why don't you go with her, Alec? I'll follow in the car.'

Her reward, if such it could be considered, was in her daughter's smile. She stood watching while Harriet was wheeled out of the front door and lifted gently into the waiting vehicle. As the ambulance doors were closed she blinked hard, and turned blindly to Liz. Mike had joined them, and Ruth was now within the circle of his arms. 'I see your daughter likes her father best, too,' she said. She sounded more bewildered than embittered, as though it had never occurred to her that such a thing could be possible.

'Well, she's not really my daughter,' responded Liz vaguely. 'It's natural that she should prefer her father.' She saw Christine's expression. 'That's the way it usually goes, isn't it?' she added in encouraging tones. 'Girls prefer their fathers, boys their mothers . . .'

'I'd have liked a boy . . .'

'Well, it doesn't always happen, of course. And I know you get on very well with your other daughter, don't you?'

'Yes. Yes, I suppose I do.'

'There you are, then.' It wasn't entirely logical, but Christine seemed to be comforted. Her own inability to deal with this crisis had shaken her to the depths of her being. It had never happened to her before, and she had never imagined that it could. As she saw it, she was the driving force in the family, the decision maker, even, in some senses, the provider. Alexander was . . . well, Alexander. She loved him, of course she did. He was her husband, her children's father, and more than that he was a kind, thoughtful man. She saw and acknowledged all his good qualities, but she had always taken it rather for granted that he was somehow less important, in the general scheme of things, than she was.

Now, for the first time, she was forced to confront the fact that her elder daughter, her firstborn child whom she had carried in her body and given birth to and seen through the delights and hazards of babyhood, toddlerhood and early childhood, was in many ways a complete stranger to her. She had been aware, of course, that she didn't really understand Harriet, but she had seen this as a lack in Harriet rather than in herself. Seeing herself as the leader, the power figure, she had somehow felt that it was up to Harriet to make herself understandable, to be what her mother wanted. It had never really occurred to her that Harriet might have wishes and hopes that could differ so fundamentally from hers. She supposed she knew, intellectually, that her children would grow up and have lives of their own that were separate from hers. She, certainly, had never felt herself to be particularly part of her own parents' life and had established her independence at an early age. It was not that she wanted to deny her daughters that same independence, merely that she was so sure that she, and she alone, knew what was best for them that there could be no need for them to break away.

This had been at the heart of her inability to cope with Harriet's disappearance. Her first thought, that the child had been abducted by perverts or kidnappers, had thrown her into a terror that was heightened by the deep down feeling that she hadn't loved Harriet enough, that this was her punishment for preferring Georgie. The discovery that her daughter had run away and that, worse, her own cleaning lady had felt the need to protect the child, however erroneously, from Christine's anger, had devastated her. Was she really so harsh, so insensitive? The honesty which sometimes made her an uncomfortable companion forced her to admit that perhaps she had appeared so.

'Hadn't you better get to the hospital?' Mike, looking up from comforting Ruth was surprised by the lost look on Christine's face. From the little he had seen of her, she was not a woman to stand around wondering what to do, and from the depths of his own terror and guilt about his daughter he was able to imagine how devastated Christine might be.

'Yes – yes, of course. Oh dear, where are the car keys?' She looked helplessly about her, then down at her hands which were empty, without even a handbag. 'Alexander must have gone off with them in his pocket . . .'

'He didn't have them – we were in my car,' Mike pointed out. 'Um, you were in such a hurry, do you think you might have left them in the car?'

'Oh no! It could have been stolen!'

'Let's go and see. I'm sure it's all right. Would you like me to drive you?'

'But your daughter . . .'

'She'll be fine with Liz. I don't think you should be driving, you've had a bad shock.' He gave Ruth a little squeeze, then nudged her towards Liz.

'I'm very sorry, Mrs Blake . . .'

Christine looked at Ruth blankly.

'That's all right,' she said, as though Ruth had been apologising for breaking a cup. Ruth opened her mouth to say more, but Liz squeezed the hand that she held and Ruth kept quiet.

Paul was left in the empty bungalow. Methodically he found a brush and dustpan and swept the broken glass from the kitchen floor, brushing the soles of his shoes to make sure that he carried no sharp splinters into the rest of the house. As an afterthought he vacuumed the hall, where other people's shoes might have taken fragments. Only then, like a child rewarding himself for good behaviour, did he allow himself to go into the sitting room to see whether Archimedes was all right.

As he opened the heavy door the parrot shifted on his perch and took his head from under his wing. He blinked as Paul switched on the light – obviously all the comings and goings had failed to rouse him. After regarding Paul blearily for a few moments he appeared to decide that the prospect of some company was better than sleep. He sidled along his perch and put his head on one side like a child actor doing 'coy'.

'Biscuit?' he wheedled. 'Just a small one?'

Paul opened the cage door and held out his hand for the parrot to step on to. Having checked the hand for food the bird ignored it completely and flew round the room. Finding nothing to eat he perched on the back of an armchair.

'Well, nuts to you,' he remarked crossly. Paul wondered, yet again, how much the parrot was aware of the meaning of what he was saying. He had always understood that birds simply repeated a known sequence of sounds, but Archimedes always seemed to say uncannily appropriate things.

Paul remembered that he had some grapes in the car, bought earlier in the day when he had expected to call in at the bungalow on his way home from work, and spend a peaceful half a hour with the parrot. He had even brought a bottle of wine to open for himself, since he knew he wouldn't be able to bring himself to drink Mrs Holt's though she had repeatedly pressed him to help himself. He thought he might as well fetch them. Accustomed to the dangers of vandalism in empty houses, he always kept some pieces of board with a set of basic tools in the boot of his car. It would be easier to board up the broken door himself than to telephone around and then wait for a reluctant, and at that time of night expensive, carpenter or glazier.

It was the sort of job he rather enjoyed, the kind of simple carpentry that his own little house seldom needed, and it was soon done. Before re-locking the door he took the torch and went down to the air-raid shelter. The remnants of the girls' adventure were still as they had left them, a warm smell of burnt sugar hung in the air. The candles had blown out when Ruth flung open the door. The remains of their picnic were neatly stacked away, and their sleeping bags carefully folded, contrasting shockingly with the splashes of blood and the litter of broken glass. It would have to be cleared up before Mrs Holt came back but it could wait. Paul shut and locked the door, then went gratefully back to his bottle of wine and the self-serving affections of Archimedes.

He was sipping the remains of a second glass, and regretting that the need to drive himself home meant that he could not allow himself a third, when the telephone rang. He hesitated to answer it, but when it continued to ring he picked it up, trying to pitch his voice so that he sounded inoffensive and as unlike a burglar as possible.

'Hello?'

'Mr Kingswood.' Mrs Holt's voice came vigorously down the telephone line. He glanced at his watch, seeing to his astonishment that it was after eleven.

'Oh, Mrs Holt. I was going to ring you in the morning. There's been a bit of bother here, but you don't need to worry, everything's fine. Um, how did you know I was here?'

Her voice was unruffled. 'Well, I didn't obviously. Beth and I have been out all evening, and we came home to rather a melodramatic message on her answerphone, one of my neighbours talking about cars and lights and ambulances . . . ?' Her voice rose into an amused query. Paul thought how very fortunate it was that she was such a calm, detached person. He had been the one, after all, who had brought Harriet there in the first place.

He gave her a succinct account of the evening's events. She listened in silence, with neither shocked gasps nor angry tuts, until he had finished.

'Heavens,' she said at the end. 'That little Harriet. I wouldn't have thought she'd do a thing like that. It was the older girl, I suppose. Well, thank goodness she knew about the air-raid shelter.'

Paul blinked at her matter-of-fact acceptance of what was, after all, a case of trespass.

'I hadn't seen it quite like that,' he said cautiously.

'Think where they could have ended up,' she pointed out. 'The world's a dangerous place for young girls on their own. At least they were safe there . . . well, safe from everything but themselves, that is. Let's hope they've learned something from all this, anyway.'

'It's a bit of a mess out there. Broken glass, and blood. I'll come back tomorrow and clear it up for you.'

'Certainly not! You've already secured the back door, and if you'd be kind enough to contact a glazier for me I'd be most grateful, but that's quite enough. No, let the girls clear up their own mess. Good for them, part of their punishment, if you like, to confront the results of their actions. And of course I shall expect them to come and apologise to me in person, when I get back. That can be another part. After that, it's up to their parents.'

He was amused.

'Retribution – with you in the part of Nemesis?'

'Well, I wasn't proposing to follow them around, exactly. But I do believe that children should learn to consider the consequences of what they do, and if possible deal with them. I don't go in for all that 'Oh, poor things, they've had a difficult childhood' stuff, or not beyond a certain point, at least. So scrubbing off the blood stains and picking up the bits of glass might be a bit horrific for them, but I don't believe it would do them any harm.'

He agreed with her, but wondered whether the parents would.

'What shall I do about your neighbour? It's a bit late to knock on the door and reassure her but I could write a note and put it through.'

'Don't worry, I'll ring her in the morning. I expect she enjoyed every moment of the drama, and she'll love being the only one in the road who knows what really happened.'

He would have liked to ask about her daughter, but it was late and hardly the time for idle chat. He said good night, with some regret, and went to put Archimedes back in his cage.

In the hospital, Harriet blinked at the nurse in the casualty department. They had taken her glasses away, and her eyes were slightly unfocussed, the pupils large and dark. Was it the blurring that made his hair gleam so brightly, and his eyes look so blue?

'Hi, Harriet, my name's Jason.'

'Oh, of *course*,' she said without thinking, then blushed miserably. Young as she was, she had learned very early that the adults she had been brought up to respect quite often didn't know very much – at least not the kind of things that she knew – and that they generally resented being enlightened by a child. He grinned at her.

'S'right,' he said. 'I did the hair to go with the name, but don't tell anyone. I want them to think it's natural.'

She smiled with delight. Poor little thing, he thought, so small and plain, but how her face lights up when she smiles. Alec, watching them, also saw the unguarded pleasure in his daughter's face and thought how rarely he saw her look like that. From now on, he thought firmly, I'm going to make sure she smiles more, a lot more.

In another ward, Philippa was also smiling. She had a dull, throbbing pain in her stomach, her head felt as though it had been stuffed with damp cotton wool and her mouth tasted furry and disgusting, but in spite of all this she was happy. The operation was over. A large cyst had been removed and the surgeon had told her that while he couldn't make any promises, he was pretty certain that it wasn't malignant. That, on its own, was enough to make her smile, but in fact she scarcely gave it a thought. Instead, she fixed her eyes on the arrangement of freesias and hot-house roses on her bedside cabinet.

Earlier in the day, waiting to be wheeled down to the theatre and half-doped with pre-med, she had struggled to contain the tears that kept wanting to roll down her face into her hair. She told herself firmly that she was alone because that was what she had wanted, that it was better this way. It had been a relief when they came to fetch her, she had welcomed the prick of the needle with its promise of quick oblivion. Her last thought, before the black curtain descended, was that once it was over she would be able to tell George.

Coming round, as always, had been a slow process, a gradual ascent through layers of unconsciousness that were as like sleep as heavy oil is like water – both are liquid, but they are different in every other respect. Reluctant to return to the world, she gradually became aware that someone was holding her hand. A nurse, she thought. That's what nurses do, they pat your hand and call your name to wake you up again. There was no patting, however, and the hand that held hers was large and somehow familiar. With an effort she turned her hand a little, shifting so that her little finger fitted in the gap next to his.

There was a rustle of uniform.

'Speak to her, Mr Denton. Say her name, wake her up.'

Philippa heard the smile in his voice. 'No need,' he said. 'She knows I'm here.' He gave her hand a small squeeze, and she twitched her fingers back, one at a time, something that they had done for so long she had forgotten that they had started doing it when she had been learning to type, and had found her fingers typing words all the time. She spoke without opening her eyes.

'How did you know?' Her tongue felt thick, her words were slurred.

'You didn't seriously think I believed all that rigmarole about health farms? Silly girl, I know you too well. I went to Malcolm.'

'Hmf. What's become of a patient's right to privacy? Dish – disgraceful.'

'Shocking. Except that he flatly refused to tell me anything. So, of course, I knew that there was something going on, so I rang the hospital, said I was checking what time you had to be in. Bluffed them, and it worked. So here I am.'

At last she opened her eyes. He sat at her bedside, leaning back in his chair, as relaxed as if he were in the little sitting room at home.

'That's better,' he said easily.

'I really thought I had you fooled.' she complained.

'Can't pull the wool over my eyes that easily,' he said. 'Silly girl,' he said again.

'Not really a girl,' she pointed out.

'All right. Silly old bat.'

'That's better. Ouch! Don't make me laugh!'

Now she closed her eyes again. Sleep drifted over her like a warm soft cloud. The operation was over, for good or ill, and George had been here with her. How ridiculous, she thought. I still don't know for certain whether I've got cancer or not, my mouth's dry and my stomach hurts, but I'm happy. It must be something in the anaesthetic.

217

I wonder what all those young nurses would think if they knew that sitting and holding hands with my husband could make me feel like this, at my age. Daft old trout.

As she fell asleep, she was smiling.

Chapter Twenty

Ruth walked into her home, the house she had left only that morning, and looked around her as if she had never seen it before. For the first time she noticed that it was a bit shabby. The curtains were faded, the carpet marked with wear and stains that even the fiercest carpet cleaner couldn't shift. It was clean and tidy, but somehow sad looking, a left-over from another life. She felt a kind of pity, as for an old pet that once ran and played, and now could do no more than doze by the fire. It made her feel unreasonably angry. She went through to the kitchen, thinking it would be better, but even there the cupboard doors were chipped, the laminate worktop scratched, and two of the tiles on the wall behind were cracked.

'Do you want a hot drink?' Liz had followed her.

'No.' The word came out more abruptly than she had meant. 'No, thank you,' she amended, trying to sound less aggressive but managing, even to her own ears, to sound no more than sulky.

Liz sighed. Obviously, she thought, the change in Ruth's attitude towards her had been no more than a temporary aberration brought on by fright.

Ruth heard the sigh. 'We could have a cup of tea,' she suggested, with an effort. Liz, who was also suffering from reaction, suppressed the desire to say 'Don't do me any favours', and filled the kettle. Ruth, unbidden, took out mugs and milk from the fridge.

'Do you want anything to eat?'

'No, thank you. We had a meal before . . .'

Liz, who hadn't eaten anything, wondered whether to make herself a sandwich, but the thought of sitting and eating while Ruth watched her made her throat close up. She would wait until Mike came back.

They sat in awkward silence, sipping their tea. Liz felt that saying, 'We need to talk' would make her sound like a character in *Neighbours*. Ruth didn't know how to start a conversation. The silence between them stretched like a piece of elastic until neither of them could bear the tension, and with an almost audible *twang* they both spoke at the same time.

'I didn't mean . . .' said Ruth.

'You don't have to . . .' said Liz.

They stopped.

'Carry on,' said Liz.

'No, no, it's all right, you go on.' Ruth spoke hurriedly, eager to cede since she didn't know how to find the words to apologise.

'Well,' said Liz, who didn't really know what to say either, 'I suppose I just wanted to say that it's all right. You've won. We'll stay here.'

A few hours ago, it would have been a victory. Ruth would have expected to feel delight, triumph, a surge of power. Instead she understood for the first time a phrase she had read and dismissed in old books, about pleasure turning to dust and ashes. She could taste them in her mouth, dry, gritty, utterly savourless. She shook her head.

'I don't want to.'

Liz could feel her self-control shredding away, like rotten fabric that looks sound but disintegrates at a touch.

'What do you mean, you don't want to?' Her voice was harsh. Ruth responded to the anger with equal aggression. She had thought she was conceding, was making a sacrifice of her own hopes and feelings and her gesture was being thrown back in her face. 'What I said, of course!' She stood up, pushing her chair back roughly so that it screeched on the floor and then crashed over. Ruth ignored the noise – she didn't even hear it – and leaned forwards, her hands flat on the table top for support. Her throat felt tight and painful, she had to shout to get the words out. 'I just . . . don't . . . want . . . to.'

Goaded beyond bearing, Liz reached up and slapped her face.

'How *dare* you!' she shouted back. 'How *dare* you go off like that, frighten us all half to death without a second thought, and then have the nerve to come back and say you've changed your mind, it was all done for nothing at all! Tell me we've been through all this . . . this *agony* . . . for you to *change* your *mind*?'

Ruth gave a wail, crying like a small child with a square, wide mouth.

'You hit me! It's not *fair*! *You* haven't been frightened! I expect you were glad I'd gone!'

'What do you mean, I wasn't frightened! You may be a little cow, but you're my family! I was terrified, I thought you'd been abducted, raped, murdered . . . I – oh, no . . .' Liz stood up and Ruth instinctively flinched back, but Liz turned away and ran from the room. Ruth heard her retching, and remembered how she herself had been sick on the evening when her father had told her about the coming baby. Ruth dithered, feeling that she should go and help but fearing that her presence would make things worse. She rubbed her eyes childishly with the heels of her hands, smudging away the tears. Her nose ran, and she sniffed. In her head, she heard her mother's voice speaking clearly and crossly.

'For goodness' sake, Ruth, don't sniff,' she said. Ruth snatched a piece of paper off the roll on the wall. All this time she had longed to hear her mother speak again, and now that she did it was just to tell her off.

'Mummy?' she whispered, in her head. 'Mummy? Are you there?'

'Of course I am. Where else would I be? You know I told you I'd be there as long as you kept me alive in your memory.'

'Why couldn't I hear you before, then?'

'You were too busy shouting, weren't you?'

Ruth could hear that Liz had not come out of the cloakroom, although she was no longer being sick. The silence was unnerving.

'I don't know what to do.'

'Nonsense, darling.' It was the voice she had forgotten, not the saintly figure she had created and enshrined in her memory but the practical woman who had loved her enough to tell her off. 'Of course you do.'

It was true. Ruth knew, deep down, that the voice she heard was not some angelic communication from her mother's spirit, but simply a creation of her own mind and memory, speaking with the common sense that she too possessed but preferred not to listen to. She filled a glass with cold water, and damped a clean tea towel, remembering how she had done the same for Louise Johnson.

Liz was sitting on the closed lid of the lavatory, her arms clasped protectively round her stomach and her head lowered to her knees. She did not move when Ruth came in.

'Do you want some water?'

Liz did not speak, but held up her hand for the glass. When she sat up to drink Ruth was shocked by her face, which was greenish white. She saw how Liz's hand shook, and put her own over it, laying her other arm round Liz's shoulders to support her as she sipped. Liz drank half the water, then put her head down to her knees again. Ruth kept her arm in place, crouching down to bring her face level with the older woman's.

'Are you all right? Shall I call the doctor?'

Liz shook her head.

'I'm all right,' she managed to say. 'It's going off now.'

'You're not bleeding, or anything?' Ruth had a vivid memory of Louise's miscarriage. 'I mean, you'd feel something, wouldn't you, if there was anything wrong with the baby.'

Liz sat up again.

'No, it's nothing like that,' she said more strongly. 'Just my stomach – the eating part of it, that is.' Her face was a better colour now, though still yellowish pale under the ineradicable Australian tan. Ruth offered the tea towel, which she had dumped on the wash basin, and Liz wiped her face, pressing the coolness to her eyes for a moment. 'There. I'm right. Sorry about that. And sorry I hit you.'

'It's all right.' And amazingly, Ruth thought, it was. Looking back, she realised that one of the problems had actually been Liz's patience, her acceptance of Ruth's behaviour. Ruth, childishly, had taken this for lack of caring rather than for the adult self-control that it actually was. The fact that it had seemed impossible to upset or hurt Liz had made it seem to her that she didn't matter to Liz at all. Ruth had felt that she was being treated as a stranger, an unwanted visitor who must be politely endured because it wasn't worth getting annoyed with her.

The shock of Harriet's accident had made Ruth see that she wasn't quite as grown up as she thought herself, and Liz's subsequent anger and distress showed Ruth that like it or not they were each involved in the other's life. Liz's offer to abandon the new house finally made Ruth confront the knowledge she was clinging to her old home like a hermit crab that refused to admit it has outgrown its old shell.

It was an extraordinary moment. She could almost feel the hard casing of her pupal shell cracking and splitting, falling away. Her body felt light and free – she straightened her spine and stretched her arms up and out – an imago spreading her new wings to dry in the sunshine. Then she stood still, her hand unselfconsciously stroking and patting Liz's shoulder as Liz, earlier, had comforted her. Liz leaned her head against the skinny body of her step-daughter, and closed her eyes. There was the sound of a key in the door, but neither of them moved as Mike came in. He stopped in the doorway of the cloakroom. He was pale and tired, but his eyes lit into a smile as he saw them.

'What's this? A party? Is it private, or can anyone join in?'

Ruth was the first to pull herself together.

'Liz should be sitting down, putting her feet up,' she said bossily. Mike and Liz exchanged glances that were a mixture of amusement and dread. Ruth, they thought, having done her best to absent herself from their lives altogether, would end up running them if they weren't careful. Wisely, however, Mike said nothing. He could see that some kind of breakthrough had been achieved, and it was enough for him to have his daughter back safely, and to see her fussing like a prematurely mature mother hen over the step-mother she had professed to hate. He took himself quietly off to the kitchen. There was a bottle of champagne in the fridge. He had intended to save it for the day they exchanged contracts on the new house, but on second thoughts now seemed like the perfect time to open it.

Harriet was in bed in the hospital. Her arm was sore now that the anaesthetic they had given her for the stitches had worn off but she didn't mind. The bed was hard, the stiff sheet slipping on the plastic-covered mattress, the pillows were unyielding and the cotton blanket was light and insubstantial, so that she felt rather insecure on her high bed, but she didn't really mind that either.

The hospital had insisted on keeping her in, because she had lost a lot of blood and had been unconscious for some time. Her mother had wanted her to be in a private room, and would have stayed with her, but there were no rooms available. The children's ward was bright and cheerful, with big cartoon paintings on the walls and toys everywhere, not at all like the white antiseptic look that she had expected. A small girl in the bed next door had smiled at her when she was brought in, and seeing that she had none of her own things with her had offered one of her soft toys for company. Harriet, who thought she was a bit too old for such things, had accepted the bright pink cat out of politeness but had found it curiously comforting.

Her parents had sat one on each side of the bed. They hadn't seemed to know what to say, which was odd. Harriet realised that for once she would have to take the initiative.

'I'm very sorry I ran away,' she said. Her mother leaned forward to stroke her face.

'Darling, it's all right, you don't have to apologise . . .'

Alec frowned slightly.

'Yes, she does,' he said. Harriet was so amazed to hear her father disagreeing with her mother that she scarcely took in what he had said.

'But she's been hurt, she's in hospital . . .' Harriet would never have believed that she would hear her mother, generally so strict, pleading for clemency from her easy-going father.

'I know.' His face softened, and he put out a hand to take Harriet's. 'You know how thankful I am that she's safe and not too badly hurt. But she put herself in danger, real danger, by behaving very stupidly.'

'Yes, but . . .'

'I'm not saying she should be punished. I'm not even saying we're cross with her – though goodness knows we've had enough anxiety in the last few hours to send our hair white. I'm just saying that it doesn't need to be like this. I just can't believe that we're such ogres that Harriet feels she has to run away rather than to tell us about what's bothering her.'

'It was that other girl,' said Christine defensively. 'That Ruth. I blame myself. I should have known there was something wrong with her. She pushed Harriet into doing this, she'd never have done it otherwise.'

Alec looked at Harriet. Her little pale face on the hospital pillow made his whole body contract with love and anxiety but he was determined to persuade Harriet to talk. He, perhaps more than Christine, was profoundly hurt to think that his daughter didn't trust him enough to confide in him. He, too, felt guilty, knowing that for too long he had allowed Christine to take charge.

Christine's inability to cope with Harriet's disappearance had changed him profoundly. In fact, the little seed of increased self-confidence Shelley had planted had put down roots and sent out branches – he literally felt himself to be a different person. Why this should be he was at a loss to know. Christine rarely refused his sexual advances, while Shelley had made it clear that she was not available. She had made him feel attractive, however, even desirable, while so often with Christine he felt he was just a kind of habit. Shelley had acknowledged him as a potent, available male. That she had not wanted to go any further was immaterial. Other than physically, he hadn't wanted to either. The element of 'we could have done, but we didn't' somehow empowered him.

The fact that Christine had turned to him and had needed him to take charge, had completed what Shelley had begun. No longer would he allow himself to be emasculated by the trust. Even that had dwindled in his mind and no longer required capital letters. He felt he could accept the financial help it gave without his own position in the family being weakened, in the same way that he could accept that Christine could cook better than he did.

The change he felt within himself was too new, he was still learning how to use the strength that his access of confidence had given him. However, as he saw it, Harriet had asserted her independence by running away, now it was up to her to use it.

'Harriet may be younger, but she's not stupid. I don't believe that anyone could persuade her to do something she really didn't want to do. I think she should tell us for herself what happened.'

Harriet was dazed. For the first time in her life her father was treating her, not as a beloved infant, but as an adult. Rather than making excuses for her, as her mother had done, he expected her to take responsibility for her actions. It was frightening, but flattering as well. Clearly, neither letting Ruth take the blame nor, 'I'm sorry, I won't do it again,' would be sufficient. She thought for a moment.

'It was Ruth's idea,' she said carefully, 'but she didn't make me do it. We nearly didn't but I broke my piggy bank to get the money out, and then we had to carry on.'

'But why? Why did you have to?' Alec kept his voice very gentle.

Harriet frowned. Looking back, it was hard to remember why she had ever thought it necessary to run away. Talking like this, quietly and reasonably, seemed so easy that it was difficult to put herself back into that earlier frame of mind.

'It just seemed . . . the only way,' she said slowly. 'We didn't know what else to do.' Wisely, Alec said nothing, and Harriet struggled to continue. 'Ruth was so unhappy, her mother dying and then having a step-mother, and now selling the house . . . it's where her mother died . . . I felt so sorry for her . . .'

'But that's Ruth – what about you?' Christine could not keep quiet any longer. 'You didn't have anything like that. So why did you do it? Was it just to keep her company, to be kind to her?'

Harriet shook her head. 'No. It was a bit that, but not really. It's . . . I put it in my letter.'

'But darling!' Christine was astonished. 'All that stuff about a big house, and ponies . . . you can't be serious! It's a lovely house! I thought you liked it! It was you we wanted it for – well, Georgie too, of course – we thought . . . I thought,' she amended, glancing at Alec, 'I thought you could have such fun, such a wonderful time . . . It was for *you*!'

'I know.' Harriet wriggled uncomfortably. 'It's not the house. It's me. I don't want to be like that.'

'Like what?' Christine's voice was rising. Alec put out his hand and touched her. 'Like what?' she repeated, more quietly.

'Like . . . oh, I don't know. Like ponies and tennis parties and things.'

'But Harry, these are such *little* things.'

'Not to me.'

'And anyway, I'd never have *made* you do them, you must know that. I mean, they're extras, you don't have to do them. Surely you knew you only had to *say* . . .'

Harriet was silent, looking at her, and Christine's voice tailed away. She looked from Harriet's anxious, pleading eyes to Alec's carefully neutral expression, and knew that it wasn't true. She would have dismissed or ignored Harriet's fears and dislikes, have jollied her along with brisk phrases like, 'Of course you want to learn to ride – most little girls would love to have the chance'. It was beyond her comprehension that Harriet should feel so strongly about something so trivial.

'I promise you don't have to learn riding or tennis,' she said. 'All right?'

'And . . . boarding school?'

Christine frowned. 'Well, that's rather a different thing, isn't it? I mean, it doesn't really matter if you don't learn to ride or play tennis just yet, but your education's very important. I'm sure Daddy agrees with that?'

Alec nodded. 'Very important. But not so important that we would make you go to a school you hate.'

'Well, of course not! We wouldn't do a thing like that!'

Harriet looked at her.

'Well, of course we wouldn't! Not if we knew you didn't like it!'

'But . . . would you know?' asked Harriet helplessly.

'Of course I would! I'm your mother!'

Harriet said nothing.

'I mean, you'd tell me, wouldn't you?' Christine was floundering. Harriet looked sad.

'Yes, Mummy.' The words, 'But you wouldn't listen,' hung in the air, unspoken but palpable to all three of them.

Christine's lip trembled. 'I don't mean to be bossy,' she said childishly. 'I'm your mother, I'm responsible for you. I want all the good things for you, the best there is. Because I love you so much.'

'I know you do, Mummy.' Harriet reached out, and Christine at the same moment did too so that they hugged, not so much as mother and child but as two women friends might share an embrace. Christine clung to Harriet, feeling the slender bones within her slight body, surprised by the strength of her arms.

'I will listen,' whispered Christine. 'I really will. I promise.'

Harriet tightened her arms, then winced as her newly stitched cut throbbed. 'Ouch!'

'Oh, be careful, darling!' Christine loosened her arms and laid Harriet gently back against the pillow.

Roger lay in the dark. It was after midnight, but he felt wide awake. An early riser by habit and inclination, he normally fell asleep before eleven, almost as soon as his head touched the pillow. Tonight, however, he couldn't even close his eyes for more than a few seconds before they flew open again as if on springs. He told himself that he would regret it tomorrow, that he would be tired and scratchy, but the blood felt as though it was fizzing in his veins and his brain was twice as alive as usual. He thought that he could do anything – solve the most difficult crossword, say, or learn a new language in a matter of hours. It was as though he had discovered a whole new dimension inside himself.

Mum had noticed the difference in him as soon as he walked in through the door. He was sure she had, though she'd said nothing beyond her usual enquiry. 'Had a good evening? Class go well?'

'Very well.' He had felt his lips curling up into a smile. 'My pastry turned out beautifully.' To distract her, he had held out the tray with the savoury puffs and the Gateau Pithiviers he had made.

'They *do* look good!' She had nodded approvingly and he had been pleased, knowing she was a critical judge and that her admiration was sincere. 'Can I try them?'

'Isn't it a bit late in the evening for you to be eating pastry?' He was always anxious for her health. 'Mightn't it give you indigestion?'

'Indigestion?' She had laughed. 'It's only sad pastry that lies heavy on the stomach. I don't need to taste that to know it's light as a feather. You put the kettle on, we'll have a nice cup of tea with it, and you can tell me what you're making next week.'

And the pastry had been good. Tasting it at the class, he had thought it was his own happiness that made it seem so good. Now, sitting cosily with Mum and laughing like a pair of kids having a midnight feast, he had been proud of it. Crisp and lightly flaky to bite into, it had melted richly in the mouth.

'Better than mine,' Mum had said judiciously and Roger glowed with pride.

It was extraordinary, now that he came to think of it, that he'd never taken more interest in cooking. It was true to say that living at home meant that he never had to give a moment's thought to his meals, which appeared on the table before him as soon as he sat down. Mum prided herself on being what she called a good, plain cook, which in her terms meant making things herself rather than buying ready-made, and serving the slightly unimaginative menus that she had learned from her own mother before the war. As a concession to modern trends she now undercooked her vegetables rather than boiling sprouts and cabbage to the yellowish mush of her childhood, but otherwise her meals displayed the solid virtues of pre-war cookery.

Roger had grown up on stews, pies and roasts, the remains of the Sunday joint thriftily re-presented as rissoles, cottage pie or curry, on steak and kidney puddings steamed to a delicate gold, and followed by crumbles and tarts made with fresh or home-bottled fruit, always served with smoothly stirred custard just as milk puddings always had their dollop of home-made jam. His school friends had always liked to come to tea, knowing that there would always be a cake in the tin, and often scones or flapjacks as well. It was fortunate for Roger that his metabolism burned calories as efficiently as it did, or he would have been as plump as one of the cushions that his mother pummelled into roundness on the sofa and armchairs.

An affectionate son, with no hang-ups about macho status, Roger had always helped round the house and in the kitchen. Since the onset of his mother's illness he had done more, though generally under her direction. Some of her skills, certainly, had been inherited or absorbed, for from the very first cookery class he had found himself enthralled. Not just enthralled, but relatively expert. While the rest of the class struggled, cutting their fingers while chopping, forgetting to add the baking powder, rushing sauces so they curdled or forgetting to stir them so they caught at the bottom, Roger seemed unable to make a wrong move.

Beneath his deft fingers, fat and flour amalgamated effortlessly into the light breadcrumb texture required; souffles and sponges rose to puffy perfection; cloves of garlic crushed to a purée beneath his knife blade while all around him they shot like small out-of-control missiles, and he managed to do all this without covering his clothes with flour,

227

splatters of oil, or globs of tomato purée. The teacher smiled encouragingly and his class-mates vied to share his table. Somehow, though, for the last two classes it had been Sam who had won the coveted place, sharing worktop, cooker and sink in the home economics room of the comprehensive school.

The first time, Roger had been pleased but had assumed it was an accident. He had already noticed Sam, of course – among a group mostly made up of couples and elderly single people it was good to see someone about his own age. He liked the way she looked, too - quietly dressed, even old-fashioned, but neat and pretty. She was shy, like him, but the shared activity made things easy. The week before they had worked well together, chatting with an increasing lack of restraint, exchanging shy smiles when they bumped into one another at the sink. It had been pleasant, with an overtone of slightly shivery excitement, a kind of 'what if?' and 'I wonder?' sort of feeling. When he saw that Sam was making a determined effort to pair with him this week, Roger had made no attempt to hide his delight. Sam had responded at once, with a smile that seemed, to Roger, to light up the room.

Working side by side, sharing a flour shaker and a rolling pin, their hands touched and sprang apart, touched again. Their talk, confined the previous week to cooking, became more personal, an exchange of interests and ideas. Neither was particularly surprised to find how much they had in common. By the time the pastry was in the oven, Roger had told Sam more about himself and his life than he had ever revealed to anyone before, and heard in return about Sam's family of brothers and sisters. Each was intrigued – Roger, an only child, had always secretly longed for siblings, while Sam had grown up the third in a rowdy family of six. Fending off teasing from the younger ones and bullying from the older had naturally led to dreams of the pleasures of being an only child. They laughed about it, comparing memories of the past and thinking of unspoken possibilities for the future.

They shared their washing up amicably. Sam, drying up the mixing bowls, spoke shyly.

'Perhaps we could get together some time? Have a drink . . . or, what about cooking a meal? I've only got a bedsit, but you'd be surprised what I can produce – my landlady lets me use her kitchen sometimes.'

'That would be nice.' Roger's temperate words were belied by his flushed face – he bent over the sink, scrubbing at a baking sheet to hide the tremble in his hands. 'And I can cook something for you when I move into my new flat. Unless . . .'

'Oh, couldn't I come and meet your mum? She sounds great! And you might not get into your flat for weeks, yet.'

Sam spoke unselfconsciously, making it clear that she didn't want to wait that long. Roger blushed again, but lifted his head to smile at his new friend.

'She'd like that too,' he said. 'And so would I.'

Chapter Twenty-One

'Wotcha!'

Paul's spirits lifted as Shelley bounced into the office. She manipulated the baby buggy through the door and round the empty central desk with remarkable dexterity, considering that she held several bulging carriers in one hand and the buggy itself was hung with several more. Her little boy – Niall? Sean? No, Liam, Paul remembered belatedly – was mercifully fast asleep, almost invisible inside layers of clothes. Shelley herself, her face glowing from the cold, was cockatoo-bright in a ski suit of brilliant blues and yellows. The office, which had seemed as gloomy as the December afternoon outside despite all its lighting, suddenly seemed brighter and more cheerful.

Shelley parked the buggy by the wall, dumped her extra bags next to it, and flopped into a chair with an exaggerated sigh of relief.

'That's better. I've been shopping,' she informed Paul and Melanie unnecessarily. 'Murder out there, it is,' she added cheerfully. 'Makes you wonder why we do it every year. Still, it's for the kiddies, innit?'

'Go on with you, Shelley. I bet you love Christmas too, don't you?'

Shelley grinned. ''Course I do. Any excuse for a party, eh?' She looked round the office. 'No tree? No lights?'

Paul shook his head.

'Estate agents hate Christmas. It's bad for business. Like summer holidays.'

'Oh, go on with you. Christmas, maybe, but summer holidays? All those long days, and people with free time on their hands?'

'People with free time on their hands don't seem to buy and sell houses. They might go and look at some, as a day out, or to be nosy – but mostly they go to the sea, or abroad, or do the garden. If the weather's good they stay at home and sunbathe, and if it's bad they stay at home because it's raining. You can't win.'

'Poor old you. I never thought of it like that.' Shelley, always sympathetic, looked quite worried, and Paul hastened to reassure her.

'Don't take any notice of me – I'm just an old Scrooge. At least, that's what my daughters tell me.'

Shelley brightened. She loved to gossip. 'Daughters? How many?'

231

'Two. Both grown up, of course – in fact, one of them's getting married soon, and the other one's expecting twins.'

'Twins! That's lovely, really lovely. You must be really thrilled. I always fancied twins, though it's a lot of work, of course.' She glanced at Liam, who continued to sleep.

'Is there any problem with your sale and purchase?' Paul was superstitiously afraid that his recent sales, the best business he had done for months, might still fall to pieces.

'No, no problem. Why, is there likely to be?'

'No, no, of course not.' Paul spoke rather too heartily and Shelley, who was no fool, looked anxious.

'You sure there's nothing? I heard about those girls, poor little things. Naughty, of course, but still . . . it must have been frightening for them. It didn't make the families change their minds, did it?'

'No, thank goodness.' Paul reflected, not for the first time, how impossible it was to keep anything quiet in this town. The population might be large and growing, but in many ways it was still village-like in its propensity for everyone to know everybody else's business. 'Roger told you, I suppose?'

'Yes, 'sright. Proper little gossip he's getting to be. Came round to measure again for furniture, brought me a cake he'd made. Lovely, it was. Says he's going to evening classes, learning to cook.'

'Yes, he told me.' A connection of ideas, and the fact that Liam still didn't stir, made Paul offer Shelley a cup of tea.

'Don't mind if I do. If it's not too much trouble,' Shelley added politely.

'Well, I think I can fit it in with this mad rush of clients. We can always tell them to form an orderly queue outside the door.' Shelley glanced round at the silent phones, the empty office, and Melanie who had been reading a magazine and who now went to put the kettle on. At least, thought Paul, Shelley was always cheerful company.

They sipped their tea companionably. Rose, who always rather disapproved of socialising with clients (unless they were cash buyers wanting substantial houses), would have pursed her lips and been suddenly very busy but Melanie loved it, and volunteered to look up everyone's stars. She was reading out Shelley's when the door was pushed open with such force that it banged against the table behind it, and a man walked in. Oh dear, thought Paul. Mr Jones.

Paul Jones walked over with his peculiarly bouncing, self-satisfied walk. He pushed the door shut behind him, giving it a shove so that it only closed three-quarters of the way, and not bothering to look behind to see whether it was shut. A bluster of cold, damp air came through it and Melanie went to shut it, her silence eloquent. When she returned to her desk she assumed an air of great business, typing rapidly on her keyboard with her eyes fixed on the screen.

Mr Jones ignored Shelley, pushing past her chair as if she didn't exist, and planted himself in front of Paul's desk.

'What about my offer, then?' he barked, jutting his jaw.

Paul thought for a moment. Offer? What offer?

'I'm afraid it was unacceptable,' he said, finally remembering the insultingly low sum Mr Jones had offered two weeks earlier on a pleasant house on the edge of the town.

'Didn't you tell them I'm a cash buyer?'

'I certainly did, Mr Jones, but I'm afraid even that didn't sway them.'

'Don't they want to sell their house, then?'

Melanie gave a little grunt of disgust and muttered something to herself. Paul spoke in the voice of exaggerated calm that was intended to cover feelings of near-homicidal fury.

'They do want to sell their house, Mr Jones. They just don't want to sell it for twenty thousand pounds less than it's worth.'

'Less than it's worth? Who says it's worth that ridiculous amount?'

'I do, Mr Jones. And so, as you would see if you would care to read the property pages of the local paper, do other agents selling similar properties.'

'You agents, always pushing prices up. It's disgusting.'

Melanie's rapidly moving fingers made a loud clatter. Paul knew that she was typing rude words on to her screen, probably in capital letters. Paul remembered how tactfully he had managed to argue with the owners of this particular house and persuade them that to put it on the market at the even higher price they wanted would mean that no one would be interested even in going to look at it. 'It would never get through the survey,' he had told them firmly. 'Mortgage companies are fanatical about finding similar places that have sold for the same price. Comparables, they call it. And frankly, they wouldn't be able to find any.'

Shelley was watching, wide-eyed. Mr Jones's harshly raised voice made Liam whimper in his sleep. She jiggled the buggy, and he subsided into snuffles.

'You are entitled to your opinion, Mr Jones,' said Paul now, insincerely.

'And my opinion is that you'll never sell that house at that price.'

'Perhaps not. But I have, in fact, sold it at something not far short of it.'

It was almost worth all the aggravation, Paul thought, to see Jones's face at that news. Shelley was grinning and Melanie had stopped her typing to watch. Mr Jones's jaw was thrust so far forward that it looked like the shovel front of a JCB. A purple tinge clashed in an unlovely way with his yellowish teeth.

'This place,' he said in disgust, 'is the arsehole of the universe.'

Liam gave a fretful wail and Shelley jiggled him again.

'Just passing through, are you?' she enquired brightly. Melanie gave a stifled giggle that she tried to pass off as a cough, and Paul could feel his diaphragm trembling with the effort to restrain his laughter. Mr Jones turned and glared at Shelley, with a look of uncomprehending irritation. Vaguely aware that some kind of attack was in progress, he was not quick-witted enough to interpret Shelley's words. Presumably, though, he soon would. Paul stood up.

'I mustn't detain you,' he said as firmly as he could. Mr Jones looked round with baffled fury.

'You won't be getting any more of *my* business, I can tell you that,' he said venomously.

'Splendid,' said Paul heartily. Mr Jones marched out, leaving the door wide open. Paul shut it, then leaned against it in case his erstwhile visitor should experience a flash of comprehension and come back to avenge the insult. The two girls were giggling.

'If a man's gotta go . . .' said Paul. Shelley and Melanie wailed with laughter. Paul glanced out of the window, and saw that the street was empty. He went back to his chair and gave himself up to laughter.

'Sorry,' said Shelley when she could speak. 'I don't know what came over me. It just slipped out.'

'In a manner of speaking . . .' said Melanie, with another burst of giggles.

'No, but I wouldn't want you to lose business because of what I said. I mean, he said he'd never come in here again and he was a cash buyer.'

'Don't give it another thought,' Paul reassured her. 'The way he's going, he'll never buy anything. Even if he does get an offer accepted – which is unlikely – he'll fiddle and faddle and nitpick and you can be quite sure he'll annoy the vendor so badly the sale won't go through. I'm glad to see the back of him.'

'That's all right then. What a horrible man. Get a lot like him, do you?'

'A few, but not too many. The trouble is, they're the ones you remember, while the nice ones don't stick in your mind. Unless they're particularly nice, like you.'

'Ooh, you are awful!' The catch phrase came out automatically. Shelley flirted as naturally as she breathed, and with as little self-consciousness. Shelley was still laughing when the door opened. Half expecting the return of Mr Jones, Paul was relieved to hear Alec Blake's voice.

'Is this a private party, or can anyone join in?'

Shelley looked round, her face pleased.

'Hi, Alec! How you doing? How's your little girl?'

Alec, who hadn't realised who Shelley was until she turned and spoke, felt his face grow slightly pink. He hadn't seen her since his visit to value her flat, though he had thought of her – thoughts in which warmth and gratitude were mingled with a kind of amused regret. The sight of Shelley brought back a sudden vivid memory of her body sitting, warm and soft, on his lap. His skin still seemed imprinted with her, his hands curled involuntarily as if stroking the firmly curved limbs, even cupping the generous breasts that his face had been pressed to . . . he gave himself a little shake.

'Shelley! Good to see you!'

His voice sounded over-hearty in his own ears, but nobody else seemed to notice. Melanie, without being asked, was already heading for the kitchen to make another cup of tea. Alec sat in the chair Paul indicated with a nod of his head, and accepted the steaming mug gratefully.

'Thanks! It's freezing out there.'

'So how is she?' Shelley leaned forward in her chair. Alec, still fazed by seeing her, was confused.

'Oh, fine,' he said vaguely. 'Busy, of course, with Christmas and everything. Looking forward to doing up the new house, of course, lots of plans for curtains and things. Though I think I've persuaded her not to do anything too over the top,' he added with some pride Christine, if she had considered the matter at all, would have said that her new willingness to listen to (and even act on) Alec's wishes dated from Harriet's running away. Alec, privately, thought that it started with the change in his own personality that his encounter with Shelley had brought about.

'I think,' said Paul, noticing Shelley's confused expression, 'that Shelley was asking about Harriet, not Christine.'

'Harriet! Yes, of course! Silly of me. You heard about that, then?' Alec glanced at Paul with mild criticism.

''Course I did! Young Roger told me about it!' Shelley, blithely, as always assumed that everyone knew the people that she knew.

Alec turned his eyes to Paul, with an expression of surmise. Young Roger? Could this, he wondered, be some kind of nickname for Paul? Paul, reading his mind with an inward laugh, shook his head slightly.

'Roger Selby. He's buying Shelley's flat – you did the survey on his behalf. He was in here when you telephoned about Harriet.'

Alec's face cleared.

'Of course! Stupid of me! Yes, she's fine. A nasty scar, of course, but the doctor's assured us it will soon fade. The mercy is she didn't damage any of the tendons or anything, so really it could all have been a lot worse.'

'Frightening for her, though. And for you and your wife. You must have been terrified.' Shelley looked fondly at Liam, one hand moving to her stomach in an unconsciously protective gesture. Alec nodded, his face sombre.

'Yes, it was awful. The worst few hours of my life – I hope I never have to go through anything as bad again. The uncertainty, wondering what might be happening to her . . . still, all's well now, both girls safe and sound and no harm done, or hardly any. And in Harriet's case, in a funny sort of way I believe it's done her good. She's more confident, more outgoing, even.'

'Growing up.' Shelley nodded wisely. 'Sometimes having a bit of a fright does that for a kid. Like my mum says, you can't wrap them up in cotton wool for ever.'

'I ran away once,' put in Melanie unexpectedly. 'Just about Harriet's age, too. My mum wouldn't let me go to a pop concert, so I upped and went by myself.'

Paul looked at her in amazement. 'What happened?'

'I got lost,' Melanie admitted. 'I got myself to London on the train, but I'd never been on the underground by myself before. I thought it would be easy, but somehow I got on District when it should have been Circle, or the other way round, I forget, and I ended up in Wimbledon! Terrified, I was! Some man tried to chat me up on the train, and I just got off at the next stop and ran out of the station to get away from him, then I found I'd dropped my ticket.' She shuddered at the memory.

'What did you do?'

Melanie looked embarrassed.

'What she'd always taught me. I asked a policeman. He gave me a real telling off, and the end of it was I got taken home in a police car. Furious, Mum was! It was bad enough frightening her half to death, but coming back in a police car for all the neighbours to see . . . I couldn't sit down for three days, and I wasn't allowed out on my own for a month. I had to have my big sister with me if I went anywhere – you can imagine how much she loved that! Made my life hell, it was easier to stay in.' She shook her head, sighing. 'Happy days,' she concluded, without sarcasm.

Beep beep. Beep beep.

'Hensham Homes, good afternoon?'

'You sound very cheerful. Business must be good.'

'Mrs Holt! How are you?'

'Very well, thank you. I thought you would like to know that I have definitely chosen one of the new places, the ones they're just building. They say they'll be ready in February, so I expect to move in about April.'

'You might not have to wait that long. I know those builders, they're pretty good about keeping to time.'

'Well, it doesn't really matter. I've decided to stay with Beth anyway.

No point in making all those people wait when they all want to get into their new places.'

'Wonderful! I'll give all the solicitors a chivvy, then, and see when they'll be ready to exchange. I imagine nobody will want to move until after Christmas. As a matter of fact, two of the people in your chain are here with me now – no, no problems, just called in as they were passing. As a matter of fact, it was really quite funny . . .' Paul recounted the story of Shelley's *bon mot*. Alice Holt enjoyed it, as he had known she would.

'It sounds fun in your office,' she said rather enviously. 'I'm glad the people in the chain are so friendly. I wish I'd come in now, instead of telephoning you. It would have been interesting to meet them.'

'You've met one of them, he's Harriet's father.'

'Yes, a nice man. Oh, well, I suppose it's silly to want to meet the other people. It's a funny kind of relationship, isn't it, being in a chain together? There's a kind of intimacy, all of us depending on each other, moving into each other's homes . . . It makes me curious about them all.'

Relaying the news to Shelley and Alec, Paul found himself wondering whether, when Mrs Holt had moved out of her bungalow and was staying with her daughter, he might be able to make the parrot an excuse to go and visit them. Since the night of the girls' adventure, he had spoken several times on the telephone to Beth Oldham, but still had not managed to meet her. It had been disappointing to find out, too late, that she had actually accompanied her mother home and stayed for two days. Busy with other things he had not visited, and thus missed his chance to meet the woman he felt he was beginning to know quite well, but who seemed so elusive to see face to face.

'That's really nice of her,' Shelley said. 'Saying she'd go and stay with her daughter, I mean, so we can all move. Lots of people wouldn't dream of doing that. I wish she'd come in, we could have thanked her.'

'Funnily enough, she said much the same thing. Oh, not that you could have thanked her! Just that she wished she'd come to the office, she'd have liked to meet you.' Paul told them what Mrs Holt had said. 'I suppose I'm more conscious of all of you being linked together because it's so unusual to have the whole chain under one roof. Usually it's three or four different agents involved in a chain like this, and then I only get to speak to them, not to the actual buyers.'

'How many of us are there, then?'

Paul counted up on his fingers.

'Seven. Well, six lots of sellers, and six lots of buyers. Only one of the buyers – Roger – isn't selling anything, and at the other end Mrs Holt, who's selling her bungalow, is buying a retirement home from a developer. It's pretty amazing, really. Perhaps I should contact the Guinness Book of Records.'

'The local paper,' put in Alec. 'Bit of free publicity,' he pointed out.

'We should have a party!' put in Melanie. Paul laughed and shook his head, but Shelley was quick to take up the idea.

'Yes! Why not? A Chain Party – sounds good, doesn't it?'

'The Chain Gang,' said Alec dreamily.

'I see it more as a Marley's Ghost kind of thing,' said Paul, giving in to the mood. 'With me as Marley, trailing a heavy chain with houses instead of cash boxes.'

'Pulling the chain,' giggled Shelley, happy to join in.

'I still think we should have a party,' repeated Melanie stubbornly. 'After all, Mr K, it *is* pretty special, now you come to think of it. And look at everything that's come of it, with the two girls and everything! And it could be a good bit of publicity, like Mr Blake said.'

'I agree,' Alec said unexpectedly. 'I think it's a great idea. Once we've all exchanged contracts, and we've set a date for completion.'

'But where?' Paul thought helplessly of his own tiny house.

'Here, of course. Don't worry, it needn't cause too much havoc. We could all bring something – no need for you to go to a lot of expense. A bottle of wine, or glasses, or something to eat. I've got some sparkling white I bought last time we went to France, it would do fine. And I'm sure Christine would do some food.'

'I wouldn't want to put her to any trouble . . .' Paul had a vision of Christine Blake taking over.

'Roger!' exclaimed Shelley. 'He'd love it! He's dying for a chance to show off his cooking, and his Mum would help. You should get him to bring her along so he doesn't have to come on his own – she's great. And I could bring some music. Don't worry!' she added with a grin, correctly interpreting Paul's expression, 'I won't bring anything too loud! Some nice old fifties and sixties stuff, my Mum's got loads.'

Paul followed his usual habit, and let himself be carried along with the flood. However unwilling he might be, he could see that this party was going to happen, so he might just as well sit back and enjoy it. And, he thought more cheerfully, this might at last be the chance he had been hoping for. Surely Mrs Holt would bring her daughter to it? After all, you could say that Beth, as the owner of the bungalow, was obliged to be present. Paul smiled with genuine pleasure. Maybe the party wasn't such a bad idea, after all.

Chapter Twenty-Two

'This is madness,' grumbled Paul, an unexpected attack of nerves ruffling his normally equable temper.

'No, no, it's going to be fun, come on, Dad.' Dizzy, on her own because Jeremy had once again been summoned by 'the Big Cheese' – Paul saw him as a rotund barrel of stilton, into which judicious quantities of port had been dripped – had come early to help set things up.

'Fun? Filling a small room with an assortment of people of all ages who have absolutely nothing in common except that they're moving . . . All they've got to talk about is how awful their agent is, and they can't even do that with me here. At least, I hope they can't.'

'Of course they won't, why should they? They've all got buyers for their houses, they've all found something else they really like, they'll all love you to bits.'

'But what will they *talk* about? And the children . . . we shouldn't have invited the children as well. They'll be bored. They'll create havoc. Liam will eat too much and be sick, Harriet will go all silent and look miserable, the boy – can't remember his name, Ruth's brother – he'll sneak a drink or two and probably be sick as well, and Ruth – she's the difficult one, the teenager from Hell – will have a mood and probably say something unforgivable to someone . . .'

'Dad!' Dizzy's laughing voice brought him up short. She put her arms round him, the bulge of her stomach pressing warmly against him. 'Dad, calm down! You know Rose and Melanie have promised to watch Liam, and Max will keep an eye on the drinks to stop the youngsters getting at them.'

'Max the Lax,' groaned Paul, though his self-pity was largely put on. It was nice being hugged by Dizzy, and – 'I felt that!' he exclaimed suddenly. 'I felt them kicking! Oh, Dizzy!' He put his arms round her and hugged her fiercely, more moved than he would have believed possible.

'Steady on, Dad! You're squashing us!' Dizzy laughed, but did not draw away when he slackened his hold.

'Sorry, love.' He was apologising for more than the over-enthusiastic embrace, and she knew it.

239

'You should entertain more, Dad. Give a few parties. You're out of practice.'

'Yes, you're right. It's laziness, really. And lack of space at home. As a matter of fact, I'm thinking of looking for something a bit bigger.'

'Oho! Business looking up, or is there another reason? A touch of romance? Someone new in your life?' She tickled his ribs.

'Oho to you too, madam. And yes, there is someone new in my life, or rather, two someones.' He patted her stomach. 'How are we going to fit you all into my little rabbit hutch, when you come to see me? How can I play cricket or football with them in that tiny garden? I intend to take my duties as a grandparent seriously, you know.'

Her eyes filled with unexpected tears.

'Bother these hormones!' She dabbed carefully with a tissue, wary of smudging her eye makeup. 'Everything makes me cry! That's so sweet, Daddy, and I can't wait to bring them to see you. But don't forget, they won't be up to cricket or football for a year or two yet. Don't move for us!'

Paul felt a twinge of guilt, knowing that his main reason for thinking of a new home was to provide space, not so much for Dizzy's twins, as for a large parrot cage . . . It was true that Beth had said she was willing to take Archimedes, but he still had hopes of giving it a home, even if only when she had to go away.

The door opened and he looked up nervously, saved from having to answer. His other daughter came in, her face glowing with health and cold. The emerald and diamonds in her engagement ring caught the light as she lifted her hand in an extravagant wave – she wore no gloves, in spite of the cold, he noticed with an affectionate smile.

'Hello, Grandpa! And Dizzy, the Mummy-in-waiting!'

'Father of the Bride, if you don't mind. And where are your blushes, pray?'

She came to kiss him. 'Forgot to put them on this morning. How's it going? Anything I can do? John's got a few bottles, he's just parking the car.'

'Oh, Judith, you shouldn't have bothered. One of the clients has sent a case of rather good Australian sparkling white, another some red, and I got Max to get some beer.'

'Sounds good! But don't worry, the bottles are from Mum. A last-minute Christmas present. She sends her love, by the way, says she's glad the market's picking up at last. She's gone to New York for Christmas, you knew that, didn't you?'

'Yes, she told me. She's getting very jet-setty these days, isn't she?' Paul spoke without envy, more with a kind of wonder that the woman he had been married to for all those years should suddenly have sprouted these glittering wings.

'It's sweet of you to put us up tonight, Dad, but I still don't want

240

you to get up at the crack of dawn to drive us to the airport. We can just as easily get a taxi. Of course, if you'd agreed to come with us, that would be different . . .'

Once again, Paul was touched by his daughters' loving ways. Judith and John were going to France, hoping to get a few days of skiing over Christmas and making the most, so they said, of their carefree days of being single. Since Jenny was in New York, Dizzy and Jeremy were spending Christmas with Jeremy's parents and Paul suspected the two sisters had conspired along the lines of 'poor old Dad, all alone for Christmas'. The result had been a warm, even pressing, invitation for him to join the skiing trip.

'It's sweet of you, my dears, but quite apart from the fact that I don't want to play gooseberry, I've never been all that keen on skiing. The wrong shape, you know.'

'Dad, you wouldn't be a gooseberry, we're going with a group, so you wouldn't be interrupting love's young dream. And there's no guarantee that any of us will be skiing, there may not be any snow, but there's always things to do, and wonderful food. If . . . um, if it's a question of the money, I'm sure we could chip in a bit . . .'

'Darling, the money's got nothing to do with it. Things aren't great, but I'm not on my uppers yet, don't you worry. No, to be honest I'm quite looking forward to a few days at home, just pottering, you know. Not that I don't want to be with you, of course, but it's just not my sort of thing.'

'That's what Mum said. Oops. Didn't mean to let that slip out. Sorry.'

'That's all right. You should listen to her. She still knows me better than anybody, I think. So, thanks, but no thanks! But I'll enjoy having you for the night, I'll book a table somewhere, make it the beginning of your holiday.'

In the event, it had seemed the only possible evening to have the Chain Gang party, as it had somehow become known. Contracts were to be exchanged the day before, and since it was the last proper working day before closing for Christmas it wouldn't matter if the office was left slightly bomb-struck. Miraculously, everyone involved in the chain had said they were free to come, and even that they were looking forward to it; Beth Oldham had sent a message via Mrs Holt that she would be there. Hence, probably, Paul's nervous state.

At least the place looked good. An attractive room in its own right, he had allowed Melanie and Rose a free hand with decorating it. The result was an interesting blend of traditional – a real Christmas tree and bunches of holly and ivy (Rose) decorated with themed ribbons and baubles in gold and blue (to match the Hensham Homes sign and letter heads) arranged by Melanie. The discovery of some blue and gold striped candles in the local market had been greeted with acclaim and Paul kept to himself his suspicion that they would burn badly and dribble wax everywhere.

Paul, smitten with a last minute attack of Christmas hysteria, had rushed out and bought little gifts for the children who would be there. Mainly, it was true, because he wanted to give Harriet something (a book on parrots). Liam had been easy to buy for, and after some hesitation he had purchased joke tricks for Georgina and for Ruth's younger brother. Ruth, however, had caused him some anxiety. In the end, running out of time and patience, he had opted for a very modern and rather sophisticated clock, in matt black, from a gadget shop in the town centre. These gifts, inexpertly wrapped, were sitting round the base of the tree. His presents to Rose and Melanie, of a more substantial nature, had been given earlier in the day.

A blast of cold air came in as John backed through the door, his arms full of bottles. Paul took a quick look – real champagne, and a good one too – and hid them out in the back office. It would scarcely be tactful to bring them out in competition with Alec's sparkling white. Paul glanced at his watch – half an hour to go. He went to switch on the music – the tapes provided by Shelley played on her ghetto blaster – and once he had adjusted the volume downwards found that it was pleasant, filling such silence as was left behind Dizzy and Judith's animated chattering.

A knock at the door. Paul opened it. Roger Selby smiled shyly over a tray swathed in cling film. An elderly woman with a startlingly similar smile in a drawn, sickly coloured face carried a similar large plate, and behind them a girl, small and quietly dressed, bore a large tray of small bowls.

'Mr Kingswood, I hope you don't mind, I've brought my friend Sam. We did all the cooking together and Mum said she was sure you wouldn't mind. Oh – this is Mum, by the way.'

'Mrs Selby, please come in. I've heard a lot about you from Shelley. Of course it's all right, Roger, in fact, I'm glad you brought a friend. Come in, come in.'

Mrs Selby stepped over the threshold. The whites of her eyes were tinged with yellow, but the eyes themselves twinkled at him.

'I told him you wouldn't mind – he's said often enough what a nice man you are. You bring your Sam, I said. After all, who knows? If you're talking of being partners.' Her bright eyes looked directly into his, telling him that she knew what she was saying, and was happy about it. 'They're thinking of setting up a little catering business,' she said guilelessly. 'Just part-time for now, evenings and weekends. Party stuff, like this, or private dinners, that kind of thing.'

Paul watched as the cling film was stripped away to reveal an artistically arranged selection of home-made canapés. Tiny blinis with a piping of sour cream flecked with chive held red or white lumpfish roe, decked with sprigs of dill. Miniature choux pastry balls had pink prawns nestling in a delicate sauce, pastry boats held chunks of chicken and avocado, little cherry tomatoes had been scooped out and filled with herb cheese. It was like an edible mosaic, and Paul's mouth watered.

'If this is the standard they're setting themselves, I should say they'll be rushed off their feet in no time,' he said sincerely. 'They look wonderful.' Dizzy and Judith came to admire, further delights were revealed when the other containers were uncovered, and Paul noticed that Roger and Sam were pink with delight. They stood close together, for mutual support, while the two girls enthused. Words like 'wedding' and 'christening' floated in the air. It was, though Paul was only to realise it later, the beginning of a very successful enterprise.

Melanie arrived, closely followed by Rose and Max. Neatly dressed for once, no doubt nagged by Rose, Max went straight to the table set up as a bar, and popped open the first bottle of the wine that was chilling in a plastic container of ice. Glasses were distributed, and already the place took on a festive air. Paul need not have worried about conversation – his daughters were still discussing buffet menus with Roger and Sam, Rose was talking to Mrs Selby, and Melanie was flirting happily with John, who was happy to humour her while safely under the eye of Judith.

Within half an hour, the whole chain was present. All, that is, except Beth Oldham.

'She's hoping to get here,' Alice Holt said. 'A last minute editorial problem – you know the kind of thing. I said I'd come down in a taxi, and she's hoping to meet me here if she gets away in time. If not, perhaps you'll come and have a drink with us over Christmas?'

'Thank you, I certainly will,' Paul lied with as much sincerity as he could muster. If Mrs Oldham – in his mind he had reverted to distance and formality – didn't manage to get to this party, he thought that she must for some reason prefer not to meet him. And why, after all, should she want to? A few telephone conversations, however friendly they might have appeared, scarcely constituted a relationship. Concentrate on the parrot, he thought. You know where you are with parrots.

Amazingly, the party was going with a swing. The sparkling wine added its festive touch, the food proved to be as delicious as it looked, so that Roger and Sam were inundated with compliments. Christine Blake had already booked them to do the catering for her house-warming and Max was angling for a job as their barman. Paul had been surprised by Max's efficiency – he handled the champagne-style corks with aplomb and with a good regard for safety. Paul had had a friend who, having survived a blow from a cricket ball with no more than a black eye, had been blinded in one eye by a champagne cork which was small enough to fit into the eye socket of the skull. Max kept a careful eye out for empty glasses and provided soft drinks, red wine or beer as needed. He had tactfully given Ruth a Buck's Fizz that was mostly orange juice and a shandy to her brother that was equally weighted in favour of the lemonade. Was it because he was under Rose's eyes, or had he actually turned over a new leaf?

Liam, having eaten what by an adult's standards would have been a three-course meal of canapés – not a fussy eater, Shelley had proudly pointed out – had now settled into a corner with the toy car from under the Christmas tree, under the benign supervision of Roger's mum. She had succeeded in persuading him, without raising her voice, that he didn't really want any more lumpfish blinis and that a third cola would be a bad idea. He sat at her feet, running the little car carefully over the bridge she had built him out of a dictionary and two telephone directories.

'Are you quite comfortable there, Mrs Selby? Can I fetch you anything?'

The sparkle in her eyes seemed to belie the sign of illness so clearly apparent in her face.

'Not a thing, Mr Kingswood. I'm full as an egg.'

'I should think everyone will be – they can't resist Roger's food. Roger's and Sam's, that is.'

She nodded. Her neck was so wasted and frail he almost feared the weight of her head would snap it.

'He's been a good son to me,' she said, with seeming irrelevance. 'I'm glad to see him happy. Funny, isn't it, I never believed all that stuff about going to evening classes and finding friends, but it's worked this time, anyway.'

'Think they'll make a go of it?' Paul thought that she could take that question in what ever way she chose.

'Who can say?' Her look was very direct. 'Madly in love with Roger's dad, I thought I was. Before I found out what he was like. I stuck it out – that's what we did, then. Stupid, they'd say today, but there, things change, don't they? Lots of things.' Her smile was positively wicked. 'His dad would go wild if he could see Roger now! Half kill him, he would. He was a nasty old devil,' she finished, reflectively. 'Hated to see anybody else being happy. He thought cooking was strictly women's work, wanted Roger to be a bricklayer, something like that. I used to wonder,' she looked at Paul very directly with her bright, yellow-tinged eyes, 'whether Roger might be gay. He's never had a girlfriend before, and I wasn't sure . . . I don't know that I'd have minded, so long as he was happy, but he seems to be getting on like a house on fire with Sam.'

Paul looked at her with respect. 'You're very up to date,' he said. 'And very open minded.'

'All those years of living with a bigot! Besides, I just want him to be happy. And I hope he will be.' She glanced down at Liam, who had stuck his thumb in his mouth and was leaning against her legs, his eyes glazing with sleep. 'There'd be grandchildren, too. Not that I'll be around to see them, but still.' Her matter-of-fact acceptance robbed the remark of any self-pity, and Paul felt none of the embarrassment usual on such occasions.

They sat peacefully together, while the conversation ebbed around them. Across the room, Jason caught Paul's eye and smiled. He was talking to Harriet as if she were an old friend. Paul saw her pull up her sleeve and show him the scar on her arm, and remembered that he was a nurse in the Casualty department. Louise was next to him, not saying very much but smiling with a look on her face that Paul had never seen there before. They were talking to Judith and John, and from the few words he could pick out they seemed to be happily comparing wedding stories. He saw Harriet leave Jason with a smile and wriggle her way through the clusters of people to reach Mrs Holt.

Liz and Michael Hartwell were talking to Dizzy, and he was in no doubt that their conversation was largely obstetrical. The boy – Paul still couldn't remember his name – was looking bored. He kept looking longingly at the selection of jokes and tricks that Paul had given him, but both his father and Christine had made it clear to their offsprings that none of these delightful fake dog dirts, fizzing sugar lumps, tooth-dyeing chewing gums or water squirting cameras was to be used during the party. Paul was just wondering whether he ought to find the boy something to do – after all, there were no other boys there for him to talk to except Liam – when he saw Max beckoning. After some earnest instructions, a white napkin was draped solemnly over the boy's arm and he was sent off with a bottle to replenish glasses, a job which he did solemnly and with tremendous care. Shelley, who flirted with anything male however young or old, soon had him laughing.

The Blakes, predictably, were talking to George and Philippa Denton. Christine was much less forceful than before, and was listening quite meekly to Philippa, who looked surprised. George, his eyebrows and moustache bristling, was concentrating all his attention on his wife. As Paul watched, he bent and spoke in her ear, then led her to a nearby chair. She smiled up at him, looking suddenly more like a girl than a grandmother. Christine and Alec followed as if in attendance on royalty. After a few minutes they were joined by Mrs Holt, who had been carrying on an animated conversation with Harriet.

Paul knew from Mrs Holt that both the girls had written to apologise to her and that they had visited the bungalow to clear up the air-raid shelter.

'I was quite stern with them,' she had told him on the telephone. 'I must say, it made me feel quite awful but I knew it was better that way. I sent them out with buckets and so on to scrub the place down – they both came back looking very green round the gills. All that blood, dried on to the wall and the floor! I did wonder whether it wasn't too gruesome for them, but both the parents had said they thought the girls should do it. Ruth did more than Harriet, of course, because she still had to be careful of her arm but then Ruth is older anyway. They asked me, very meekly, to come and see that it had been done properly, so I did. I don't think that old shelter has ever been so clean! They'd even washed down the ceiling, and polished up the door handle – I'd quite forgotten it was an old brass one on a reclaimed door. It was quite touching.'

'Tough love, I think they call it,' murmured Paul. 'Making children take responsibility for their own actions.'

'Well, it was certainly tough. So then I gave them some tea, and cake, and we all had a chat. Harriet went all embarrassed, and wanted to tell me that she'd been to the lavatory among the rhododendrons and should she do anything about it. I told her it was fine, the rhodies would appreciate it, and managed to keep a straight face. What a delightful child she is! Her letter was charming, and when I offered to let Archimedes out for her to feed she told me, very seriously, that she didn't think she was worthy of it. Worthy! So I told her that apologies were one thing, but self-flagellation was going entirely too far, so Archimedes got half a bowl of nuts and an apple. He even did his trick for them.'

'How did Ruth behave?' Paul was curious, having gathered that Ruth was making a big effort to behave better. He wondered whether the shock of Harriet's injury had left some permanent benefit, or whether she had reverted to her old sullen ways.

'Rather quietly, but very politely. She didn't say very much at first, beyond apologising. She opened up a bit more over tea, though. And when Archimedes did his trick – you know how teenagers suddenly plunge straight back into childhood, and are about a hundred per cent nicer? That's how she was. For a moment her face was quite lit up.'

'I'm glad to hear it. I suppose she was just going through a bad patch. I must say, I always thought she was a nightmare when I was trying to sell the house, but I suppose from her point of view I was her nightmare too.'

As if summoned by his thinking of her, Ruth appeared at his side. He stood up politely, which flustered her.

'Oh, please don't . . . I mean, I didn't want to disturb you . . .'

'Not at all. I'm the victim of an outmoded upbringing, but the instincts are so ingrained that I'm like one of Pavlov's dogs.'

'I wanted to thank you. For the clock.' She still kept her head down, as if unable to meet his eyes, but her hair had been cut and shaped to a neat, shining bob that framed her face becomingly. He smiled encouragingly.

'I didn't know what to get you,' he admitted.

'I know, I'm at a difficult age.' For the first time she lifted her head and looked him in the face. The difference, he thought, was amazing. 'I do like it, though. It's really . . . different.'

'I thought,' he said, chancing his arm, 'that it might go in your new bedroom. When you move.'

Her eyes wavered, and she kept her head up.

'Yes. I'm not sure how it's going to be, yet. They said I could chose the colours and things, but I don't know . . . It's difficult to choose. I'm used to the old room.'

'Well, black goes with everything, really, like white. I just thought black was more sophisticated.'

'Yes, it is. Black and white . . . I wonder. Do you think black and white would be good?'

'I don't know much about interior design, but black and white is a very smart combination. I'll tell you what – my wife, my ex-wife, that is, is an interior designer. She's in New York now, but she'll be back after Christmas. Would you like to talk to her about it? You could go and see her, perhaps, in London. She's got plenty of books and pictures you could look at, get some ideas.'

'Wouldn't she mind?' Ruth blushed painfully. 'I haven't got much money. I know that sort of thing is very expensive.'

'Only if you actually employ her to do the room for you. I'm sure, if I ask her, she'll let you see her books, maybe make a few suggestions. She's good at working out cheap ways of getting a good effect, and she's really very nice. She won't patronise you.'

Ruth smiled, a flashing grin that transformed her face.

'It would be really good! Thank you! If you're sure she wouldn't mind . . .' The smile vanished in a renewed loss of confidence.

'She'd be delighted. It will make a nice change from middle-aged ladies with more money than taste.'

Ruth smiled again. She's really not so bad, thought Paul.

Ruth moved away. Next to Paul, Liam had somehow managed to climb into Mrs Selby's lap and was fast asleep on her knee, his thumb plugged into his mouth.

'Is he too heavy? Shall I take him away?'

She shook her head.

'No, he's fine. I'll tell you if he gets too heavy. He knows me a little bit – Shelley's been round to our house once or twice. Someone wants to speak to you.'

'I beg your pardon?'

Mrs Selby nodded her head. Paul looked round and saw Harriet, too diffident to interrupt an adult conversation, waiting patiently beside him. Behind her was Alice Holt. Paul stood up again.

'Thank you very much for my book.' The formal words were unimportant – it was her glowing look that thanked him.

'Harriet has something to ask you,' said Mrs Holt. Paul looked enquiringly at Harriet.

'What,' she asked carefully, 'do you call a parrot that can say words in several languages?'

Paul went through the mime of racking his brains, knowing that he was not required to find an answer.

'I give up. What do you call a parrot that can say words in several languages?'

'Glot.'

This time, Paul thought in earnest. Mrs Holt and Harriet waited and watched him, their eyes bright with identical mischief. He could feel them willing him to work it out. Light dawned.

'Polyglot! I like it!' He thought. 'What about a parrot with a college education?'

'Polytechnic!' Harriet was there in no time. The three of them looked at one another in a moment of complete harmony.

'A parrot you plant in the garden?' A new voice chimed in, a voice that was familiar to Paul although for a moment, distracted, he couldn't place it.

'Polyanthus.' He spoke absently, looking round as he did so. She stood to one side of him. They were eye to eye, being the same height. Her eyes were a warm brown, the few fine lines around them caused, he could see, by the smile that was a rearrangement of all her facial muscles so that even with the bottom half of her face hidden you would have known that she was smiling. Her skin, though etched with the first tracery of lines round her mouth and beneath her chin, had the glow and softness of a young child's, a glow that came from health and humour rather than from any skilfully applied cosmetics. The humour and intelligence in her eyes was far from childish, however, and there were strands of grey in her hair.

Like Paul himself, she was plump. Not fat – it was more that her body was rounded over her bones. He thought that it would feel firm but soft, not flab but sweetly moulded flesh that Rubens would have painted as deliciously as if it had been ripe fruit. He put out his hand, and it was taken in one that felt just as he had expected, a handshake that was firm without being aggressive, warm but not flirtatious. He smiled.

'Mrs Oldham.' It was not a question, more a recognition of an old friend, not seen for a long time but unchanged to the eyes of affection.

'Beth!' cried out Mrs Holt at the same moment. 'I'd just decided you weren't going to make it!'

'Yes, I'm sorry.' Her apology was shared between all of them. 'I know I'm disgracefully late, but I thought I'd at least get here for a few minutes.'

'It's good to see you.' Like Harriet's earlier words of thanks, Paul's sincerity could not be doubted.

She raised one eyebrow. 'When you called me "Mrs Oldham" I thought I must be so late it was unforgivable.'

'Not at all – let me get you a drink! There's some sparkling white . . .' He wanted to offer the champagne he had hidden, but common sense told him it would be over the top.

'Thank you, that would be lovely.'

'I'll go!' Harriet was eager to help. 'Please let me, I'll be very careful.'

'Thanks . . . now you must be Harriet? I'm Mrs Holt's daughter, Beth Oldham.'

Harriet blushed.

'I know. I'm sorry I used your air-raid shelter.'

'My dear, you're welcome for my part, though we'd all prefer you not to injure yourself there. Is it healed now?'

'Yes.' Harriet nodded. 'Um, how did you know who I am?'

'The parrot book, of course.' Beth nodded to the book that Harriet held clutched under her arm. 'My mother told me you loved Archimedes.' Tactfully, she suppressed the fact that her mother's description – 'a funny little thing, all skin and bones and brains' – had been what she recognised.

'Oh, I do. And so does Mr Kingswood,' Harriet replied artlessly. 'He gave me the book. I'll go and get you a drink.' She eeled off between the close-packed bodies.

Mrs Holt sat in the chair Paul had vacated, and began to talk to Mrs Selby. Paul looked at Beth Oldham, and felt suddenly tongue-tied.

'Tell me who everyone is,' she demanded cheerfully. 'I'm fascinated by the idea of this chain. I think it's a brilliant idea to get them all together.'

Quietly, he did as she asked, starting with Roger and working his way through the chain. Beth nodded, her eyes moving with his descriptions, assessing, remembering.

'You're not going to write about it, are you?' he asked, in some alarm.

'Why not? It's all good human-interest stuff. No names, of course, unless I can put yours in? A bit of publicity? After all, it isn't often you give a party like this, is it?'

'It's never happened before,' he admitted. 'And it will probably never happen again. It's almost unheard of to have a chain this long all with one agency. It's been . . . interesting.'

'So I hear! But rewarding?'

'Financially, yes. The best month I've had for several years, in fact. But rewarding in other ways too. I've met some interesting people – and that doesn't always happen, sadly. Maybe I just got the chance to get to know them better than usual, because of all the problems, I don't know. But it's been . . . different.' He thought about it. 'I feel different,' he admitted, surprised by the thought and by the fact that he was voicing it.

'Better? Worse?'

'More alive.' He wondered at the thought. 'More involved in life,' he amended.

'It changes you, moving house. You become a different person, in a way. Different in the way you see yourself, and in the way other people see you. After all, most people nowadays move house for a *reason*, don't they? Not just for a whim, like they did in the boom years. Now it's the significant things – a marriage, or the end of one, a new baby, divorce, illness, death . . . it must affect you.'

He nodded. 'I shall be sorry, in a way, when all these sales complete. I should like to think . . .'

'What?'

'That we could keep in touch.' The words came out in a rush. He felt as awkward as a schoolboy.

'We?'

'The people I've got to know. Mrs Holt. Harriet. You . . .'

She laughed at him.

'Go on, you can't fool me! You want to keep in touch with Archimedes!'

He laughed, feeling suddenly comfortable and easy, as if he had come home after a long journey.

'Of course! What other reason could I possibly have?'

'Parrots,' she said thoughtfully, 'sometimes live for a very long time.'

'I know.' He laughed back at her. 'Lucky, isn't it?'